Beyond
the
Hardwood

L.M. NELSON

Beyond the Hardwood
Copyright © 2016 L.M. Nelson

ISBN: 0692811532
ISBN-13: 978-0-692-81153-5

1 2 3 4 5 6 7 8 9 10

This is a work of fiction. The events and characters described
herein are imaginary and are not intended to refer to specific
places or living people.

Cover Design Assistance by: Rachael Ritchey
Cover artwork courtesy of Pixabay:
alles/PDpics/cameonaton/Abdecoral

Other Books in the Series

Scrubs
Sand & Sutures

ACKNOWLEDGMENTS

Thanks to Alex, for his expertise about basketball.

CHAPTER ONE

Surrounded by family and friends, Nathan Hanson eyed eighteen candles flickering on the cake in front of him.

"Happy birthday, Nathan," his mother said. "Make a wish."

Nathan thought about this for a minute before he blew out the flames.

His father pulled a set of car keys from his pocket and handed them to Nathan.

Bemused, Nathan stared at his father. "What are these for?"

"Go look out front."

Nathan gripped the keys in his hand and dashed out the door. A cherry red 1969 Ford Mustang Mach One was parked in the driveway out front. Nathan's jaw hit the ground. "Are you serious?"

"Happy birthday, Son."

"Oh, sweet! Thanks, Dad."

"Why don't you take it for a spin?"

Nathan gazed at his girlfriend with an enticing smile. "Wanna go for a ride?"

She nodded, full of anticipation.

He unlocked the car and presented his hand to her, helping her ease into the passenger seat.

Once she was secured, Nathan walked around to the opposite side of the car. He sat in the driver's seat and revved up the engine, letting the car idle for a minute so he could hear it purr. "Listen to that engine, Gab."

"I can't believe your dad bought you a car."

"My dad is awesome." He gripped the steering wheel with one hand and held Gabriella's hand with the other. Then he glanced over his shoulder, backed out of the driveway, and drove down the street.

"You're so lucky your dad is a doctor," Gabby remarked.

"Why do you say that?"

"Because you and your family go on cool vacations, you live in a nice house, and your parents bought you a car for your birthday. They do all kinds of things for you."

"Your mom does things for you too."

Gabby shook her head and snorted. "Not like your parents do."

He signaled to turn right, checked the rearview mirror, and switched lanes. "She sends you to cheer camp. That counts."

"I guess."

Gabby's despondency led Nathan to believe something was bothering her. "What's the matter?"

Not wanting to burden him with her problems, she stared at her hands with a dejected expression on her face.

Nathan pulled into the closest parking lot and put the car in park. He turned to face her, insistent that she talk to him. "What's wrong?"

Gabby sighed. "My mom lost her job, and she pretty much told me she won't be able to pay for any of my college expenses. Either I live off loans and work my way through school or I don't go."

"When did she lose her job?"

"Last week. And she refuses to let me work. Aside from my college problem, I don't have any money to get a dress for the winter dance, so I won't be able to go."

Offering support, he took both of her hands in his. "We will get you a dress. That is not a big deal."

"Really?"

"Of course. There is no way I'm going without you."

Those were the exact words she wanted to hear. "Thank you."

"We'll figure it out. We always do." He drew her closer and tenderly kissed her on the lips.

Nathan came home a little after 10:00 P.M. that night. He removed his letter jacket and slipped his car keys in the pocket of his jeans. "It's cold out tonight," he said to his father as he draped his jacket over the back of a chair.

Dr. Randy Hanson looked up from the medical article he was reading. "Is it?"

"Yeah."

He set the medical journal on the coffee table and focused his attention on his son. "Did you have a good day?"

"I had an awesome day. That car is amazing. Thank you so much."

"You're welcome. I had a Mustang when I was your age. It's a nice ride."

"It is," Nathan agreed, taking a seat on the couch next to his father.

"How was the movie?"

"It was good. A few parts scared Gabby. She jumped and spilled popcorn all over herself then wouldn't let go of my hand for the rest of the night."

"Scary movies are good for that." With a more serious tone, Dr. Hanson looked his son in the eye. "Nate?"

"Yes, Sir?"

"You're a senior now. You have important decisions to make about college and career choices."

"I know. We've already discussed this."

"Yes, but you haven't told me what you've decided," he insisted on knowing.

"Gabby and I are going to UW together."

"And have you made any other decisions?"

Nathan knew exactly what his father meant. "Biology I think, with emphasis on pre-med."

Dr. Hanson grinned, thrilled that his son showed an interest in pursuing a medical career. "Have you filled out scholarship applications?"

"Yup. Found a few I qualified for." Nathan had something else on his mind that he wanted to discuss with his father, but since it was a sensitive subject, he wasn't sure how to bring it up. "Dad, I need to talk to you."

"About what?"

"Gabby and I have been talking."

Dr. Hanson bobbed his head. "Talking is good."

"You know, we've been together for over a year now."

"I know. I like Gabby. She's a nice girl, and I think she's good for you."

Nathan sat up to instill more confidence. "Gabriella and I…we…" He breathed in deeply before he said, "We want to have sex."

Dr. Hanson knew his son was old enough to think about this, but wasn't expecting Nathan to be quite this open about it. Seeking clarification, he asked, "She wants to or you want to?"

"We both do," Nathan affirmed.

Dr. Hanson wasn't convinced. "You're not pressuring her, are you?"

"No, I'm not. She's actually the one who brought it up."

He snorted under his breath, not believing Nathan's claim for one second. "Oh really?"

"Dad, I know what you're thinking."

"No you don't," he scoffed. "You have no idea what I'm thinking."

"Then what are you thinking?"

Nathan's father was an obstetrician who saw young pregnant girls in his office on a weekly basis. Nathan was convinced his father was about to lecture him about teenage pregnancy, or even worse, give him the abstinence speech. But his father did neither of those things. Instead, he simply said, "I understand. I was eighteen once."

That was not the response Nathan expected.

Hoping his son had considered every aspect of this decision, Dr. Hanson threw him a thought-provoking question. "Have you considered what that means for Gabby?"

"What do you mean?"

"Son, once a girl loses her virginity, that's not something she can ever take back. It's done. And have you thought about contraception?"

Nathan knew the whole pregnancy issue would pop up sooner or later. "You mean condoms?"

"Yes, condoms. Be smart about this, Nate. Protect yourself, protect her. And for god's sake don't get her pregnant."

"Dad."

"I'm serious, Nathan. Use a condom, all the time, every time," Dr. Hanson insisted. "Is she on the pill?"

"No."

"If you two are going to have a sexual relationship, she should be. I'll be more than happy to get her a scrip for birth control pills, but I'm not going to do it without her mother's consent," he sternly stated. "Has Gabby talked to her mother about this?"

If Gabby's mother knew they were even considering having sex, she would throw a conniption. Panic-stricken, Nathan replied, "Dad, she can't."

"Why not?"

"Because. Her mom isn't the most understanding person in the world, especially with sensitive issues like this."

"Gabby should discuss this with her mother." Dr. Hanson reached for a cup of coffee. "We're going to get you a box of condoms. I want both of you to be safe."

Nathan could see the seriousness in his father's eyes. Dr. Hanson wasn't about to let his son be the reason for another teenage girl having a baby. With a nod of understanding, Nathan replied, "Yes, Sir."

CHAPTER TWO

Monday morning, Nathan had a hard time concentrating in class. He zoned in and out of discussions, and when one of his teachers called on him, he wasn't paying attention. "I'm sorry, Sir. Could you please repeat the question?"

Several classmates laughed at him.

Michael Lynott, Nathan's best friend since childhood, noticed how distracted Nathan was. When the bell sounded and they all crowded into the hallway to switch classes, Mike ran to catch up with him. "You alright, man?"

Nathan turned his head. "Yeah. I'm fine. Just tired. Haven't been sleeping well lately." He lied through his teeth, but knew Mike wouldn't question him about it.

"You and Gabby want to double up this weekend?"

"Where do you want to go?"

Mike lifted a shoulder. "I dunno. Whirlyball maybe?"

"Sounds fun. Let me talk to Gabby and I'll get back to you."

The two friends knuckle bumped and each reported to his next class.

Nathan couldn't focus on anything. All he could think about was Gabby and the brief moment of physical intimacy they shared over the weekend. The experience of losing their virginity together wasn't quite the firework show he expected it to be. In fact, the whole experience was a bit awkward and clumsy, and it didn't last as long as he thought it would. The more Nathan thought about this, the more distracted he became. For his own reassurance, he had to make sure Gabby wasn't feeling embarrassed or experiencing pangs of guilt about it, but because of schedule conflicts and lack of privacy in the crowded high school hallways, he hadn't had an opportunity to talk to her.

Before he went to basketball practice, Nathan caught up with Gabby at her locker. He snuck up behind her and whispered, "Hey."

She whirled around and smiled at him. "Hey, you."

"Can I talk to you for a minute?"

"Sure." She took his hand and led him to a secluded corner of the hallway where they could have more privacy.

Finally alone, Nathan took her in his arms. "I've been thinking about you all day. You ok?"

Gabby wrinkled her forehead and cocked her head at him. "Yes. Why wouldn't I be?"

"Because yesterday…"

Fully understanding now why he asked her that, she offered reassurance. "I'm fine."

"Are you sure? No regrets?" he asked, hoping she wasn't uncomfortable about the situation.

"None at all. If I didn't want to, Nathan, I wouldn't have."

Hearing those words made him feel better. "Good. That's what I wanted to hear."

Gabby returned the question to him. "Why, do you have regrets?"

"No," he declared. "I just wanted to make sure you were ok."

"I'm fine." She leaned a bit closer and whispered, "I want to do it again."

A seductive grin slowly crept onto his face. "I might be able to arrange that. But we will have to wait, because I have practice and so do you."

She giggled. "Meet me after practice?"

"Absolutely." He kissed her lovingly but firmly on the lips then released her and headed toward the gym.

"Nathan?" Gabby called out to him.

He pivoted around to face her. "Yeah?"

"I love you."

His heart raced and his smile grew wider. "I love you too."

Weeks later, Nathan's mother set a pile of folded laundry on Nathan's bed. An open box of Trojans peeked out from the partially opened drawer of his bedside table. She sighed in disbelief, pressed her lips together firmly, and exited the room.

Later that evening, when she and her husband were alone in their bedroom, she said, "Do you know what I found in Nathan's room this morning?"

Dr. Hanson unbuttoned his shirt. "No. What?"

"He has a box of condoms in the drawer by his bed."

"I know," he replied. "I bought it for him."

"You what?"

"I bought it for him," he repeated.

"Why?" she demanded to know.

Removing his shirt and tossing it in the hamper, he said, "Janey, you know as well as I do that we aren't going to be able to keep him from having sex if that's what he wants to do, but we can protect him."

"By buying him a box of condoms and encouraging him?"

"I'm not encouraging him," he argued. "I'm just not discouraging him."

"Randal!"

"What?" he teased, not seeing the problem.

She rolled her eyes and stormed into the bathroom.

He followed close behind her. "What's the matter?"

"I can't believe you did that."

"Would you rather he had unprotected sex and got Gabby pregnant?" he asked her.

"No, but…"

"Ok then." Dr. Hanson could tell by the look on his wife's face that she wasn't satisfied with that response. "Honey, he's eighteen now, and he and Gabby have been together for a long time. It was bound to happen sooner or later."

"That's not the point. I wish you would have discussed this with me."

He openly laughed. "Nathan was embarrassed enough when he asked me for advice. Do you really think he would have been put at ease if his mother knew about this?"

Jane's mouth dropped. "He asked you for advice about sex?"

"Being his first time, he didn't know what to do. He was afraid he'd screw it all up, so he asked me for pointers."

"You didn't offer any, I hope"

"Sure I did," he confidently replied.

"You gave our son pointers about sex?" she raged, upset that her husband responded to that outrageous request.

"I simply told him to relax and do whatever came naturally. Gabby wouldn't know the difference anyway."

"Dammit, Randy."

"Baby, come on. It's not that big of a deal. I'm glad he feels comfortable enough to talk to me about things like this." He wrapped her in his arms and nibbled on her neck.

"Stop it," she insisted.

"You're freaking out."

"No I'm not," she denied.

"Yes you are. Besides, I think he loves her."

"Pfft," she mocked.

"What? You don't think he does? Have you heard the way he talks about her?" he reminded her. "Watch them together. He's in love with her, Babe."

"He's just a boy."

He shook his head, contradicting her opinion. "No, he's a young man. And he has a wonderful young woman he cares for very much."

"I don't doubt he cares about Gabby," she admitted.

"Then what's the problem?" His lips rubbed across her forehead. "Let it go, Babe. You can't stop the inevitable."

Meanwhile, Nathan was out with Gabby. They snuggled on a blanket by the lake staring at the stars and the moon. The air was crisp. To keep warm, Gabby wore Nathan's high school varsity letter jacket; he was bundled up in a thermal winter coat.

"Did you sign up for the SAT next Saturday?" Gabby asked him.

"Yes."

"I did too, but I'm nervous about it."

Nathan reassured her, "You'll be fine. As long as you prepare for it, it isn't that bad. I took it last year and did ok. My dad bought me a book with sample questions, review sections, and practice tests. And he hooked me up with the on-line study course. I've been doing really well."

"I don't have any material to practice with, and I don't feel prepared," Gabby admitted.

"Do you want to borrow my book?"

"Could I?" she asked.

"Sure," he replied, happy to give her whatever she needed.

"Thank you."

Gabriella was not as spunky as she normally was, which made Nathan wonder what was on her mind. "You ok? You're not very talkative tonight."

"I tried to talk to my mom about getting on the pill."

By the look on Gabby's face, Nathan had the feeling their conversation didn't turn out well. "Uh oh. What did she say?"

"She wasn't happy," Gabby admitted. "In fact, she's pretty angry about the entire situation. She seems to think you're a bad influence on me."

This didn't really surprise him. Her mother wasn't particularly thrilled that their relationship was as serious as it was anyway. The fact that sex had been added to the equation must have put her over the edge. Nathan began to assume the worst. "Do you think she'll try to keep us apart?"

"She threatened. I don't know if she'll actually do it, but I think she's going to make things a lot harder for us now."

"Like they weren't difficult enough already," he snarled.

Gabby didn't find his smart-aleck comment amusing. She stood up and strode down the beach without him.

Nathan couldn't figure out why Gabby reacted that way. He rose to his feet and ran after her. When he caught up with her, her arms were folded across her chest and she was staring down at the sand. He pulled her close and sheltered her in his arms. "I'm sorry."

She nuzzled into his chest. "She acts that way because of my dad."

"But you've never met your dad," Nathan told her. "What does he have to do with this?"

"My mom got pregnant when she was seventeen. As soon as he found out, he dumped her and ran off. She never saw him again."

Nathan hadn't heard this story before. "She was only seventeen?"

"Yes."

Since Gabriella's mom became pregnant at a young age, it was safe for Nathan to assume that she was afraid the same thing would happen to Gabby. "I would think that would make her all the more willing to let you go on the pill."

"You'd think."

"You told her we use a condom, right?"

"Yes, but that didn't make her feel any better about it." Gabby hesitated for a moment before she said, "She's mad at your dad too."

"My dad? Why?"

"Because he didn't tell her about this."

That was the most ridiculous thing he had ever heard. He couldn't help but laugh. "My dad is not going to say something like that to your mother, Gab."

"Well, she seems to think he should have." Frustrated, Gabby trekked further down the beach.

Nathan walked faster to catch up with her. "Wait a minute, she's pissed at my dad because he didn't tell her about this?" he said, trying to keep a straight face. "Dad's gonna love that."

Gabby sneered at him, unamused. "This isn't funny. She said she was going to call him."

Nathan rolled his eyes, knowing that Gabriella's mother always blew things out of proportion. "Great."

The phone in Randy's clinic rang non-stop all morning. The receptionist, posed with pen in hand, stared at a computer monitor while she answered yet another call. "Dr. Hanson and Dr. Hutchins' office. May I help you?"

"May I speak with Dr. Hanson, please," chimed a female voice on the other end of the line.

"Dr. Hanson is with a patient. Would you like me to take a message or would you like to speak to a nurse?"

"I'd rather talk to him," the woman insisted.

"He has appointments all morning, Ma'am."

"I am aware that he has appointments. But I need to speak with him."

"Are you a patient of his?" the receptionist asked.

"No, I'm not a patient of his."

"May I have your name so I can tell him you're on the line?"

"Theresa Pervis," the woman replied.

"Please hold, Ma'am." When Randy stepped out of an examination room, the receptionist relayed the message. "Dr. Hanson?"

He lifted his head. "Yes?"

"I'm sorry to bother you, but Theresa Pervis is on line one, and she's pretty persistent about speaking to you."

Theresa Pervis. Randy recognized that name. "Did she say what she wanted?"

"No. But she doesn't sound happy."

"I'll take it in my office." Randy slipped into his office, closed the door, and picked up line one. "Ms. Pervis."

"Dr. Hanson. You and I need to talk," she demanded.

"This isn't the best time. I have patients waiting."

She didn't care. "Explain to me, please, why you knew our children were sexually active yet did not bother to tell me?"

"Because it was not my place to tell you," Randy replied. "Nathan came to me and discussed the issue. I assumed Gabby would have done the same with you."

"Well, she didn't, until yesterday, long after the fact. I'm very upset that our children are having sex, and even more so that you knew about it but didn't inform me. Gabby tells me you offered to put her on the pill."

Her tone was extremely bitter. He wasn't sure how far he was going to get with her, but he remained professional. "Ms. Pervis, please calm down. I told Nathan I would write Gabby a prescription, but not without your consent."

"If your son gets my daughter pregnant..." she threatened.

"He won't. Nathan is more responsible than that, but we can protect them even more if you let me put Gabby on the pill. All I have to do is write a prescription."

She was outraged that he even suggested that. "You're encouraging this behavior with your son?"

"We can't stop them if that's what they want to do. You know that as well as I do. I'm just glad Nathan came to me about it so I could help him get protection. He cares about Gabby and wants her to be safe. In all honesty, Ms. Pervis, it took a lot of courage for the kids to come forward with this. Let me help them."

"I think you've done enough, Dr. Hanson. I'm not sure I want my daughter around your son."

Gabby's mother had the authority to keep the kids apart if she really wanted to. Randy didn't want to be the cause of that, so he tried a different approach. "Maybe you're right. Maybe I should have told you. I'm sorry you're so upset about this."

An uncomfortable silence resonated for several seconds. Randy hoped she hadn't hung up on him. "Ms. Pervis? Hello? Are you there?"

She broke the silence by saying, "Does she need to have an appointment to get a prescription?"

"No. I'll write her a scrip without one. Has she ever been to a gynecologist?"

"No."

"I would strongly suggest that she does, especially now that she's sexually active," Randy advised.

"I can't afford that right now. I have no medical coverage."

"Have her come to me," he stated. "I'll see her free of charge."

"Really? You would do that for Gabby?"

"Yes, Ma'am," Randy declared. "I certainly will."

"I'll bring her in tomorrow after school."

"I can't see her tomorrow. I'm at the hospital all day working with medical students. What about Wednesday? I have an opening around 3:30. Can you bring her in then?" he asked.

"Yes."

"Great. I'll connect you to my receptionist and she'll put you on the schedule. Thank you, Ms. Pervis, for working with me on this."

She grumbled into the phone.

Randy transferred her over to the receptionist desk then peeked his head out the door. "Stephanie, schedule this woman's daughter in. No need to collect insurance information because I'm not charging her."

"Yes, Doctor." She picked up the phone and added the girl to Randy's scheduled appointments.

Randy's medical partner, Greg Hutchins, overheard this conversation. "Not charging who?"

"Nate's girlfriend," Randy replied.

"Is that who was on the phone?"

"No. Her mother was on the phone. And she is livid."

Greg shot a questioning glance Randy's way. "Why?"

"Because she found out that her daughter and my son are having sex. I knew about it, didn't tell her, and she feels it's my fault."

Greg didn't understand why Randy wasn't more concerned about this. "Nathan and his girlfriend are having sex and you're ok with that?"

"What am I supposed to do about it, Greg? He's eighteen. It was bound to happen sooner or later. At least he opened up to me about it."

"This is true. Why is his girlfriend coming in?" Greg wanted to know.

"Because I'm going to put her on the pill."

Greg nodded in agreement. "Good call."

Randy took a quick breath. "My son's definitely not a baby anymore."

"Nope. He's sure not."

CHAPTER THREE

"Daddy!"

Wondering what all the commotion was about, Randy emerged from his home office. His two teenage daughters were throwing a fit about something, and Nathan was smack in the middle of it. "What is going on in here?"

Nathan held something over his sister's head so she couldn't reach it.

She stretched for it, trying to pull it out of his hand. "Nathan took my uniform. And he won't give it back!"

Her twin sister, Lauren, jumped up to grab it, but she couldn't reach it either. "That's not yours."

"I know it's not mine," Nathan said. "What would I do with a leotard?"

"Nate," Randy said to his son. "Give it back to her."

"But it's green and yellow," Nathan declared. "Those are Rough Rider colors. She can't wear those tonight."

"It's her dance outfit, Son. She needs it for her routine. Shouldn't you be getting ready for your game anyway?"

He handed the tights and leotard back to his sister, who immediately ran upstairs. "Yup. We're gonna kill Roosevelt. You coming to the game?"

Nathan had his first basketball game of the season that night, and Randy was pumped about it. "I'm planning on it, but you know I'm on-call tonight. Hopefully my cellphone will stay silent. I want to see your game and watch Lacy's dance team during the halftime show."

Nathan picked up his basketball and spun it on his finger. "Gabby's cheering squad is performing a routine during halftime too. They're making a huge pyramid with Gab on the top. It looks awesome, from what I saw from their practices."

"Good," Randy acknowledged. "Can't wait to see it. Uncle Jim is coming to the game."

"He is?" Nathan asked excitedly.

"Yup." Jim Ryan wasn't really their uncle; he was Randy's best friend. They had been friends since their freshman year in college. They were also former roommates and attended medical school together. The two men were like brothers. "He wanted me to tell you he'd be wearing a kangaroo suit tonight," Randy teased him.

Nathan hoped his father wasn't serious. "Oh good lord."

Randy laughed as Nathan went up to his room to prepare for his game.

Although Jim was crazy enough to come to the game in a kangaroo suit, he didn't. He arrived in his normal attire instead—a brightly colored Hawaiian shirt, baggy jeans, a shark tooth and pukka shell necklace, and a pair of Vans. His blonde hair was spiked in front, with Quicksilver sunglasses propped up on his head. He stepped up the bleachers, fighting his way through tons of high school kids, and greeted Randy with a thumb and pinky fist. "Yo, man. What's up?" They shook hands then Jim took a seat next to Randy. "How's Nathan feelin'?"

"He was feeling pretty good when he left."

"Sweet." Jim looked down at the cheerleaders and spotted Gabriella stretching and doing some warm up cheers with her squad. "How are he and Gabby doin'?"

"Doing well. They're both scheduled to take the SAT this weekend."

"Didn't he already take that?"

"Yeah, but he wasn't happy with his score, so he's trying to improve it."

"Has he made any decisions about college?"

"At this point, it looks like UW. He wants to major in Biology with emphasis on pre-med," Randy said with a grin.

"A third generation doctor. You should be proud of that choice."

"I am proud of him, but I hope he's making that decision for himself and not for me."

"He's always had a fascination with science and medicine, Dude. Medical school makes sense for him. Gotta feed the kid's interests. When Chris wanted to go to Botswana to do some Peace Corps work, I didn't like the fact that he was shipping off to some far away land and I'd never see him, but I knew it was somethin' he really wanted, so I supported him."

Christopher Ryan was Jim's son. He held a Master's Degree in Sociology and was a world philanthropist, always giving to charities and trying to help third world countries. He joined the Peace Corps and was now living in Africa.

"How's Chris doing?" Randy asked.

"He's happy. He's got some woman over there he's involved with."

"Really?" Randy snickered. "An African girl?"

"No, some Peace Corps volunteer he's workin' with. He seems pretty serious about her."

"Uh oh," Randy teased. "Marriage serious?"

"Maybe. Too soon to tell, but he's definitely in love with her."

"How's Sabrina?"

Sabrina Ryan, Jim's daughter, recently graduated from medical school. She was currently working through a Hematology and Oncology Residency Program at the University of Texas Health Science Center in San Antonio. "She's not particularly fond of the weather down there, but she enjoys her placement."

"I bet she does. Oncology will keep her busy."

"It certainly will." Jim quickly scanned the stands. "Where's your wife?"

"Lacy's dance team is performing the halftime show tonight, so she's helping the girls with their uniforms."

"Oh, that's right. I forgot Lacy had a performance tonight. Where's Lauren?"

Randy pointed to the student section of the bleachers. That's when he noticed his daughter getting cozy with the teenage boy sitting next to her. "Who the hell is that?"

Jim turned his head to look. The young man put his arms around Randy's daughter and moved his lips close to hers. "Don't know. He sure seems to like Lauren though."

"He needs to get his damn hands off my daughter."

Jim laughed. "Teenagers, Dude. Been there, done that." He took a moment to watch the cheerleaders, paying particular attention to Gabby. "You do realize, don't you, that your son is involved with a hottie."

Randy scoffed at Jim's statement. "It's funny you say that."

"Why is that?"

"Because his girlfriend has an appointment to see me tomorrow. I'm putting her on the pill."

Jim busted out laughing. "Are you serious?"

"Yup. A few weeks ago, Nathan informed me that he and Gabby wanted to have sex. I bought him a box of condoms and suggested she get on the pill."

Surprised by this sudden news, Jim sputtered, "God damn, Dude. How did Jane react to all this?" He assumed that she probably had a panic attack when she discovered her son was having sex while he was still in high school.

"She had a mini meltdown. It didn't help that she found out by finding a box of condoms hidden in the drawer by Nathan's bed. She kinda got upset with me when I told her I bought them for him."

"You got those for him without her knowin' about it? That's ballsy."

"Once I explained the situation to her, she was ok with it. She's not particularly thrilled that he's having sex, but she feels better knowing he's using protection."

"That's good."

Gabriella spotted Dr. Hanson and Dr. Ryan in the stands and waved to them.

Randy waved back. "I like Gabby. She's a sweet girl. What's more important is Nathan loves her, and they're happy together. That's all I care about."

The following week, Nathan was at his locker grabbing materials for his next class when his friend, Todd, walked up behind him. "Is it true?"

"Is what true?"

"That you and Gabby did the nasty?"

Nathan pretended he had no idea what Todd was talking about. "Where'd you hear that?"

"Word is out all over school. It was the topic of talk in the locker room before practice yesterday."

"You shouldn't believe everything you hear." The fact that his teammates chose to spread ugly rumors about him made Nathan angry. He closed his locker, scrambled the combination, and strode down the hall.

Todd called out, "So you're saying it isn't true?"

Nathan stopped and stood tautly. "I'm saying it's none of anyone's damn business what Gabby and I do." Ignoring any further remarks, he stepped into his class right as the tardy bell rang.

Nathan shared this class with Gabby, who immediately noticed the troubled look on his face. She leaned over and said, "You ok?"

Hiding behind a fake smile, he set his supplies on his desk. "I'm fine."

"No you're not."

Nathan's eyes met hers. "It's nothing. Just some guys being jerks."

With a flirtatious blink of her eyelids, she asked, "Are we still on for tonight?"

"Definitely." He combed his hair off his forehead with his fingers. "And I have a surprise for you."

"Ooh, what is it?"

When the teacher began instruction, Nathan opened his notebook and whispered, "Not now. I'll tell you later."

After practice, Nathan stood on the basketball court skimming through his text messages. Gabby ran up behind him and covered his eyes with her hands. "Boo!" she said.

Nathan removed her hands and turned around. "Hey."

"What is this surprise you said you had for me?"

"Oh," Nathan said, recalling what he was going to tell her. "Remember that dress you were looking at last week, the one you said you wanted for the dance?"

"Yes."

"I bought it for you."

Gabby beamed. "Really?"

"Yup. I took care of it. I told you I would."

"Where is it?"

"At my house. You wanna come over?" he asked.

"Yes."

"Alright. Let's go." Taking her hand, Nathan escorted her to his car.

When they arrived at his house, he and Gabby ambled inside, greeted by his mother. "Hey, Mom."

"Hi, Nathan. How was your day?"

"Had a good day. Practice went well." Getting straight to the point, Nathan said, "I brought Gabby over to see the dress."

Excited to show her, his mother said, "Nathan picked out the perfect dress for you. You're going to love it." She traipsed upstairs to get it.

Gabby eagerly waited for Mrs. Hanson to return. When she saw the beautiful royal blue gown on the hanger, her mouth gaped open. "Oh my god, that's my dress!"

"Yup." Nathan flashed a crooked grin. "It's the one you said you wanted."

Gabby took the dress in her hands and held it up, admiring the dazzling strapless, slim-fitting bodice covered in sparkling accents and layered with a tulle skirt. "It's perfect!"

"Put it on," Nathan suggested.

Gabby ran into the bathroom.

While Gabby was changing, Jane told Nathan, "That was a wonderful thing you did for her."

"We're not going to miss the dance just because Gabby can't afford a dress. She fell in love with that one. I had to get it for her."

She kissed him on the cheek. "You're a good man."

"Thanks, Mom."

When Gabby emerged from the bathroom, Nathan couldn't keep his eyes off of her. She was the most beautiful girl he had ever seen, and that dress was perfect for her. It accentuated her beautiful blue eyes and hugged every curve of her body. He was speechless and probably looked like a codfish with his mouth gaped open like that.

Gabby brushed the layers flat as she twirled around and posed for him. "What do you think?" she asked. "Do you like it?"

Nathan paraded around her and carefully placed his hand on her waist. "You are beautiful, and that dress makes you look hot."

Gabby lifted her chin and tilted her head so they were face to face. She closed her eyes inviting Nathan to kiss her. He gladly complied. As their lips met, his hand slowly moved across her tummy, stopping right under the curve of her breast.

They stayed embraced like this for several minutes before Dr. Hanson walked in the door and cleared his throat, cutting their kiss short.

Randy raised an eyebrow. "Nice dress."

Before either of them could respond, Randy left the room just as quickly as he entered. Nathan or Gabby both looked at each other and laughed.

Nathan took Gabby out to dinner that evening. On their way out to the parking lot, Gabby bundled her arms around herself, trying to keep warm. Nathan pulled his letter jacket off and wrapped it around Gabby's shoulders. "That better?"

"Yes, thank you."

He quickly escorted her to the car, out of the cold air. As soon as they were buckled in, Nathan turned on the ignition and cranked up the heat.

"Where we going now?" Gabby asked.

"Home." He backed out of the parking space and drove into traffic.

"Already?" She checked the clock on the dashboard. It was only 8:30. "I don't want to go home yet."

With a mischievous grin, he replied, "We're going to my house."

When they arrived, every light in the house was off, except for the front porch light. "Where is everybody?" Gabby asked.

"My sisters are at a sleepover and my parents went out tonight. We have the whole house to ourselves." Nathan unlocked the door, stepped inside, and turned off the house alarm. With Gabby in his arms, and his lips pressed against hers, he slid his keys in his pocket and slowly led them toward the stairs. Since it was dark, and he couldn't see where he was going, he almost tripped over a pair of shoes at the bottom of the staircase.

"Nathan," Gabby said between kisses.

"Hmm?"

"Are you sure your parents aren't coming home?"

He pulled her upstairs with him, carefully treading one step at a time. "I'm sure."

When they made it to the top, Nathan slipped his letter jacket off Gabby's shoulders and watched it fall to the floor in the hallway.

"What if they come home while we're up here?"

He dragged her into his room. "They went out with some friends. They'll be gone all night." He sat her down on the bed and eased her onto the mattress.

"But what if they catch us?"

"They won't," he assured her, reaching for the switch on his bedside table lamp. "I told you they went out. Stop worrying."

He kicked off his shoes and scooted up to give their bodies more support. In one swift motion, he pulled his shirt over his head and reclaimed her lips, kissing her fervently.

Gabby kicked off her shoes and tightened her grip around him. "I don't want your parents to walk in and catch us."

He moved his hands up the back of her shirt, fumbling for the strap of her bra. "They won't." He stopped long enough to look into her eyes. "I promise."

She grinned at him, feeling more at ease.

Gabby helped him out by unbuttoning her blouse. She pressed her pelvis against his warm body while he reached down and searched for the button of his jeans. With one hand, he tried to unbutton his pants, which proved to be more challenging than he anticipated.

Watching him struggle with his zipper made Gabby laugh.

"Oh, ha ha, that's very funny," he joked with her. "You gonna lie there laughing at me or are you gonna help me?"

She loosened his pants for him. Once free, he stripped them off and kicked them over the end of the bed.

They helped each other remove the rest of their clothes until they were finally flesh to flesh. Nathan stumbled through the nightstand drawer for the box of condoms.

When he was able to grab one, he sat on his knees, straddling Gabby's legs, and ripped it open with his teeth.

Gabby watched him unroll it. When he was ready, she repositioned herself to allow him better access. Lying over top of her with his arms on either side of her head, he supported his weight on his elbows. In a loving gesture, he rubbed his thumb across her cheek. "You know I love you."

"I love you too."

Without further delay, he held Gabby in his arms and kissed her. She gladly welcomed him into her body.

Nathan and Gabby had done this often enough that he was better able to control his urges. He could last for longer periods of time, allowing Gabby to experience the full ecstasy of climax.

"Oh my god, Nathan." Her chest rose and fell rapidly. "That was amazing."

Nathan struggled to catch his breath. "You think?" He crawled off the bed and reached down to pick up her clothes. He tossed her jeans and blouse to her then stood over his wastebasket and removed the used condom. "Did you ask your mom about next weekend?"

"Yes."

When Nathan looked up, Gabby was on the bed in only her undergarments. For a seventeen-year-old girl, she had an amazing body. Grinning at her, he stepped into his underwear. "And what did she say?"

"She won't let me go."

This didn't surprise him. "Of course not.

"I'm sorry. We can hang out Friday after the game if you want."

He leaned over the bed and kissed her. "Absolutely." The alarm clock emitted a bright red 9:42. It was almost her curfew. "I need to get you home. I don't want you to be late."

As Gabby pulled her tee-shirt over her head and tucked it into her jeans, Nathan chuckled.

"What?" she questioned, wondering what he was laughing at.

Her ponytail was hanging off the side of her head and her hair was all disheveled. "You might want to fix your hair. If you walk into the house like that, your mom's going to question what you've been doing."

The next day, while Nathan was at work and Randy was on an emergency call at the hospital, Jane roamed around the house dumping all the wastebasket contents into a garbage bag. When she leaned over to pick up Nathan's trashcan, the condom he used the night before was in plain sight. She tightened her jaw and set the wastebasket back on the floor.

When Randy came home an hour later, he didn't even have time to set his stethoscope on the table before Jane confronted him. "I need to show you something."

"I just walked in the door."

"I know, but this important." She took his hand and directed him to Nathan's room. Once inside, she pointed to the wastebasket. "Look in there, please."

Randy thought this was an odd request. "In the trashcan?"

"Yes."

"Why?"

"Just do it," she insisted.

Randy peeked into the wastebasket and immediately saw what his wife was riled up about.

"You see it, right?" she questioned.

"Yeah, I see it."

"Will you talk to your son about this please?"

Randy took a deep breath. "Yes. I'll talk to him."

When Nathan got home from work that afternoon, he stepped into the kitchen and poured himself something to drink.

Randy picked up his car keys and twirled them around his finger. "Get in the car, Nate. We're going for a ride."

Although Nathan loved riding in his father's sports car, he hated when his father asked him to get in the car. It usually meant he was in trouble. "Yes, Sir." He quickly chugged down his drink then followed his father out to the garage.

Randy drove for a while without saying a word. Nathan glanced over at his father several times, hoping to get some kind of indication—a look, a word, something—to let him know why he was asked to go for a ride. Unable to take the silent tension, he asked, "Am I in trouble?"

"No, you're not in trouble. But your mom asked me to talk to you."

"About what?"

"Before I tell you, let's see if you can figure it out," Randy declared. "I'll give you a hint. Your mom was cleaning up the house this morning and went upstairs to dump your trash."

Randy didn't have to say another word. Nathan's mouth dipped into a sour frown. He wanted to crawl under the seat and disappear. "Oh crap."

"You know what I'm talking about, don't you?"

"Dad, I…"

Randy stopped him. "It's ok. I'm not upset with you. I think your mom is, but I'm not." Randy gathered his thoughts before he continued. "Leaving a condom in your trashcan wasn't very wise, Son."

"I didn't mean to. I wasn't using my head."

Randy tried to ease the tension by adding his perverted sense of humor. "Oh you were using your head alright, just not your brain."

"It's hard sometimes."

Randy continued to tease his son, "Kinda difficult to use a condom if it's not."

"That's not what I mean," Nathan declared. "I mean finding privacy, places where we can be alone. We can't go to her house. And there's not enough room in my car."

"Oh, I know. You have to be a contortionist or something to be able to stretch like that."

Although Nathan found this conversation embarrassing, he could no longer maintain a straight face. "Very funny, Dad."

Getting serious, Randy firmly stated, "Nate, you're eighteen now. Your mother and I want to give you more freedom and allow you more privacy, but giving you that freedom means you have to be more responsible. You have to consider all options and think about your choices wisely before you make decisions. And when you make these decisions, you need to keep in mind that you have younger sisters in the house, and I'm sure you can picture the look on your mother's face when she found that."

"Yeah. I'm glad I wasn't there to see it."

"Be responsible, Son. And for god's sake, don't throw a used condom out in the open where your mom can see it."

"Yes, Sir."

When they stopped at a red light, Randy smiled at his son. "I could go for some ice cream. You want some?"

"I would love some."

CHAPTER FOUR

Friday night, while Nathan warmed up on the court with his team, Gabby, in her purple and white cheering outfit, squatted down on the sidelines to tie her shoe.

Nathan loomed closer. "Hey."

She looked up at him and smiled. "Hey, Superstar."

"Meet me outside the locker room after the game?"

She picked up her metallic purple pompoms and rose to her feet. "Ok."

Nathan gazed at her with loving eyes. "Wish me luck."

"I'm always cheering for you." She poked him in the chest with her pompom. "You know that."

He leaned in to kiss her then headed to the locker room with his team.

The game itself was fast-paced and energetic, and Nathan was on his mark tonight, making several layups, sinking three-point shots, and nailing all four of his free throws. By the end of the first half, the Lake Washington Kangaroos were ahead by seven points.

Nathan and his team returned to the locker room, and Randy turned to his wife. "He is hot tonight."

"That three pointer he made at the buzzer was amazing," Jane remarked. "Where'd he learn to play like that?"

"Gee, I can't imagine. Seems like a woman I know used to make shots like that all the time. And she'd get pissed off if she'd lose."

"I don't like to lose," she retorted. "If a team wanted to win on my court, they had to get past me."

"No shit. You are aggressive on the basketball court, Babe. Jim's afraid to play with you. Last time he did, you knocked him on his ass. He's convinced you dislocated his shoulder."

"He's a wuss."

Randy chuckled and patted her thigh. "I'm gonna run to the restroom and grab something to drink. You want anything?"

"A Diet Pepsi, please."

"Ok. Be back in a bit." Randy stood up and hopped down the bleachers to the restrooms.

When he stepped into the crowded concession area, he saw his daughter, Lacy, in a nearby corner making out with some boy he had never seen before. He advanced toward them. "Well, what have we here?" he said, startling them.

"Daddy!"

Randy gave the young man an icy glare. "Who are you?"

The boy staggered. "Spencer."

Trying to intimidate this boy, Randy towered over him. "Well, Spencer, you do realize that's my daughter you have your hands on, don't you?"

The boy moved his hands and stepped several feet away.

Randy snarled at his daughter, "I want to talk to you." He stepped outside expecting her to follow him. Reluctantly, she complied.

Stiff-faced and confrontational, she placed her hands on her hips and huffed, "Dad, listen…"

Before she uttered another word, Randy interjected, "First off, cool the attitude."

Lacy relaxed her stance.

"Secondly, who the hell is that?"

"His name is Spencer," she argued.

Wanting a better explanation than that, Randy demanded more information. "Does he go to school here?"

"Yes. He's a junior."

"How long have you known him?"

"I met him at the game tonight."

Randy's lips drew a hard line. "You just met this boy, yet you let him rub his hands all over you?"

"So?"

"You don't know him, Lacy."

"Neither do you!" Lacy folded her arms across her chest, rolled her eyes, and turned away from her father.

Randy wasn't about to tolerate disrespectful behavior from his daughter. "Oh no, Ma'am. You most certainly will not raise your voice at me, nor will you turn your back when I'm speaking to you. Turn around."

Out of respect for her father, she did. But she kept her arms crossed.

Giving her the evil eye, he warned, "That tone you're taking with me is inappropriate. I strongly suggest you modify it before you open your mouth again."

Lacy inhaled heavily. "This isn't fair. How come Nathan can have a girlfriend, but I can't have a boyfriend?"

"A boyfriend?" Randy scoffed, thinking that was the most ludicrous thing he ever heard. "He is not your boyfriend. You've known him for, what, five minutes?"

"Why does that matter?"

"You know nothing about him, Lace. How do you know you can trust him?" he questioned, trying to get her to think this through rationally.

She shifted from one foot to the other.

"A boy like that will lie to your face and say anything you want to hear. Then without a second thought, he'll badmouth you in front of his friends the very next day. He doesn't care about you, and he doesn't respect you."

Lacy looked down at her hands and fiddled with her fingers.

The distraught look on his daughter's face made Randy wonder if maybe he was too hard on her. "I'm not meaning to sound like an overbearing dad here, Lace. I'm trying to protect you. I don't want you to get hurt."

After considering everything her father said, Lacy realized he was right. She fell into his arms and cried. "I'm sorry, Daddy."

In an attempt to comfort his overly emotional fifteen-year-old daughter, Randy wrapped his arms around her and kissed the top of her head. "Don't be in such a hurry to grow up, Baby. Someday you'll meet a boy who will treat you with the respect you deserve. Wait for him. Don't jump on the first opportunity that pops up."

Lacy lifted her chin. "I love you, Daddy."

"I love you too."

After the game, Nathan drove Gabby down to the waterfront. Lake Washington was one of Nathan's favorite places to hang out. Waterfowl filled the area, and great blue heron were often spotted near the shoreline. The night was clear, and the glowing stars reflected off the smooth surface of the water. Nathan and Gabby held hands and strolled along the water's edge.

"I wish I could go with you tomorrow," Gabby declared.

"I wish you could too. How come your mom wouldn't let you go?"

"I don't know. She wouldn't give me a reason. She just said no and told me not to ask again."

"I don't think your mom likes me," he scoffed. "Every time we plan something like this, she waits until the last minute then decides you can't go."

"I can't wait 'til graduation so I can get away from my mother."

Nathan chuckled, "You in a hurry to get out of the house?"

"Wouldn't you be? You said yourself she never lets me do anything."

"She is restrictive. But I never had that problem. My parents have always given me quite a bit of freedom."

"Your parents are so cool. They come to all your games, they support you in school. You and your dad talk all the time, and your mom is always so nice to me."

Nathan agreed with her. "Yeah. My parents are pretty cool." He put his arm around her and kissed her head. "I'm hungry. You wanna grab some tacos?"

"Mmm, that sounds good."

While they munched on tacos, they talked about future plans. Both were excited about attending college in the fall, but shared their fears about this transition in their lives.

With late night munchies satisfied, Nathan took Gabby home. He pulled into the driveway of her house, turned off the ignition, and stepped out of the car. He went around to the passenger's side and offered his hand to her. Together they walked up to her front porch.

"I wish you were coming this weekend," he said.

"I wish I was too, but you know how my mom is."

Nathan wrapped her in his arms. "I'll miss you, Gab. Won't be the same without you."

"I'll miss you too."

Nathan leaned closer, closed his eyes, and touched his lips on hers. Her kiss was enticingly sweet. They stood on the porch embraced like this for a solid five minutes before Nathan pulled away. "I'll call you tomorrow."

"Have fun. And be careful," Gabby advised.

"I will." Nathan didn't want to let her go, but knew he had to. If she walked in the door even a minute late, he wouldn't be able to go out with her for several weeks. "I love you."

"I love you too."

The moment Gabby was safe inside, Nathan returned to the car and drove home.

When he walked in the house, his dad was sitting on the couch reading one of his medical journals. "Hi, Dad."

Randy looked up from his reading and focused his attention on his son. "Hi, Nate. Great game tonight."

"Thanks." Nathan draped his letter jacket over the back of the chair and put his keys in a glass bowl on the table. "I wish Gab and I could spend more time together, but her mom always gets in the way. I don't think she likes me."

"What makes you think that?"

Nathan plopped down on the couch. "Every time Gab and I make plans, her mom always finds a way to ruin them. Like last winter when we all went on that ski trip and you invited Gabby, but in the morning, right when we were getting ready to leave, her mom decided she couldn't go. The family barbecue on the 4th of July, that weekend a bunch of our friends got together and went waterskiing, and now this camping trip. It's like she goes out of her way to keep us apart."

Randy set his medical journal on the coffee table to give Nathan his undivided attention. "Nathan, let me tell you a story. When your mother and I first started dating, your grandfather hated me."

Nathan gave his father a confused look. "Grampa Davine?"

"Yes. The first time I met him, he shot me the nastiest glare and spent the entire evening grilling me with 20,000 questions, including demanding to know how much money was in my bank account. I felt like I was in an interrogation room, afraid to say or do anything. And every time I'd try to touch your mom, he'd scowl at me with these evil eyes. I was terrified of him."

"Really? I find that hard to believe. You two get along so well."

"We do now," Randy said. "But it wasn't always like that. The longer your mom and I dated, the worse his attitude became. He basically told me to stay away from his daughter."

If his father was trying to encourage him with this story, it wasn't working. "What did you do?"

"Your mom and I continued to build our relationship, hoping his attitude would improve. But as time moved on and your mom and I became more committed to one another, his attitude became so bad that he and your mother went a long time without speaking to each other. And when we moved in together, oh man did that open a can of worms. That man was furious. Yet despite all of this, and the fact that I was convinced the man hated me, the day your mother and I exchanged vows, your grandfather shook my hand, called me son, and told me he trusted me to take care of his daughter."

"Whoa. Why the sudden change of heart?"

"Turns out it wasn't me he had a problem with. It was his misbelief that I was trying to steal his daughter away from him. He loved her and was afraid to lose her, but overtime he realized I loved her too. My point is it's always been Gabby and her mom, and you pose a threat to that."

Nathan hadn't considered this. "So how do I handle this?"

"Let Ms. Pervis see your dedication to Gabby. Prove you care about her."

"I do care about her. I love her, Dad," Nathan said.

"I know you do, but Gabby's mom needs to be convinced."

Nathan nodded. "Gabby was telling me she wants to live in the dorms."

"And what about you?"

"I don't know what I want to do yet. I like living at home, but I want to be able to spend more time with Gabby."

"Consider your options carefully," Randy advised. "I'll support whatever you decide, aside from you and Gabby living together, which I don't even want you to consider because you are not ready for that."

"But you and Mom lived together."

Randy laughed. "We were both in grad school at the time, and I was seriously considering proposing to her."

"Obviously that worked out for you."

"Yes it did. Your mother and I have a great marriage. But it requires patience, compromise, and communication to keep that fire alive. I show her and tell her every day that I love her."

"Thank you for that. I learned how to treat a woman by watching you and Mom," Nathan said.

"You are doing a great job, Nathan. It's very obvious you love Gabby."

Nathan grinned proudly, glad he was making a positive impression.

Randy checked the time on his watch. "I need to get some sleep. I'm on-call tomorrow. Gotta be alert to welcome those babies into the world."

"Yeah. I need to get some sleep too. We're leaving early tomorrow morning."

"Be safe, please. Make sure you have your phone, and call us when you get there."

"I will," Nathan replied.

Randy stood up. "Goodnight, Nathan. In case I don't see you in the morning, have fun this weekend."

"Thanks, Dad."

CHAPTER FIVE

Camping with his friends was something Nathan had been looking forward to for weeks. They were going to roast hotdogs and marshmallows by a campfire, hike through the woods, fish, and enjoy the wonderful wilderness. Even though Gabby wasn't there, Nathan was determined to have a good time. He and his friends, Mike and Todd, were pitching tents by the lake when Mike asked, "How come Gabby didn't come?"

Nathan hammered a tent stake into the ground. "Her mom wouldn't let her."

Todd teased, "Probably because she found out you two have been getting naked together."

Nathan abruptly looked up, offended by Todd's rude remark. "Shut up and mind your own damn business."

Taking Nathan's side, Mike intervened, "Todd, lay off, man."

Todd closed his mouth and resumed tent setup.

"Why wouldn't her mom let her come?" Mike asked.

"I don't know," Nathan replied. "Her mom does this all the time. It's frustrating. Every time Gabby and I make plans, her mom makes up some lame ass excuse and won't let her go. She's a real buzzkill."

"That sucks."

Nathan couldn't have agreed more. "Yes it does."

As night fell and the temperature began to drop, they bundled up in jackets and built a campfire to stay warm. Mike and his girlfriend snuggled together by the fire while

Todd cuddled under a sleeping bag with his. Nathan felt out of place being there without Gabby. He used this awkward moment to call her. With his cellphone in his hand, he walked over to a large boulder. Minimal coverage. He moved closer to the edge of the lake, more out in the open, and his signal bumped up from one bar to two. He dialed Gabby's number.

Thrilled to hear his voice, she answered. "Hey, Superstar. Are you having fun?"

"I'm a bit uncomfortable at the moment."

"Why?"

"Everyone is gathered around the campfire kissing and cuddling, but I'm here by myself. I feel like the third wheel."

"I tried to come, Nathan," she declared.

"I know. It's not your fault." To fight the chill in the air, he put the hand that wasn't holding the phone in his pocket. "It's cold out tonight."

Concerned about his wellbeing, she asked, "Are you warm enough?"

"Yes, I'm fine. Would be warmer if I had you to snuggle with. But there's a fire rolling, and I have a nice cozy sleeping bag. Don't worry."

"Of course I worry. I don't want you to turn into a Popsicle."

Nathan chuckled. "I won't turn into a Popsicle. You know my mother. She insisted I pack wool socks, gloves, a knitted hat, insulated boots, long underwear...you know, the usual camping attire."

"She only does it because she cares about you."

"I know she does." Nathan released a long drawn-out sigh.

Gabby knew something was wrong. "You ok?"

"Kinda bummed."

"About what?"

What he was about to divulge was probably going to shake her up a bit. He had to tread carefully. "There's something I need to tell you. I want you to hear it from me before you hear it from someone else."

"What is it?"

"Some of the guys have been spreading rumors about us."

"Rumors?" she asked. "What kind of rumors?"

"Apparently word is out around school that you and I are having sex. I swear I didn't tell anyone, and I don't know who started it or why, but it's out there."

The line grew silent.

Gabby's lack of response worried him. He thought she was mad. "Gab?"

"Guess that explains the funny looks I got yesterday."

"I'm sorry, Babe. I don't know how this happened."

"So someone just made this up?"

"I guess. I'm really sorry."

"Why are you apologizing? You said you had nothing to do with it."

"I didn't, but people are saying mean things and disgracing your reputation. That bothers me."

"Someone at some point would have started a rumor about it regardless. That's how people are, Nathan. There's always some juicy story going around."

Nathan chuckled a little. "Seems juvenile to me."

"It is."

"I didn't want you to find out by hearing it circulate around school," he stated.

"Thank you for telling me. I appreciate your honesty."

They talked for another thirty minutes before Nathan's fingers became numb and he had to return to the fire to unthaw. By this time, the two couples were roasting hotdogs and marshmallows and telling scary stories by the campfire. Nathan grabbed himself a stick and joined them.

Monday after basketball practice, Nathan trotted out of the locker room prepared to drive Gabby home. As he walked across the gym, one of his teammates, Derek, said something to Gabby that obviously upset her. Nathan walked closer to them, hoping to intervene, but he was too late. Gabby threw her pompoms on the gym floor, covered her mouth with her hand, and ran away crying.

Nathan sped up his pace and immediately confronted Derek. "What did you say to my girlfriend?"

Derek stepped back, unaware that Nathan was standing there watching. "I didn't say anything to her."

"The hell you didn't. Gabby doesn't run off crying for no reason. You had to have said something to her."

With a derisive sneer, Derek replied, "Maybe you should ask her."

"Maybe I will." Nathan searched the school for Gabby, checking every location he could think of. In the hallway, he bumped into one of her cheerleader friends. "Hey, Naomi, did you see which way Gabby went?"

Naomi pointed toward the bathroom. "That way."

"Thank you." Nathan headed that direction. When he got to the girl's bathroom, he leaned against the doorjamb and put his ear against the door, trying to listen in. "Gab?"

No one answered.

A girl Nathan knew walked out of the bathroom. "Alondra," he said to her. "Is Gabby in there?"

"Yes." She snarled at him, as if he was a bloodsucking leech. "What'd you do to her?"

In his defense, he replied, "I didn't do anything to her."

"Then why is she crying?"

"It wasn't me. Is anyone else in there?"

"No."

Nathan opened the door and was about to walk inside when Alondra stopped him. "What are you doing?"

"Going in to talk to Gabby."

"But that's the girl's bathroom. You can't go in there."

"Oh yeah? Just watch me." He barged right in.

Gabby was on the floor hugging her knees; tears streamed down her face. Nathan sat on the floor next to her and reached out to hold her hand. "What's wrong?"

She sniffled and wiped her eyes. "I hate my mother."

Well, this was a bold and hurtful statement, not like her at all. Nathan wondered what happened that made her snap like this. "What's going on?"

"All of my friends have their licenses except me. They all get to hang out with friends after school and stay out past ten and go to the after game party, but I don't. Then Derek accused me of keeping you away from your friends because if I don't go to the party on Friday then you won't go. He said all I do is drag you down and prevent you from focusing on your game," she wailed. "I'm going to mess up your chances of getting a basketball scholarship, and all your hopes and dreams will disappear because of me."

How dare Derek say that to her? He moved closer and pulled her into his arms. "You don't drag me down at all. You lift me up. When I see you standing on the sidelines cheering me on, it makes me play harder."

"But Nathan," Gabby cried into his shoulder. "He said…"

He didn't let her finish. "I don't give a crap what Derek said. He doesn't know what he's talking about. He's had a problem with me ever since basketball season started because I made captain and he didn't." Nathan lifted Gabby's chin and looked at her pretty face. It was all wet with tears. "Don't worry about Derek. What he said wasn't nice, it also isn't true." He wiped her tears away and tenderly kissed her on the lips. "As far as your mother is concerned, there isn't much we can do about that. We only have six more months of high school, then you can get away from her and you and I will have more time together. We need to hang on a little longer. And for the record, I wasn't planning on going to that party anyway. The way the guys were talking, it sounded lame." Nathan lifted himself to his feet and held his hand out to Gabby. "Come on. I am dying for a milkshake. Wanna share one with me?"

"Can we get chocolate?"

"We can get whatever flavor you want." She took his hand, and he pulled her off the floor.

When Gabby realized where they were standing, she started to giggle. "Nathan, what are you doing in the girl's bathroom?"

"I came in here to find you," he replied.

"You're gonna get in trouble if a teacher catches you in here."

"Then we better get out of here." They held hands and exited the bathroom together.

The next day, Nathan confronted Derek in the hallway. "Can I talk to you for a minute?"

Derek followed him to a less crowded location. "What's up?"

"What you said to Gabby," Nathan shook his head. "Not cool."

"The only reason you aren't coming to the party Friday is because Gabby isn't going."

"I'm not going because I don't want to. I have better things to do with my time."

Derek grumbled, "You're the team captain. You should be with your team. But little miss perfect drags you away all the time."

Trying to be civilized and resolve this dispute diplomatically, Nathan said, "If you have a problem with me, then come out and say it. Don't drag Gabby into this."

"You think you are some kind of bigshot, don't you?"

Nathan hardened his expression. "What?"

"You are coach's little pet. You have your nose shoved so far up his ass."

Derek was about to storm off, but Nathan grabbed his arm. "What is your problem?"

Derek turned around, fuming. "You have no fucking clue, do you? You're the local superstar. Your face is plastered on every sports page in town. Hanson scores the winning point. Hanson wins MVP. The whole damn town adores Nathan Hanson."

"Is that what this is about? Because if it is, that's asinine."

"Your life is perfect. Even your girlfriend is perfect—she's the prettiest cheerleader on the squad, and she puts out for you."

"I told you to leave her out of this. You can talk smack to me all you want, but don't drag my girlfriend into any stupid issue you have with me." He ended the conversation and marched to the locker room.

During practice, Nathan's basketball coach sensed the tension between him and Derek. He blew his whistle and shouted, "Alright, gentlemen. Take five and hydrate. Hanson, come here."

Nathan rushed over to see what his coach wanted. "Yes, Coach?"

"What's going on with you and Hampton today?"

"Nothing. Just a personal issue."

"You need to handle it," his coach insisted. "Now."

"Yes, Sir." Nathan took a cleansing breath then headed back over to the side of the court to grab a Gatorade. He opened the bottle, chugged down a huge gulp, then took a few strides toward Derek. "Hey."

Derek refused to acknowledge him.

Trying to break the ice, Nathan offered him a compliment. "Nice steal."

"Thanks."

"Gabby and I are going to catch a movie and hang out by the lake Saturday night. You wanna snag a date and come along?"

Derek glared at Nathan. "Why would I want to do that?"

Nathan lifted a shoulder. "I don't know. To get out and do something fun." Derek stared at him derisively. Obviously this wasn't working, so Nathan tried a different approach. "You know, if something was bothering you, all you had to do was come talk to me about it. We've been friends for a long time Derek."

"I know."

"Why don't we get some burgers after practice and we'll talk."

Reluctantly, Derek agreed, "Alright."

To make peace, Nathan offered his hand.

Derek stared at it before he shook it.

Coach Dolan witnessed this whole encounter, satisfied with the outcome. Nathan was a wonderful leader, doing whatever he could to maintain comradery among the players.

At the end of practice, as the boys scrambled off the court and herded to the locker room, Coach Dolan pulled Nathan aside. "Hanson, stop by my office before you leave."

"Yes, Sir." Since Nathan was the team captain, it wasn't unusual for the coach to call him into his office. They often discussed game stats and personal issues. And sometimes the coach sought his help when other players needed to brush up on their game.

After a refreshing shower, Nathan stopped by his coach's office. The door was partially ajar, so he tapped lightly on the door frame. "You wanted to see me, Coach?"

"Yes," Coach Dolan replied. "Come in and sit down."

Nathan took a seat on the opposite side of the desk.

The coach sat back in his chair and crossed his arms, grinning at Nathan. "This morning I received a phone call from a basketball scout who came out to see you play last week. He informed me that he was sending a recruiter out for Friday's game."

Nathan wasn't sure how to react to this news. His heart rate accelerated and his stomach fluttered. "This Friday?"

"Yes. Pretty exciting, huh?"

Nathan wavered, unsure what to think. "Well, yeah. I mean…" The significance of this slowly began to sink in. "What school is he from?"

"University of Washington."

Nathan's eyes widened. He couldn't believe a basketball recruiter from UW was interested in him. "UW? Seriously?"

"Yes," the coach replied, knowing Nathan had dreams of playing college basketball. "I know this is big news for you, and a great opportunity. You're a good player. You dominate the court and you know how to lead a team. But you also have a good head on your shoulders. I know you'll impress them."

"I'll certainly try."

"Play your ass off Friday night," Coach Dolan bluntly stated.

This comment made Nathan laugh. "I always do."

"Congratulations."

"Thanks, Coach."

On his way out of the locker room, the varsity cheerleaders had mats spread out on the gym floor, practicing a new pyramid they were planning to perform at the upcoming game. The moment Nathan spotted Gabby, he smiled widely. Hoping he could offer her a ride home, he stuck around and waited for them to finish.

When the girls concluded their practice session, they filed into the locker room one by one. Nathan snuck up behind Gabby and tickled her. "Hey, Beautiful. Can I offer you a ride home?"

She plastered a smile on her face. "Of course."

He rested his hands on her hips. "Coach Dolan called me into his office today and you'll never guess what he told me."

"What did he tell you?"

"A basketball recruiter from UW is coming to watch me play this week."

Gabby's jaw dropped. "Are you serious?"

"Yup."

"Oh my god, Nathan." She hugged him tightly. "That is awesome."

"It is, but I'm a little nervous."

"Why?"

"Well, think about it, Gab. This guy is coming to watch me because he wants me to play basketball for UW. This is what I've always wanted. What if I have a bad game or we get our asses kicked and I make a poor showing?"

She offered reassurance. "You are always strong on the court. And you handle pressure well. The higher the stakes are, the more intensely you play. I stand on the sidelines and watch every game, remember?"

Exhaling heavily, he said, "I don't want to screw this up."

"You won't. You will shine like you always do."

"Thank you. It means a lot knowing you believe in me."

"I've always believed in you."

It was moments like this that made Nathan love Gabby. Not only was she his biggest fan, she was also the one person he could always count on no matter what was going on in his life.

Back in eighth grade, Gabby stood on the sidelines waving her pompoms while Nathan pounded the hardwood. Ever since that day, a mutual friendship formed between them that eventually developed into a committed partnership of mutual trust, undying support, and genuine love. They were inseparable.

Nathan leaned in closer and embraced her with a kiss. "I love you," he said.

"I love you more," she teased.

Playing along, he retorted, "I love to infinity and beyond."

"You sound like Buzz Lightyear," she giggled.

Nathan chuckled and kissed her again. "I'm gonna stop by The Slip and grab some burgers with Derek."

"Derek?" she questioned, wondering why Nathan was hanging out with him.

"Yes. He and I haven't really sat down and talked in a while. We need to catch up and rebuild our relationship."

Although she didn't really like Derek, she was glad Nathan was making an effort to fix the distance between them. "Alright."

"Can I offer you a ride home first?"

"Of course. Let me get my stuff."

Nathan walked in the door of his house around 6:30 that night. He set his backpack on the dining room table and called out, "Mom!"

"Up here," her voice trailed from the second floor.

Nathan tromped up the stairs and found her in the bedroom sorting laundry.

"Hi, Sweetie. How was school?"

"Coach Dolan called me into his office after practice today."

She immediately stopped what she was doing. "Is everything alright?"

"Yeah," Nathan replied. "He told me a recruiter from UW is coming to the game Friday night."

Since she had played starting point guard for UC Berkeley, she understood the significance of this. "That's great, Honey. How do you feel about that?"

"I'm excited, but I'm nervous."

"What are you nervous about?"

Nathan sat on his parents' bed with one leg bent under him and the other dangling off the edge. "You know how much I want to play college ball. I can't believe this opportunity has actually presented itself to me. I don't want to mess it up."

Jane sat down next to him. "If the recruiter is coming, then someone has already read your stats and watched you play. They must've liked what they saw. If they didn't, they wouldn't be sending a recruiter out for you."

"But I want to show him what I can do. I want to play my best."

"You always give your best on the court, Nathan. You won't give anything less than that. You're a lot like me in that respect."

"I need to work on my three pointers. I've been off lately. Will you help me?" he pleaded.

"Of course," she said with a smile. "Let me change into basketball worthy attire and I'll meet you out front."

"Thanks." Nathan went into his room and changed into sweats, a sweatshirt, and a pair of basketball shoes. He grabbed his basketball and went out to the driveway, shooting a few baskets into the hoop before his mother joined him.

When Randy drove up to the house in his red convertible, his son and wife were out on the driveway playing a game of one-on-one. Trying not to disturb their game, he parked out by the curb. He stepped out of the car right as Nathan spun a 360, dribbled the ball, and ran up to the basket making a backward layup. "Wow, nice one, Nate."

Nathan retrieved the ball and held it under his arm. "Thanks."

Randy walked over to his wife and gave her a kiss. "The kid is better than you, Babe," he teased her. "You might want to brush up on your game."

She smirked at her husband's orneriness. "Hush!"

"You know I love you. I wouldn't tease you if I didn't."

"Just remember, what comes around goes around."

Moving closer to his wife, he whispered in her ear, "Oh, I'm counting on it." He gave her a seductive wink and patted her on the butt before he went inside.

Later that night, as the Hanson family was enjoying a quiet evening together, Randy's cellphone went off. With a coffee cup in his hand, he looked down at his phone. "Damn. I was hoping she could hold off for a few days."

He gulped down the rest of his coffee, slid his cellphone back in his pocket, and fumbled around for his stethoscope.

This clumsy juggling act made Nathan laugh. "That was graceful, Dad. I hope you don't stumble around like that when you catch babies."

"That would be bad, wouldn't it?" He kissed his wife goodbye. "I'm off. Duty calls."

As Randy was about to leave, Nathan reached into a glass bowl in the center of the table. "Uh, Dad? You might need these."

Randy turned around to see Nathan holding up his car keys. "Yes, that would be helpful." He grabbed his keys, mussing up Nathan's hair as he did. "Thank you, Son."

"You're welcome."

"Love you guys. Be back in a couple hours." He closed the door and took off to bring another baby into the world.

Nathan's sisters shuffled up to their rooms, but Nathan hung out in the living room with his mother. He pulled a chapter book for his English class out of his backpack and began reading it. With the million thoughts rolling around in his head, he had a hard time concentrating. He read the same page three times and still didn't know what it said. Frustrated, he placed a bookmark in his book and set it on the coffee table. "Mom?"

She looked up from the book she was reading. "Yes?"

"Can I talk to you about something?"

Jane placed the book beside her on the sofa. "What is it, Sweetie?"

"I'm worried about Gabby."

"Why?"

"Because her mom never lets her do anything. Gabby doesn't get into trouble, she's responsible and reliable, and she's a good student. Yet she can't go to parties, can't attend sleepovers, and she's not allowed to invite friends to her house. She can't watch R rated movies, and she has to ask her mother's permission before she can read a book because her mom insists on checking it to make sure it's appropriate. She can't go on class trips, and her mom wouldn't sign any permission forms for the movies we watch in health class. And on the weekends, she can't stay out past ten. Her mom won't let her get her driver's license or a job. How come Gabby doesn't have any privileges? It's like she's being punished when she hasn't done anything wrong. I don't understand the rationale behind that."

Jane heard the vexation in Nathan's voice and did her best to soothe him. "If that's the way Ms. Pervis wants to raise her daughter, there's nothing you can do about it."

"She broke down in tears after school the other day."

"Who? Gabby?"

"Yes," Nathan said. "She was upset because her mom won't let her go to the after-game party Friday night. It didn't help that Derek had to be a jerk to her about it. All of her friends have all these privileges, especially now that we're seniors, but her mom treats her like a child and doesn't let her do anything. It's not fair."

"No, it's not, but it's out of your control."

"I can't stand to watch her being treated so unjustly. I want to get her out of that situation."

"Sweetheart, you can't control the way Gabby's mom is. But what you can control is your reaction to it."

"My reaction?" Nathan asked. "What do you mean?"

Jane explained, "You can either let it get in the way and allow it to control your relationship, or you can work around it and not let it be an obstacle."

Nathan didn't understand what his mother was trying to say. "Work around it?"

"If you want to be with her, you'll find a way to make it work. It may take time, but in the end it will be worth it."

Nathan leaned back. "It's already worth it. I'm going to do whatever it takes to be with Gabby."

"Sounds like you have the right attitude."

CHAPTER SIX

Friday night, while Nathan was packing up his athletic bag in preparation for the big game, his mother stepped into his room. Even though Nathan tried to hide the stress and tension he felt, Jane could tell he was nervous. "Hi, Honey."

"Hey, Mom."

"How are you feeling?"

"I'm ready for the game tonight."

"You're not nervous?"

"No. Why would I be?" he stated confidently.

"Just do your best. Remember, they already like what they see."

"I know. You told me that already." Jane had an anxious look on her face, which Nathan found amusing. "You're the one who looks nervous."

"I've been where you are. I know how it feels. Don't let the pressure get the best of you tonight."

"I live for pressure." Nathan threw his bag over his shoulder and reached into his pocket for his keys.

Before Nathan left the house, Randy caught up with him in the living room. "Nate."

"Yes, Sir?"

"Focus on your defense tonight, and be the master of your offense."

Randy's words of advice made Nathan laugh. "Um...ok. I'll try."

Kidding around with his son, Randy said, "Do or do not. There is no try."

Nathan stared at his father, thinking he'd lost his mind. "You've been watching Star Wars again, haven't you?"

"Just trying to get you to relax. Your mom said you might be nervous."

"Did you see her face?" Nathan remarked. "She's the one who's nervous. I'm excited about the game tonight. We're gonna kill Bellevue."

"Good. I would love to see a Kangaroo kick a Wolverine's ass."

"So would I," Nathan said. "See you tonight, Dad."

"Good luck. We'll be rooting for you."

The Lake Washington High School Kangaroos were the conference dominators this season. They had a 14-1 record and were ranked among the top ten teams in the state. Their goal was to hoist the Championship Trophy, and they were well on their way. But first, they had to get past Bellevue.

Some pretty intense basketball games were played between Lake Washington and Bellevue. The two teams were rivals. But for Nathan, this was more than a rivalry game or a chance to increase their ranking. He was on his way to the NCAA.

Nathan played the game of his life. Throughout the entirety of the first half, he was aggressive on the court and accurate at the hoop, both inside the key and at three point range. His defensive skills were on target, and he almost seemed angry as he trotted back and forth from one end of the paint to the other. He vocalized orders to his team and successfully directed them around the half court. By the end of the game, all ten suited up Kangaroos scored at least four points, led by Nathan with a season high of thirty-nine. It was one of the best high school basketball games Randy had ever seen, and it boosted Lake Washington's record to 15-1. Surely that game made an impression on the recruiter.

Randy rose early the next morning, awakened by a call from the hospital informing him that a patient of his had checked in. He siphoned coffee from the brewing pot, added sugar and creamer, then sat at the dining room table to read the paper. Under the local high school sports section, the morning headline accompanied a photo of Nathan making a layup. ***99-80—Lake Washington vs. Bellevue.*** The article ran a play by play of the game and posted an interview with the coach and some of the players. Randy smiled smugly as he read through it.

After checking on his patient, Randy hoped to catch Jim in the ER. Dr. Ryan was just finishing up with a patient when Randy walked through the main doors. Jim greeted him with a knuckle bump. "Hanson. What's up, Bro?"

"Can you sneak away to get some coffee with me?"

"Sure. Let me finish up here first. I'll meet you in five."

Randy marched down to the coffee shop and claimed a table. It wasn't long before Jim joined him. "Dude, I read the paper this morning. That son of yours is a badass basketball player."

Randy stirred sugar into his cup. "You should have seen him last night, Jim. He was phenomenal."

"Wish I could have been there."

"A recruiter from UW came to watch him play."

"Is that right?"

Randy set his stir stick on the table and lifted the cup to his lips. Right as he was about to take a sip, his cellphone rang. He didn't recognize the number. Assuming it was a consultation call, he answered, "Dr. Hanson."

"Hello, Dr. Hanson. This is Joseph Malone. I'm a basketball recruiter from the University of Washington."

"Good afternoon, Mr. Malone. What can I do for you?"

"I watched your son's game last night. Impressive," Mr. Malone said. "He's quite the player."

"We're proud of him."

"As you should be. I would like to speak to Nathan, with you and your wife present of course, about the possibility of having him play for the University of Washington," Mr. Malone offered. "Are you available sometime this weekend or next week to meet with me?"

Elated by this news, Randy grinned. "With my on-call schedule, this weekend would work best for me. I insist on being there."

"Absolutely, Doctor. What about tomorrow afternoon, around 1:00?"

"Tomorrow will be fine."

"Sounds great. Thank you for your time, Doctor. I look forward to meeting both you and Nathan tomorrow."

Randy hung up his phone and took a sip of his coffee.

"What's goin' on tomorrow?" Jim asked, eavesdropping on the conversation.

With a self-satisfied smirk on his face, Randy replied, "That was the recruiter. He wants to meet with Nathan tomorrow afternoon. My boy is going to play college ball."

"That is hellatiously cool!" Before Jim could get in another word, his beeper went off. "I'm bein' paged."

"I heard."

Jim stood up with his coffee cup in his hand. "You headin' upstairs?"

"Yup. Have a baby to deliver."

"Tell Nathan congrats for us."

"Will do."

When the recruiter showed up Sunday afternoon, the UW men's basketball coach and the Huskies' team captain came with him. Nathan and his parents sat around the coffee table in their living room discussing basketball with these people while they looked over paperwork, brochures, team stats, academic programs, and scholarship deals. For the most part, Jane and Randy sat back and let Nathan do the talking. They only interjected if they had a concern or pressing question. When all was said and done, the university offered him a full ride scholarship, including room and board on campus.

Before the band of Huskies cleared, the coach laid a letter of intent in Nathan's hand. Daunted, Nathan sat on the sofa staring at the paperwork in front of him.

Jane and Randy each took a seat on either side of him.

"Penny for your thoughts?" Jane said to her son.

Nathan's head spun. He didn't know what to say. "I can't think straight right now."

Knowing exactly what her son was going through, Jane offered him some sound advice. "This is a huge decision, but one you should not take lightly. Playing for an NCAA team will require a great deal of commitment on your part. Hours of practice, both before and after class, spending the entire game day at the gym, traveling out of town. Yet despite your practice schedule, you are still responsible for the class load you carry. And I know you want pre-med. I don't know exactly what that entails, but I do know the time commitment involved is going to be a huge factor for you."

"Nathan," Randy cut in. "Pre-med requires a lot of upper division science and math classes, both of which require you to study extensively. The coursework involved is not something you can neglect or put off for another day. If you let it slide, it will pile up quickly and you will fall behind, which is next to impossible to recover from." Randy could sense Nathan's stress, so he tried to ease the tension. "Your mom and I think this is a once in a lifetime opportunity that you should take advantage of. But we want you to see the reality of this and consider what you are going up against."

His mother interjected, "And what about Gabby?"

Hearing Gabriella's name got Nathan's attention. "What about her?"

"With the pre-med requirements, you will already have a loaded schedule. You add an NCAA basketball schedule on top of that, you're going to be one busy guy. Your decision affects her too. Have you and Gabby talked about this?"

"Yes," Nathan replied. "She's aware of the time commitment involved. And she's prepared, as am I, to work with that."

Randy added, "You need to look at this realistically, Nate. Weigh your options carefully. Read through all the information and consider every avenue. Come to us if you have any questions. The decision is yours. Whatever you decide, your mother and I will support you."

In an attempt to comprehend the full picture, Nathan sat with his father to discuss pre-med requirements, then he had a separate conversation with his mother about college basketball obligations. All the information Nathan received and the conversations he had with his parents constantly rolled around in his head. He and Gabby looked over paperwork together and discussed all of the options further. "What do you think I should do?" he asked.

She tried to offer the best advice she could. "An opportunity like this doesn't come along every day."

"I know, but college ball is a big commitment, Gab. Hours of practice, out of town for games and tournaments. All of that, along with the pre-med courses I'll be carrying, will keep me pretty busy."

"And I'll be right by your side through it all. You can't pass this up, Nathan. We'll make it work."

After practice, Nathan stopped by his coach's office, hoping he wasn't busy. "Hey, Coach. You have a minute?"

Coach Dolan greeted him with a friendly smile. "Sure, Nathan. Come on in."

Nathan pulled up a chair and sat down.

"What's on your mind?"

"Playing basketball for UW is something I've always dreamed of, something I've talked about since I was old enough to hold a basketball. But this whole college recruitment business has really got me thinking about my goals and my future." He rested his elbows on his knees and sat forward. "From a very young age, my parents instilled in me a strong work ethic that has stuck with me my entire life. My mother always set high expectations and told me, that with hard work, I can accomplish anything. She's an incredible basketball player and taught me everything she knows about the game. She showed me the value of teamwork and constantly offers undying encouragement and support. She's convinced I have the skills and desire necessary to be successful, and thinks I should follow my dream."

"I think that's sound advice."

"But there's more to it than that," Nathan declared. "I have another dream, one that will be much harder to achieve."

"What dream is that?" Coach Dolan asked.

"I want to go to medical school and be a doctor like my dad. He has an important job. He saves lives, brings new life into the world, and helps people every day. So aside from talking to my mother about basketball, I also had a heart to heart conversation with my dad about what it takes to make it through pre-med and medical school. He thinks I can do it, but I don't know if I can."

"Why not?"

"I never told you this before, when I was in grade school, I struggled with reading. My grades were far from stellar and the act of reading was physically exhausting. In second grade, my parents had me tested and found out I was dyslexic. They put me in a special reading program, and I was able to get the help I needed. All my life, I've had to work twice as hard as my peers to maintain good grades. Understanding what I read doesn't come as easy for me as it does for other people. What the average person can read in twenty minutes takes me an hour to fully comprehend. Pre-med requires a lot of technical reading and hours of studying. As much as I would love to play for UW, it will be hard for me to keep up with school when I have basketball commitments."

Coach Dolan leaned back in his chair. "Let me tell you something, Nathan. You underestimate yourself. You are a good student. You're earning A's and B's in AP classes, and that's not easy to do."

"Science and math come easy to me though. English, not so much."

"But you are diligent, hardworking, and put one hundred percent into everything you do. Even if a task seems unobtainable, you go the extra mile to get it done. With that kind of dedication, you can reach your goals. You're an all-around good kid with a heart of gold, and if anyone deserves this opportunity, it's you."

Contemplating his coach's advice, Nathan asked, "So you think I should sign?"

"I think you'll regret it if you don't."

After compiling all the information, weighing every option, and taking into account every conversation he had, Nathan finally reached a decision. At the dinner table that night, in the middle of a conversation about Lacy's dance recital and Lauren's upcoming musical, he blurted out, "I've decided to sign with UW."

All conversation ceased.

"I've discussed it with my coach, read through all the information at least fifty times, and have considered everything everyone has said to me." Nathan nodded his head and definitively stated, "I'm gonna sign."

Lauren gasped and stood up to give her brother a hug. "That's fantastic, Nathan! Congratulations!"

"We'll go to every game," Lacy added. "I'll even bring my purple pompom."

Randy smiled at his son, proud of the choice he made. "I know this was a difficult decision. Your mother and I will be here to support you and offer any help we can."

"Thanks, Dad."

Before he went to bed that night, Nathan signed his commitment letter and placed it in a manila envelope. But instead of putting a stamp on it and sticking it in the mailbox, he decided to hand deliver it.

After school the next day, he and Gabby hopped in the car and drove over to University of Washington.

"Wow," he said, gripping the steering wheel. "I can't believe this is really happening."

"I know," Gabriella replied. "I'm so happy for you. Now I can officially say my boyfriend plays basketball for the Huskies."

Nathan chuckled. "Not yet. Let's get through this season and get that State Championship first."

Nathan and Gabby plodded into Alaska Airlines Arena, where Nathan turned in his commitment letter followed by a brief conversation with the basketball coach. Before he left, the coach gave him a firm handshake and a purple *Washington Basketball* tee-shirt. On their way home, they stopped by Swedish Medical Center to catch up with his father.

Holding hands, Nathan and Gabby walked through the main doors of the hospital and over to some chairs in the waiting room. Nathan pulled out his cellphone and texted his dad to let him know they were downstairs.

Gabby had driven past this medical facility many times, but had never been inside. On the wall near the front entrance were a bunch of pictures of doctors affiliated with the hospital. Among the framed photographs were two faces she recognized—Dr. James Ryan and Dr. J. Randal Hanson.

After waiting a few minutes, Randy popped out of the elevator dressed in a white lab coat with a stethoscope draped around his neck. "Hey, Nate."

"Hi, Dad."

"Did you turn your letter in?"

"Yes, I did. Got a cool tee-shirt too," Nathan grinned.

"Good." Randy looked over at Gabriella. "Hello, Gabby. How are you?"

Gabby liked Dr. Hanson. He was always very kind to her, and he could make her laugh with some of the funny things he said. "Doing well, thank you."

Randy glanced at his watch. It was almost 5:30. "I have one more thing I need to do before I can get out of here, but if you want to hang around for a few minutes, we can grab some dinner."

"Alright."

Randy shifted his attention to Gabby. "Would you like to join us?"

Gabby nodded in agreement.

Randy turned to Nathan and said, "Call your mom. Tell her and the girls to meet us at Lai Tai's."

"What about Gabby?" Nathan asked. "Her mom is expecting her home by 7:00."

"I'll call Gabby's mom."

Nathan smiled appreciatively. "Thanks."

Nathan wore his *Washington Basketball* tee-shirt to school the next day. When Mike saw him, he gave him a congratulatory high-five. "Nice shirt, Dude."

"Thanks," Nathan replied.

"I guess your college plans are all secure now. One less thing on your plate."

Nathan breathed a sigh of relief. "Have to wait and see if Gabby gets accepted now. That would be the icing on the cake."

"No doubt," Mike said. "Is she gonna try to get on the cheerleading team? I heard the Husky squad is one of the most difficult teams to earn a spot on. The competition can get pretty intense."

"She wants to," Nathan replied. "Tryouts aren't until spring though. Right now, she'll just be happy with an acceptance letter."

The two boys walked to their lockers together. "What is Gabby going to do after graduation? Is she planning to live with her mom?"

Nathan snorted derisively. "No. She's looking into the dorms."

"The dorms?" Mike questioned, curling his lip. "Why?"

"Because it's close and convenient, and living in the dorms will be cheaper for her in the long run. It will get her out of the house, which is what she wants. Can't say I blame her. Her mom drives me crazy."

Mike had also applied to UW. Anticipating getting an acceptance letter soon, he and Nathan made plans to get an apartment together. "What about us?"

"I'm looking into university housing at this point."

"But an apartment will give you and Gabby more privacy, if you know what I mean," Mike teased.

"Getting an apartment also means we have to work a lot of hours to pay for it, and I don't want to do that. Honestly, Mike, I want to focus on basketball and school, not worry about paying rent. My basketball scholarship will cover housing costs. I'm getting a full ride, remember?"

Mike grinned. "Oh yeah."

"They have apartment-style housing on campus. We'll have plenty of privacy," Nathan explained. "And I'd rather avoid the commute into Seattle every day. University housing makes the most sense."

"You gonna ditch your job at Safeway?"

"Yup," Nathan replied. "I'll need some sort of part time job though if I want spending money, so I'm looking for something closer to campus."

"Like what?" Mike asked.

Nathan gave a half shrug. "I don't know. I'll have to look around and see what's available."

The headline on the sports page of the local paper made the entire Hanson family celebrate. Randy cut out the article and proudly displayed it on their refrigerator.

UW Lands Hanson! Music to Nathans's ears. Dream one, accomplished. Dream two…in the making.

CHAPTER SEVEN

Since the entire Hanson family was off Friday due to a holiday, Randy decided to take advantage of this three-day weekend by planning a family ski trip. He invited Gabby to come with them. As of yet, Ms. Pervis hadn't made any decisions indicated whether or not Gabby would be joining them.

Trying to get confirmation, Nathan met Gabby outside the school gymnasium. "What did your mom say about skiing this weekend?"

"She won't even consider letting me go if she doesn't talk to your mother first."

When Nathan got home that afternoon, he tossed his letter jacket of the couch and headed to the kitchen to grab something to eat. "Hey, Mom," he called out to her while he reached into the fruit bowl for an apple.

"Yes."

"Gabby asked about skiing with us this weekend, but her mom won't let her go unless you call her."

Jane reached for her cellphone. "I'll take care of it."

"Remember last year when her mom said she could go, but at the last minute she changed her mind and decided not to let her come?"

Jane remembered that calamity all too well. It caused quite a stink. "Oh yes."

"She might be less tempted to change her mind if Gabby is already over here. So maybe we can convince her to let Gabby stay here tonight."

"That's a good idea. I'll suggest that to her."

As Jane spoke to Ms. Pervis, Nathan listened in on the conversation, trying to read his mother's face for any signs of a positive response.

"I understand your concern, Ms. Pervis, but I assure you they will be sleeping in separate rooms," Jane said. "And they will be closely monitored."

Nathan took a bite of his apple and slid to the edge of his seat.

"Yes, Ma'am. I promise we'll keep her safe."

He had a hunch he knew what that meant. He hoped he was right. When Jane hung up, Nathan stared at his mother. "What did she say?"

"You need to pick her up in twenty minutes."

"Seriously? She agreed?"

"Yes."

Nathan bounded to his feet and gave his mother a huge bear hug. "Thank you so much, Mom. You're awesome!" He grabbed his jacket and headed out the door, taking his apple with him.

When he pulled up to Gabby' house, she was standing on the porch with a duffle bag over her shoulder and ski equipment spread out across the front porch.

He turned off the ignition and stepped out of the car, twirling his keys around his finger. "I can't believe your mom agreed to this."

"There's one stipulation," Gabby said. "I have to call her twice a day and keep her updated on my whereabouts."

"Your whereabouts? You're going to be on a mountain all weekend. Where are you gonna go?" He took Gabby's duffle bag from her, grabbed her skis and ski poles, and headed to his car.

"I'm just glad she let me come. I didn't think she would."

Nathan popped the trunk and stuffed Gabby's duffle bag inside. He placed her ski boots and backpack full of ski gear on top of her bag then laid her skis across the backseat. "Hopefully she won't change her mind by morning."

Even though Crystal Mountain ski resort was only a few hours away from home, Randy booked a cabin for the weekend. The cabin had three bedrooms, and before retiring for the night, Randy made it very clear to everyone what sleeping arrangements would be. He and Jane claimed the master bedroom. Lauren and Lacy shared a room with Gabby, and Nathan took occupancy in the smaller room with one double-sized bed.

Randy pulled Gabby and Nathan aside and gave them a strict mandate. "You are to stay in your own rooms all night, no exceptions."

"I know, Dad. We will."

"I mean it, Nathan." He gave his son a firm stare. "Get some sleep. I'll see you in the morning."

Nathan retreated to his room but had a difficult time sleeping. He tossed and turned for a few hours, then finally, around 1:00 A.M., he sent Gabby a text. *Are you asleep?*

It took her a minute to reply. *No.*

Come over here, he coaxed.

Your dad said not to leave this room. We'll get caught, she warned him.

No we won't. Everyone's asleep. I'll meet you at the door.

She carefully crawled out of bed and tiptoed toward Nathan's room.

Awaiting her arrival, he cracked his door open and peeked out. When he saw her, he held his index finger up to his lips. "Ssh."

She crept into his room and quietly closed the door behind them.

Nathan awoke in the morning to the smell of freshly brewed coffee. He slipped on a pair of sweats and reported to the kitchen. "Good morning."

Randy sat at the table reading the Seattle Times. When he saw Nathan, he looked up. "Morning, Nate."

Nathan picked a grape off its stem and popped it in his mouth. "What's for breakfast?"

Instead of responding to Nathan's question, Randy folded his newspaper and set it on the table. "Was Gabby in your room last night?"

Nathan pulled the innocent act. "What are you talking about?"

"I would strongly suggest you think this through carefully and choose your words wisely before you answer." Randy crossed his arms. "Was Gabby in your room last night?"

Obviously his father knew something, and lying about it was only going to make matters worse. Nathan decided it was best to tell the truth. "Yes, Sir."

"What were my specific instructions to you before we went to bed last night?"

Nathan swallowed hard, prepared to face his father's wrath. "That I stay in my room and Gabby stay in hers."

"Then am I to understand that you heard me but chose to ignore my request?"

Trying to weasel his way out of this, Nathan replied, "I didn't ignore you. I just…"

"You thought you wouldn't get caught."

Nathan hung his head. "Yes, Sir."

Nathan's direct disobedience and lack of common sense in this situation made Randy's face tighten. "What was she doing in your room?"

Nathan fidgeted in his seat, but didn't respond.

"Answer me, Son," Randy insisted. "What was she doing in your room last night? And don't lie to me either."

Although he didn't want to, Nathan told him. "We were having sex."

"Oh, I know you were," Randy said, not at all surprised by this news. "Because I heard you."

Nathan's cheeks turned bright red. He wished he could crawl under the table and disappear. "You did?"

"Every moan." Randy combed his fingers through his hair, trying to figure out how to handle this. "We assured Gabby's mother that the two of you would not be sharing a bed. Her mother entrusted us. You violated that trust."

"I'm sorry."

Being firm, Randy ordered, "This will not happen again on this trip. If it does, Gabby will never be invited to join us again. Am I clear?"

Nathan nodded compliantly. "Yes, Sir."

After disciplining his son, Randy began to chuckle. "Well, on a positive note, at least your plumbing works."

Although Nathan was horribly embarrassed by this situation, he found his father's comment amusing. It took every ounce of effort he had not to laugh.

"Why don't you scramble up some eggs for everyone," Randy suggested. "I'll slice up some fruit. Let's get everyone fed so we can hit the slopes early."

"Yes, Sir."

Out on the slopes, Randy had a quick family meeting before everyone parted ways. "Ok. We will meet at the lodge at one o'clock. Does everyone have a phone on them?"

Everyone did. So they all took off in different directions and enjoyed their morning of skiing.

Nathan and Gabby headed to the chairlift. On the way up, Nathan was quiet. In fact, he hadn't said much of anything all morning. Gabby wondered what was wrong. "Nathan? Are you ok?"

He took a cleansing breath but refused to look at her. "My dad heard us last night."

"What do you mean he heard us?"

"In my room…he heard us. I should have known, when their room is right next to mine."

Gabby covered her mouth with her hand and gave him an interrogating stare down. "I told you we were going to get caught."

"And you were right. I'm sorry."

She began to panic. "If he tells my mother."

"He won't, but he did say that if it happens again, he will no longer invite you on family vacations."

"It was your idea," she accused.

He desperately tried to defend himself, "I know, and I told you I was sorry. I should have listened to you."

"Are you grounded when we get home?"

Nathan eyed her uncertainly. "Hopefully not." The ski lift came to the top of the run and Gabby and Nathan hopped off together. "Come on," he said. "Race ya down the hill."

CHAPTER EIGHT

The last week of February, Nathan and Gabby met at his house several times to prepare for their AP Physics exam. Nathan loved this class. Not only did it provide him with a foundation in Physics for his upcoming pre-medicine courses, but with the AP status of the class, there was a definite payoff in his preparedness for college. Advanced placement classes helped him develop strong study skills and time management habits, and they looked excellent on his high school transcript. Throughout high school, Nathan was able to attain college credit for the Advanced Placement science and math classes he took. These courses required more time and effort than the average high school class, but because Nathan was willing to put the proper amount of effort into these classes, he definitely reaped the benefits.

Nathan and Gabby spread Physics books, study guides, and notes all over the dining room table. Gabby had been struggling to understand vectors. To help her, Nathan drew two arrows on her paper, each pointing a different direction. He labeled them A and B. "A vector is represented by an arrow which defines the direction, and the length of the arrow defines the vector's magnitude. Two vectors are equal if they have the same magnitude and direction, regardless of whether they have the same initial point."

Gabby wrinkled her forehead. "What?"

He could see she was confused, so he tried a simpler approach. "Remember when we learned about transformations in Geometry? It's the same thing. Vectors depend on a coordinate system. When the coordinates are transformed by rotation, displacement, or stretching, the components of the vector also transform. The vector itself doesn't change, but the coordinates of the vector must change to compensate."

Gabby dropped her pencil on the table. "I am going to fail this test."

"No you're not. You're going to be fine."

She plopped her head on her textbook, ready to give up.

"Maybe you need a break." He walked into the kitchen and pulled a freshly baked plate of cookies off the counter. "Here." He set the plate in the middle of the table. "My mom makes awesome cookies. Try one."

Randy's voice trailed from the living room, "Don't eat all my cookies."

"They're not your cookies. Mom makes them for all of us." Nathan picked one up and took a big bite.

"Dibs on the chocolate chip. Those are mine," Randy proclaimed, staking claim to his property.

Nathan's sister, Lauren, ran down the stairs, almost running into her father.

"Whoa there, Speedy," Randy said. "What's your hurry?"

"Daddy, I need to talk to you."

"Ok," he said. "If something makes you move that fast, it must be pretty important."

"I just got off the phone with Drew."

Drew. Drew. Where had he heard that name before? "Who's Drew?"

"That guy in theatre I told you about. The one I said I liked, but I didn't think he liked me because he kept talking to Cassie all the time."

Randy tried to remember, but nothing rang a bell. "Ok."

"He asked me out, and I really want to go. Can I? Please?" she begged her father.

Nathan overheard this conversation and couldn't control his burst of laughter. "Isn't Drew that geeky guy who wears superhero shirts all the time?"

"He's not geeky," Lauren disputed.

Nathan begged to differ. "Yes he is. He quotes Sci-Fi movies and has a comic book collection."

"He's really smart and he's cute and he…"

"Hold on one second," Randy said, ceasing the conversation. "Who is this guy?"

"Drew. He's in theatre with me."

Knowing nothing about this kid, Randy probed for more information. "How long have you known him?"

Lauren couldn't believe her father didn't remember. "Daddy, he's been in theatre with me since last year."

"Yeah, Dad," Nathan added with a smartass smirk on his face. "She talks about him all the time."

"Shut up!" Lauren snapped.

"Nathan, leave her alone," Randy said to his son. Then he turned his attention to his daughter again. "Where does he want to take you?"

"To a movie."

"When?" he asked.

"Next Friday night."

"Does he drive?"

Lauren replied, "Yes."

"Have I met this guy?

"No."

"Well, I want to meet him before you go out," he insisted.

"Does that mean I can go?" she asked, feeling hopeful.

"Yes. You can go."

"Thank you, Daddy." Lauren hugged her father tightly and ran back upstairs to her room.

Randy let out a heavy sigh. "I am not ready for this."

Nathan tried to suppress a laugh.

"You find this funny, do you?" Randy asked.

"A little," Nathan admitted.

Randy didn't think it was funny at all.

Lacy stormed down the stairs, riled up. "How come Lauren gets to go out on a date, but when I want to be with a boy, you won't let me?"

Randy raised an eyebrow. "Excuse me?"

Nathan cringed, knowing his sister was in big trouble for speaking to their father like that.

"Get that scowl off your face and lose the tone now," Randy demanded. "You do not storm down the stairs of my house and cock an attitude with me, young lady."

"This isn't fair!"

Randy immediately interceded. "Stop talking, right now, before you say something you regret."

Lacy huffed and held her hands on her hips.

"Lauren is being given permission to go out with this boy because she approached it the right way, the respectful way. He asked her out properly. She asked me for permission. At no time did she allow some boy she barely knew to pull her off the bleachers and drag her into the hallway to make out with her in public. When you start thinking and approach this in a reasonable manner, then we will talk. In the meantime, you are grounded for speaking to me in that disrespectful tone."

Lacy rolled her eyes.

"What was that? I didn't hear you," Randy corrected.

"Yes, Sir." She stomped back up to her room, grumbling under her breath.

Nathan sat there grinning, trying to keep a straight face.

Randy jerked his head Nathan's direction, not amused by his laughter. "Get that smartass smirk off your face."

Not wanting to get in trouble like his sister did, Nathan immediately wiped the smile away. "Yes, Sir."

During Friday night's game, the crowd rose to its feet, led by the cheerleaders who waved their purple pompoms on the sidelines. This game was vital for the boys. It would determine which team would go to the state playoffs, and Bellevue was the only rival standing in their way.

With fifteen seconds left on the game clock, the Kangaroos were down by one point. Nathan dribbled the ball midcourt, trying to set up a screen by directing his team to various positions on the court. After a quick scan of the situation, he passed the ball to Derek, who dribbled toward the hoop but was immediately blocked by an opposing player. With no access to the net, he passed the ball back to Nathan. Only seconds remained on the clock. Nathan seized the moment. He dribbled to an open spot and jumped for a three pointer. Right before the buzzer sounded, the net swished the sweetest sound Nathan had ever heard. Cheers from the crowd echoed off the gym walls. Lake Washington High School was on their way to the state basketball championships.

Gabby ran across the court and jumped into Nathan's arms. "Oh my god, you did it!" She squeezed her arms around his neck and kissed him with such fervor that Nathan could barely breathe.

The crowd went wild, but Nathan didn't even notice the noise or the hundreds of screaming fans jumping up and down in their elated victory dances. He was too entranced by Gabby.

Mike tried to get his attention. "Holy shit, Dude! Nice damn shot! You totally owned that ball!"

Nathan reluctantly broke away from Gabby and offered his friend a high five. "We're goin' to state, Baby!"

After the game, Nathan's parents went out with some friends and both of his sisters attended the post-game dance. Nathan and Gabby took advantage of this opportunity and celebrated on their own.

Heavy breathing emanated from behind the closed door. On the bed, Gabby moved her hips to meet Nathan's thrusts, taking in the delight of the moment.

Skin on skin, they lay on the bed trying to regain much needed air. With their bodies intertwined, Nathan glanced over at the clock on his bedside table. In a state of panic, he quickly hopped out of bed. "Get up. Get dressed."

Gabby peeked over at the clock, wondering what Nathan was freaking out about. 9:52 P.M. They had eight minutes until her curfew, and her house was at least ten minutes away. "Oh no." She hopped off the bed and quickly dressed herself.

"Where the hell did the time go?" Nathan said. "Were we really up here that long?" He quickly slipped on his clothes and handed Gabby her shoes. "Here. Just put them on in the car."

They ran down the stairs and out to Nathan's car.

"We better hope I hit every green light on the way, or we are screwed." He backed out of the driveway and sped down the road, squealing the tires behind him.

When Nathan got home from work the next day, he received a phone call from Gabby. "Hey, Gab. You ready for tonight?"

"Actually, that's why I called. My mom won't let me go."

He grabbed a glass out of the cupboard and poured milk into it. "Why not?"

"Because I was late last night."

Late? She wasn't late. Nathan had her home by ten o'clock like he was supposed to. "You weren't late."

"My mom said standing on the porch with you didn't count. I wasn't in the house until 10:01."

"You have got to be kidding?"

Gabby's voice became brittle. "I'm sorry, Nathan."

"Why are you sorry? It was my fault. I should have kept a closer eye on the clock."

74

"It's as much my fault as it is yours."

"No. I should have had you home on time and I didn't."

"I'm grounded all weekend. I can't even text you because I won't have my phone."

Trying to stay calm, Nathan took a cleansing breath. "I'm sorry."

"It's ok," she assured him. "I have to go."

"I guess I'll see at school on Monday then."

"Yeah," Gabby confirmed.

"I love you, Gab."

"I love you too."

Nathan hung up his phone and muttered, "She was standing on the porch. How does that not count?"

Jane overheard the bitter edge of cynicism in his voice and questioned his mood. "You alright?"

He slipped the milk carton back in the fridge and gripped the glass in his hand. "Gabby's grounded this weekend and it's my fault."

"What happened?"

"Her curfew is ten, which in itself is ridiculous," he griped. "Anyway, I pulled up to her house, walked her up to the door, and gave her a kiss goodnight. She went straight inside after that, but her mom says she didn't get in the house until 10:01. Now she's grounded all weekend. This sucks."

"I'm sorry, Sweetie."

He gulped down his milk and set the glass in the sink. "Is Dad home?"

"He's out back."

"Thanks."

Since Nathan couldn't hang out with Gabby, he went fishing with his dad instead. Fishing on Lake Washington not only gave Nathan a chance to spend time with his dad, it also gave them time to talk in private.

Nathan tossed his line into the calm lake waters. It landed with a splash. "Mike told me his parents are getting divorced."

"I'm sorry to hear that."

"It made me think. You and Mom have been married nearly twenty-three years. You talk all the time, and you actually enjoy each other's company. I want Gabby and me to have a relationship like that," Nathan said.

"I think you already do," Randy remarked. "You two have known each other for a long time. You communicate, you spend time together. You're friends first."

"She's my best friend."

"I know she is. And that's good. A relationship won't grow if you're not."

"Gabby and I talk about everything. We always have."

"And you should. Communication is important," Randy advised.

Wanting his father's advice about something, Nathan said, "I want to show Gabby I can be romantic by giving her a night she'll never forget, but I don't know how to do it."

Nathan often asked for advice in this area. Although Randy did his best to guide him, romance was not Nathan's strong suit. "You don't have to do anything fancy, Nate. Keep it simple."

"By doing what?"

"When your mom and I first started dating, even though I detest yogurt, I knew she loved it, so I made it a point to always have some in my refrigerator."

Nathan laughed. "That's really cheesy."

"But it's effective. Mom appreciated it, and it made her feel like I went out of my way to do something for her. It's the little things that matter most. Something as simple as a text that simply says I love you or leaving her a note to tell her you're thinking about her will have more meaning than an elaborate dinner date. You're trying to make this more complicated than it has to be. Think smaller. Get a blanket and spread it out in front of the fireplace. Turn down all the lights and sip on hot cocoa together. It doesn't cost anything and it's really romantic. Leave her little gifts, things you know she loves. These may seem like simple things, but they let her know she's special." Randy could see the gears turning in Nathan's head. To help him along, he said, "What's Gabby's favorite soda?"

"Diet Coke."

"Favorite candy?"

"M&M's. Why?" Nathan questioned.

"Buy her a Diet Coke and a package of M&Ms. Tie a bow around them and leave them in her locker or on her desk in class. It will make her feel special knowing you took the time to think about her. It's simple, and it works. Little things go a long way. And you have to keep the passion alive in your relationship. The strongest, healthiest relationships involve physical intimacy."

Nathan eyebrows bowed downward. "Actually, I was kinda hoping you could help me out with that. What positions are good?"

Randy shook his head. "We are not having this conversation."

"Come on, Dad. Help me out."

The expression on his son's face made Randy laugh. "This discussion can never leave this boat, do you understand? If your mother finds out we had this conversation, she'll kill me."

"Don't worry, Dad, I won't tell her."

Monday at school, Gabby caught up with Nathan in the hallway between classes. "Hey," she said, touching his arm to get his attention.

"Hey, Babe." He greeted her with a kiss. "I missed you this weekend."

"I missed you too." She handed him a legal sized envelope. "Look what I got in the mail Saturday."

Nathan stared at it, confused. "What's this?"

"Open it."

Inside was a letter from the University of Washington's admissions office. As Nathan read the letter, the corners of his lips curved upward. "Alright, Baby! You got in!" He grabbed Gabby in his arms and spun her around.

"They're giving me an academic scholarship, and I qualified for a grant, so the majority of my tuition will be paid."

"That's great. Congratulations!" He folded the letter and slid it back in the envelope. "When are cheerleading tryouts?"

"Next week."

"Do you want me to go with you? I can give you a ride if you want."

She gladly accepted his offer.

CHAPTER NINE

"Who says cheerleading isn't a sport?" Gabby complained at the lunch table. "I don't know any other sports where you have to do flips all day, dance for three hours straight, sweat like crazy, and you still have to look good."

Nathan interjected, "That's definitely true."

"It bothers me that every sport can earn full ride scholarships, but according to NCAA logic, cheerleading isn't a sport, so we don't get a dime."

"I'm sure they have their reasons behind it."

"Well, it isn't fair," she complained. "We compete like other sports. We have the same risks. In fact, there are more risks of serious injury being a cheerleader than for you guys out on the court. Two-thirds of all catastrophic sports injuries are due to cheerleading."

Trying to defend his sport, Nathan said, "Hey, we have injuries. We get broken noses, jammed fingers, sprained ankles, torn ligaments, and damaged ACL's. We get slammed by other players, fall into walls and bleachers, and have you ever gotten a brush burn from skidding across a hardwood court? Those hurt like hell."

"I have never seen a basketball player get a broken tailbone from doing a layup. We practice five days a week, just like you do, and our practices are just as physically demanding with stunts, tumbling, working on cheers and dance routines. There's much more to being a cheerleader than just waving our pompoms at stands full of screaming fans."

Nathan couldn't hold in his amusement any longer. "Oh, I know. You also get to wear those skimpy uniforms that drive me wild while you shake it on the court."

Mike thought Nathan's retort was hysterical.

But Gabby didn't think it was funny.

Sensing her irritation, Nathan leaned over and whispered, "You know I'm teasing."

"Speaking of which," Mike turned his attention to Gabby. "Have you heard anything from UW yet about your tryout?"

Nathan chuckled, "Oh, man. Don't get her started, Mike."

"Why?" Mike asked.

Gabby told him why. "I have gone through the most intense physical training with gymnastics and tumbling classes and have been to every type of cheer camp imaginable, but that tryout was stupid. There were fifteen judges sitting at this long table in a huge gym, and I auditioned by myself in front all of these people. It was like being on trial, but instead of defending myself verbally, I had to perform standing back flips and do the splits on a cold ass hardwood floor. It was the most nerve-wracking thing ever."

Nathan had already gotten the receiving end of this experience right after her tryout. It was evident that Gabby was not at all impressed with the undertaking of trying out for collegiate cheerleading. Of the hundreds of people who tried out for the twenty-eight cheerleading slots at the University of Washington, only the best were offered spots. Despite the fact that Gabby spent years in gymnastics and had solid cheerleading experience, she wasn't one of them. At the time, she was really disappointed, but now she seemed more pissed off about it.

Nathan fought hard to keep a straight face.

"It's not funny," Gabby demanded. "It makes me mad. Give me a megaphone and I'll show them where they can shove it."

Nathan burst out laughing. "Wow! Getting a little hostile there, aren't you, Gab?"

She growled in frustration as she stood up and left the table.

Gabby's foul and sudden departure took Mike by surprise. "Dude, what's with her?"

"I don't know." Nathan stood up and followed her. When he caught up with her, he said, "Gab, come on. I was just teasing."

"That's not funny," she said, unimpressed with his bantering.

"Why are you getting so upset?"

"Because I don't feel like I was given a fair opportunity."

"There's nothing you can do about it now," Nathan reminded her. "It's over. Quit dwelling on it."

"But now I can't cheer for you during your games," she cried.

"You don't have to wear a cheerleading uniform or carry pompoms to cheer for me. Just knowing you're in the stands and rooting for me is all I need. I don't care about any of that glorified crap. All I want is you."

Gabby stared at him, overwhelmed by his loving sentiments. "Really?"

"Yes. Really. To me it's not about the glory, it's about the game and sharing that experience with you, whether you are standing on the sidelines or sitting in the stands. I just want to know I have your support."

"You have always had my support. I'm your biggest fan."

"That's all I want. You're the most important thing. If I have no other fans in the world other than you, I will be happy."

Nathan had never said anything this sweet before. She felt truly loved by him. "You really mean that?"

"Yes," he said with a smile. "I wouldn't have said it if I didn't mean it. I love you, Gabby."

After practice that day, Nathan snuck up behind Gabby and nibbled on her neck. "I have something for you."

"What is it?"

"Close your eyes." While her eyes were closed, Nathan pulled a gold chain from a black velvet box. On the chain was a gold pendant with two interlocking hearts. He unclasped the necklace and hung it around her neck. "Ok. You can open your eyes now."

Gabby looked down at the necklace. "Oh my god, Nathan. This is beautiful."

Trying to be poetic, which he wasn't, he touched the pendant with his finger and said, "Look, it has two hearts. You know, my heart, your heart, they're connected."

This was the cutest and most romantic thing Nathan had ever done. "I love you, Nathan Hanson." Before he had time to respond, Gabby kissed him, but this was not an ordinary kiss. This was a deep, tongue in mouth kiss, firm and purposeful.

He willingly took it all in.

Every high school basketball player in the state of Washington dreamed of playing in front of hundreds of fans under the lights of the famous Tacoma Dome. Stepping into the gym back in November, each team had one goal—to hoist the state championship trophy. This year's tournament featured eight of the top ten high school teams in Washington. Teams from all over the state were represented, and each team came into this tournament with a solid chance of taking home the hardware. The competition was going to be fierce.

The always dominant Metro League featured the most teams with three—Seattle Prep, Rainier Beach, and O'Dea.

These were big name schools from Seattle that made it into the state championship almost every year. Other schools represented were Mountlake Terrace, Kennedy Catholic, Kamiakin, University High School, and Lake Washington.

Closing the season with a 23-3 record, Lake Washington High School had the best point guard in this tournament. Nathan Hanson had great court vision and averaged 23.7 points per game. He rarely met a last minute shot he couldn't sink.

Aside from Nathan, this team featured seniors Derek Hampton, Michael Lynott, Todd Collier, and DeShawn Ellis, as well as juniors, Darien Staudacher, Cory Ferguson, and Adrian Schruele. The strength of this team was its outstanding defense and athleticism, which allowed the boys to set a fast-paced tempo and wear out their opponent. The talent was definitely there, but the Kangs sometimes struggled with inconsistency. When they got on a roll offensively, the boys were nearly impossible to stop, but if they lost their stroke, the offense quickly fell apart. To win the title, Nathan needed to maintain his leadership on the court and the team as a whole needed to rediscover its consistency at the hoop.

Lake Washington easily took down their opponent in the first round and managed to survive the succeeding rounds to qualify for the championship game. The last roadblock they had to face was the toughest, most frightening team in the state—Rainier Beach.

Rainier Beach had a 24-2 record. They were ranked number one in state and were the defending champions. They has some of the best guards in the division, who could easily get to the basket with their athleticism. This team was a serious threat from behind the arc and loved to use the fast break to put pressure on the opposing team's defense. Overall, Rainer Beach was a better, stronger, more experienced team when it came to state-wide tournaments.

The Kangaroos were the underdogs, and they were going to have to work their tails off to take home that trophy. But they were determined, and refused to go home without a fight. It was definitely going to be a battle for the state title.

Part of the excitement of the state competition was the forty mile bus ride to the Tacoma Dome. The cheerleaders, the basketball team, and the coaches all traveled together. Athletic bags full of balls, uniforms, and basketball gear were stored in the storage compartment underneath the bus, and one seat housed all the cheerleaders' pompoms.

Gabby and Nathan shared a seat on the bus. Nathan leaned back, with his knees bent, resting his shins on the seat in front of him. Gabby faced him, sitting with one knee bent under her and the other leg dangling down to the floor. They both held UNO cards in their hand with the draw pile between them. Nathan had an overabundance of cards in comparison to Gabby's three. It didn't appear this game was going to be a victory for him. "Man, you are kicking my butt," he complained. "Why do I play this game with you? You always win."

She laid down a Draw Four card. "Yellow."

Nathan shook his head in defeat and painstakingly drew four cards, adding to his already full hand. "I think you're cheating. How is it possible that you get every freakin' wild card in this deck and I can't even get one?"

"You have no one to blame but yourself. You're the one who shuffled." She laid down a card with a yellow five on it. "Uno."

He was certain she had another yellow card in her hand, so he perused through the cards he had, hoping to find a five. When he found a green one, he laid it down.

Gabby developed an evil grin on her face as she placed a red five on top of his green one. "Ha!" she boasted. "I win."

"As always." He picked up all the cards, organized them into a neat pile, and put the rubber band back around them. "My family is having a spring celebration next weekend. We're gonna take the boat out and barbecue some burgers. You think your mom will let you come?"

She lifted a shoulder. "I don't know. I can ask her."

"Your mother treats you like a criminal," Nathan complained. "Keeping you locked up and sheltered from life."

"She's always been that way," Gabby stated. "I wish she'd learn to trust me. I don't know what I have to do to earn that from her. Why did she let me take Driver's Ed if she had no intention of letting me drive? Doesn't that defeat the whole purpose of the class?"

"Yes," Nathan concurred.

"She's never going to let me get my license. After graduation, that is the first thing on my list of things to do."

"Do you think she'll extend your curfew for Prom?" Nathan asked, feeling hopeful.

"I doubt it," Gabby grunted. "That would be asking a lot, wouldn't it?"

"We can try, can't we? It's Prom. It doesn't make sense to have a ten o'clock curfew for an event that doesn't end until midnight. She's gotta give in at some point."

"When has she ever given in? That woman is stubborn and set in her ways. She doesn't give in to anything."

"I still think we should ask her."

"She won't listen to me, Nathan," Gabby griped. "She doesn't care how I feel. If I argue with her, she gets mad, then I end up grounded and can't leave the house."

"I'm not saying to argue with her. Just talk to her."

"I can't," Gabby stated.

"Why not?"

"My mother doesn't talk to me."

That was a ludicrous thing to say. "Of course she talks to you."

"No, she scolds me and criticizes everything I do. That's not talking. Every time I try to talk to her about something, she shushes me and tells me she's busy. The only time she notices anything I do is when I break one of her stupid rules. Otherwise she doesn't care. She sends me to cheer camp every summer to get rid of me."

"Gab, come on. That's crazy. She sends you to cheer camp because she knows you love it. She paid for tumbling and gymnastics lessons so you could get better at what you love to do. She wouldn't have done that if she didn't care about you."

"If she cares so much, how come she never lets me do anything?"

Nathan didn't have an answer. "I don't know."

"I hate my mother. I can't wait to get out of that house."

"I'll just be glad when we don't have to fight a curfew anymore."

Gabby smiled, looking forward to their future together. "Then I can spend more time with you."

"Yes, you can."

Nathan leaned in to kiss her, but as soon as he did, Mike peeked over the back of his seat, interrupting them. "Hey! No canoodling on the bus."

"Says who?" Nathan said, annoyed by Mike's meddling.

"Says me."

"Since when are you my boss? I didn't ask for your opinion anyway," Nathan teased.

"Well, you're gonna get it, whether you want it or not," Mike retorted.

"Why does that not surprise me?"

Trying to be witty, Mike replied, "My words of wisdom are profound and life changing."

Nathan laughed. "Oh, they're life changing alright. Your BS makes my ears bleed. If you actually said something worth hearing, maybe I'd listen to you more often."

Mike dropped his jaw and looked at Gabby. "You're gonna let your boyfriend talk to me like that?"

She teased, "There is some truth behind what he's saying. You do offer your opinion a lot when people don't ask for it."

"Ooh," Nathan laughed. "She burned you, Chump!"

These two young men teased each other all the time, only because they adored each other. They had been friends since childhood. Behind closed doors, when no one else was around, Nathan and Mike were extremely close and talked about their fears, relationships, and future plans. They shared celebrations, mourned losses, and bragged about first kisses. They encouraged each other through tough times, pushed each other when they felt like giving up, and backed each other up in a fight. One would gladly take a fist for the other.

"You going to Prom?" Nathan asked Mike.

Mike had recently gone through a bad breakup with his long-term girlfriend and was still hurt over the fact that she dumped him for what he thought was no reason. He hadn't dated since the breakup. "I don't know."

"You know, Mike," Gabby interjected. "I know someone who would die to go to Prom with you if you'd ask her. She's always liked you."

"Who?" Mike asked.

"Emily." Emily was on the cheerleading squad with Gabby and often sat at the lunch table with them.

Mike peered over at her. "Really?"

"Yes. But she never pursued it because you had a girlfriend."

Nathan tried to entice him. "You should ask her out."

"After what Rachel did to me, I really don't know if I'm ready to jump into that right now," Mike said.

"You know she wants you," Nathan teased, noticing how Emily was giving Mike flirty eyes. "Look at her."

Gabby added, "She's sweet, Mike. And she really likes you."

Piling onto the sell job, Nathan said, "She's pretty too. And she looks hot in a cheerleading skirt."

Mike stared across the bus at Emily.

"Go for it, man," Nathan encouraged him. "You have nothing to lose."

After some thought, Mike jumped out of his seat and hobbled across the moving bus.

Gabby and Nathan looked at each other and laughed.

The Tacoma Dome, located in one of Washington's most vibrant waterfront communities, was one of the largest wood-domed structures in the world. With numerous seating configurations, the Tacoma Dome was the preferred concert venue of the Pacific Northwest. The Dome hosted the Goodwill Games, the NCAA Women's Basketball Final Four, and the United States Figure Skating Championships. This week, it hosted the State of Washington Boys High School Basketball Championship Tournament.

Under the lights of the mighty Tacoma Dome, the boys warmed up for their final game of the season. Nathan felt confident as he took practice shots and stretched on the floor with his teammates. Considering the stakes involved in this game, he remained calm and collected.

"He seems pretty poised down there," Randy said to his wife while he watched his son warm up for the big game.

"He looks relaxed. Confident," Jane added.

Randy was excited about this game, anxious to cheer the boys on as he sported his Lake Washington Kangaroos tee-shirt. Lake Washington High School was his alma mater. He was once a shooting guard on the Varsity basketball team, but he was never as good as his son. "This is so cool. What a great way for Nate to end his high school basketball career."

"Wouldn't it be wonderful if they walked out of here tonight with that trophy?" Jane proclaimed.

"Oh, man," Randy said dreamy-eyed. "That would be awesome."

This year's Varsity boys' basketball team had a tremendous season, perhaps the best hardwood season in the history of the school. The quality of players truly distinguished this season's crop of ballplayers from previous years. And Nathan was the most highly ranked among this amazing group of young men. It was well worth the price of admission to see the LWHS boys play.

"I can't believe how much his game has improved over the last four years. Coach Dolan is amazing."

"He is a great coach. But you contributed too," Randy told his wife. "Nathan has learned a lot from you over the years. You've given him shooting tips and imparted him with pointers about how to lead a team. Your prowess on the basketball court rubbed off on him."

Jane smiled widely. "He's worked so hard. I'm glad he decided to sign with UW."

"Me too. I couldn't be more proud of him."

The big game was about to tipoff. The cheerleaders lined up in two parallel rows at the corner of the court allowing room for the players to run between them. Nathan led his team onto the court, with Gabby happily shaking her pompoms for him as he trotted across the hardwood. The other players followed.

As soon as the coaches and players were situated on the sidelines, the starting lineup for both teams stood center court. When the jumpball was tossed into the air, Lake Washington gained possession. Within a minute, Nathan hit a three pointer for the first bucket of the game; the brutal competition had begun.

The Kangaroos started out with good defense and set a fast-paced tempo for the game. Midway through the first quarter, Rainier started to get a strong offense going, which made maintaining a tough defense much more challenging. The boys were going to have to tighten things up.

Offensively, the Kangs were on their A game. Nathan made solid passes and nailed several shots. He made an impressive behind-the-back pass to Mike for a layup then scored his own layup on the return run. Despite these efforts, Lake Washington was down 23-20 by the end of the first quarter.

This game proved to be difficult for the Kangs. If they wanted that trophy, they were going to have to play with sweat and blood. At the beginning of the second quarter, Rainier attempted a three-point shot that missed. Nathan snagged the defensive rebound and was instantly fouled and sent to the line.

Nathan had a standard routine he used on the free-throw line. He dribbled the ball twice, eyed the hoop, then held the ball in his hands for a second before he made his shot. He had never played in front of this many screaming fans before. All fourteen thousand of them had their eyes on him right now, which was a bit intimidating. Before he released the ball, he took a deep breath. It grazed the rim and went in. One more to go. He followed the same procedure, nailing his second shot as well. Even with these two shots, the Kangs ended the half trailing by four.

Nathan and his team developed a hot streak in the third quarter leaving Rainier Beach unable to match up against their offense. The boys quickly passed the ball around and nailed their shot attempts, effectively taking the lead in a fast-break third quarter.

Lake Washington was so inferior to Rainier Beach that they should have been run out of the building. But by the grace of God, the Kangs shot better than ninety percent from the field in the second half. Offensively, Nathan showed great diversity, which made him difficult to defend. One minute he was canning deep-range three pointers and the next, instead of taking shots himself, he made unexpected passes to his teammates, which tripped up Rainier's defense. The Kangs tightened up their defense, making it difficult for Rainier to land buckets. The fourth quarter proved to be athletically challenging. Tension was high and the boys were exhausted, but they were determined to win.

With eight seconds remaining in the game, the score was tied. Coach Dolan called a timeout; his last one. This was their final opportunity to score, and they needed a bucket to win.

"Own this, Hanson," Coach Dolan said to his star point guard.

"Don't worry, Coach," Nathan responded confidently. "We got this."

Nathan led his team onto the court and took possession of the ball. With a fast breakaway, he dribbled down court then immediately passed to Mike, who quickly busted through the double team and fired a shot. Nathan held his breath, praying it would go in. The shot cleared the rim right as the buzzer went off.

The excitement level in the Tacoma Dome was over the top. The Lake Washington fans screamed and noisemakers echoed through the arena. This was the biggest upset of the tournament, and the biggest victory in Lake Washington High School history.

The boys huddled together center court, cheering in celebration. Nathan had never been as excited as he was at this moment. And the best part was, he got to share this experience with Gabby.

Gabby ran over to Nathan and threw her arms around him. "Oh my god, Nathan! That was the most amazing play ever. My heart is still pounding."

"Your heart is pounding?" Nathan said. "Holy crap. My heart stopped when Mike tossed that shot."

The bus ride back to Kirkland buzzed with celebration. The state trophy glistened on the front seat and celebratory high fives circulated all around. Even Coach Dolan and the bus driver got in on the action. The radio played, but no one paid much attention to it until *We Are the Champions* came on. Everyone joined in, singing at the top of their lungs. At that moment they were champions. They had the state championship trophy to prove it.

This was a first state title for the Kangaroos, so to celebrate, students attended a special pep assembly in the team's honor. Since Nathan was the team captain, Coach Dolan asked him to address the student body.

After the cheerleaders performed a pyramid cheer and the band played the fight song to welcome the players onto the gym floor, Coach Dolan said a few words before he introduced Nathan.

Nathan confidently approached the podium, making as grandiose an entrance as possible. "Hello, Lake Washington!"

The student body went wild, which was the reaction Nathan was shooting for. He let them get the excitement out of their system and waited for the volume to subside before he continued.

"Four days ago, we lucky few, we band of brothers, went to the state championship for the first time in Kangaroo history. We were told we made it in on a whim or a streak of pure luck. Competing against big name schools, we didn't have a prayer in the world. At the start of this tournament, the fans of our opposing teams boasted 'the Kangaroos suck', but today, from this time and this place, to friend and foe alike, the proudest boast in this world of basketball is 'I'm a Kangaroo.'"

The entire student body rose to their feet and chanted, "Kang-a-roos! Kang-a-roos!"

The energy in the room was awe inspiring. Nathan had never seen the students of Lake Washington High School this excited.

When his high school comrades settled down a bit, he concluded his speech. "On behalf of my teammates, I want to say how much we appreciate all the support each and every one of you gave us this season. When the chips were down and we were up against what seemed like impossible odds, when things went wrong and the breaks were beating us, all of you were right there with us every step of the way. And even though this season is over, this is not the end. It's not even the beginning of the end. It's the start of a legacy." Nathan picked up the trophy and held it above his head, showing it off to the entire student body. "A legacy of champions."

School spirit resonated throughout the entire gym. Pompoms waved frantically and students jumped up and down in the stands. Every clique and class, from freshmen to seniors, put their differences behind them and came together to celebrate. The scene was epic. This victory wasn't just a win for the boys, it was a victory for the entire school, a moment in time when everyone was a champion.

They proudly displayed the championship trophy in a large trophy case in the main hallway, with all of the boys' names carved on nameplates attached to the wooden base. The members of boys' basketball team would forever be cast in Lake Washington High School history.

CHAPTER TEN

Nathan woke up the following morning feeling fatigued. All the stress and physical exertion of basketball season finally caught up with him and made his rundown body rebel. He was congested, his throat was sore, and he had a throbbing headache. He cleared his throat a bit to try to loosen the tightness in his chest then slowly tumbled out of bed. Before he hopped in the shower, he trekked downstairs to the kitchen to get a drink of water. When he reached into the cupboard for a glass, the congestion in his chest made him cough.

Randy had just picked up his car keys and was about to head out the door when he heard Nathan's deep chest cough. "That doesn't sound good."

With a hoarse, dry throat, Nathan replied, "Not feeling all that great." He filled his glass with water and chugged it down. As he swallowed, his body developed chills. "It's freezing in here."

Randy pulled out his stethoscope. "Come over here and sit down."

Nathan coughed again and set his glass on the counter. "Is that really necessary?"

"Yes, it is. Now come here."

He walked over to his father and sat at the dining room table.

Randy held the bell of his scope on Nathan's chest.

Nathan protested. "This is ridiculous."

"Stop talking and take a deep breath."

"Dad, I'm fine," he said gruffly.

But Randy remained persistent. "No, you are not fine. Last time I checked, I was the doctor in this house, not you. Deep breath."

Nathan humored his father and complied. But breathing in deep like that tickled his throat and made him cough again.

Randy moved the bell to the other side of Nathan's chest and ordered him to take another deep breath. "Hmm." He grabbed a thermometer and handed it to Nathan. "Put this under your tongue."

Even though he didn't like it, Nathan did as he was told.

"Sit there for a minute. I'll be right back." Randy stepped into the bathroom while Nathan sat in the chair with a thermometer hanging out of his mouth.

When his father returned, he read the temperature—100.2. "Oh, yes. Just as I thought." He set the thermometer down and gently felt around Nathan's throat with his fingers. As suspected, his lymph nodes were swollen.

Randy held a tongue depressor and a pen light in his hand. Although Nathan already knew the answer, he asked, "What are you doing with those?"

Randy grinned slyly. "Open wide."

"You can't be serious," Nathan complained.

"Come on, Nate. I have to take a look."

Hesitantly, Nathan opened his mouth.

Randy checked his son's tonsils and throat—enlarged and red. This, along with the cough, hoarseness, and fever, confirmed his diagnosis. "You aren't going anywhere today." Randy turned off his pen light and slipped it in his pocket. "You need to stay home and rest."

"I have exams coming up," Nathan objected. "I can't miss school."

"This is not a debate, Son. You have an upper respiratory infection, and you're running a fever." Randy tossed the tongue depressor in the trash and washed his hands. "You're not going to school today."

"Can I at least call Gabby so she can pick up any classwork I'm missing?"

"Yes. You can call Gabby." He dried his hands with a paper towel then turned off the water in the kitchen sink. "I'm going to run upstairs and grab you some meds. Lie on the couch and get some rest."

While Randy was upstairs, Nathan grabbed his cellphone and dialed Gabby's number.

"Hi, Nathan," she answered.

"Hey, Gab." He coughed into the phone.

"You sound terrible."

"Not feeling well. Dad says I have an upper respiratory infection and is forcing me to stay home today. Can you pick up homework for me and get any notes I miss?"

"Sure," she willingly agreed.

"I'm apologizing to you ahead of time if I gave this to you."

"It's ok," she said. "Just feel better."

Stuffed up, he coughed again.

"Get some rest, Nathan. I'll stop by after school."

"Thanks. Love you, Gab."

"Love you too. I'll see you this afternoon."

Nathan hung up his phone and set it on the coffee table. He grabbed a blanket and shuffled the pillows around on the couch, plopping himself down with the TV remote.

Meanwhile, Randy dug around in the medicine cabinet. "I'm keeping Nathan home today," he told his wife.

"Why?"

"URI."

Sympathizing with her son, Jane replied, "That's not fun. Poor baby."

He pulled out a bottle of Tylenol and a package of Mucinex then closed the cabinet. "I gotta head out." He leaned over and kissed her softly on the lips. "Love you, Babe."

"Love you too."

Randy trotted back down the stairs and grabbed a bottle of water from the refrigerator. He handed it to Nathan, along with a Mucinex tablet and two Tylenol capsules. "Here. Take these. It will lower your fever and loosen up your congestion. You need to rest today," Randy ordered.

"I know, Dad. I will."

"I mean it. Increase your fluid intake and don't overexert yourself. No hanging out with your friends tonight either. Your body needs rest."

"Gabby's gonna stop by after school to give me the work I missed."

"If you've been kissing her, she's probably going to catch this."

"I know."

He kissed his son on the forehead. "Get some rest, please."

"I will."

Carrying three spiral notebooks, a Calculus textbook, and a Tupperware container, Gabby was able to bum a ride from a friend to get to Nathan's house after school.

Upon her arrival, Jane answered the door. "Hi, Mrs. Hanson. How's Nathan feeling?"

"Better. He slept most of the day."

Gabby placed Nathan's work and the Tupperware container on the dining room table. "Is he sleeping now?"

"I don't think so. He's in his room."

"No, I'm not." Nathan tromped down the stairs, cracking a smile the minute he saw Gabby. "Hey, Gab."

Gabby turned around. "Hey, Champ. I brought you some soup." She handed him the container. "My mom made chicken noodle soup last night. When you called and told me you were sick, I snagged some for you."

He gazed at Gabby with loving eyes. "Thank you."

"A lot of people asked about you today."

Nathan laughed. "I'm glad I have so many concerned friends." He pranced into the kitchen to warm up his soup. "Have you talked to your mom about this weekend?"

"Yes." She sat on a barstool at the kitchen island. "She said I can only come if your parents are here."

"My parents are the ones hosting the party," Nathan replied.

"That's what I told her."

"She's actually letting you come?"

"As long as I'm home by…"

Interrupting her, Nathan said, "I know. Ten o'clock."

Gabby giggled. "Yeah."

"Mike is coming too."

"Is he bringing Emily?"

"I don't know," Nathan said. "He told me he asked her to Prom."

"And did she agree?"

"Yes. He's excited about it." When the timer went off on the microwave, Nathan carefully took his hot soup out and sat it on the kitchen island. He grabbed a spoon from the drawer and pulled up the barstool next to Gabby. "Speaking of which, where did you want to go for dinner on Prom night?"

"I don't know."

"Come on, Gab, help me out here. What do you feel like? You want Chinese, Seafood, Mexican, Italian…"

"Mmm," she stopped him. "Italian sounds good."

Grinning at her, he concurred, "Italian it is. What about Calabrias?"

"Calabrias is expensive," she told him.

"I don't care. It's Prom. This is the only time we get to do this so I wanna do it right. I'll make a reservation. They're going to start selling tickets next month."

"I know," Gabby said. "I can't wait."

He slurped down a spoonful of soup. "I'll come get you at 1:00 on Saturday."

"Do I need to bring anything?"

"Nope," Nathan said. "Just yourself."

CHAPTER ELEVEN

Spring get-togethers at the Hanson home had become a yearly tradition. The entire family, including Nathan's grandparents, aunt, and cousins, all came over to barbecue, take the boat out for a joyride, and celebrate life. Many of their closest friends often attended this event.

Nathan's parents owned a house on Lake Washington. With sixty-eight feet of low bank waterfront, including a private beach, the house was designed for an indoor/outdoor waterfront lifestyle. The walls of oversized windows throughout the three-thousand square foot home captured the ever-changing beauty of the lake, bringing the outside view in. The dining room had a gorgeous wraparound view with French doors that opened to an inviting spacious private entertainment deck. The deck, which faced the lake, overlooked a huge multi-leveled backyard. Lush gardens and tons of greenery surrounded the area. On the deck was a private hot tub, gas grill, outdoor glass-topped dining table with chairs, and a comfortable sitting area. This home was a true water haven for the water sports fanatic, which the Hansons definitely were. It had the best view with tons of opportunities to enjoy water sports. The home quickly became the gathering place of choice for all of Nathan's friends.

With burgers grilled, sodas and beers dispersed, and side dishes served, Nathan, Gabby, and Mike sat in lawn chairs by the lake chatting about school, upcoming events, and college plans.

Mike glanced over to the deck and saw Nathan's parents kissing. "Dude, your parents are totally making out."

Nathan turned to look. "Yeah, so what? They do it all the time."

Mike cringed, thinking that behavior was inappropriate. "They're your parents. That doesn't gross you out?"

"No. I'm glad they show affection toward each other. It means they're still in love."

"My parents can't stand each other." Mike stated. "They're constantly fighting. My dad finally got fed up with my mom's constant nagging and moved out of the house."

"At least you have both of your parents in your life," Gabby interjected. "My dad abandoned me."

"Do you ever see him?" Mike asked.

"No. My mom was young when I was born," Gabby explained. "She was still in high school, and when my dad found out about me, he left. At least that's what my mom told me."

Nathan questioned her cynicism. "You say that as if you don't believe her."

Gabby scoffed, "I really don't know what to believe. All I know is she was forced off the cheerleading squad, had to give up college, and the man she loved left her because of me. No wonder she keeps me from doing things. It's her way of punishing me for ruining her life."

Gabby was taking this personally, and Nathan didn't like her negative attitude. "Where did that come from?"

"She tells me all the time she wishes she could have gone to college."

"That doesn't mean she blames you," Nathan explained.

"She makes it a point to emphasize how lucky I am to have the opportunity to go because she was never given that chance."

"Did you ever stop to think that maybe she's trying to make your life better than hers was?"

Gabby scrunched up her face. "Why do you always side with my mother?"

"I'm not siding with her, I just find it hard to believe that your mom would do that simply to satisfy her own selfish regrets. Seems to me like she's made a lot of sacrifices for you because she loves you. That's why the early curfew and the overprotectiveness, Gab. She's not doing it to punish you. She's doing it because she loves you and wants to keep you safe."

Mike agreed with Nathan. "That makes sense."

"Of course it makes sense," Nathan remarked. "It makes perfect sense."

Gabby didn't seem as convinced. "I don't know. She's pretty harsh."

"Tough love," Mike said. "Some parents are like that."

"You and your mom really need to talk more," Nathan suggested.

After all the guests left, Nathan helped his father clean up. "Can Gabby and I take the boat out for a bit?"

"Sure." Randy reached into his pocket and handed his son the boat keys. "Fill it up with gas and dock it for me."

"Ok." Nathan took the keys, and he and Gabby went for a ride.

After filling up the boat and driving around the lake for a while, Nathan parked it in the middle of the water, offshore from his parents' house.

"Why did we stop?" Gabby asked when Nathan turned off the motor.

"Come here." He signaled with his index finger for her to join him.

Gabby moved to his lap, straddling him.

Nathan pulled her body closer to his and kissed her rather intensely.

She wrapped her arms around his neck and reciprocated with the same intensity. The heat of passion grew quickly, and before they knew it, they were both naked from the waist down. Gabby maintained her straddled position as he gently eased inside. Their bodies moved rhythmically, totally in sync with one another. Nathan looked into Gabby's eyes while he held her tightly in his arms. This experience was incredibly bonding, and the pleasurable sensation was intense.

While Nathan and Gabby enjoyed a little private time, Jane and Randy cleaned up the backyard. When Jane looked out and saw the boat floating in the middle of the lake, she squinted, trying to figure out why it wasn't moving. "What is Nathan doing out there? Are they stuck?"

Randy knew exactly what Nathan was doing. "They're fine, Jane. Leave them alone."

Shocked by what her husband implied, she blurted out, "Are they…?"

Randy laughed at her. "Like you and I have never had sex on the boat."

"But we're married."

He laughed even harder. "Wow, how quickly we forget. If I recall, you and I did that exact same thing while we were still dating, and don't even tell me you didn't like it," he suggested, winking at her.

She glared at him. "That's different."

"No it's not. We were young and in love. Nathan's no different. Why are you bringing this up again?" he asked her. "You know he and Gabby have been doing that for months now. Let it go, Babe. You are trying to fight a battle you have already lost."

But Jane was worried. "Is he wearing a condom? What if he gets her pregnant?"

"He won't."

"How can you be so sure?" she asked, not nearly as convinced.

"Because she's on the pill."

"How do you know that?"

"Because I'm the one who wrote her the prescription."

Outraged that he would do such a thing, Jane questioned his judgement. "Randal Hanson! Does her mother know about that?"

"Yes. I wouldn't have done it without her consent. She wasn't happy about it, but she's not an ignorant woman. She cares about Gabby and doesn't want to see her get pregnant any more than we do. Putting Gabby on the pill was the smart thing to do."

"Randy."

"Honey, relax. He's being safe. I'd rather he was having sex than drinking or taking drugs, wouldn't you?"

"Yes, but..." She had a hard time relating to Randy's coolness. "I can't believe this doesn't bother you."

"It's not a battle worth fighting," he stated. "We have to choose our battles, Babe, and this is not one of them. He's young. Let him enjoy himself."

The house buzzed Monday morning with everyone trying to get ready for work and school. Randy was downstairs talking on his cellphone, sipping on a cup of coffee. Jane was in the kitchen unloading the dishwasher, and Lauren and Lacy were fighting over the bathroom.

Nathan gulped down a glass of orange juice then set his glass in the kitchen sink. "Won't be in 'til eight or nine tonight, Mom."

"Why is that?" Jane asked.

"Workin' 'til six then meeting Mike at the library to go over an English project we're working on."

"Do you want me to save dinner for you?"

"What are we having?"

"Tacos."

One of his favorite meals. "Can Mike come over here and have dinner with us instead?"

"Sure, Honey," Jane said.

"Sweet! See you later, Mom." He grabbed his letter jacket off the back of a chair, slipped his cellphone in his pocket, and kissed his mother on the cheek. Trying not to disturb his father's phone conversation, he grabbed his keys and headed toward the door waving goodbye.

Randy waved back. His attention was quickly diverted when his daughter, Lacy, came down the stairs wearing super tight skinny jeans and a very low cut, form-fitting tee-shirt. The words *HOT STUFF* were printed in glitter letters across the front of her chest, deliberately drawing attention to her breasts. "Uh, Jim, I'll call you back in a minute." He hung up his phone and scowled coarsely at his daughter. "You are *not* wearing that."

Lacy didn't see anything wrong with her outfit. "Why not?"

"Because those jeans are too tight, you're wearing way too much makeup, and there is no way in hell I'm letting you out of this house in that shirt. Go change your clothes and wash that crap off your face."

"Daddy," Lacy argued. "What's wrong with this shirt?"

"Hot stuff? Really? That's the kind of message you're trying to send? And it is far too low cut. Where did you get that shirt?"

"It's Jackie's."

"You're not wearing that."

"Why not?" she asked, not understanding his logic.

"Because my teenage daughter is not going to advertise herself as a sex object, that's why."

"Daddy, it's just a shirt," Lacy argued.

"It's inappropriate. Go change."

"But, Dad…"

"Now!" Randy demanded.

Lacy huffed and headed back up the stairs.

Randy turned to his wife for answers. "What makes her think she can wear stuff like that?"

"It's the latest style," Jane replied. "All of her friends are wearing clothes like that."

"I don't give a crap if her friends dress like that or not. My daughters are not advertising themselves as hot, baby, sweet, sexy, juicy, or any other word that insinuates sex and draws attention to their ass or their chest."

Jane tittered under her breath. "I'll help her change." She gently touched his shoulder then marched up the stairs to help her daughter find more appropriate clothes.

Randy stood there baffled as he finished his coffee.

"Daddy," Lauren called when she walked into the room. She handed her father a necklace, turned her back to him, and lifted her hair up. "Can you clasp it for me?"

"Sure." Randy fastened the necklace around her neck.

Lauren was the more subtle of the twins. She had a more laidback personality, was more modest, and far less argumentative. "I have theatre rehearsal after school. Last week until opening night."

"Are you nervous?" he asked his daughter.

"I'm excited about it. Tech week is always busy though. You're coming to my play this weekend, right?"

Randy smiled proudly. "Of course. I wouldn't miss it." The Lake Washington High School theatre department was performing *Bye, Bye Birdie* this coming weekend, and Lauren had been cast as the female lead. Randy had never missed a single performance by her, and wasn't planning on missing this one.

"I love you, Daddy."

"Love you too, Baby."

Even though Lauren and Lacy were identical twins, they had very different tastes, different interests, and unique, distinctive personalities. Randy had noticed this about his girls from the day they were born. They had their own language and an unspoken ability to communicate their thoughts and emotions in a way that only they understood—it was almost like telepathy. It was not only a message that could be shared between the girls but an impulse to do something at a certain time, such as sharpening a pencil or eating the same thing for lunch. This connection sometimes extended to feeling physical pain the other twin was experiencing even when oblivious to the situation. Each girl could sense what the other one was feeling without being in the same room. This ability proved to be beneficial on many occasions. Today was one of those days.

Lacy had a get wrenching feeling that something was wrong. She knew Lauren had theatre rehearsal after school, and although she had to report to dance practice, intuition told her to hold off and look for her twin. She found Lauren sitting alone in a corner of the auditorium, crying and hugging her knees. "Lauren, what's wrong?"

"He's such a jerk," Lauren replied.

Lacy sat down next to her. "Who?"

"Damien." She sniffled and wiped her eyes.

Sympathizing with her sister, Lacy gently touched her arm. "What did he do?"

Lauren told her what happened.

After hearing Lauren's story, Lacy texted her brother. Nathan was out in the parking lot joking around with his friends when he received her message. *Come to the auditorium ASAP. Lauren needs you.* He quickly ended his conversation and headed that direction.

In the auditorium, he saw both of his sisters sitting on the floor. Lauren was in tears with Lacy trying to comfort her. He knelt down beside them. "What's going on?"

Lacy told him. "You know Damien Schreiner, right?"

"Yeah, I know him. He's one of the fastest runners on the track team. Didn't Lauren go out with him this weekend?"

"Yes, she did," Lacy confirmed. "And he's a total ass."

"Why? What did he do?" Nathan asked, ready and willing to battle it out with any guy would dare hurt his sister.

Lauren shook her head. "You haven't heard what he's been telling everyone?"

"No."

"I'm surprised. It's all over the school now and everyone's making fun of me."

Lacy interposed, "He told everyone that he and Lauren had sex this weekend."

Nathan drew back. "That's not true, is it?"

Lacy snarled at her brother, shocked he had made that assumption. "Of course not, and that's the point. She only went out with him that one time, but he bragged to all of his friends, saying he did her faster than he ran the 400."

Appalled by that blatantly disrespectful remark, Nathan asked for clarification. "He actually said that?"

"Yes," Lacy continued, "And he's going around telling everyone how studly he was, making up a bunch of phony, dirty details."

Lauren added, "Everyone is calling me a slut and saying how easy I am when I didn't do anything. He tried to push me to have sex with him, but I told him I didn't want to. He went off on me, ended our date, and drove me back home. Now he's making up a bunch of stuff to make it look like we…"

Nathan had heard enough. Making sure he correctly understood the situation, he summarized, "He pressured you, you denied him, so he spread false rumors about you?"

"Yes," Lauren confirmed.

Fuming at the unmitigated gall of this asshole, Nathan said, "What a dick." Nathan was extremely protective of his sisters, and since he was a big name at Lake Washington High School and people respected him, he had a lot of clout in the ranks of the cliques. He hugged his sister, and assured her, "It's alright, Lauren. I'll take care of this."

Damien had track practice that afternoon. Undoubtedly, he was talking smack and trying to look like a big shot in front of his friends, but Nathan was fully prepared to put him in his place.

When Nathan sauntered into the locker room, he advanced straight to Damien. "Hey, Asshole!"

Damien was down on the floor tying his shoe, but looked up when he heard Nathan's voice. "You talkin' to me?" "Yeah, I'm talking to you. What kind of bullshit lies did you make up about my sister?"

As the scene unleashed, everyone in the locker room stopped what they were doing to watch.

"Your sister? I didn't even know you had a sister." Damien's retort made him look like a moron. Everyone in that school knew Nathan had twin sisters.

"Who the hell do you think Lauren Hanson is, Dumbass?" Nathan pointed out. "It really didn't dawn on you that she and I share the same last name? Are you that fucking stupid?"

"I don't know what you're talking about."

But Nathan knew better. "You know damn well what I'm talking about. No one says shit like that about my sister," he bellowed, wanting to rip this guy a new asshole.

Everyone in the locker room heard the sexual prowess Damien bragged about, but now the star basketball player was calling him out on his own bullshit.

"You're a selfish ass," Nathan added. "Do you really think you are such a stud that a girl will spread it for you on a first date? No girl is that stupid or that desperate, least of all my sister. When you tangled with Lauren, you tangled with me."

"I had no idea she was your sister," Damien tried to defend himself.

But Nathan wouldn't hear it. "It shouldn't matter whose sister she is. The point is you made up shit about her because you forced yourself on her and she denied you. She didn't just deny you, she totally blew you off. And what do you do? You retaliate by making up some juicy, fake ass story to try to make yourself look good in the eyes of your friends. But what pisses me off is you smeared my sister's name unjustly. Only a selfish douchebag does shit like that."

"I'm sorry, man," Damien begged for forgiveness. "I wasn't trying to…"

By now, the entire locker room was laughing at him.

"Have a taste of your own medicine, Schreiner, and see what if feels like to have people laugh at you and make fun of you, all because you don't have the balls to be a man and treat a girl the way she should be treated. You damn well better get your story straight and get my sister's name out of your lame ass lies. Everyone here knows damn well that you are full of shit. There's not a girl in this school who will go within ten feet of you once news gets out about how you make up shit about them. And believe me, word can spread about you just as quickly as your lies can."

Humiliated by everyone's snickering, Damien's face turned bright red.

Nathan shook his head in disgust. "Not cool, Dude. Not cool at all. You're lucky I don't kick your ass right now."

"I'm sorry," Damien said, desperately trying to redeem himself.

"You are apologizing to the wrong person. Lauren was really hurt by what you did. She doesn't deserve that, and you know it."

Damien closed his eyes and sighed deeply, knowing Nathan was right.

"You better fix this," Nathan demanded, "And if you ever go near either of my sisters again, I will give you a serious smack down." Nathan exited the locker room, leaving Damien to ponder his poor choices.

That evening, after dinner, Nathan relaxed on his bed, tossing a basketball into the air and catching it a few times.

Lauren knocked on his bedroom door. "Nathan, are you in there?"

"Yeah."

Lauren peeked her head inside. "Are you busy?"

He set his ball down and sat up. "No. What's up?"

Lauren closed the door and joined him on the bed. "Thank you for dealing with Damien today. He called me to apologize."

Nathan was happy to hear that. "He needed to. The guy's an ass."

"Why do you have to live on campus? Why can't you just stay here?"

Nathan raised an eyebrow and chuckled. "It's not like I'm going that far."

"I know, but I don't want you to leave. I'm gonna miss you."

"Living on campus is more convenient," Nathan explained. "I won't have to commute to Seattle every day, and Gabby and I will have more privacy. She and I want some alone time, and we can't really do that here."

"I like Gabby. She's really nice," Lauren said.

Nathan smiled thinking about her. "I like her too."

Curious about her brother's relationship with Gabby, Lauren asked, "Have you and Gabby ever…" She couldn't finish her sentence.

"Ever what?"

Lauren shook her head wishing she hadn't said anything. "I'm sorry. It's really none of my business."

He chuckled at her discretion. "Why do you want to know?"

"It seems like a lot of guys brag about it, but none of them have a clue what it's really like 'cause they haven't actually done it. They just boast about it to their friends, like Damien did. But I never hear you talk about it, ever."

"You promise to keep this conversation between you and me?"

"Yes," she promised.

Knowing Lauren wasn't the kind of person to blab, Nathan divulged the truth. "Gabby and I have had sex.

And you're right, I don't talk about it. I have told no one and I will deny it if they ask me. I'm certainly not going to run around bragging to all of my friends about something intimate, private, and very personal that Gabby and I share. I love her and respect her too much."

"That's because you're not an arrogant jerk," Lauren declared with a hostile tone. "Unlike most guys I know."

Her antagonistic attitude toward boys made Nathan laugh. "Gabby seems to think I'm a pretty good guy."

"Because you are. She's lucky to have you," Lauren declared. "It's not going to be the same around here without you."

"I'll be around. This is my family. I'm not gonna be a stranger."

She gave him a hug. "Thank you for what you did today."

"That's what big brothers are for."

"I'm heading off to my room." She rose to her feet and took several strides toward the door. "Love you, Nathan."

"Love you too, Sis. See you in the morning."

CHAPTER TWELVE

Everyone at Lake Washington High School anticipated the end of the school year and the start of summer. The hallways buzzed busily as students were released from classes.

Gabby forced her way through the crowd and caught up with Nathan at his locker. "Hey, Superstar."

Nathan turned to her voice. "Hey."

"Are you going home right away?" she asked him.

"No, why?" He opened his locker and placed his textbooks and notebooks inside. "What did you have in mind?"

"I was hoping you and I could hang out for a while before we meet everyone for pizza tonight," she suggested.

"Alright." Nathan opened his backpack and shoved one of his books inside.

With basketball season over, Nathan didn't have practice and Gabby didn't have cheer commitments. Both were looking forward to a rare Friday night off. They made plans to join a group of friends for dinner before they went to Par 3 Mini Golf and Arcade for some Friday night entertainment.

Nathan put on his letter jacket and threw his backpack over his shoulder. "You ready to go?"

"I need to stop at my locker first."

"No problem. Get what you need then let's get out of here."

When Randy pulled into his driveway that evening, his dark eyes hardened. He pulled the Jaguar into the garage, but instead of going through the door that led into the house, he walked around the perimeter of his property. His yard always looked like it had been professionally landscaped. He took care of his plants and trees and kept his lawn cleanly cut. But right now, the grass needed to be mowed, the beach had loose sticks and large rocks scattered around it, and the flowerbeds needed to be weeded. He grumbled a little, irritated by this untidy sight.

He entered the house and set his keys in the decorative glass bowl in the middle of the dining room table and placed his stethoscope on the kitchen counter. Before he did anything else, he went upstairs to his son's room.

Nathan was sitting on his bed tying his shoes when Randy walked in. "Going somewhere?" he asked his son.

Nathan looked up. "Oh, hey Dad." He planted his feet on the floor, grabbed his letter jacket, and slid his car keys in his pocket. "Gabby and I are going to meet some friends for pizza and go to Par 3 tonight."

"Is that right?"

Nathan didn't understand the inexplicable mockery in his father's voice. "I told you about this last week, remember?"

As Nathan was about to exit the room, Randy looked his son in the eye. "What did you tell me you were going to do this afternoon?"

By the distinct look of scorn on his father's face, it must have been something important, yet Nathan couldn't recall what it was.

After waiting several minutes with no response, Randy concluded that Nathan had no idea what he was talking about. He refreshed his memory. "You promised me you were going to mow the lawn and pick up the beach after school today."

That's what he was supposed to do. "Oh, man. I totally forgot."

"Did you?"

"Yes," Nathan tried to justify himself, feeling like an idiot to forget something like that. "I got sidetracked and it completely slipped my mind. I'm sorry, Dad."

"I bet you are, and because of your lack of recollection and irresponsible neglecting of this task, you are not going anywhere tonight," Randy firmly stated.

Nathan desperately tried to eradicate his mistake. "But Dad, you can't..."

Before Nathan could get another word in, Randy said, "You weren't about to argue with me, were you?"

Nathan decided it was best to just shut up. "No, Sir."

"Good. Now, do you mind explaining to me what was so distracting that it caused you to neglect your duties here at home?"

Nathan didn't answer.

"I asked you a question," Randy demanded. "Questions require answers, Son."

Knowing his father wasn't going to like the answer he gave, but also knowing he didn't dare lie or he'd be in far worse trouble than he already was, Nathan replied, "I was with Gabby."

Randy nodded his head, not surprised by the answer Nathan gave. "Uh huh. That's what I figured." He scowled at his son, disappointed by his lack of responsibility. "Well, I hope it was worth it, because you are not leaving this house all weekend. And since you will have so much time on your hands, you can spend tomorrow doing the yard work you were supposed to get done this afternoon."

"I have to work tomorrow," Nathan refuted.

Aggravated by his son's smartass tone, Randy shot Nathan an eye-piercing glare. "That sounded an awful lot like attitude to me, young man."

Realizing that yes, it probably did, Nathan hung his head. "I'm sorry."

"What time do you get off work?"

"1:30."

"You are to report straight home afterwards," Randy insisted. "And you better be in this door no later than 2:00. Not only will you be mowing the grass and picking up the beach like I asked you to, but you have just earned yourself an extensive list of other chores as well."

No longer trying to argue with his father, Nathan accepted the consequences. "Yes, Sir."

"Out of common courtesy, you are going to call Gabby and tell her you aren't coming tonight so she can make other arrangements. When you are finished, you are surrendering your phone. You have two minutes, so make it quick." Randy left his son's room to change out of his work attire.

Nathan took a deep breath and sat on his bed, staring at his phone for a minute before he dialed Gabby's number.

She answered joyfully. "Are you on your way?"

"Actually I'm not going to make it tonight."

"Why not?"

Not wanting to admit his error to her, Nathan said, "My father just grounded me."

"What did you do?"

"I don't have time to explain right now. I'm sorry, Gab. I know I told you I'd pick you up and we'd go together, but…"

"It's ok," she assured him. "I'll call Amber and see if I can get a ride from her."

"I'm out of commission the whole weekend." Nathan heard his father holler his name from the bedroom demanding that he get off the phone. "Look, I have to go. I'll explain everything on Monday."

"Ok. I love you," she said to him.

"I love you too." Nathan hung up right as his father walked back into his room.

Randy held out his hand. "I'll take that now."

Nathan handed over his phone.

"Not only have you disappointed me, but you have disappointed Gabby as well. Are you proud of yourself?"

Nathan sat stone-faced, not feeling proud at all. "No, Sir."

"I strongly suggest you get a good night's sleep tonight," Randy advised. "You are going to be busy tomorrow." He put Nathan's phone in his pocket and reported downstairs to help his wife prepare dinner. He snuck up behind her and took a whiff of the meal she was concocting. "That smells amazing."

She fed him a sample from the spoon. "How was your day?"

"My day was ok," he stated. "Fell behind a little this afternoon, but I was able to catch up by four." Jane returned to making dinner while Randy pulled a coffee mug from the cupboard. "Nathan is not to leave the house this weekend."

"Why is that?"

"He shirked his responsibilities and didn't do what he told me he was going to do."

"Ok," Jane replied. "I'll support you on that. What didn't he do?"

Randy proceeded to explain the situation while he made himself a cup of coffee. "I'm disappointed," he said, sipping from his mug. "I really thought Nathan was more responsible than that."

"He's a good kid," she argued.

"I know he is, but he has to learn to balance his responsibilities. I need to sit down and have a talk with him about the realities of adulthood and the many hats he will have to wear and maintain. That's something he and I have never really talked about."

"Well, it looks like your Sunday afternoon bonding time is all planned out then," she teased.

Randy mumbled under his breath, "Not quite the quality time I was hoping for."

Saturday evening, around 6:00, Nathan was tired, hot, and hungry from a long morning of bagging groceries and a long afternoon of yardwork. Aside from mowing and picking up loose debris off the beach, Nathan had to trim hedges, weed and mulch flowerbeds, sweep the deck and driveway, edge around trees and the front lawn, and clean out the storage shed where all of the yard care gear and watersport equipment was stored.

Watching Nathan diligently working, Jane poked her head out the back door and called out to him, "Nathan, come inside and get something to eat."

Nathan ambled over to his mother and took a big swig from the water bottle he had in his hand. "I have to get this done."

"You can't function very well without food to give you energy," she insisted. "Come inside and grab a quick bite."

While Nathan sat at the kitchen island chugging down the rest of his water, Jane dished up a plate for him. She frowned at the pitiful look on his face. "You know why he's so upset with you, don't you?"

Nathan set the bottle on the counter. "He asked me to do something. I forgot about it and didn't get it done."

"This isn't about you not doing the chores your father asked you to do."

"It's not?"

"There's more to it than that," she explained. "You broke his trust."

Nathan didn't see how this was a trust issue at all. "What do you mean, I broke his trust? I don't understand."

"Your father assigned you that task because he trusted you would get it done. But instead of relying on you to be the responsible person he thought you were, you showed him you weren't dependable. He was hurt by that."

Nathan hadn't thought about it that way. "I wasn't trying to be untrustworthy. I just forgot."

"Not forgetting is part of being responsible." She handed him a plate. "It's going to take a while to earn his trust back."

Nathan hung his head. "I know."

As Jane walked out of the kitchen, she lovingly put her hand on Nathan's shoulder. "Eat up, Sweetheart, then finish outside."

Nathan nodded and did as his mother asked.

By the time the sun went down, Nathan had completed everything on his father's list. He came inside dirty, sweaty, and tired. "I'm finished," he said to his father.

"Good. We'll talk when you're cleaned up."

"Yes, Sir."

After a hot shower, Nathan sat on his bed trying to ease some tension by tossing a basketball into the air over and over again. He dreaded the 'talk' he was about to have with his father, although he knew it was inevitable.

Before Randy headed up to Nathan's room, Jane touched his arm to get his attention. "Randy, don't be too hard on him."

"I'm not going to be hard on him. I'm just going to talk to him."

"He really is trying to please you. He wants nothing more than for you to be proud of him."

"I am proud of him," Randy declared. "But if he's going to function in the adult world, he needs to understand what it means to be a responsible and trustworthy person." He kissed her then traipsed up the stairs to Nathan's room. He lightly tapped on the door. "Nate?"

Nathan caught the ball one last time then dropped it on the floor. "Yes, Sir. Come in." He sat up respectfully as his father entered the room.

Randy took a seat next to his son.

"Dad, I'm really sorry," Nathan said with apologetic eyes. "I know I betrayed your trust."

"That you did." Randy proceeded to explain a few things, "Nathan, I want you to think for a minute about all the responsibilities I have as an adult."

"You have a lot," Nathan said.

"That I do. First and foremost, I'm a husband, which means I need to be available for your mother when she needs me. I contribute to keeping our marriage growing strong, show her daily that I love her, and together we work at rectifying any problems or differences we may have. I'm also a doctor, which means I have commitments to my patients and to my colleagues when they need me for consultation purposes. I'm an attending physician, which means the university entrusts me to educate the medical students under my supervision. I'm a homeowner who is required to maintain upkeep on the house so it doesn't fall apart, and I have certain utilities to pay so we can all live comfortably. And I'm a father who provides for his children, supports you and your sisters in your individual interests, disciplines you when necessary, and no matter what, loves you unconditionally. All of these duties I have require different types of responsibility, and each is just as important as the next. Part of growing up means learning how to balance the responsibilities you have. And when you are able to do that, you become a trustworthy adult people can depend on."

"I'm aware of that, Dad, and I'm trying."

"I know you are," Randy confirmed. "And you have many responsibilities to maintain. You're a student who is working hard to keep your grades up and performing well on exams so you can be successful in college. You are also an athlete, which probably requires the most discipline on your part. Becoming a member of an NCAA team is going to require even more self-discipline because you'll need to learn to balance your time wisely. You are a son, an older brother, and a contributing member of this family, which means you have certain responsibilities at home that need to be taken care of. And I know how important your responsibility to Gabby is. That requires commitment and dedication from you, and it takes time. But something you absolutely cannot do is neglect one responsibility to satisfy another one. Think about it this way, what would happen if I got a call from Jim about an emergency situation where my expertise was needed, but I didn't respond because I didn't feel like having doctor duties that day?"

Nathan chuckled a little. "That's absurd and unrealistic, Dad, because you would never allow that to happen."

"And why is that?"

"Because it's your responsibility to save lives. It's what you do," Nathan explained.

"Ok. Good." Trying to use analogies his son could relate too, Randy offered, "Here's another example. Suppose Gabby wanted you to hang out with her on game day, so you, fulfilling your boyfriend responsibilities, don't show up for the game. What would happen?"

Nathan carefully analyzed this scenario. "Besides the fact that we'd probably lose, I would disappoint all of my teammates, my coach, and the fans, and I'd be benched and might even get kicked off the team. Likewise, I would give up my leadership position and would most likely lose my basketball scholarship. But she would never ask me to do that."

"Why not?" Randy asked, trying to get his son to think.

"Because she knows I have responsibilities to my team. I wouldn't do that anyway, even if she asked me to."

"If the roles had been reversed and Gabby would have told you yesterday that she had other commitments at home, what would you have said to her?"

"I would have told her to go home and take care of them," Nathan admitted.

"Why?" Randy probed.

"Because I know she has responsibilities to her family." This was all starting to make sense now. "I see your point."

"It's all about balance. And if Gabby really cares about you, she'll understand." Randy ended his discussion with some words of advice. "Being a responsible adult means many things, Nate. It means you take action when you need to, you're available to the people who depend on you, you're a man of your word, and you accept responsibility for your actions without making excuses. Only then will you be a dependable adult people trust. Do you understand what I'm saying?"

Acknowledging his father's words, Nathan replied, "Yes, Sir. I do."

"Good." Randy stood up.

Nathan probed for his father's attention. "Dad?"

"Yes, Son?"

"Thanks." He smiled as his father left the room.

Monday morning, Nathan had some explaining to do. When he picked Gabby up on his way to school, he proceeded to tell her what happened. "Were you able to find another ride?"

"Yes," Gabby reassured him. "Amber picked me up and Mike gave me a ride home."

Grateful for his helpful friends, Nathan replied, "Remind me to thank them later."

Gabby sat in the passenger seat and stared at Nathan.

Her gawping eyes made him uneasy. "What's that look for?"

"If you had something you needed to do, why didn't you just tell me?" she asked.

"I told you, I forgot about it," he justified. "It's not like I neglected it deliberately."

"I bet your dad was mad," Gabby deduced. "Are you still under house arrest?"

"No, but building back my father's trust is not going to be easy."

CHAPTER THIRTEEN

Celebrating the culmination of high school, the Prom was the most awaited event among teenagers. It was the time of year when high school seniors scrambled to make sure they had the perfect dress, shoes, jewelry, and tux picked out. It was a night of dancing, socializing with friends, and creating lasting memories. Everybody had high expectations of what their Prom would be like, and all wanted the night to be memorable and unique. Nathan and Gabby were no different. They had planned for Prom night and looked forward to it for months.

Gabby gazed into the mirror one last time, primping her hair and turning from side to side to check the fit of her dress.

Her mother walked into the room and looked her over from head to toe. "You look nice."

Gabby smoothed down her dress. "You think so?"

"Yes, you look very nice. That is a beautiful dress."

"Nathan helped me pick it out."

"He really cares about you, doesn't he? He's polite and well mannered. He's good about getting you home on time and doesn't appear to be a troublemaker."

Gabby was expecting her mom to say something derogatory about Nathan, but she didn't. Although Gabby talked about Nathan all the time, her mother never really paid much attention. Most of the time she failed to acknowledge him and found excuses to keep them from seeing each other. It had gotten to the point where Gabby had become resentful of her mother because of it. "He's my best friend, and he cares about people. He's smart, funny, and very motivated. He's an amazing basketball player too. He's going to play for UW next year."

"You've mentioned that before," her mother remembered.

"I'm really proud of him." Gabby's face lit up, excited that her mother was taking an interest in Nathan. "He's such a hard worker. He wants to be a doctor, you know, and he has the competitive drive to do it. He's already been accepted to the pre-med program."

"He's ambitious," Gabby's mom signified, impressed by what Gabby was saying about this young man.

"He is," Gabby concurred. "He tutors people in science if they don't understand. He's been helping me with Physics."

"I saw that your grade went up."

"That's because of Nathan," Gabby declared. "He's really a great guy. If you'd take the time to get to know him, you'd like him."

A knock on the door ended their conversation. "Speak of the devil," Ms. Pervis declared. "Your prince has arrived."

Gabby giggled.

Ms. Pervis opened the front door and invited Nathan inside.

She had never allowed him in the house before, so he wasn't quite sure how to react. "Good evening, Ma'am," he said politely.

"Good evening, Nathan."

"Is Gabby ready?"

Gabby stepped into the room in a long blue strapless gown with beaded sequins and mini pleats that crossed in the front. She had on matching heels. Her glowing blonde hair and dangly crystal earrings sparkled in the light.

Nathan eyed her dotingly, awe-struck by her beauty. "Wow. You look amazing."

Gabby straightened his tie. "So do you."

Nathan snuffed, "I feel like a penguin in this monkey suit."

She laughed at him. "You look very handsome."

"Here." He handed her a box. "I got this for you."

Inside the box was a stunning blue orchid flower corsage tied with dainty white ribbon. The flexible wrist band was made from a double layer of pearls. "This is gorgeous."

"It matches your dress, and your pretty eyes." He took it out of the box, slipped it on her wrist, then spun around to face Ms. Pervis. "What time do you want her home tonight?"

"What time is the Prom scheduled to end?" Ms. Pervis returned.

"12:00," he replied, although he knew there was no way Gabby's mom was going to let her stay out that late.

"How far away is it?"

"Bellevue Hilton. I'll get her home on time, I just need to know when," Nathan said.

Ms. Pervis looked at her daughter and smiled. "You'll need time to get through traffic. Does 1:00 sound fair?"

Nathan and Gabby could hardly believe their ears. They stared at each other in complete surprise. "Yes, Ma'am. Thank you."

"Be safe, please," Ms. Pervis insisted.

"Always." Nathan took Gabby's hand and headed to his car.

Gabby shrieked in excitement. "Oh my god. Can you believe this?"

Nathan shook his head in disbelief. "No, actually, I can't. One o'clock? That is unbelievable."

"Tonight is going to be awesome."

"Yes it is." Nathan kissed her then opened the passenger side door. "Let's get this night started, shall we?"

Nathan promised his parents he would stop at the house after picking up Gabby so his dad could take pictures. Following the picture taking session, they hopped in Nathan's Mustang, had a nice Italian dinner together at Calabrias, then drove to the big event, ready to enjoy a night they would never forget.

Upon arrival at the Bellevue Hilton ballroom, Nathan proudly walked in with Gabby on his arm. The Prom theme was Midnight in the Garden. The entire room was decorated in low-lit white lights surrounded by a midnight blue glow. It had a darkened sky, starry night appeal to it. The white linen tablecloths and flickering candles added to the romantic aura of the scene.

"Wow. This is quite the setup," Nathan said. "Tonight is gonna be fun."

They joined a group of their friends and pulled a few tables together, staking claim to their seats.

Several hours into dancing, they took a break to get drinks and refresh. The catering for this event included a dessert bar and punch. Nathan snagged a cookie from the tray and handed it to Gabby. "A sweet treat for my sweetie."

"Aw, thank you."

They sat at the table conversing with friends until a slow song came on. Nathan broke the conversation and extended his hand out to Gabby. "Dance with me."

She gladly accepted.

On the dancefloor, her pretty blue eyes and beautiful, bright smile gazed at him hypnotically. "You look gorgeous tonight."

"You told me that already."

"I'm telling you again." He drew her closer and gently touched her cheek with his hand.

Gabby rose to her tiptoes and closed her eyes, inviting Nathan to kiss her. He gladly accepted her invitation.

What started out as a loving, tender embrace quickly ignited. Nathan locked himself in her embrace, and, as the kiss became more and more heated, he had a hard time suppressing his desire. "Baby, don't kiss me like that. You know what that does to me."

"Maybe that's the idea." She kissed him again, sinking in deep with her tongue.

The yearning deep within drove him mad, and the middle of the dancefloor during Prom was not the appropriate time or place for that to happen. He broke their embrace and inhaled deeply to regain his composure. "We can't do this here, but I have an idea. Come on." He took her by the hand and escorted her out of the ballroom toward the front desk of the hotel.

"Where are we going?" she asked, hoping he had a brilliant plan.

"We're getting a room."

"Here?"

"Yes. This is a hotel, isn't it?"

Indeed he was brilliant.

As soon as they received their room key, they hurried to the elevator and up to their room. They kissed as they stumbled in the door. Fighting his lustful desire was next to impossible. He removed his suit coat and tie then pulled her into his arms. Now that they were alone, he gave in to her completely. He plunged in with a passion-filled kiss and slowly led them to the bed. "You've got me so hot."

Gabby rubbed her leg on his thigh, tantalizing his senses. "What are you going to do about it?"

His hand roamed up her dress to skim her hips and thighs. Then he reached around and unzipped her dress, slowly stripping it off. With his tongue, he traced a sensuous path from her breasts all the way down to the lacy fabric of her panties. He gripped them in his hands and pulled them over her hips, exposing her soft, curvy body to him.

She spread her legs, trying to get a rise out of him. "Do you want it?"

Panting heavily, he replied, "You have no idea." His impatience grew to explosive levels. Craving flesh on flesh contact, he stood up long enough to remove the rest of his clothes.

"Nathan," she called out in a sing-song voice.

"I'm coming. Not soon enough, but I'm coming." Discarding his clothes, he stared at her in lustful delight. He couldn't hold out much longer. As soon as he was naked, he re-joined her on the bed, kissing and caressing her entire body from head to toe. He pressed his pelvis against hers, and a tormented groan fell from his lips.

She gasped.

Craving every inch of her, he closed his eyes, taking in the full sensation. His heartrate skyrocketed, and agonizing pleasure filled his entire body.

The more he and Gabby shared intimate moments like this, the more Nathan discovered her drive was just as rampant as his was. She was spontaneous and carefree in the bedroom and had no fear of exposing herself to him. Her sexuality flowed through her. She loved trying new things, and Nathan loved finding new ways to please her. They explored different positions often and learned each other's likes, which kept their sex life exciting and fun.

Gabby rested her head on his chest, listening to his racing heart. Her cute laugh resonated through the room.

"What are you laughing at?" he asked, trying to catch his breath.

"Do you remember homecoming when you grabbed my pompoms and started cheering, trying to get the crowd riled up?" she replied.

Nathan chuckled. "We were getting our asses kicked and everyone was bummed. I had to do something to pump up the crowd."

"You were perfect. That little cheer you did was so funny."

Nathan chanted, "Rah, rah ree, kick 'em in the knee. Rah, rah rass, kick 'em in the other knee."

"Everybody thought you were crazy."

"Hey, it worked, didn't it? By the end of the night, the crowd was pumped."

"I can't believe that guy ran across the field and kicked Bellevue's mascot."

"I didn't mean to literally kick the guy. Moron." Reminiscing this fun time with Gabby made Nathan laugh. "We've had some good times together."

"We have." She snuggled against him and their legs intertwined. "Tonight was incredible, Nathan. Thank you."

"You don't need to thank me, Babe." He kissed her softly on the lips. "I do these things because I love you and I want you to be happy."

"I am very happy," Gabby declared.

"Good. Then I'm doing my job."

Nathan and Mike met for burgers and milkshakes the following afternoon. Between bites, Mike set his burger down and wiped his hands on his napkin. "We were all looking for you and Gabby at the Prom. Where'd you guys go?"

"We left early."

"Gabby's curfew?"

"No. In fact, her mom let her stay out 'til 1:00. I was surprised."

"Then where'd you go?"

"We didn't feel like hangin' out there anymore. We wanted to be alone," Nathan replied with a mischievous grin on his face, completely giving himself away.

"So the rumors are true." Mike grinned right back at him. "I suspected as much. How long has this been going on?"

"Since the rumor first started. I denied it then and I will continue to deny it if anyone says anything about it."

"That's respectable, and I don't blame you. But that's kind of a big thing. How come you never told me?"

"Because I respect Gabby," Nathan replied, taking a sip of his milkshake. "I don't want her name and reputation smeared all over that school. You know how people are, Mike. Word spreads quickly. There's already talk about it, and I haven't said a thing."

Mike was offended that Nathan had kept this from him. "I can't believe you didn't tell me. You're my best friend. You know I would never say anything to anyone."

Deep down, Nathan knew that. Mike had never exposed a secret between the two of them, and never would. Conversations between them stayed between them. "I know, and I'm sorry I didn't tell you. But I refuse to subject Gabby to people's smack talk. It's not like she had sex with some random stranger she hardly knows. It was with me."

"And that makes sense. You and Gabby have liked each other from the day you met. You've 'officially'," he said with little finger quotation marks, "been together for a year and a half now, so it doesn't surprise me you two are having sex." With a cunning smile, Mike inquired, "So, what's it like?"

"What? Sex?"

"Yeah. You've experienced something I never have. I bet it's pretty intense."

Nathan chuckled at Mike's inquisitiveness. "It's hard to describe." He paused for a moment to gather his thoughts. "It's a feeling I've never felt before—bonding, intimate. It allows Gabby and me to be as physically close to each other as possible. We kiss, touch, explore every inch of each other. It's the most incredible, exhilarating rush of pleasure I've ever experienced. It feels incredible, and it gets better every time."

Mike let his imagination run wild. "Damn."

"We're exploring new things as we go. My dad's been helping me out in that department."

"Your dad?" Mike exclaimed, shocked by the words that just came out of Nathan's mouth. "Are you shittin' me? Your dad knows you and Gabby are having sex?"

"Yeah."

"And he doesn't care?"

"No. He's the one who wrote her a prescription for the pill."

Mike shook his head in disbelief. "Your dad is so cool. I always liked him."

Nathan popped a French fry in his mouth. "How did it go with Emily last night?"

"We had a good time."

"Did you kiss her?"

"Yup," Mike boasted happily. "We're going out next weekend. Wanna double up?"

"Sure. Sounds fun. What do you want to do?"

"I don't know," Mike shrugged. "What about the aquarium or the zoo?"

"Sounds great."

A few weeks prior to Prom, Mike received his acceptance letter to UW. He and Nathan planned to be roommates, and since Nathan had a choice of resident halls to occupy, they chose Mercer Court. It provided apartment-style housing right on campus. Both were excited about this opportunity to explore independence while sharing living quarters. It had been a topic of conversation for weeks now.

Finishing the rest of his burger, Mike proclaimed, "Two more months."

"I know," Nathan replied. "My parents want to take us shopping sometime next month to get the stuff we'll need for the apartment."

"Cool. Did you find a job close to campus yet?" Mike asked.

"No, not yet. I need to get a job that will work around my schedule, but that might be kinda hard to find."

"Your schedule is gonna be crazy busy. I don't know how you're gonna do it."

"Can't be any worse than the schedule I have now," Nathan said. "I'll figure it out."

CHAPTER FOURTEEN

There was a pretty good chance that if anyone had a heart attack at this moment they would be dead fairly quickly. That message applied to everyone in the country, except those who happened to live in Seattle.

Many years ago, Seattle was declared the best place in the world to suffer a heart attack. The city gained this reputation because of a big revolution in medical care, led by a cardiologist from the University of Washington. First came the invention of CPR—pumping the chest to save someone's life. Around the same time, a new medical gadget emerged, called an electronic automatic defibrillator, or AED, which was a machine that delivered electric shocks to jumpstart someone's heart. The cardiologist worked with the Seattle Fire Department to mix up the components and put them in a truck. It developed into the Medic One unit. This small hospital room on wheels allowed firefighters to deliver CPR while following a doctor's instructions over a two-way radio, reviving people outside the hospital. Before long, cities around the country were setting up emergency systems.

Despite this nationwide medical revolution, Seattle managed to save more victims of cardiac arrest than any other city. Nathan was about to find out why this reputation held true.

Nathan wanted a fresh pair of basketball shoes to break in before he started practice for UW. To accomplish this task, he and his father went shopping for shoes. He needed something lightweight with a good fit and feel, and they had to be purple to match UW's uniforms.

Randy held up a stylish pair of purple and black Nikes. "Hey, Nate, what about these?"

Nathan took a look at his father's find. "These are nice."

Randy's attention quickly shifted to a man gripping his chest and gasping to get air. Within seconds, he collapsed to the floor. Randy dropped the shoe and rushed to the man's aid. Nathan ran right behind him.

The man was unresponsive, and his skin was a bluish-gray color. Randy knelt down beside him and checked for a pulse. Nothing. He looked up at Nathan and said, "Call 9-1-1."

Nathan pulled out his cellphone, and his father began CPR.

While Randy gave chest compressions, he addressed the store clerk. "Is there an AED around here?"

Without reacting, he store clerk stared at him.

If this man had to wait five minutes for Medic One to arrive, he may not survive. Randy needed an AED and he needed it now. He addressed the store clerk again, more demanding this time. "This man needs help. I'm a doctor, dammit. Get me an AED!"

Horrified, the clerk ran to get it.

"Nate, ETA on that ambulance?" Randy asked, sustaining chest compressions.

"It's on its way. Less than five minutes."

When the store clerk brought the AED, Randy quickly ordered Nathan to come help him. By this time, a crowd had gathered around the lifeless man. "There should be a pair of scissors inside that AED unit. Cut the front of his shirt and hook him up."

Nathan gripped the scissors in his hand and cut the man's tee-shirt away from his chest. In less than five seconds, he systematically removed the pads from the

AED storage box, peeled the adhesive covering off the back of each one, and applied the pads to the bare skin. "Powering on," he warned. He pushed the green button to charge the AED.

Randy waited for the unit to administer an electric shock. The victim was still nonresponsive. But Randy kept at it, meticulously prolonging CPR and giving an occasional rescue breath. This man's heart underwent another agonizing electric shock. This time his eyes blinked open. The bluish-gray color disappeared almost instantly.

Nathan always assumed his father could save lives, but never actually witnessed him do it before. Watching Randy easily and calmly administer chest compressions to this victim gave Nathan a new level of respect for his father. He saved that man's life.

Randy pulled his car keys out of his pocket and handed them to Nathan. "Run out to my car and grab my medical bag," he instructed. "Move quickly."

Nathan dashed out to the parking lot.

Randy stayed by the man's side, closely monitoring him. He was not one hundred percent alert yet, but at least he was alive.

Nathan returned in less than a minute with his father's black medical bag in his hand.

"Hand me my scope," Randy instructed.

Nathan reached into the bag and pulled out his father's stethoscope.

Randy listened to the man's heartbeat. Steady rhythm. He pulled out a portable blood pressure monitor and checked the man's vitals. Everything was stable.

Within minutes, Medic One arrived. Randy identified himself as a physician and showed the Medic One personnel his hospital badge, at which time he helped the EMT's strap the victim onto the stretcher. The EMT's hooked the man up to oxygen and a Lifepack monitor then wheeled him out to the ambulance while Randy offered consult. When the victim was loaded, Medic One took off with sirens blaring. Randy called the hospital and spoke to the receiving ER physician to give him a heads up on the situation. His job was complete. This man would be yet another one of King County's good statistics.

After the commotion settled, Randy and Nathan went back inside the store. Everyone cheered when they entered. "No applause please," Randy said. He squatted down and removed the used pads from the AED, replacing them with new ones.

Nathan bent down to help. "Dad?" he said, eyeing his father admiringly.

"Yes?"

"That was amazing," Nathan boasted, proud of his father's heroic deed. "You saved that man's life."

Randy stopped what he was doing and looked up. "It's my job, Nathan. This was not the first time, and, unfortunately, it will not be the last. He was lucky. In a situation like that you have to act quickly. When the heart stops, the lack of oxygenated blood can cause brain damage in a matter of minutes. Death can occur within four to six minutes. Time is critical when you're helping an unconscious person who isn't breathing."

"But you were so cool about it. You maintained your composure through the whole thing and never flinched once. I don't think I could have done that as calmly as you did," Nathan remarked.

"I'm a doctor, Son. That's what I do." Randy put the pads back in their place and closed the AED. With the unit in his hand, he carefully stood up and handed it back to the clerk. "You did a fantastic job, by the way," he said to his son. "Thank you for your help. Now, let's get you some basketball shoes."

Randy put his arm around Nathan's shoulders, and together they returned to shoe shopping.

On the drive home, Nathan fiddled with his cell phone. "I want to find a part time job that might be able to help me get the medical field experience I need, but it must work around my basketball and class schedule and has to be fairly close to campus. Any suggestions?"

"You could come work for me," Randy offered.

Nathan looked away from his phone. "Doing what?"

"I need someone in the clinic who can restock supply closets, prep exam rooms, wash and fold gowns, keep track of inventory, and order supplies when we need them. Little things like that need to be done, but they take time away from patients. There'll be some other tasks associated with the job too, but you'll learn how my clinic runs and I'll teach you a few things about medicine along the way." Randy came to a red light and stopped. "You can come in whenever you have time during the week. I'll work around your schedule. I'll even offer you weekend work, if that would be easier. You interested?"

Nathan's face lit up. "I'm very interested. How much you willing to pay me?"

"Twenty-five dollars an hour?" Randy suggested. "If you're dedicated and show up consistently."

"Oh, I'll show up. I need the money." The thought of working in his father's clinic intrigued Nathan more than the generous salary did. "I'll get to work with you?"

"Yes you will," Randy affirmed.

"That's awesome. When do I start?"

Randy laughed at Nathan's enthusiasm. "You can start right after graduation if you want."

"I'm in," Nathan agreed.

"Speaking of graduation," Randy said as the light turned green. "I've purchased an extra airline ticket for our Cozumel trip, and I've decided to get you your own room this year. Think Gabby might be interested in coming with us?"

Nathan's jaw dropped. "Are you serious?"

"Yes, I'm serious. You're older now, more responsible. Your mother and I thought you might want to spend the annual Hanson family vacation with Gabby."

Gabby spent so much time around the Hansons that everyone in the house had pretty much taken her in as one of their own. In Randy's eyes, Gabby was family.

Nathan was in total shock. "Oh my god, Dad. Gabby is going to be jacked. This is so cool."

"Is that a yes?"

"Yes!" Nathan confirmed. "Yes, I will definitely talk to her."

"Alright. Consider it my graduation gift to both of you."

"Thank you so much. This is awesome!"

That night, when Nathan pulled up to Gabby's house, she ran out the door to greet him. "Hey, Champ."

"Hey, Beautiful."

Nathan stepped out of the car and opened the passenger door for her. After she was seated, he took position behind the wheel, but he didn't say a thing. He didn't start the car and didn't pull out of the driveway. He just sat there with his hands on the steering wheel wearing an ornery grin.

Gabby knew he was up to something. "What are you grinning about?"

"My dad and I had an interesting conversation this afternoon."

"About what?"

"He bought an extra airline ticket to Cozumel this summer. He's inviting you to come with us."

Nathan patiently waited for her reaction.

She stared at him, not sure she heard him correctly. "What?"

"My father is inviting you to come to Cozumel with us," Nathan repeated. "What do you think?"

She threw her arms around him excitedly. "Oh my god, Nathan. I get to go to Mexico with you?"

"Yes, Ma'am, if you want to come. But it gets better." He released his grip on her and met her gaze. "He also told me that I get my own room this year. Which means you and I will get to spend two weeks together in Mexico in the privacy of our own our hotel suite."

A dreadful thought came to her that immediately drained the excitement from her face. "What about my mother? She's never going to let me go."

"I've considered that." Nathan started the car and backed out of the driveway. "All you need to do is explain to her that you want to celebrate graduating by getting away to relax for a while before you start college. I'm sure she can understand that."

"This is my mother we're talking about," Gabby grumbled. "I can't reason with her."

"Then I'll talk to her."

"You and I have known each other since eighth grade. When has my mother ever sat down and carried on a conversation with you? She doesn't know anything about you."

"That's not entirely her fault you know," Nathan admitted. "I've never taken the time to talk to her either."

"So?"

"So, relationships are a two way street. And if she and I are going to get to know one another, we have to talk. But that will not happen if neither one of us opens the door and takes the initiative to communicate."

"Well, my mother won't do it."

"Then it's time I do," Nathan declared.

Gabby thought he had lost his mind. "What are you talking about?"

"Maybe I need to initiate the conversation. Let her get to know me, let her see that you and I are serious about each other. Maybe then she'll be more understanding about plans we make together. I think part of the problem is she doesn't know me, therefore she has a hard time trusting me."

Gabby scoffed at his plan. "Talking to her isn't going to change anything."

"You don't even want me to try?" Nathan asked, bothered that she shot down his idea so quickly. "I think it might help. The last thing I want to do is cause problems between you and your mom, Gabby."

"You don't cause problems between me and my mom," Gabby corrected. "My mother does. She's a control freak and enjoys having power over me."

"Don't let her," Nathan suggested.

"Like I have any control over that."

"You have more control than you think you do. Think about it, Babe. In about a month she won't have much to say about it anyway. You're going to be eighteen, and legally you'll be an adult. You'll be old enough to make your own decisions, which means she can't keep you from going to Mexico with us. She might fuss about it a lot and try to make you feel guilty, but ultimately the decision will be yours."

Gabby hadn't thought of that. "True."

"It's not the decision that's a problem, it's the fuss and guilt she'll try to place on you. How you handle telling her can make a significant difference in the way she reacts, which is where I come in."

"You?" Gabby queried.

"Yes, me. You and I are going to sit down with her, together, and talk. Let her warm up to me. Let me show her she can trust me."

She doubted the effectiveness of this plan. "I don't know about this."

"Do you trust me?" he posed.

"Of course I do."

"Why?"

"Because we're friends, Nathan. We've known each other for years. I know you are true to your word and I can depend on you to do what you say you're going to do."

"But that trust we have didn't develop overnight. It took us building a friendship and strengthening our relationship for that to happen, which is what I want to do with your mom."

That was the most absurd thing she'd ever heard. "You want to be friends with my mom?"

"No, I want to establish communication with her, build that relationship, create that trust."

Nathan had a valid argument. And the more Gabby thought about it, the more she considered the possibility that his idea might actually work. "Do you really think this will work?"

"Well, it certainly won't hurt. I want your mom to trust me, Gabby. I want her to know that I won't let anything happen to you, that I really do love you and care about your wellbeing. When she believes that, she won't fight us so much."

"How are we going to do this? When?" Gabby asked.

"What about next week? I'll come over after school and the three of us will sit and talk."

Gabby shook her head. "You know my mom doesn't like me having friends over."

"But I won't be coming over to see you. I'll be going over there to talk to her."

Gabby seemed doubtful. "I don't know, Nathan."

"You said you trusted me."

"I do," she declared.

"Then let me do this."

CHAPTER FIFTEEN

Just like every other high school student in America, Nathan and his friends had daily conversations at the lunch table. The topics of discussion tended to vary from day to day, but one thing remained consistent—girls.

"No, it's not that she couldn't dance, it's that she actually attempted to do it in that super tight miniskirt with her belly bulge sagging over the top," Todd said, laughing. "It jiggled like Jell-O."

"Dude," Mike scoffed. "TMI. That's nasty."

"Not any worse than girls who wear skinny jeans when they shouldn't," Todd added. "Or fat chicks in bikinis. That should be outlawed. They also shouldn't be allowed to try out for the cheerleading squad."

"Hey now," Nathan interjected, trying to get his shallow-minded friend to be more accepting of others. "Just 'cause a girl is heavy doesn't mean she's not pretty. Megan Garrison has a beautiful face. She's a little robust, but you guys can't deny she has gorgeous eyes, and one of the prettiest smiles I've ever seen."

"Who cares if she has a pretty face? That doesn't mean she should be on the cheerleading squad," Todd argued. "She can't cheer worth a crap and she looks horrid in that uniform."

"I never said she should be on the squad," Nathan retorted. "Lots of girls try out for the team, but that doesn't mean they'll make it. At least Megan had the balls to give it a shot, no matter how embarrassing it might have been for her. I have to respect her courage on that one."

"That's true," Todd agreed.

"Hey," Mike cut in. "I still don't understand why Gabby didn't make the UW squad. She's the best cheerleader we have. She certainly has the gymnastic capability, and I don't know how she does so damn many handsprings without getting dizzy. And those splits she does, she's one of the most flexible people I've ever seen."

Nathan grunted. "Oh, she's flexible alright."

Mike chuckled, knowing exactly what Nathan was implying. "She stands on top of that pyramid with her pompoms and cheers her heart out. She's knows how to pump up a crowd."

"Hell yeah, she does," Nathan said. "I think the whole situation and the newness of it all intimidated her to the point where she got nervous."

"Is she going to try out again next year?" Mike asked.

"I'm gonna try to convince her, and I think she'd make it, but she told me she's not good enough to cheer for UW."

Gabby walked up to the lunch table right as Nathan said that, however she didn't hear the entire conversation. All she heard was, 'she's not good enough to cheer for UW.' With a hostile tone in her voice, she questioned his bold statement. "I'm not good enough?"

Nathan had no idea what she was talking about. "What?"

"You said I wasn't good enough to cheer for UW."

Having come into the conversation at the very end, Gabby completely mistook what he said. "That is not what I said."

"I heard you."

"No, you heard the end of my statement. What you failed to hear was the conversation before those words. I was simply repeating something you had said to me."

She persisted, "I know what I heard, Nathan."

"And I know what I said," he defended.

She sneered at him and stormed off.

Shocked by Gabby's overreaction, Mike said, "I think she's pissed at you."

Nathan scowled at him. "Oh, you think? Thank you, Captain Obvious."

"What is she so pissy about? You didn't do anything," Todd added.

"I know." Nathan looked over at Gabby and sighed. "I'll talk to you guys later." He left his lunch bunch and took a few strides to the other side of the cafeteria. "Gab?"

Gabby snarled at him. "I can't believe you said that."

"I didn't say anything," he retorted in his defense.

"Do you always have those kinds of conversations about me in front of your friends?"

Gabby's accusatory tone was unfounded. She was huffing over something completely unjustified, and in Nathan's eyes, she had no right to be upset with him. "That's ridiculous. You know damn well I would never say anything like that about you."

"I was standing right there. I heard what you said."

"Well, you heard wrong," he contended. "All I said was that I thought you could make the team if you tried out again, then I recapped the conversation you and I had when you told me you didn't think you were good enough to cheer for UW." Nathan took a deep breath, trying to remain calm.

Gabby just stood there gawking at him.

Nathan shook his head in disbelief and folded his arms across his chest. "I can't believe you think I would say something derogatory against you. What kind of asshole do you think I am?"

They stared at each other in awkward silence. They had never had communication problems before, and had always been able to talk things out, but right now he didn't know what to say to her.

She closed her eyes and started to cry. "I didn't mean it like that."

There was nothing Nathan hated more than seeing Gabby cry. Yet somehow he knew it wasn't their little spat that caused her to tear up. Something else was bothering her. He pulled her into his arms and kissed the top of her head. "Gabby, what's wrong?"

She sniveled, "Nothing."

"I know you better than that. Something is bothering you." He pulled her into the hall, away from the crowded lunch room. Now that they had a bit more privacy, he asked her again. "What's going on?"

"I hate my mother."

Of course it was her mom. Why did this not surprise him? "What happened now?"

"Know what I found out?" she wept. "My father has been trying to contact me for years, and my mother kept him from me."

Nathan listened in dazed exasperation. "What?"

"All this time I thought he just abandoned me and didn't care at all, but that's not at all the case. He didn't want to leave me, but my mother dumped him when she found out she was pregnant. Then after I was born, she wouldn't let him have any contact with me."

Nathan didn't know what to say. "Why the hell did she do that?"

"I don't know," Gabby cried, "But I hate her. She lied to me."

Nathan tried to get her to calm down by gently rubbing her back. "How did you find out about this?"

"From my father," she replied.

Without turning his eyes away, Nathan pulled back slightly. "Your father?"

"Yes," she explained. "He sent me a letter."

"How did he get your address?"

"He said he looked it up."

None of this make any sense. "How is that even possible, Gab? If he didn't know you were in Seattle, how would he even know where to look to find you?"

"I don't know, but he did. He told me about himself and enclosed baby pictures of me, a high school homecoming photo of him and my mother, and sent a recent picture. He looks just like the photographs I've seen. And he knew everything about me. My birth place, my middle name, who my grandparents are. He is nothing like what my mother led me to believe."

Nathan released his tight grip and stared at her, seriously concerned over this turn of events. "Wait a minute, are you sure this is legit? This sounds hokey to me. The guy sounds like a stalker. Do you know for sure he's your dad?"

"Yes. I confronted my mom about it and showed her the pictures he sent. She admitted it was him."

Perplexed, Nathan stood deep in thought, trying to put all the pieces together. "Does she know what he told you? Did you question her about that?"

"Yes. She read the letter."

"What did she say about it?"

"She didn't deny it," Gabby replied, distressed about this entire situation. "She knew he was trying to contact me, but refused to let him talk to me. Instead she made up some stupid story about how he left us, because she didn't want me to find out the truth."

Nathan couldn't believe Gabby's mom had kept this from her all these years. This deceitful lie was bad enough, but he was more upset over Gabby's reaction to it all. What kind of mother would deliberately keep a daughter away from her father and lie to her about his whereabouts? Gabby had always thought her father didn't care about her, had abandoned her, and wanted nothing to do with her. All the feelings of rejection and abandonment could have been avoided if Gabby's mother would have just allowed Gabby to see her father. "What the hell?"

"He gave me his e-mail address so I sent him a message. He wants to see me," Gabby declared.

Nathan wasn't sure how to react to that. "He told you that?"

"Yes. He said he wants to catch up and get to know me, since he missed seventeen years of my life."

"And how do you feel about this?"

"I want to see him too. He's my dad, Nathan. You know I've always wished I knew him. And now I'll finally have a chance to talk to him in person."

"Ok. But," Nathan interjected. "You don't know this man. You've never met him."

"So?"

Nathan tried to reason with her. "There is no way I am letting you go off by yourself to meet a man you don't know. That is not safe, and I will not let you do that."

"But I want to meet my dad," she argued.

"And you will, but not alone. I'm coming with you," Nathan insisted.

Gabby smiled. "I was hoping you'd say that."

"When does he want to meet?"

"This Saturday."

Nathan nodded. "Ok. Set it up with him. I'll be there."

After school, Mike met Nathan at his locker. "Everything ok on the relationship front or is she still pissed at you?"

Nathan chuckled. "We're fine. Turns out there were other things going on and it wasn't really me she was mad at."

"Let me guess," Mike suggested, "Somehow her mom is involved. Am I right?"

Laughing, Nathan confirmed Mike's theory. "You nailed it."

"Her mom is really weird."

"You will get no argument from me on that one, my friend. That woman makes me exceedingly uncomfortable." Nathan opened his locker and grabbed his letter jacket. "Gabby and I are gonna go grab a soda. You and Emily wanna come?"

"Sure. Let me shoot her a text and have her meet us over here."

"Great." Nathan closed his locker and pulled his car keys out of his pocket. "I'll drive."

Saturday, just before noon, Gabby was full of smiles, yet her tummy was tickly with nerves. Nathan sensed she had mixed emotions about the encounter she was about to have with her father, so he did his best to ease her anxiety.

"You're nervous," he said.

Hiding behind a smile, she admitted he was right. "A little."

"It'll be alright. I'll be right there with you."

She gave him a kiss of appreciation. "My mother doesn't know I'm meeting my dad today. She thinks we're going out for coffee and doughnuts."

"We are going out for coffee and doughnuts. We're just meeting someone there." Nathan's tone became more serious and a momentary look of suspicion crossed his face. "Look, Gab, if things get weird or uncomfortable or I get a bad feeling about this, we are leaving immediately. I don't care if he's your father or not. Your safety comes first."

Nathan always had her back. That was one of many things Gabby loved about him. "Thank you for doing this with me."

"I wouldn't have it any other way."

They planned to meet her father at the Bedlam Coffee Shop, which was a small, quaint atmosphere in a trendy downtown waterfront neighborhood. The name Bedlam was echoed by the interior design. The walls were adorned with an assortment of found objects as well as pieces from local artists, which ranged from a bicycle mounted on the wall to a stuffed deer head. The furniture was mismatched, but comfortable, and there were plenty of cozy corners to plant in.

"You're going to recognize him, right?" Nathan asked, making a quick scan of their surroundings.

"I think so."

"Do you see him anywhere?"

Gabby checked every corner but didn't see any familiar faces. Then she spotted a man sitting on a leather seat by the window. She pointed him out to Nathan. "He's over there."

Nathan squinted to get a better look. "Are you sure?"

"Yes."

Holding her hand, he led her toward the booth.

A gut wrenching feeling in Gabby's stomach made her queasy. She pulled Nathan back. "I can't."

"Why not?"

"What if he's not who he says he is? What if he doesn't like me?"

Nathan squeezed her hand to offer reassurance. "Relax, Babe. I'm sure he's nervous too. If things don't go the way you think they should, we'll leave. And if that happens you have lost nothing. Keep in mind that all this time you thought he didn't care about you. He took the initiative to contact you and was willing to meet you here. At least give him a chance."

Gabby took a cleansing breath, trying to release some tension. "I feel nauseous."

"That's understandable. You're meeting your father for the first time."

"What am I supposed to say to him?"

"Just talk to him. It's gonna be ok." Offering his support, he calmed her with a kiss. "Come on."

As Gabby approached the booth, she squeezed Nathan's hand. Nathan squeezed back—his way of telling her it was ok.

"Go ahead," he encouraged.

She took a deep breath and stepped closer.

The moment this man saw Gabby, a huge smile filled his face. "Gabriella?"

Gabby breathed a sigh of relief. "Hi."

The man stood up and attempted to give her a hug, but Gabby wasn't quite ready for physical contact, so she took a seat across from him instead. "I want you to meet someone. This is Nathan Hanson."

Nathan offered a friendly handshake and sat in the booth next to her. "Pleasure to meet you, Sir."

"You're a friend of Gabby's?" her father asked.

"You could say that. We've known each other since we were thirteen. Been dating for almost two years now."

"So you're her boyfriend."

"Yes, Sir," Nathan confirmed.

They talked for several hours while they sipped coffee and munched on pastries. Even though Gabby spent her entire life having no contact with her father, there was a certain comfort between them, as if they had once been close but somehow drifted apart. Gabby had a bit of her father in her—his eyes, his smile, and his interest in sports. Through the conversation, Nathan learned that Gabby's father played basketball in high school, something the two of them had in common. Gabby's father not only caught up with the events in her life, he actually took an interest in getting to know Nathan as well.

"Once you get settled into your dorm, let me know if you need anything…money for books or supplies," Gabby's father told her.

She finally gave him a hug. "Thank you."

"And Nathan," her father said. "Thank you for looking out for my daughter."

"It's my pleasure, Sir."

As soon as her father left, Nathan and Gabby headed back to the car. Joy resonated from Gabby's eyes, and a smile decorated her face. Nathan wondered what she was thinking. "How do you feel?" he asked.

"I'm so glad I did this. I can't believe he offered to pay for my books."

"Let's hope he sticks to his word." Something Gabby said during this visit put Nathan on edge. Trying to understand her logic, he questioned her actions. "I can't believe you invited you dad to graduation. How are you going to explain that to your mother?"

"She doesn't need to know."

"You really think she's not going to see him there?" Nathan warned.

Gabby defended her decision. "He's my father, and he's a part of my life whether she likes it or not."

Obviously she had gotten to the point where trying to please her mother was not high on her priority list. Although Nathan didn't necessarily agree with this decision, Gabby's obstinate resolve made him laugh.

CHAPTER SIXTEEN

Graduating from high school was a lot like running a marathon, and Nathan and Gabby were about to cross the finish line. Unlike his father, school never came easy for Nathan. He dedicated several hours a day to completing homework and spent many late nights studying for exams. In the end, it was worth the time and energy, because he walked across the stage carrying a high school diploma in his hand.

Thrilled with his accomplishment, Nathan found Gabby and embraced her with a huge hug. "We did it, Gab. We're finally finished with high school."

"I know. I'm so excited."

He looked around the immediate area for other familiar faces. "Did your dad show up?"

"I don't know. If he's here, he didn't tell me."

"Where's your mom?"

"She's meeting me out front."

"Cool. Let's go find my parents." Proudly holding his diploma, Nathan clasped Gabby's hand with his and met his parents outside.

"Congratulations, Honey," Jane said, squeezing her son tightly. "I'm so proud of you."

"Thanks," he replied, wearing a satisfied smile. "This is the best day of my life."

"It's about to get better." Randy reached into his pocket and handed Nathan an envelope.

Nathan stared at it for a minute before he opened it. Inside was a graduation card with a two-hundred dollar check enclosed. "Thanks, Dad."

"You're welcome. That will give you some spending money in Mexico next week." Randy handed a second envelope to Gabby. "We got a little something for you too."

While Gabby opened the card, Randy simply grinned. She too received a two-hundred dollar check, which made her whole face light up. "Oh my god. Thank you so much." She hugged Nathan's parents, one at a time.

Gabby's mother soon joined them, and they all stood around chatting for a few minutes. When the crowd began to clear, Randy announced, "We need to get going. Dinner reservations await us." He offered Gabby's mother an invitation as well. "We are celebrating the graduation of Nathan *and* Gabby, and we would love it if you joined us for dinner."

With a bit of persuasion, Ms. Pervis agreed to come.

Over the last five years, since Gabby and Nathan had known each other, Gabby and the Hanson family became quite close. Her mother, however, had never taken the time to befriend any of them. Every time she was invited to events hosted by the Hansons, she turned down the invitation and refused to attend. Nathan hoped that by being around him and his family, she would see that he truly cared about Gabby and would do everything he could to put her needs before his own.

Trying to impress Gabby's mother, Nathan held the door open for her, pulled her chair out so she could sit down, and poured her a glass of wine. He was just as chivalrous toward Gabby. Ms. Pervis hadn't seen this kind of gentlemanly behavior in a young man in years.

Aside from watching Nathan, she closely observed the dynamic of the Hanson family. Dr. Hanson was a well-educated man who was very down to earth and easy to talk to. He constantly joked around with his kids and treated his wife with love and respect. Mrs. Hanson was a kind woman who, based on the interactions she had with her children, would do anything for her family. The twins were sensible and polite young ladies who didn't seem to suffer from an attitude of privilege that so many teenagers these days seemed to possess. Nathan was an outspoken young man who was polite and well-mannered. As the evening progressed, Ms. Pervis came to realize that the Hansons were a close knit, supportive family who were gracious with their time and money and kind to everyone they met. More importantly, every one of them cared about Gabby. They spoke to her and about her as if she was a part of their family

"Bullfighting, to me, seems pointless and cruel for the bull, but at least it's limited to trained professionals," Nathan stated. "But the encierro of Pamplona, anyone over the age of eighteen can participate in that. Nothing like a relaxing vacation running through the streets with an angry bull charging behind you."

Randy chuckled at his son's description. "It is completely inconceivable to me why a person would want to do that. I have no desire to be gouged by a rampant bull whose only desire at that particular moment is to wage war on any person standing in his path. One would have to be seriously lacking in common sense to even consider that as a pastime. The only thing that will do is get you dangling from the horns of a bull like tandoori chicken on a skewer, and will definitely earn you a trip to the ER, if it doesn't kill you."

Gabby found this conversation hilarious. "It's good to have people like that around though," she said. "They keep Emergency Room doctors employed."

"Isn't that the truth," Randy replied. "Believe me, I've heard my share of stories about stupid things people do to earn themselves a trip to the ER."

Ms. Pervis hadn't said anything to anyone all night, so the family was surprised when she openly contributed to the conversation. "Have you ever encountered anything like that, Dr. Hanson?"

Randy smiled at her inquisitiveness. "In my specialty, no. When I was in medical school, I saw my share of pretty unusual injuries, ranging from a woman biting her boyfriend's fingers off to a man stapling his hand to a two-by-four."

"Well, you certainly don't have a dull job, do you?" she asked.

"No, I do not," Randy replied. "Every day is full of surprises."

After dinner, Ms. Pervis said goodbye to the family and graciously thanked Dr. Hanson for dinner. Gabby stayed with Nathan.

Both were about to embark on a major life milestone—moving out of their parents' homes, starting college, and heading down their chosen career paths. They had many things to look forward to, yet many fears accompanied their excitement. Grateful they had each other to lean on, Nathan and Gabby held hands and strolled along the shoreline, sharing their thoughts about their future.

"I got a phone call from Brett Sorenson yesterday," Nathan declared.

"Who's that?"

"The starting point guard for UW. He wants to get together to talk about the team. He said the guys are looking forward to meeting me."

Gabby couldn't have been more thrilled for Nathan. Yet, he didn't have much excitement in his voice. "And how do you feel about that?"

"This is a different league of hoops, Gab. It's NCAA, not high school. This is a once in a lifetime opportunity not everyone gets. I don't want to screw it up."

"You won't," she assured him. "You love the game too much. You've never been in it for glory."

"Yet somehow I've established some kind of superstar reputation on the court. It's that image the guys are expecting to see."

"You are better than you think you are, Nathan, and your humility is what makes you a good leader."

"But I'm not the leader anymore. I'm the rookie, the new guy," he stated. "They're expecting a certain caliber of player. What if I don't fit that bill?"

Nathan tended to doubt himself and question his skills on the basketball court if he felt nervous or anxious. Gabby tried to calm his fears. "You don't give yourself enough credit. There's obviously something they see in you and your abilities on the court. If they didn't like what they saw, they wouldn't have chosen you."

"But why me?" Nathan asked, not feeling worthy of this honor. "There are a ton of other guys out there who are better than I am who would give anything to have this opportunity."

She claimed, "You've worked hard for this, and you've earned it."

"And they haven't?" he questioned. "Mike worked just as hard as I did, but he didn't get chosen."

This was a once in a lifetime opportunity that he had dreamed of for years. Gabby didn't understand why he was getting hostile and defensive. "I know he's your best friend, Nathan, but Mike has always been inconsistent on the court. He's not as good as you are."

"He scored the winning bucket during the state championship," Nathan reminded her.

"Yes he did, but you totally owned that game. You led your team to victory."

Full of discontent, Nathan let go of Gabby's hand and walked ahead of her.

Nathan didn't see the talent he possessed; he played basketball simply because he loved the game. The fact that he was chosen to play because of his talent was hard for him to swallow. Worried about his sudden apprehension and avoidance of the issue, Gabby ran to catch up with him. "Nathan, please talk to me."

He stopped in his tracks and turned to face her. "I'm not this glorified superstar people have made me out to be. I'm not the star of the show. I'm just a guy on the court trying to win with his team. I don't deserve this."

"Yes you do," she proclaimed. "What are you so worried about?"

Nathan stared at Gabby, scared and unsure of himself. "Not being good enough. Letting everyone down. What if I can't uphold my reputation? What if I suck on the court and the team loses because of me? What if I can't cut it in college ball?"

Eyeing him sympathetically, Gabby uttered, "You're going to be fine."

"I want to make a good impression on these guys. I want to be a part of their team, someone they can trust on the court, a positive contributor. I'm nervous as hell that I won't be able to do that."

She put her arms around him, offering support. "It's ok to be nervous. But I know you can do this. You have a lot to offer them, Sweetie. Just relax and be yourself. Show them who you are and what you're made of." She gently kissed him on the lips to reassure him.

"Thank you for believing in me."

"I've always believed in you," she affirmed.

Sunday afternoon, Jane held a graduation party for Nathan and some of his friends. She ordered a cake in the shape of a purple graduation cap and made cupcakes with yellow and white frosting, signifying Nathan's transition from Lake Washington purple and white to University of Washington purple and gold. Purple, white, and yellow *Congratulations Grad* balloons and strings of purple streamers hung all over the deck and dining room.

Nathan and his friends spent the day waterskiing, swimming in the lake, and munching on fun party treats, enjoying their last get together before they went their separate ways in the world. Although Nathan was excited about his future prospects, this moment was bittersweet.

Nathan and Mike lounged in lawn chairs on the beach while they watched Emily and Gabby splash around in the lake.

"When are you guys leaving for Cozumel?" Mike asked.

"Thursday." Nathan popped the top on his soda can and took a drink.

"I can't believe your dad invited Gabby to come with you guys. How did you manage to get that past her mother?"

"That was an interesting conversation, actually," Nathan said. "It wasn't really a matter of asking for permission. Rather, it was a case of telling her mom that we already purchased the tickets. How could she possibly deny her daughter the opportunity to go on a vacation that was fully paid for?" Nathan explained.

"Wow! Bet that didn't go over too well," Mike said.

"Her mom wasn't happy about it, but she really doesn't have a choice. Gabby is eighteen now. There isn't a whole lot she can say about it," Nathan honestly stated. "Did I tell you Gabby met her father last week?"

"I thought her father abandoned her?"

Nathan tried to explain the situation. "That's what she was led to believe, but as it turns out, that's not actually the case. Her dad contacted her and she met him at a coffee shop, but her mother doesn't know she went and saw him."

"Did you go with her?" Mike wondered.

"Of course. I wasn't going to let her meet some strange man by herself. He turned out to be a cool guy and," Nathan laughed, "he actually likes me."

"Imagine that."

"He told Gabby he wants to help her with college expenses."

"That'll be nice," Mike remarked.

"I hope he's sincere about that. I'm not going to be very happy if he disappoints her." He glanced over at the girls again, who were now chatting on the beach. "Seems like you and Emily are getting along. I saw the way you were looking at each other."

A bit red-faced, Mike admitted, "Things are going really well."

"Good. I'm glad to hear that," Nathan stated. "Which reminds me, you are aware that Gabby will be over at our apartment a lot, right?"

"I've been meaning to talk to you about that. I don't want to disturb you guys or walk in on anything, so I think you and I need to come up with some sort of signal to let the other one know when we have a girl over," Mike suggested.

"Hmm, that's a good idea. What did you have in mind?"

"I don't know," Mike shrugged. "Tying a sock on the doorknob or something. And I think we need to agree to keep all sexual activity confined to our individual bedrooms."

Nathan grinned mischievously. "I don't know, Mike. That might be challenging for us. We like to experiment with different locations—the couch, the table, in the shower, on the kitchen counter, and we might have to try out your bed too."

Mike cringed with his mouth gaped open. He looked like he was about to gag.

The look on Mike's face made Nathan roll with laughter. "I'm joking. But, man, you should see your face right now."

"Dude…that's not funny."

Nathan continued to laugh at him. "Don't worry. Gabby and I are pretty discrete. We'll keep it confined to the bedroom." Nathan chugged down the rest of his soda and grinned mischievously. "Watch this." He rose to his feet and snuck up behind Gabby. Being sneaky, he picked her up and playfully tossed her into the lake, soaking her from head to toe. When she popped out of the water, she retaliated by splashing him.

It wasn't long before Mike and Emily joined them.

CHAPTER SEVENTEEN

In preparation of his week-long vacation, Randy spoke to several of his patients and gave them alternative plans just in case things got exciting while he was gone. Aside from one patient, who was due within the next ten days, he wasn't anticipating any action.

"Alright, Margie. Everything looks good." He set his laptop on the counter and wheeled a stool over to her. "I told you I was going on vacation next week. I'm hoping you can hold out until I get back."

"As am I," she replied.

"If you need anything, contact Dr. Hutchins. Here's his direct number." He pulled an appointment card out of his pocket and handed it to her. "If you happen to go into labor while I'm gone, you'll be in good hands."

"Thank you, Doctor. I appreciate all the work you've done to prepare for this."

He rolled the stool back where it belonged and picked up his laptop. "Call if you need anything." Randy left the room and joined Dr. Hutchins, who stood near an exam room skimming through a patient's file. "Thanks for holding down the fort while I'm gone, Greg."

Greg closed the file and looked up. "No problem."

"I'll have my cellphone with me if anything unusual happens."

"I am not going to bother you while you're on vacation. You need to enjoy your time with your family, not worry about what's going on here," Greg insisted.

Randy removed his stethoscope, slid his laptop in his bag, and pulled his car keys out of his pocket. "Well, I'm off. Have a good weekend, Greg."

"I'll try. Have fun."

"Thanks." Before Randy headed home, he stopped by Swedish Medical Center. When he walked through the Emergency Room doors, Jim was at the front desk filling out paperwork. "Hello, Dr. Ryan."

Jim signed the last form and clicked his pen closed. "Hey, Bro."

Only one patient was sitting in the waiting room, which was unusual for a Friday night. "Slow today?"

"Yeah, but that's not necessarily a bad thing."

Randy pulled a key ring out of his pocket and handed it to Jim. "Here's the key. I'll set the alarm before we leave in the morning. You know the code, right?"

"Yes, Sir."

"I'm going to park the Jag in the garage while we're gone."

"Good idea," Jim concluded. "Your bird better not bite me."

"No guarantees there, Jim." Randy remembered the last time Jim took care of his parrot when he went out of town. The animal bit down on to his knuckle and refused to let go, leaving Jim with broken skin and a scarred ego. "And while you're over at my house, why don't you mow the grass, water my flowers, and wash my car for me."

Jim laughed at him. "Mow your own damn grass."

One of the ER nurses popped her head out and said, "I'm sorry to bother you, Doctor, but we just got a call about a massive freeway pileup."

"Alright. I'll be right there." He slipped Randy's keys in his pocket and glanced at the patient board. "Sounds like I'm about to get busy."

"Yes it does," Randy chuckled. "Thanks, Jim."

"No problem, man. Have fun hangin' out with your kids and makin' love to your wife in Mexico."

"I fully intend to."

Jim flashed Randy a fist wave with his pinky and thumb. "Later, Bro."

"Later."

"Nathan!" Randy called to his son from his bedroom as he packed last minute items for their trip.

Nathan entered his parents' room. "Yes, Sir?"

"You've talked to Gabby about packing for an international trip, right? She knows about customs and what's allowable?"

"Yes," Nathan replied. "She knows."

"Good. I want to get to the airport early tomorrow. You're going to have to pick her up by 5:00 A.M. Remind her to bring her passport and picture ID."

"Yes, Sir," Nathan replied. "I will."

Their flight to Cozumel required a plane change in Dallas, Texas. That flight alone was almost four hours. After an hour layover in Dallas, they boarded another plane for a three hour flight that would take them to the Cozumel International Airport.

Upon landing in Cozumel, they spent two hours going through customs and baggage. By the time they were done, it was close to 8:00 P.M. Randy rented a seven passenger minivan, piled everyone inside, and drove to the hotel.

The hotel they were staying in, the InterContinental Resort & Spa, was a five-star resort. The minute they walked in the door, Gabby was immediately drawn to a huge tree sculpture in the middle of the lobby. It served as a centerpiece to the open lounge area. The room had stone-patterned floors, lots of ambient lighting, and several potted palm plants. Unique art pieces hung on the walls and a brightly colored bouquet of fresh flowers welcomed guests at the front counter.

Gabby had never experienced a luxury hotel before. She was in complete awe over the splendor of it all. "Look at this place."

Nathan wheeled his suitcase over to her. "Nice, isn't it?"

Randy stepped away from the counter and handed Nathan two room keys. "You are right next to us."

"Thanks." Nathan put one key in his pocket and gave the other one to Gabby. The long day of traveling took a toll on his body. He held his hand on his stomach and said, "Is anyone else hungry?"

"I am," Randy replied. "Let's bring our bags upstairs and grab some dinner before we settle in for the night."

"Sounds good," Nathan agreed.

They all went up the elevator together and Nathan and Gabby reported to their room. When Nathan opened the door, Gabby's eyes widened. "This is our room?"

The look on her face made him laugh. "Yup. Pretty cool, huh?" He plopped his suitcase on the bed and rummaged for a fresh shirt.

Gabby explored all eight-hundred square feet of this spacious suite. The balcony had a breathtaking ocean view. The décor, in its shades of orange, yellow, and blue, matched the sunsets of the Caribbean. The furnishings were a dark wicker, and potted palm plants added a tropical touch to the already fabulous room. Gabby had never experienced anything like it. "Can you believe this?" she said, bounding from one side of the room to the other.

"Looks comfy to me."

She threw her arms around Nathan, excited about this new adventure. "This is going to be the most amazing vacation ever, and I get to spend it all with you."

"Yes you do. But the best part is, we get this whole room to ourselves, and we get to spend the whole night together in that bed," he said with a seductive grin.

"This is so exciting."

Nathan shoved his hands in his pockets and leaned against the wall, eyeing her dotingly. The child-like excitement in her eyes was adorable. She bounced around opening every drawer and looking in every closet. She even ran out to the balcony and peeked over the edge to soak in the view. "You're adorable," he said.

"I've never been on a vacation like this before. The closest I've come to a beach vacation was the weekend my mom and I went to the coast."

He offered her a sweet kiss. "Dad wants to treat us all to dinner tonight."

"Right now?"

"Yes, Ma'am."

"Do I have time to freshen up first?"

"Sure. We have a few minutes."

While Gabby was changing her clothes, Nathan went next door to his parents' suite. This room was similar to his except the master area offered a king-sized bed and had a connecting bedroom. "These rooms are nice, Dad," Nathan said, giving his opinion of their accommodations. "You should see the look on Gabby's face. She's already having a great time, and we haven't even left the hotel yet."

Randy got a chuckle out of that. "I'm glad she's enjoying herself. Do you guys have everything you need?"

"Think we'll get along quite nicely," Nathan replied.

Traveling all day without a constant caffeine supply left Randy feeling edgy. The tee-shirt he had on described his coffee addiction quite accurately—*Warning: Physician Without Coffee!* He did not function well without it. "I need coffee."

"I'm sure you can get some at the restaurant."

Even though Randy was on vacation, he never traveled without essential medical supplies. He'd only had to use his physician skills while on vacation twice in the past. He set his medical bag on the dresser, hoping his services wouldn't be needed during this trip. "Where's Gabby?"

"She's coming. She wanted to change first."

Before retiring for the night, Randy pulled Nathan into the hallway. "Are you sure you two have everything you need?"

"We're good," Nathan assured his father.

"We'll be right next door should you need us."

This was Nathan's first time staying in his own room on a family vacation. He could tell his father was a bit apprehensive about that. "We'll be fine, really."

"Get some sleep tonight. I want to get an early start tomorrow."

"What time?" Nathan asked.

"Let's sleep in a little. 9:00ish?"

"Nine sounds good to me."

"Goodnight, Nathan," Randy said as he headed toward his room.

"Goodnight, Dad."

Nathan awoke from peaceful slumber to Gabby's naked body sprawled out all over the bed. Her yoga-like stance made him chuckle under his breath. He left her in peace while he hopped in the shower.

The sound of running water woke Gabby up. She stretched gracefully and took in a deep breath of fresh morning air. Letting out a content sigh, she sat up, slipped on the white terrycloth robe the hotel offered, then stepped onto the balcony to gaze at the spectacular view.

Nathan came out of the shower with a towel wrapped around his waist. He spotted Gabby on the balcony and smiled. "Morning, Babe."

She pivoted her body and peered at him intently, gawking at his broad shoulders, muscular chest, and toned arms. "Good morning."

He pulled a pair of underwear, shorts, and a tee-shirt out of his suitcase. "Did you sleep well?"

"Yes, I did. Slept like a rock."

"I noticed. You were knocked out when I woke up." Bare-chested, he joined her on the balcony. Tracing kisses down her neck, he reflected on the night they shared together. "Snuggling in bed, feeling your body against mine as I slept, waking up to your pretty face...I could get used to that." He moved his hand across her tummy and rested it on the soft skin above her navel. His lips gently grazed her ear. "Shower's all yours."

She turned her head and touched her lips onto his. "Thank you."

He stepped back into the room and removed the towel from his waist. His powerful, well-toned body moved with easy grace.

Gabby sized him up for a few minutes before she made her way to the shower.

Watching Gabby prepare herself in the morning was a sight Nathan thoroughly enjoyed. Simple tasks such as dressing herself or brushing her hair, things he could easily accomplish in ten minutes, took Gabby three times as long to perfect. Every button had to be straight, every seam even with the opposite one, and every strand of hair had to be combed down perfectly. He tried to maintain a straight face as she pulled makeup out of her toiletry bag.

"What are you laughing at?" she asked.

"I've never watched you primp yourself before. Why do you go through all this?"

"So I can look pretty."

Nathan stared at her, baffled. "Gabby, you are beautiful." He stood behind her, took the makeup compact out of her hand, and set it on the counter. "You don't need this. You look prettier without it."

"Really?"

"Yes. Don't mess up your gorgeous face with all this cosmetic crap. I love you the way you are."

With their vacation in full swing, Nathan and Gabby took the rental car and cruised the highway in search of adventure. On their drive, they stopped to visit the San Gervasio ruins. Located in the lush sub-tropical forest, the serene ruins were once a ceremonial center where the

Mayas worshipped the goddess of fertility. As the highway turned, they found the national wildlife refuge of Punta Sur Park where they saw the ancient Mayan lighthouse, El Caracol. The paved highway turned east and became an unpaved road which lead to an unspoiled beach. This secluded haven offered them the peaceful hideaway they were searching for.

Nathan held Gabby's hand as they waded in the waves, feeling the smooth white sand between their toes. "This is perfect," Gabby declared. "I could stay here forever."

"Mexico is one of my favorite places," Nathan said. "My parents love Mexico too. I wouldn't be surprised if they retired down here."

In the horizon, the sunrays appeared to splinter through the clouds. The sun, with its amazing display of pink, purple, light blue, and orange, took merely fifteen minutes to set. Nathan was able to capture a few shots with his camera before it completely disappeared.

"That is gorgeous," Gabby remarked. "You don't see sunsets like that in Seattle."

"No," Nathan agreed. "You most certainly do not."

When the rainbow display was over, Nathan and Gabby strolled along the beach, splashed each other in the warm ocean waters, and kissed under the moonlit sky. With Gabby sitting between his legs, Nathan leaned against a palm tree. He wrapped his arms tightly around her and enjoyed the relaxing calmness of the beach. "You know, Gab, once we start college, things are going to be a lot different for us. Each of us will be traveling down our own path and pursuing our own dreams."

"But that's not a bad thing," she told him. "This is what we've waited our whole lives for."

"Yes, but the reality of it all has finally sunk in. We have no choice but to grow up and face adulthood. It's kind of scary knowing we're going out on our own."

"I'm excited about it."

"I am too. It's just…" he paused to gather his thoughts. "My family has always been close. It's going to be weird not being around them all the time."

"You'll be working with your dad a few days a week," she assured him. "And knowing you, you'll be over there every weekend."

While Nathan and Gabby lounged on the beach, his family enjoyed some quiet time at the hotel. Lauren and Lacy hung out in their room watching a movie, and Jane and Randy shared a bottle of wine together in their huge jetted bathtub. The full moon reflected off the water emitting a romantic glow. Randy grazed his lips across Jane's ear then took a sip of his wine.

"When's the last time you heard from Nathan?" Jane asked, concerned about her son.

Randy set his glass on the edge of the tub. "A couple hours ago. Why?"

"They've been gone a long time."

"Jane, he's fine. Nathan is responsible. I wouldn't have let him take the car if I didn't trust him."

"Do you know where they went?"

"The last time he checked in they were hanging out at a beach on the southeast side of the island. They've been there most of the day." When it came to the kids, Jane was an excessive worrier. Randy had told her several times not to hover over the kids so much. She needed to let go and let them figure things out on their own. "Let him enjoy himself. Once school starts, he's going to be a busy young man. With Biology classes, fulfilling pre-med requirements, carrying a part time job, and his basketball schedule, I wonder how much we'll see him."

"He'll come by. I know he will."

"I'm gonna miss him," Randy confessed. "It's always been Nathan and me."

"I know. He's been your buddy from the time he was little. It kinda made me jealous."

"Jealous?" Randy questioned. "Of Nathan?"

"Of your relationship with him. He's always been closer to you than he was to me. When he was a little boy, he followed you around everywhere. He'd stare out the window waiting for you to come home. He looks up to you, Randy. You are his hero."

A tear formed in Randy's eye. "He's grown up," he said. "And he's an amazing young man. I'd say we did a pretty good job raising him. The twins, on the other hand, that is exhausting. Teenage girls wear me out. From the day they were born, they've kicked my butt."

Randy's surrender to parenting the twins made Jane laugh. "You love being a dad to girls and you know it."

"Oh, I love them to death," he affirmed. "And I would do anything for them, but this dad is having a hard time watching his daughters grow up. It was bad enough when they began wearing bras and started their periods almost simultaneously, but seeing them in bikinis out on the beach today, that was difficult to swallow."

"They are beautiful young women who will be wives someday," she teased him.

His eyes widened. "Don't say shit like that. Those are my little girls you're talking about, Jane. You know how hard this is for me—the dating, the phone calls from boys." As Randy thought about this, he realized how ridiculously overprotective he sounded. "I'm proud of our girls. Both are incredibly talented young ladies. Lauren has one hell of a voice. I love watching her plays. It wouldn't surprise me if we saw her name on a Broadway theatre marque someday. That girl is gifted and sparkles on a stage. She definitely did not get that from me," Randy chuckled. "And Lacy...that girl can dance. She is so creative. Her dance classes have been worth every penny we paid for them. Between Lauren's plays, Lacy's dance team performances, and Nathan's games, I feel like one of those soccer dads being dragged in twenty different directions at once. But with my unpredictable schedule, I can't always be there. I feel like I let them down."

"The kids know you'll be there if you can," Jane reassured him. "You're a good father, Randy."

"I have to admit, I wouldn't trade this whole parenting thing for the world. When I look at Nathan and the twins, I can't imagine our lives without them." Randy swallowed down the rest of his wine then took Jane's glass out of her hand and set it on the floor. Eyeing her lustfully, he signaled with his index finger for her to come closer.

She bit her lip and straddled his lap with one leg on either side of him. Her arms went around his neck. Her wet naked body, along with the full moon, the rhythmic sound of the waves lapping on the shore, and the wine, brought out Randy's wilder side. Although the passion never left their marriage, the Caribbean always reignited the fire and made them feel young again.

Randy awoke to the sound of someone hammering at his door. "Dad!" Another frantic pound followed by another, and another. "Dad! Open the door!"

Still naked, Randy slipped on a pair of athletic shorts. The minute he opened the door, Nathan ran into the room with Gabby's weakened body in his arms. Her skin was pale and clammy, her breathing labored. In a state of panic, Nathan laid her on the bed. "She can't breathe."

The commotion woke Jane up. "What's going on?" When she saw Gabby lying unconscious on the bed, she gasped in horror. "Oh my god. What happened?""

Gabby's wheezing worsened as she drifted in and out of consciousness. Randy pushed Nathan aside. "Grab my bag, quickly."

Nathan retrieved his father's medical bag while Randy elevated Gabby's feet and checked her pulse.

"Gabby, can you hear me?" Randy said, trying to wake her up. "Open your eyes, Honey."

Her body went limp.

Randy looked straight at his wife. "Call an ambulance. Get medical personnel here ASAP."

Jane picked up her cellphone and made the call.

Nathan frantically paced around the room. "What's wrong with her?"

Randy checked Gabby's heart rate and wrapped a blood pressure cuff around her arm. Her heartbeat was rapid and her blood pressure was well below normal. Her throat and tongue were swollen, and the area around her mouth was red. The skin on her hands had developed hives. Classic symptoms of anaphylaxis. "Does she have any allergies?"

Nathan stammered through his words. "I…I don't know."

"Think, Nathan. Were you guys eating something she may have been allergic to? Did she get stung or bitten by something?"

Nathan's hands shook. "We were munching on a bag of mixed nuts, but she's eaten them with me a hundred times."

"Was there something in there she'd never eaten before? Something that may have caused her to have this kind of reaction?"

"I don't know. If she had allergies to anything, she didn't tell me." Fearful images flooded Nathan's mind and his whole body tensed up.

Randy reached into his medical bag and pulled out an EpiPen, immediately injecting it into Gabby's thigh. "How long was she like this before you brought her over here?"

"It came on suddenly. She started coughing and within seconds she couldn't breathe." Seeing Gabby lying on the bed in this weak, lethargic state made Nathan's stomach lurch. Overcome with sheer, black fear, he was on the verge of tears. "Is she gonna be ok?"

Randy reassessed Gabby to make sure the epinephrine took effect then set his stethoscope on the nightstand. "She'll be alright. Your quick action probably saved her life."

With a groan, Gabby's eyes blinked open. "Nathan?"

Her breathing was shallow and wheezy, her voice hoarse. Nathan rushed to be by her side. "I'm right here, Baby."

Her groggy eyes followed his voice. "Where am I?"

"You're in my parents' hotel room." He squeezed her hand and leaned over to kiss her forehead. "Just lie still, Honey. The ambulance is on its way."

When they arrived at the hospital, the ER crew checked her oxygen levels and hooked her up to an IV solution to boost her blood pressure. Once she was stable, they ran a few tests. When the doctors left the room, and Nathan and Gabby were finally alone, he held her hand and rubbed her wrist with his thumb. "How you feeling?"

"My throat hurts."

Choking back tears, Nathan nuzzled her forehead with his. "You scared the hell out of me."

"I'm fine, Nathan."

"You weren't breathing, Gab. I thought I was going to lose you." He squeezed her tightly in his arms, afraid to let her go. Taking in the sweet scent of her hair, he kissed the top of her head. "I love you so much."

The test results revealed that Gabby had a severe allergy to pistachios, which happened to be in the bag of mixed nuts she and Nathan were eating. Since she never had a reaction like that before, they were unaware of this allergy. Now that they knew, they would have to be much more cognizant of what she ate. "Guess I won't be eating pistachios any time soon," Nathan said.

"I'm the one who's allergic to them, not you," Gabby told him.

"Well, I don't want to take any risks."

The hospital constantly monitored her vitals and kept her under close observation for the next six hours. Nathan never left her side. Upon release from the hospital, Randy stopped by the pharmacy to pick up two EpiPens—one to replace the injector he used, and one for Gabby.

When they returned to the hotel, Randy insisted Gabby rest. She curled up on the bed and closed her eyes, trying to recuperate from the traumatic, sleepless night.

"Nathan, can I talk to you for a minute?" Randy said.

"Sure." Nathan tucked Gabby in then joined his father in the hallway. "Yes, Sir?"

"You need to call Gabby's mom and tell her what happened."

Nathan didn't like that idea. "She is going to freak."

"But she needs to be notified. It's common courtesy."

Nathan rubbed his hand across his chin. "Alright, but Gabby needs to rest first. She's been through enough."

Randy agreed. "You want to join us for breakfast?"

"Think I'll pass. Might meet you for lunch later though. Depends how Gabby feels."

When Randy returned to his room, he heard giggles from the room next door. He knocked on Lauren and Lacy's door and peeked his head inside. "Good morning, ladies."

Both were still in their pajamas. "Good morning, Daddy," they said in perfect sync with one another.

"Who's ready for breakfast?" he asked.

"I want pancakes," Lacy suggested.

"Yeah," Lauren agreed. "I'm tired of Mexican food."

Randy laughed. "We're in Mexico. They're going to serve Mexican food."

"We want pancakes," Lacy demanded.

Randy grinned at his daughters, knowing damn well he was going to do whatever he could to satisfy their breakfast desires. "Ok. I'll see what I can do. Get showered and dressed. I want to be out of here in a half hour." He closed the door and left them to get ready.

By now, Jane was dressed. Randy crept behind her and gave her a kiss. "Good morning, Beautiful. The girls are up."

"I know. I heard." She gently touched his face. "How's Gabby?"

"Better. She's resting."

"Did they find out what caused it?"

"Apparently she's allergic to pistachios. I talked to her about preventative measures, and she has her own EpiPen now, in case it happens again."

"Good."

"I'm gonna run downstairs and grab some coffee. You need anything?"

"No, thank you," she replied.

"And the girls want pancakes this morning."

"Pancakes?" Jane asked, thinking that was an odd request. "Where are we going to find pancakes?"

"I'm gonna check with the concierge and see what they recommend. Be back in a bit." He left the room on a quest for a cup of coffee.

CHAPTER EIGHTEEN

When the Hanson family returned home, Nathan immediately started working in his father's clinic. After proper introductions, Randy showed him where supplies were stored, demonstrated proper hygienic disposal of medical waste materials, and taught him how to use the computerized equipment ordering system. This job required Nathan to perform specific tasks related to clinic efficiency. These included sterilizing medical equipment, restocking paper towels, wiping down sinks and countertops with bleach solution, and sanitizing common areas with antibacterial wipes. He was also responsible for maintaining general upkeep of the facility by keeping the lobby and reception area tidy, restocking exam rooms, and washing gowns. His computer skills were required for occasional troubleshooting, and he was responsible for inventory and ordering needed supplies. Needless to say, he was going to stay busy.

One of the things Nathan loved about this job was working directly with his father. He had been in his dad's clinic many times, but never really paid attention to the operational aspects or physical layout of the environment. His father and Dr. Hutchins had a very distinct methodology and rationale behind the layout and look of the clinic. They had recently remodeled the lobby to make it bigger and more comfortable for awaiting patients. The walls were painted a light beige to brighten up the area and the color palette was violet and purple with natural shades of brown. New comfortable chairs had been purchased, and a large flat-screen TV was attached to the wall for the patients' entertainment. A mini fridge full of bottled water was available for patients, and a delicate looking glass bowl full of mints sat on a table in the middle of the lobby. Potted green plants and framed artwork decorated the entire area. Large plate glass doors with natural wood trim served as a gateway from the waiting room back to the exam rooms, making the clinic more open and inviting.

The entire clinic had been modernized with high-speed technology and more energy efficient lighting. New medical equipment, including two portable ultrasound machines, compact fetal monitors, and ultrasonic pocket fetal Dopplers, made clinical work easier and more convenient for the doctors.

By the front check-in counter, a dry erase board announced, *Dr. _____ is running a little late due to a special delivery. If this delay is inconvenient, please let a receptionist know.* The blank space left room for a magnetized name plate with either *Hanson* or *Hutchins* printed on it, depending who was making the delivery at the time.

Each of his father's exam rooms had a drawer full of pink and blue infant onesie shirts with the words *'I was a special delivery by Dr. Hanson'* printed on the front. Nathan assumed his father gave these to his patients for their new babies.

Nathan stared at a bulletin board outside his father's office. Hundreds of pictures of newborns were pinned all over it. Randy was always being called out for deliveries, but Nathan never realized how many babies his father was responsible for bringing into the world, and he figured this board didn't even represent all of them. The wall next to the bulletin board was full of degrees, awards, and honors, including several framed magazine covers in which J. Randal Hanson, M.D. was named as one of Seattle's best doctors. Nathan knew all along that his father was one of the best, but seeing all of this confirmed his beliefs.

"Nate," Randy said during a break in his morning schedule. "I have to run over to the hospital and check on a patient really quick. When I get back, you wanna grab some lunch?"

"Absolutely," Nathan agreed.

"Good. Finish up in exam room two then restock the water in the fridge out front. I should be back in twenty minutes or so, unless something else pops up."

"Yes, Sir."

Randy left the clinic and headed across the street to Swedish Medical Center while Nathan cleaned up the exam room and put more water bottles in the mini fridge.

Up in Labor and Delivery, Randy saw Margie Williams, the woman who was due before he left for Mexico. "Well, well," he said with a friendly smile. "You waited for me."

"I did my best," she panted between contractions.

"Let's see how we are doing, shall we?" He assessed her vitals, examined the baby's heart rate, and checked dilation. Everything looked good. As he washed his hands, he said, "I'm going to grab some lunch with my son, but I'll be back to check on you in a bit."

"Thank you, Doctor."

"Keep breathing and stay focused. Things are progressing nicely." He draped his stethoscope around the back of his neck and left the room. Before he exited the hospital, he stopped by the nurses' station and informed one of the nurses of Margie's condition. "She should be ok, at least long enough for me to grab some lunch. Contact me immediately if her condition changes."

"Yes, Dr. Hanson. We'll keep an eye on her."

Randy left the building and went back to his office to get Nathan. Halfway through their meal, Randy's pager went off. It was the hospital. "Of course. Never fails." He stood up and slapped twenty dollars on the table. "We have to go, Nate."

"But I'm not finished," Nathan complained.

"Take it with you. We have to go now." Randy hurried to the Jaguar with Nathan trailing behind him.

"What's going on?"

"Have to go back to the hospital. Do not spill that in my car."

Nathan fumbled for his seatbelt while he fought to keep his drink from tipping over in his father's sports car.

Luckily they were only a few blocks away. Randy sped out of the parking lot and drove down the street, making a half dozen turns before pulling into the hospital. "Tell Aunt Stephanie I'm making a delivery. As soon as you finish restocking the supply closet, you're done for the day. If you see your mom, tell her I should be home on time tonight." He scampered out of the car, beeped the alarm, and shoved his keys in his pocket.

"Bye, Dad," Nathan called out as Randy dashed toward the building.

Randy waved at his son and flew through the hospital doors.

Nathan walked back to the clinic, where he informed everyone that his father was making a delivery. It took him twenty minutes to finish his restocking task, at which time he grabbed his personal belongings and headed home.

The minute he walked in the door, he called Gabby. "Hey, Gab."

"How was your first day?"

"Interesting," Nathan replied. "My dad had patients in and out of his clinic all morning. Then right before lunch, he visited a patient who checked into the hospital. But he didn't get to finish eating because he got paged halfway through and had to rush back over to the hospital. I've never seen my dad drive that fast before."

"Wow! Sounds like an exciting day," Gabby concluded after hearing the excitement in Nathan's voice.

"Sure as hell beats bagging groceries. This is a fast-paced job, and I'm learning a lot. How was your day?"

"Guess who's street legal?" Gabby declared.

"You got your license today?"

"Yes, finally."

"Alright!" he exclaimed. "Congratulations!"

"Thank you."

"What are you doing tonight?" he asked her.

"Nothing. Why? What did you have in mind?"

"Dinner. Can I pick you up at 6:00?"

"I'll be ready," she agreed.

"Excellent. I'll see you in about an hour."

The following morning, Randy stopped at Starbucks on his way to work. With a coffee cup in his hand, he reported to the hospital, where he would spend the majority of his morning working with UW medical students. Jim was working that morning too, so Randy stopped by the ER, hoping to catch him before he started his shift.

Jim acknowledged him with a knuckle bump. "Hey, Bro. What brings you down here?"

"Just stopping by to say hello to my best friend on my way upstairs. I'm conducting Grand Rounds this morning, demonstrating a procedure, and monitoring medical students all day. And earlier this morning, I had a patient check in, so most likely I'll be making a delivery sometime this afternoon."

"Sweet. You're on site all morning?" Jim asked.

"For the most part, yes."

"Good. I love it when you're close by."

"Why?"

"Because your skills are far superior to mine, and I can't possibly make it through my day without your supreme medical knowledge to guide me along in my decision making. You are the Kahuna of doctors, Dude, and when I grow up I want to be just like you."

The obvious sarcasm present in Jim's comment made Randy laugh. "You are so full of shit, Ryan."

"I know, but I like to flatter you and boost your ego."

"Asshole," Randy teased. "You know you need me."

"Maybe," Jim said. "But seriously, I hate those damn obstetrical calls. They scare the crap out of me. I'd rather call you down here. You are the best damn OB I know, and I've seen you move pretty damn fast in an emergency situation. I'd rather have you on-call than anyone else."

"Hopefully you won't need me," Randy declared.

"Hopefully not."

"If you catch a break later, shoot me a text and we'll snag a cup of coffee," Randy suggested.

"Will do."

Jim shot him a pinky and thumb wave then Randy headed to the conference room to prepare for Grand Rounds.

Grand Rounds were an important teaching tool of medical education and a common ritual in inpatient care. During Grand Rounds, the attending physician presented a medical problem and treatment of a particular patient to an audience of doctors, residents, and medical students. Since Randy was the attending physicians for most of the obstetrical and obscure gynecological cases that flowed into the hospital, he was often involved in Grand Rounds.

Following Grand Rounds, Randy went up to the Maternity Ward to conduct his daily rounds. Daily rounds were notably different from Ground Rounds. During daily rounds, the attending physician made daily visits to all his patients on the ward. The medical students under his supervision often went with him. Although rounds were an important supplement to medical school on-the-job training, its primary focus was immediate care of patients.

After demonstrating a standard hysterectomy procedure to an audience of medical students and first year residents, Randy headed back upstairs to Labor and Delivery to check on one of his patients. It was still going to be several hours before the baby was ready. While he waited, he wandered through various floors of the hospital checking up on several medical students. In the middle of a conversation with one of them, his pager went off. He was expecting it to be L&D informing him that the baby was ready for delivery, but it wasn't. It was Jim down in the ER.

Randy made his way to the Emergency Room and found Jim in an exam room treating a patient. Jim looked over at him and said, "Jill has the file. Go check it out. I'll be with you in a minute."

Randy located Jim's wife and asked her for the file. She grabbed it from the inbox and placed it in his hand. He carefully studied the information, flipping through several pages. The patient claimed she ate at a restaurant. Six hours later, she began violent fits of vomiting and diarrhea, which continued for another four hours or so before she came to the ER. She was unable to keep anything down. Underneath the patient's synopsis, Jim made some additional notes: *PCO nausea, abdominal cramping, extreme weakness, headache, vomiting, and diarrhea. BP-130/71, Temp-100.4.*

Randy was about to slip it back in the inbox when Jim walked up behind him. "So, what do you think?"

"Looks like moderate to severe food poisoning," Randy confirmed.

"That was my analysis as well."

Randy crinkled his forehead. "Why did you call me down here? This isn't my domain."

"Actually it is," Jim corrected. "This patient is six months pregnant."

Much more concerned now, Randy reopened the file. "Do you have her hooked up to an IV?"

"Yes, but there's only saline runnin' through it. I didn't wanna give her anything else until I consulted you."

While most forms of food poisoning didn't cause severe complications, food poisoning during pregnancy had the potential to cause severe dehydration, which, in turn, could lead to preterm labor, premature birth, miscarriage, and stillbirth. If a pregnant woman was treated promptly, these complications were often prevented.

"She's pretty sick, Randy," Jim added. "She's been vomiting nonstop since she checked in, and she's in a lot of pain."

"Alright. Let me have a look." With her file in his hand, Randy stepped into the examination room. A woman, with an obvious bulging belly, was curled up in the fetal position clenching her stomach and groaning in pain. "Hello, Ms. Johns. I'm Dr. Hanson."

She leaned over the edge of the bed and vomited into a bedside bucket.

"Your ER doctor called me in to check on your baby. Do you mind if I have a look?"

She nodded weakly and threw up again.

He ran a quick ultrasound and hooked her up to a fetal monitor. The baby's heartbeat was stable, but that didn't lessen Randy's concerns. "Baby sounds good, but as a precaution, I want to monitor you for a few hours." He made a few notes on her chart and exited the room.

Jim caught up with him in the hallway. "How's she look?"

Randy tightened his jaw. "Has she been able to keep any fluids down?"

"No. Anything we give her comes right back up." Jim recognized Randy's worried expression. "It's bad, isn't it?"

Randy was blatantly honest. "Food poisoning can wreak havoc on a pregnant woman. There is not enough room in there for a baby and the crazy undulation the intestines do. Honestly, my biggest concern is dehydration. That alone poses a potential threat to the fetus. We need to hydrate her as quickly as possible. I don't like that fever she's running either. That severity tells me there's some sort of infection going on. As of right now, there isn't any fetal distress, but I want to monitor the baby for a while to make sure she doesn't go into early labor."

"What do you need me to do?"

"Give her a ten cc pyridoxine injection to relieve some of her nausea and add an amoxicillin drip to her IV, lowest dose possible. Keep trying to get her to take in fluids. Even chewing on ice cubes will help."

"Alrighty."

Randy's morning turned out to be busier than he anticipated. He admitted the dehydration patient for constant monitoring and induced labor on his patient upstairs. Right as he was about to grab some lunch, the hospital paged him for another delivery. That afternoon, he reported to his clinic to complete a few appointments he had scheduled. By now, he was running thirty minutes behind.

When Randy had a moment between patients, he stepped into his office. His face showed signs of tension and he kept rubbing the back of his neck. Nathan knew he was edgy.

Wanting to assist his father any way he could, Nathan gently tapped on the door and peeked his head inside. "Dad, you ok?"

"What?" Randy said, looking up from a file.

"Are you ok? You look stressed."

"It's been a long day. There's a patient I'm worried about, I'm running behind, and I didn't have time to eat lunch."

"Would it help if I ran over to Subway and grabbed you a sandwich?"

The corner of Randy's mouth quirked up. "That would be great, Nathan. Thank you."

By the time Nathan was ready to go home, Randy had completed his last scheduled appointment. "Are you going to be on your way home soon?" Nathan asked.

"Actually, I'm about to head back over to the hospital." He pulled out his cellphone and quickly texted his wife to tell her he was going to be late. "Shouldn't be more than a couple hours. Save dinner for me, please."

"I will."

Nathan walked in the door a little after 6:00 P.M. He greeted both of his sisters, who were watching *Grease* in the living room, then moseyed into the kitchen where his mother was concocting some kind of magnificently aromatic dinner dish. "Hi, Mom. Did Dad tell you he was going to be late?"

"Yes. He texted me earlier."

Nathan pulled a stool up to the kitchen island. "That man amazes me."

"Who? Your father?"

"Yes," Nathan explained. "I never realized how hard he works. He gave some sort of seminar this morning, spent most of the day running around the hospital, and aside from everything else he does, he had some kind of emergency in the ER he had to deal with. He didn't get a chance to eat lunch because he had to make a delivery, and I know he was having some sort of caffeine withdrawal this afternoon while he tried to catch up on appointments. When he finally finished with his last patient, he went back to the hospital to check on that ER patient."

Jane set the spoon on the spoon rest. "He loves his job, and he's a remarkable doctor, Nathan. He's put a lot of time and effort into this and has made many sacrifices. He's worked hard to get where he is. The best thing we can do is offer our support."

"And I do," Nathan said. "Working in his office has made me see all of this from a different perspective. Growing up, it was cool to tell my friends that my dad was a doctor. I mean, I knew he was helping people and would get called in unexpectedly for emergencies once in a while, but I really didn't understand what he did. It was frustrating sometimes when he was late getting home or had to leave a family activity or missed the first quarter of my games because he had to be at the hospital. But I never stopped to look beyond all that. His job is important, and there's purpose in what he does, but I never paid that much attention to it, until now."

Proud of her son's epiphany, Jane said, "He does all of this for you, you know. He wants you and your sisters to have money for college and be able to live comfortably."

"And I appreciate that. I appreciate everything he does for us."

When Randy got home that night, he was mentally drained. He draped his lab coat on the back of a chair and set his stethoscope on the table.

His daughters were the first to greet him. "Hi, Daddy."

He kissed each one on the cheek. "How are my lovely girls this evening?"

Lauren replied, "Lacy and I found this amazing dress shop. I bought a new sundress. You wanna see it?"

Although he was tired, Randy tried to show enthusiasm for his daughters' find. "I would love to see it."

Lauren rushed upstairs to put it on.

On his way into the kitchen to greet his wife, Randy slipped his car keys in the glass bowl on the dining room table. "I don't know what you made for dinner, but it smells incredible."

"I'll warm a plate for you," Jane declared.

"Thanks, Babe." He kissed her then trudged upstairs to change into more comfortable clothes.

Nathan knocked on his door. "Dad?"

"Come in, Nathan."

He walked inside and took a few strides toward his father, who stood by the walk-in closet wearing a pair of basketball shorts. Randy reached into the closet, pulled a folded tee-shirt off the shelf, and slipped it over his head. "What time did you get home?"

"Around 5:30."

"How was traffic?"

"Typical weeknight." Nathan lifted his arms around his father's shoulders and gave him a long, lingering hug. "Thank you for everything, Dad."

Randy wasn't sure what to make of this unusual behavior. "Um...ok, but could you be a little more specific?"

Nathan let go and sat down on the edge of the bed. "You work so hard to provide for us. You always support me, and you listen and offer advice. Thank you."

Randy chuckled at his son's commentary. "You do not have to thank me, Son. I'm your father. That's my job."

"But you are more than just my father. You are a teacher, a friend, an encourager, and a person who knocks some sense into me when I need it. You're an amazing man, and I couldn't have gotten as far as I have or accomplished as much as I did without you to guide me. I am who I am because of you."

Randy had never heard Nathan talk like this before. It caught him a little off guard. "I appreciate your flattery, but it's really not necessary. You have made all of these accomplishments because of who you are, Nate, not because of me. You've pushed yourself and worked hard. You received good grades and scored well on the SAT all on your own. You're the one who made it into UW and earned a spot on the basketball team. I had nothing to do with that. I am very proud of everything you've accomplished. You are an incredible young man."

Hearing this compliment brought a smile to Nathan's face. "Thanks, Dad."

Randy rubbed his grumbling tummy. "I am starving. I need to eat before I collapse."

"Dinner was amazing."

"I'm not surprised. Your mother can do some incredible things in a kitchen." He put his arm around Nathan's shoulders and moved toward the door. "Come on. I'm going to grab some food then I'll beat you at a game of one on one."

Nathan laughed out loud. "Not if I beat you first."

CHAPTER NINETEEN

Saturday, Nathan arranged to meet Brett Sorenson, the starting point guard for UW, at The Burger Place in the University District. Nathan was glad Brett chose this place because it was one of his favorite hamburger joints. It made classic burgers grilled to order and offered bottomless fries.

This meeting made Nathan's nerves a bit shaky, but he knew the importance of bonding with his future teammates. Prior to this meeting, he researched UW's basketball stats, focusing particularly on Brett's. Not only would this information provide him with conversation material, it also allowed him to put a face with a name.

When he walked into The Burger Place, he recognized Brett right away. "Hey, Sorenson."

Brett Sorenson turned around, showing off a huge smile. "Nathan! Pleasure to finally meet you."

Nathan shook his hand. "Thank you for meeting me here. This in one of my favorite places."

"Mine too. Let's grab some lunch and chat."

Over burgers and fries, the two young men became better acquainted. At first the conversation involved small talk, discussing college majors, music, movies, and what they liked to do when they weren't on the court. Wanting to learn more about this incoming freshman, Brett shifted the conversation. "I hear your dad is a doctor."

"Yup. Has a private practice not far from here. He's also an attending physician for UW's Medical School."

"A UW family," Brett assumed.

"My dad completed his residency through UW's School of Medicine, and my mom earned her Master's Degree from UW, but as far as athletics go, my mom was a former Cal player."

This piqued Brett's curiosity. "Your mom played college basketball?"

"She sure did. She was their starting point guard."

"Awesome! Did your dad play too?"

"Only in high school," Nathan explained.

"Basketball is definitely a family affair then, isn't it?"

"Oh yeah. Been dribbling a basketball around since I could walk." Nathan took a bite from a French fry. "When I was a kid, my mom coached peewees. I was on her team from the time I was six until about second grade. She's the one who taught me the fundamentals of the game."

"That's cool." Getting more personal, Brett asked, "I heard you mention someone named Gabby. Is she your sister?"

Thinking about Gabby brought a smile to Nathan's face. "No, she's not. Gabby is my girlfriend. We've been together for two years now."

Curious about this young woman in Nathan's life, Brett asked, "How'd you meet her?"

"At a basketball game in Jr. High. She cheered for the team I played on. We hung out together all the time and became good friends. Then our junior year in high school, we started dating. We've been together ever since."

"Is she going to UW?"

"Yes she is," Nathan said.

"Is she on the cheer squad?"

"She tried out, but didn't get in. I was surprised. She's a damn good cheerleader."

"You should encourage her to try again," Brett suggested.

"I'm going to, but I'm not sure she will. The whole experience put a damper on her enthusiasm. I don't know if you've ever seen the way UW conducts their tryouts, but Gabby clearly was unimpressed." Nathan laughed. "In fact she was pretty pissed about the whole situation."

Brett laughed with him. "It's funny you say that, because I was just talking to a woman the other day who said the exact same thing."

"Honestly, I think her nerves got the best of her and made her falter a bit." Nathan didn't want to be the only one revealing personal information, so he probed Brett for specifics. "What about you? You involved with anyone?"

"There's someone I've been dating for a while. She's from Portland."

"Home of the Trail Blazers."

"You a Blazers fan?" Brett asked.

"They're decent. Not my favorite team though."

"Who is your favorite team?" Brett asked.

"My favorite team or the one I respect the most?" Nathan replied.

"Is there a difference?"

"Just because I like a team doesn't mean I respect the players."

This made sense, although Brett never really thought about it this way before. "Ok, which team do you respect the most?"

"The San Antonio Spurs."

Brett didn't normally hear people from Seattle say much about the Spurs. "Really? Why?"

"Several reasons. They are not the most popular team in the NBA, and in general they don't have the most popular players as far as fan base goes, but that's because they don't showboat. They're successful because all the players are selfless and work together to win games. They have solid shooters, excellent ball movement, and they build off each other's strengths. The players coming off the bench are just as strong, if not stronger, than their starters are. The team is close-knit, and each player has something special to contribute to each game. It's fun to watch them play."

Brett took a sip from his soda. "I'm not surprised to hear you say that."

"Why?"

"Because of what I know about you," Brett clarified. "I've been watching your game for quite a while, and you, Nathan Hanson, are an incredible player. You know how to lead a team. Your dominance on the court is definitely not something to be overlooked. I've seen you play against bigger, stronger teams who had more tournament experience, but that didn't stop you. You and your team proved to everyone that you were more powerful than anyone imagined."

"You're talking about the state tournament."

"Yes, I'm talking about the state tournament. You and your team had no chance of winning. In fact, most people I talked to thought you guys would be out in the first round. But I had a feeling you were going to take everyone by surprise. That final game of the playoffs was the best damn game of basketball I've ever seen."

"Wait," Nathan interjected. "You saw that game?"

"Hell yeah. The part I enjoyed the most was watching how vocal and visual you were on the court. Your passing game was insurmountable. You controlled every play, you looked for the open man, knew when to pass and who to pass to, and you also knew when to take your shot. And on the defensive end, you didn't let a shot get past you. Then in the last quarter…man, you poured it on. That assist you pulled out in the last seconds of the game was a tremendous play. You totally owned it. Watching you dice people up out there was unbelievable."

Nathan wasn't sure how to react to Brett's accolade. "Wow. I was not expecting this, but thank you for the compliment."

"You are a well-rounded player—good at offense, tough on defense. You nail every free-throw bucket put in front of you, and your accuracy from three-point range is insurmountable. Your ball handling skills and ability to pass on the fly make you a powerful point guard. You're energy level and athleticism are unparalleled. You don't fuck around on the basketball court, Nathan. You play to win. We need someone like you. You are going to be an incredible asset to this team. As your team captain and more experienced point guard, it's my job to initiate you to college caliber hoops, take you under my wing, and train you. I want to introduce you to the guys. They're looking forward to meeting you."

"When?" Nathan asked, anxious to become acquainted with his fellow teammates.

"Those of us who stay in the Seattle area during the summer like to get together for informal games. We were planning to meet tomorrow afternoon and would like you to join us," Brett declared.

"What time?"

"One o'clock. Do you know where the basketball arena is on campus?"

Nathan nodded. "Yes."

"Good, meet us there tomorrow at 1:00."

"Alright. I'll be there."

The following afternoon, Nathan showed up at Alaska Airlines Arena dressed in athletic shorts, his *Huskies Basketball* tee-shirt, and a brand new pair of purple basketball shoes. He was a little unsure about being the new guy, but anxious to develop rapport and trust with his fellow teammates. Carrying his car keys and cellphone in one hand and a bottle of orange Gatorade in the other, he sauntered into the arena. Eleven guys conversed in a circle. The minute they saw Nathan, their conversation ended.

"There he is." Brett welcomed him with a firm handshake. "Welcome."

"Thank you."

Brett introduced Nathan to all of the teammates then split the guys into two groups. "You're on point," he said to Nathan.

Nathan raised an eyebrow, not so sure he liked this idea. "You want me to take point?"

"You are a point guard, aren't you?" Brett teased him.

"Yes."

"Then lead your team." He handed Nathan the ball.

Nathan might have been a star in high school, but here he was a rookie who seriously lacked experience. He didn't know his teammates, and they didn't know him, but he did his best to take control of his team.

As point guard, it was Nathan's job to set the tone for the game. He was used to a fast-paced tempo, but was having a difficult time determining if this group of players was better with the fast-break or more effective as a slow-down team. After a bit of assessment, he found a tempo that seemed to be successful for everyone.

He wanted to get the ball to his hot shooters. Since he didn't know who the hot shooters were, he had to use his initial observations to accomplish this task. Throughout the game, Nathan did his best not to telegraph his passes. He displayed several of his offensive moves including the pump fake, the in-and-out dribble, and his behind the back pass. He also took his own shots when he could so the defense would see that he was not a force to be reckoned with. Several times he was able to demonstrate his accuracy from three-point range.

While executing an offensive drive, Nathan's defender lunged to one side attempting a steal. Nathan fought him off by throwing the ball around his body and quickly passing to an open man. He then drove past his defender and slipped into an empty space, putting himself into scoring position. When the ball was passed back to him, he was able to clear a clean fadeaway shot.

He was confident with the ball, and his teammates were responding to him. But as the game progressed, the opposition deliberately made contact and unnecessarily fouled him. Nathan, however, was not intimidated by this. He was tough right back, determined to show them he was able to absorb any contact they threw at him.

When the game was over, they all took a hydration break. As Nathan took a swig of Gatorade, one of his teammates, sophomore Andrew Garibay, joined him on the side of the court. "Damn. You are an offensive powerhouse, Hanson. You definitely know how to use the entire floor to overshift the defense, and that drive into the paint was fucking amazing."

Panting and sweaty, Nathan tried to catch his breath. "Was it just me or were they deliberately trying to beat the shit out of me on the floor?"

"Probably. They usually do that to the new guy. They can get a little feisty."

Nathan laughed. "They want to get feisty? Oh, I can show them feisty."

Andrew liked Nathan's attitude. "Good. They could use a little attitude adjustment once in a while. Great game, man."

"Thanks."

Nathan mixed well with his teammates, which Brett was glad to see. As starting point guard for Washington, Brett was responsible for promoting team spirit and unity. He wanted to make the younger teammates feel like they were contributing members of the team. But Nathan wasn't just a contributor, he was a pretty frightening force on the floor. He had his offense under control. He played smart, could hit the outside shot, attacked the paint confidently, and was in excellent physical condition with the fast-paced game he maintained. Nathan was far better than Brett or the rest of the team anticipated.

"Impressive," Brett said. "Welcome to college hoops."

"Thanks," Nathan replied. "And thank you for inviting me. This was fun."

"So, how do you feel? You ready to take this on?"

"Definitely," Nathan confirmed. "This is my kind of basketball."

"Good," Brett stated. "You want to join us again next week?"

"Absolutely." Before Nathan left, he exchanged cellphone numbers with his new teammates. He walked out of the gym that day feeling confident and very ready to learn all he could from these magnificent players.

CHAPTER TWENTY

One of the many things Nathan eagerly anticipated about college was sharing apartment-style housing with Mike. The two of them secured a two bedroom apartment at Mercer Court, located on the west side of campus near the university's main thoroughfare. Mercer Court was close to the Burke-Gilman Trail, which was a popular seventeen-mile recreational trail for walkers, runners, cyclists, skaters, and commuters. Residents of Mercer Court had access to a gym with cardio equipment, covered parking garage, and Health & Wellness offices. Mercer Court was close to the District Market, which was a neighborhood market full of fresh produce, meats and seafood, breads and baked goods, and a full-service deli. It was also within walking distance of Nathan's favorite burger joint and the Husky Grind, a full café with espresso and desserts.

Nathan and Mike were in Building B, which provided a mix of single, double, and quad apartments. Theirs was a double located on the third floor. Apartment B305 had a furnished living room, configurable bedroom furniture, and a kitchen with full appliances. The building they were in had community lounges and group study areas with rooftop terraces. All utilities were included.

To make it more like home, Nathan and Mike bought personalized bathroom accessories, matching table lamps, kitchen essentials, and decorative wall art. They split the cost for a flat screen TV and DVD player, and Mike brought his X-Box Kinect to hook up to their entertainment system. Between the two of them, they had a pretty good assortment of DVD's, CD's, and X-Box games to keep them entertained.

Randy took a day to help the boys move in. "You're all set," he said to Nathan as he set the final box on the floor. "Is there anything else you guys need?"

"Nope. I think we're good."

This was a bittersweet moment for Randy. Although he was glad Nathan was practicing independence and going out on his own, he felt a hole in his heart because he wouldn't be able to hang out with his son every day like they used to. He would still see Nathan occasionally, since he was working in his office and was only a short drive away, but not having him at home was going to require some adjustment.

"Call us if you need anything," Randy insisted.

"We will." Nathan gave his father a long, drawn-out hug. "Thanks for helping us."

Randy pulled his car keys out of his pocket. "Make smart choices please. Don't do anything to get yourselves into trouble."

"Dad, we'll be fine."

Grinning at his son, Randy replied, "I'll see you later, Nate."

"Bye, Dad."

As soon as Randy left the apartment, Nathan and Mike looked at each other and grinned. "This is so awesome," Mike proclaimed.

"Yes it is." Nathan scanned the boxes lying all over the floor, overwhelmed by the task at hand. "But now we have to unpack everything."

"But we are unpacking *our* place," Mike reminded him.

"Yes we are."

They spent the afternoon unpacking cardboard boxes and setting up their apartment the way they wanted it.

While Nathan and Mike customized their personal space, Gabby was getting settled in her dorm room. She was housed in Lander Hall, room 524. Lander Hall was great for incoming freshmen who wanted to meet a lot of people, and since Gabby was a social butterfly, this was the perfect setting for her. Each of the five floors had two study areas and a lounge with a kitchen. The main lounge, located in the lower level, offered a huge gathering room with comfortable furniture and walls of windows to let in natural light. The open courtyard on the main floor allowed plenty of opportunities for socialization. And the best thing was, she was right across the street from Nathan and Mike's complex.

Gabby shared this room with another girl. According to the nametag on the door, her roommate's name was Ashley Proctor, and she was from a place called Mayfield, Utah.

As Gabby unpacked her belongings, a vibrantly dressed, overly bubbly brunette bounded into the room. "Hi. You must be Gabriella."

"Gabby is fine," she replied.

"I'm Ashley. Nice to meet you."

Gabby took a brief break from unpacking to become better acquainted with her new roommate.

Meanwhile, Nathan and Mike continued to work diligently in their apartment, hanging artwork on walls, setting up electronics, and putting kitchenware in its proper place. Tossing another empty box aside, Mike declared, "I'm starving."

"I am too."

The two men eyed each other and in perfect chorus said, "Subway!"

Since Subway was right on campus, they decided to walk. Nathan ordered a twelve-inch sub for himself and a six-inch flatbread sandwich for Gabby. When they got back to the apartment, Nathan pulled the sandwiches out of the bag and called Gabby. "Mike and I made a Subway run. I got you a turkey and Swiss. You wanna come over?"

"Can I bring my roommate?" Gabby suggested.

"Absolutely. The more the merrier."

"Cool. We'll be over in a bit."

He hung up his phone and grabbed four sodas out of the fridge. "Gabby's coming over. You wanna call Emily and see if she wants to join us?"

Mike wasn't particularly thrilled about that suggestion. "No."

"Why not?"

After an extended silence, Mike replied, "Emily isn't speaking to me anymore."

Nathan was unaware of this situation and wished now that he hadn't brought it up. "Oh man, I'm sorry. When did this happen?"

"I don't want to talk about it."

Sensing Mike's sensitivity to the issue, Nathan dropped the subject. "Gabby's bringing her roommate over."

"Really?" This sparked Mike's interest and brought a smile back to his face. "Is she single?"

"Don't know. Haven't met her. Guess we'll find out, won't we?"

When Gabby and Ashley came over, Nathan and Mike gladly welcomed them inside. They sat in the living room drinking sodas and munching on Subway sandwiches while they tried their hand at virtual bowling. This activity brought laughter and playful teasing into the gathering and made interesting conversation between the four of them.

At the end of two rounds, Nathan busted out laughing when Mike got another gutter ball. "Dude, you suck at this game."

Mike had the lowest score of the four of them, but he didn't seem to care. "Fuck you, Hanson," he joked. "It's not even a real game."

"You're right," Nathan exclaimed. "Screw this. Let's bowl for real."

"Excellent idea."

They all piled into the Mustang with Nathan behind the wheel, Mike in the passenger's seat, and the girls in the back. Nathan cranked up the radio, and they zoomed off to the bowling alley.

The four friends were having a great time together, knocking down pins and attempting to give one another bowling tips, which was quite amusing because none of them were very good bowlers.

As the evening came to a close, Nathan held Gabby's hand while they strolled down the sidewalk. "You gonna stay at my place tonight?"

Teasing him, she countered, "I don't know. Have you been a good boy today?"

"I'm always a good boy." With his arm around her, he touched her ear with his lips. "If you stay tonight, I'll show just how good I can be."

"Prove it."

Trying to get a rise out of her, he picked her up and carried her over his shoulder.

She kicked and squirmed, trying to get loose. "Put me down, Nathan Hanson."

He gently set her down on the ground, pulled her into his arms, and claimed her lips as his own.

Mike and Ashley followed close behind, watching the lovebirds display playful affection toward one another. "Oh my god, you two. Really?" Mike complained. "Get a room."

"We are getting a room," Nathan said. "My room."

Gabby playfully smacked him on the arm. "Nathan! Don't tell him things like that."

"Why not? He offered a suggestion, I merely informed him that I was thinking well ahead of him." Together, he and Gabby ran far ahead of Mike and Ashley, gallivanting up the stairs to the apartment.

Mike shook his head, tittering under his breath as he walked Ashley home to Lander Hall.

When they arrived, she escorted him into the lobby. "What are you doing tomorrow?" she asked.

"I have a few errands to run."

"Do you mind if I join you?" she suggested.

"If you want. I can show you around Seattle a bit too, if you'd like." Since she wasn't from Seattle, he figured a personal tour would be a good way for her to become more familiar with the city. It would also give them time to become better acquainted.

"That would be great. Thank you."

Not wanting to end the evening this early, Mike suggested, "You want to sit and talk for a while?"

"I would love to."

They pulled up a comfortable couch cushion and remained engrossed in conversation for several hours.

Back at Mercer Court, Nathan lay on the pillow next to Gabby, propped up on his side with his hand supporting his head. He gazed at her pretty face and moved a few stray hairs off her forehead. "Thank you for bringing Ashley over here. Mike was kinda bummed and needed to have fun tonight."

"What was he so bummed about?"

He scooted a bit closer so their naked bodies rubbed against one another. "Did you know he and Emily broke up?"

Surprised by this news, Gabby responded, "No. Emily didn't say anything to me."

"You know, Gab, with out of town games and both of our class schedules, we probably won't see each other as often as we thought." He gently rubbed his fingertips across her lips. "I don't ever want you to think that our relationship doesn't matter to me."

She propped herself up on her elbow and looked him in the eye. "Nathan, we have been friends since eighth grade. Our schedules haven't always been in sync and things haven't always been easy, but no matter what, we've always supported each other. We have been through so much together. We'll help each other get through this too."

"But I might not get to see you every day," he griped.

"That's what a phone is for." The disconcerting look on Nathan's face had her worried. "Why are you so insecure all of a sudden?"

"It's just…" He collected his thoughts before he said, "I don't want to lose you, Gab."

She lovingly placed her hand on his cheek. "I'm not going anywhere, Sweetie. You definitely do not need to worry about that."

"You know, don't you, that I have every intention of marrying you."

Although she was thrilled to hear those words, she was a little surprised he said that. "Nathan."

"I'm serious, Gab. We both need to finish school first, but someday it will happen." He closed his eyes and leaned over to kiss her, taking her into his arms as he did.

After acquiring class schedules and picking up ID cards, Nathan and Gabby reported to the bookstore to purchase required textbooks. Nathan immediately got sidetracked when he saw a basketball with a purple *W* printed on it. He picked it up and showed it Gabby. "Here, Gab. This is just what you need."

She shook her head. "What am I going to do with that?"

"Let me autograph it for you, then one day when I'm famous, you can sell it on e-bay."

Gabby thought he had lost his mind. "If I wanted an autographed basketball, I would grab one out of your room and have you write your name on the stupid thing."

Nathan put the ball down and held up a purple and white pompom, waving it in the air. "I'll get this for you."

Unimpressed, she said, "Do you know how many frickin' purple pompoms I have?"

Her extreme lack of enthusiasm made him laugh. "Are you sure you don't want another one?"

"I thought we were here to get books?"

"We are."

"That is definitely not a book. Put it down."

He set the pompom back in its place and finished getting what they came for. "I have my first team meeting tomorrow. We're getting our pictures taken, and we're supposed to get our game schedule."

"That's exciting."

"What are you going to do while I'm at practice?"

"Look for a job. I want to earn some money."

"Good plan," Nathan said. "I'm going into work for a few hours tomorrow afternoon. Dad and I have to set up a work schedule that doesn't conflict with my classes, practice, or games. It looks like I may not be working as many hours as I'd hoped."

Once they had all their textbooks and other necessary supplies, Nathan and Gabby headed back to the residence halls. "You know, I have yet to see your room," he remarked. "In fact, I haven't stepped foot inside your dorm at all."

"Then you'll have to come take a look, won't you?" she suggested.

"Yes I will."

When they entered her dorm, a gathering room with large plate-glass windows and a clear view of the lush courtyard quickly captured Nathan's attention. "I like this room. It's airy, comfortable, and has a nice view. I could hang out here." He wandered around playing with lampshades and fiddling with various objects on tables.

Redirecting him, Gabby took his hand and led him to the elevator.

"Hey," he protested. "I was looking at that."

"You're going to break it. Leave it alone."

As soon as the elevator door closed, Nathan pulled her into his arms. "All alone in an elevator. Whatever shall we do?" He sent sensual nibbles down her neck. Right as he leaned in to kiss her, the door slid opened. "Damn. Sabotaged by the dreaded elevator ding."

They stepped off the elevator and Nathan scanned the area. The narrow hallways felt cramped, the rooms were only a few feet apart, and people buzzed around in every direction. "Wow, not much room for privacy here, is there?"

Gabby guided him to her room and unlocked the door. When they walked inside, Ashley was lying on her bed listening to her iPod. "Hey, Ashley," Gabby addressed her.

Ashley sat up. "Hi."

This small dorm room had a private bathroom, two beds, two desks, a couple of bookshelves, and two large standing armoires, each with two bureau drawers. It was too confining for Nathan's liking, but the girls had managed to make it a little homier.

Ashley's side of the room was decorated in fluffy neon pink and lime green pillows with butterflies printed on them. She had a fuzzy pink rug spread out on the floor and tons of butterfly pictures all over the walls. The quilt on her single-sized bed was bright neon pink. The bright colors gave Nathan a headache. He was glad he didn't have to look at them every day. Her shelves were neatly organized, yet she had jewelry, handbags, and shoes occupying every square inch. Obviously Ashley was a fashionista.

Gabby's side was more to Nathan's liking. Her comforter was a pretty shade of light yellow, and she tossed three throw pillows on her bed: a coral one with yellow Hibiscus flowers, a light blue one covered in fun yellow and coral colored pompoms, and a purple pillow with a gold W printed on the front. She also had a fleece Washington Huskies blanket on her bed and a fuzzy plush husky dog wearing a purple basketball jersey.

Next to her bed, an area rug covered almost the entire floor. With its light blue, coral, and yellow pattern, it complimented the sunset-colored room nicely. She had a light yellow cushion tied to her desk chair, and on the desk, she placed a small desk lamp with a light blue lampshade. Also sitting on the desk was a UW coffee mug, a pair of purple pompoms, and some fun, decorative picture frames. One held their prom picture, another contained a photograph of Nathan and Gabby hoisting the state championship trophy.

"Well, it certainly looks like home in here," Nathan said. "Much better than the hallways." Hanging on the wall next to a purple UW Basketball pendant was an oversized, beautifully framed photograph of an awe inspiring tropical beach sunset. It looked a lot like the one they witnessed together in Cozumel. Nathan stared at it, admiring the exquisite lighting and color patterns. "That looks like Mexico."

"It is Mexico," Gabby declared. "I had one your photos enlarged and framed."

Nathan did a double take, first glancing at Gabby then turning his eyes back to the picture on the wall. "That is my photograph?"

"Uh huh. I wanted to surprise you. Do you like it?"

Nathan had always been told he was a good photographer, but he never had any of his photographs blown up and framed on a wall before. "I love it. Thank you."

"You're welcome."

He leaned in to kiss her. "I'll call you after practice tomorrow."

"You better."

"I will. Love you, Gab."

"I love you too, Nathan."

He smiled blissfully as he left.

Wondering what Nathan was talking about, Ashley asked, "Practice for what?"

"Nathan is on the basketball team. He has his first practice tomorrow."

Ashley's eyes widened. "Your boyfriend is an NCAA basketball player?"

Gabby laughed at Ashley's enthusiasm. "Yup."

"That is so cool." Ashley impatiently bounced on her bed. "Mike and I spent the day together. He drove me around Seattle and showed me the sights and…" Ashley squealed with excitement. "When he dropped me off this afternoon, he asked me out. I'm so excited."

Gabby cheered. "He's a great guy, and he's super funny, once he opens up to you."

The two girls sat and talked before going downstairs to grab a soda from the vending machine.

Nathan walked into his apartment to find Mike on the couch watching sports highlights on ESPN. "Hey, Mike."

Mike looked away from the television. "Hey, man. What's up?"

"Just got back from dinner with Gabby." Nathan set his keys and cellphone on the kitchen counter. "Where you been all day?"

"Hangin' out with Ashley."

Nathan grabbed a soda from the fridge and sat on the sofa with Mike. "Speaking of Ashley, I went and checked out Gabby's room today. That chick has an obsession with bright colors and butterflies. Felt like I had walked into a psychedelic fuzz factory."

"Are you serious?"

"Made my head spin. And she has more shoes than my mother." Nathan kicked off his sneakers and got more comfortable. "Do you know what Gabby did?"

"No. What?"

"She had a photograph of a sunset I took in Mexico enlarged to ridiculous proportions, put a frame around it, and hung it on the wall in her room."

"I tried to tell you, you should go into photography," Mike stated, knowing how much Nathan loved his hobby.

"That is the most incredible thing she has ever done for me," Nathan said contently. "I can't believe she did that."

CHAPTER TWENTY-ONE

The Huskies' basketball roster was very diverse. The fourteen players on the team came from many different areas around the globe, and all had varying levels of experience. Most had played NCAA basketball before, one was a red-shirt from the previous year, three came from a college league in other countries, and two were fresh out of high school. The roster consisted of three seniors, four juniors, five sophomores, and two freshmen, including Nathan.

Their coach was Erik Spoleda. Nathan adored this man. He was down to earth and appreciative of every one of his players. He encouraged teamwork and insisted that the young men on his team connected both on and off the court.

Their first team meeting was informal. Each player was given a practice jersey with a number printed on it; Nathan's was number 23. They all put on their jerseys and took a team picture then had individual photos taken for their player profiles on the University of Washington athletics page.

Each team member was given a jumbo-sized purple athletic bag with *Washington* stitched across the front. This bag was specifically designed to store all of their uniform attire, court shoes, and other necessary gear for games and practice sessions. Aside from their practice jerseys, they had three sets of game uniforms, but they were having names printed on the back so it would be another three weeks before they saw those.

Coach Spoleda put together notebooks for each player, which consisted of a practice calendar and game schedule, a handbook of all the NCAA basketball rules and regulations, and a copy of the playbook. He briefly explained each one then told his players to study them thoroughly.

Following the team meeting, Coach wheeled out a cart of practice balls and gave the men some court time, allowing them to do a few shootarounds. Before practice ended, Coach Spoleda told his team to be prepared for a tough practice the next day, which was fine with Nathan. He was ready to work.

Starting positions had not yet been determined. As a freshman, Nathan figured he probably wouldn't get the starting slot; Brett most likely had that one, but he was going to work his tail off to get himself a position on the reserve team. There was no way he was going to settle for being a bench warmer. Because he was open to advice about his game and sought to improve in any way he could, he was a quick and willing learner who accepted constructive criticism. As Nathan headed home from his first practice session, he felt confident and ready to tackle whatever Coach Spoleda asked of him.

UW's athletic website had already posted bios on all of the players. Nathan was curious to see what the athletic department had to say about him. When he got home that afternoon, before reporting to work, he looked on-line. His picture had not been uploaded yet, but there was a description of him, along with a detailed overview of his experience on the court. Nathan couldn't wait to show this to Gabby.

He grabbed his cellphone and called her. "Hey, Gab. Turn on your laptop and go to gohuskies.com. I have to show you this." He helped her navigate through the page to find player profiles.

She clicked on his name and read his bio: *Nathan Hanson was starting point guard on Washington's Class 3A winning state championship team. During the championship game vs. Rainier Beach, he scored 32 points and had 10 assists. He was voted player of the year for Lake Washington High School, averaging 24 points, 5 rebounds, and 8 assists per game. He served as team captain for Lake Washington and was ranked as one of the top 10 high school point guards in the state his senior year.*

His mother, Jane, played collegiately at California Berkeley and works as a sports psychologist. His father, Randal, is a local obstetrician and serves as an attending physician for Washington's School of Medicine. His uncle, Brian Davine, was a former NFL Linebacker for the San Francisco 49ers.

Hanson is majoring in Biology, with emphasis on pre-med.

"Oh my god, Nathan. That is so cool."

"Isn't it?" he concurred. "We received practice gear and schedules today, and we even got some court time. Coach Spoleda is a cool guy. He made things so relaxed today. It was awesome!"

Gabby loved to see the excitement basketball always gave him. Although playing professional basketball was not Nathan's ultimate career choice, he loved the game and put his heart and soul into each practice session and every play he made. "That's great, Sweetie. Sounds like your morning went well."

"Yes it did. How did job searching go?" he asked, curious about her daily escapades.

"I turned in three applications today. One was for a teaching assistant at the campus daycare."

Gabby loved kids. She wanted to be a teacher and had committed to being an Education major. Working in a daycare center was perfect for her. "That's right up your alley."

"The job starts on Monday, so I'm hoping to hear from them by the end of the week."

"Good luck. I hope you get it."

"So do I."

"I gotta head to work. Why don't you come over tonight and we'll talk then," he suggested.

Gabby liked that idea. "Sounds good."

"Alright. Love you, Gab. I'll see you tonight."

"Love you too, Nathan. Drive safely."

When Nathan got home from work that evening, he and Gabby decided to cook dinner at the apartment. They headed over to District Market to pick up some ingredients for dinner prep—chicken breasts, salad fixings, a bag of red potatoes, a gallon of milk, and some seasonings to spice things up. They put groceries away then Nathan prepared the chicken and slid it in the oven. While it was cooking, he diced up the red potatoes and put them in a glass baking pan, seasoning them with butter and rosemary.

Gabby pulled lettuce leaves off the bunch and rinsed them in the sink. "I talked to my dad today. He wants to come visit us this weekend."

"That's fine, but I have my grandfather's birthday party on Saturday, so it will have to be on Sunday." Nathan stirred the potatoes, making sure all sides were coated. "I'm glad you're keeping in touch with him. Did he ever give you money for books?"

"Not yet. He said he was going to bring me a check when he came over this weekend."

"Hopefully he'll keep true to his word. That would definitely help you out."

Over dinner, they discussed weekend plans and future job prospects, and Nathan told her all about his day. He had worked hard for the opportunity to play in the NCAA. Gabby was glad it was turning out to be everything he hoped it would be. "Can I see your uniform?" she asked.

"Of course. I'll go get it." Nathan bounded out of his seat and went into his bedroom and put it on. When he came out, he modeled it for her, pointing out the number 23. "What do you think?"

Nathan was a handsome young man. Gabby always loved his wavy brown hair and dark grey eyes, and in that uniform, his muscles bulged. "It looks good."

"Pretty sexy, huh?"

"I don't know if I'd go that far."

"Oh, come on." He grabbed her hand and pulled her into his arms. "You know you find me irresistible."

"I might," she teased. "If you weren't so obnoxious."

"Obnoxious?" he declared. "I think you mean frisky, frolicsome, and full of fun." Between each word, he kissed her, making each kiss linger longer than the last. He slid her shirt and bra strap down, exposing the feminine curve of her shoulder.

She closed her eyes, taking in his gentle touch. "What are you doing?"

"What's it feel like I'm doing?" He lifted her hair off her neck and traced his lips across the soft skin underneath, slowly working his way to her collarbone.

His slow, drugging kisses demanded a response. Raising her mouth to his, she gazed up at him. They stared at each other for a moment before Nathan kissed the tip of her nose, then her eyelids, and finally, her mouth. Within minutes, they drifted toward Nathan's bedroom door.

Meanwhile, Mike and Ashley were strolling around Portage Bay taking in the cool nighttime air. The night was unusually clear, and the moon reflected its glint of light off the rippled water, making it look like broken glass.

"This is beautiful," Ashley said. "I can't get over how much water there is around here."

Mike reached over and clasped her hand. "That's one of the things I love about Seattle. The bay, the lake, Puget Sound…there's water everywhere you go."

"It's better than salt flats and dust."

"I have to agree with you on that." Mike snuck his arm around Ashley and drew her nearer.

"You know, Mike, you are probably the nicest guy I've ever met."

Her compliment made him laugh. "Really? That's a new one. I'm usually accused of being a smartass."

"But you're a smartass in a nice way."

He had no clue what that meant. "Is that even possible? That sounds like an oxymoron to me."

"What's an oxymoron?"

Although Mike liked Ashley, she didn't always understand his snarky remarks. He sometimes had to explain things to her and clarify his thinking.

As she melted into his arms, the flowery scent of her hair made him dizzy. He was convinced she was wearing some kind of hypnotic body spray that put him in a trance. His mind began to wander.

Mike knew the dating rules, but following these so-called rules never seemed to work out for him. He'd been told to never kiss a girl on a first date, and that he should ask a girl before he kissed her. However, contradictory advice-givers suggested he always end a date with a kiss, especially if he wanted a second date. All of the advice Mike had been given confused him, and he didn't know who to believe. When was the prime moment to kiss someone? And was it ok to kiss someone passionately on the lips on a first date? He definitely wanted to be certain that the time was right though, as to get it wrong often left him without another chance to kiss.

He and Ashley had been laughing together and generally having a good time. They were engrossed in conversation, and several times she looked directly into his eyes. He definitely felt the vibes. This was the perfect kissing moment.

Ignoring all dating advice, he leaned into her a bit and kissed her. Gradually, a little open mouth began to develop, and their kiss became extremely intense. Blood pulsed through his heart, chest, and head. His hands moved downward, skimming either side of her body.

Feeling an intense heat building between them, he broke away from her before things went too far.

Leaving a lasting impression, he touched her hand. She snuggled closer and rested her head on his chest. Under the moonlight, Mike held her, soaking in the intimacy they felt for each other. As they snuggled, Mike realized that relationships and intimacy didn't develop by a book of rules. It developed by the personality of the person he was with, and Ashley was a firecracker, something he was definitely into.

The temperature began to drop, and since Mike didn't have a jacket with him, they decided to stop by his apartment to get it. When they got there, Ashley found a peculiar object hanging on the doorknob. "Why is there a sock on your door?"

"Because Gabby is over here."

Ashley didn't understand. "So?"

Mike unlocked the door and tiptoed inside. The light above the kitchen stove was on, but the rest of the apartment was dark. "Ssh," he said to Ashley.

"Why are we whispering?"

"So they won't know we're here."

From behind Nathan's door, Mike could hear moaning and heavy breathing, which made him uncomfortable. Trying not to eavesdrop on Nathan's privacy, he stepped into the living room and quickly grabbed his jacket. As soon as it was in his hand, he crept out of the apartment and closed the door. "Guess I'm not going home for a while."

"Why not?"

"I told you. Gabby's over here." Mike slipped on his jacket and zipped it.

When Ashley finally put the pieces together, she covered her mouth and gasped. "That's what the sock is for."

Her delayed reaction made Mike laugh. "It's kind of cold out. We should go to the café."

"We should."

He clasped her hand and headed down the stairs. Together, they strolled over to Husky Grind to warm up on hot cocoa.

CHAPTER TWENTY-TWO

Nathan was anxious to dive into his schedule and begin his pre-med requirements, many of which overlapped with his required Biology classes. One of the things he was required to do was attend a pre-health information session, at which time he signed up for the pre-health e-mail list to receive important updates. When this seminar was over, he sat down with his pre-med advisor and planned out his four years of coursework.

He was also required to be involved in health related extra-curricular activities. Nathan asked around campus and did extensive research on health related student groups he could get involved in. After careful consideration, he decided to join the pre-medical chapter of the American Medical Student Association. This group was designed to encourage and educate students on issues of national and international health concerns. This particular student group not only offered services pre-med students found helpful, such as hosting health related panels, informational interviews, and group volunteering events, but also provided a community of students who had similar interests and goals.

To fulfill his community service goal, he found a group called Husky EMS, which promoted educational opportunities in emergency medical services for the students, faculty, and staff at the University of Washington. Its purpose was to increase awareness of sudden illness and to train the members of the UW community in CPR, First Aid and AED use. Since Nathan was CPR, AED, and First Aid certified, he was excited about training others.

Even though Nathan was dyslexic, he was a dedicated student and a hard worker who utilized his class time to its full potential. With all of the AP Science classes he took in high school, he was well versed in the high expectations of college coursework and felt prepared for the challenges and requirements he would be facing.

One of his requirements as a Biology major was to write extensive research papers. Writing had never been his strong suit. In order to improve his skills, he took a writing class that was specific and specialized to his needs. His schedule also included Pre-Calculus, Chemistry, Advanced Spanish, and Intro to Biology. All of this, along with his basketball schedule, was bound to challenge him and keep him busy.

Following his first day of classes, Nathan had Pre-Calculus homework, a chapter to read for Chemistry, and an essay to start working on for his writing class. But all of that would have to wait until after basketball practice.

They ran ball drills for about thirty minutes before Coach Spoleda placed the men into teams to work on offensive and defensive skills. On the court, the coach shifted players in and out so he could see who was strong in what areas. There were two other point guards besides Nathan who were given the opportunity to show off their skills. One was Brett, the other was Rajik D'Jibouti.

Nathan didn't know much about Rajik other than the fact that he was a redshirt last year, which meant he was on the team roster and came to all the practices, but sat on the bench all season. Although Rajik had some NCAA experience, Nathan had better overall stats.

Midway through practice, Coach Spoleda put Nathan to the test. "Alright, Hanson. Let's see what you got."

Nathan confidently took the court, replacing Sorenson and going opposite Rajik. This was his chance to show his coach that his reputation preceded him.

As the game progressed, Rajik struggled to keep up with the fast-paced tempo Nathan had established on offense. Rajik was generally a decent defensive player, but Nathan's quickness made defending against him next to impossible. Nathan was an effective passer. He could get the ball to his teammates then just as easily fake pass, leaving himself open for the three-point opportunity.

Offensively, Rajik was accurate with short range jump shots and layups, but long range, he was overconfident and tended to take the outside shot himself, even though someone else on the court had a better shooting opportunity. And since three-point shots were not his strongest attribute, he missed almost every one he attempted.

Rajik had more experience and was physically stronger than Nathan was, but Nathan was faster and far more accurate, making five of seven shot attempts, two of which were from three-point range. His amazing athleticism and stamina allowed him to take a beating on the court. Rajik soon realized that knocking Nathan around was not a good strategy because he had a knack for drawing fouls, which brought him to the line. On the free-throw line, Nathan rarely missed a shot. He had a superb ability to tune out everything around him and focus solely on the net, a strategy his mother taught him.

Brett stood alongside his coach and watched the head-to-head battle between Nathan and Rajik, and in this particular fight, Nathan was clearly the victor.

Coach Spoleda sounded his whistle. "Alright, nice work. We need to get faster and we need to get stronger. Shower up, gentlemen, and be at the gym by 3:00 P.M. tomorrow, ready for intense training."

While the team headed to the showers, Brett intercepted Nathan as he walked over to the side of the court to get his warmup sweats. "Nice job today. You're looking good. Raj is a tough defensive player and you were able to get through him."

"He's strong, and he's got an accurate shot, from the inside."

Brett stopped walking and let the others get ahead of them. When he and Nathan were alone, he said, "I know what you want, Hanson, and it doesn't involve a bench."

Nathan totally agreed. "I'm not sitting on the sidelines. I want game action."

"You know what you need to do to make that happen, right?"

Nathan nodded. "Yeah."

"I think you've got what it takes, but you're going to have to work harder, play smarter, and focus more on the team than you ever have before. Don't try to be a showboat. You told me yourself that you don't like showboat players."

"I don't. They're arrogant ball hogs, and they do more harm to a team than good." Brett's comment made Nathan question his performance. "I wasn't showboating, was I?"

"No, you weren't. But I know from past experience that the new guy wants so much to impress, he tends to show off instead of focusing on the team and trying to win games. You can't let any of this get to your head. That is the biggest mistake people make here," Brett warned. "You are an astounding player with tremendous leadership skills; you can lead this team. But you need to be a leader the guys can trust. It's not about stats, it's about character and your ability to work as a team."

"I'm all about team, Brett. You know that."

"I know," Brett concurred. "And that is definitely to your advantage. Just between you and me, Raj tends to be a showoff. There's a reason coach keeps him on the bench. He's so worried about his stats that he doesn't focus on the team. He's reckless and lets glory get in the way of the game. You're good, Nathan, and you have a lot of potential. If you listen to Coach, he can make you one of the best."

"I don't want fame or glory, and I'm not out to be the best," Nathan replied. "I just want to play basketball."

Brett smiled. That was the exact answer he hoped for. "And that's why you're as good as you are, because you don't let it get to your head. Coach has every intention of giving you game time if you prove to him you can handle it. Be smart, Nathan. Be the team player you already are. Don't lose that."

"I won't." Focusing on the team was always Nathan's game plan. That's who he was as a player, and why he was such an effective point guard.

During the first few weeks of practice, Nathan discovered that many of his teammates were bigger and had more solid strength than he did. Although he was fast, agile, and had a tremendous amount of stamina, Nathan had to bulk up if he was going to compete with the big boys. To gain leaner muscle mass, he diligently adhered to a sensible, specific nutritional plan. He stuck to lean protein sources and munched on healthy snack choices. Gabby helped him by going on this regimented diet right along with him.

To build muscle strength, Nathan invested countless hours, outside of regular practice sessions, in the weight room. Mike always went with him. This daily regimen allowed he and Mike the opportunity to hang out together and talk. They chatted about basketball, talked about women, and enjoyed some bonding time while Nathan worked on conditioning.

"One of our guys is being scouted by the NBA," Nathan stated.

"Are you sure it's not you?" Mike declared.

"It isn't. Even if it was, I wouldn't care. I have no desire to play in the NBA."

"You mean to tell me that if an NBA team wanted you, you would turn them down?" Mike asked.

"Yes, I would. There are other things in my life more important than basketball."

Mike thought Nathan was crazy. No one would pass up the opportunity to play in the NBA if given the chance. He certainly wouldn't. "Like what?"

"Like medical school. Like Gabby. I want to have a normal life—finish school, earn my medical degree, get married, have kids. I love to play, and I'll give it my all while I'm in it, but after college, that's it. I'm done."

Shocked by Nathan's retort, Mike reminded him, "All you talked about when we were kids was playing in the NCAA. It's what you've always wanted."

"And I am playing in the NCAA, but that doesn't mean I want to dedicate my entire life to the game. NBA was never a goal of mine."

Mike didn't understand Nathan's motivation. If he didn't want to play in the NBA, why was he sticking to a strict diet and spending hours upon hours at the gym? "Why are you trying to beef up your game then?"

"Because I did not come this far to spend my college basketball career warming a bench," Nathan insisted. "If I'm going to do this, I'm going to do it right. I want to be on the frontline and see some game action. To me, it's not worth it to come this far and never step foot on the court. So I'm going to bulk up, work my ass off, and get myself game time."

"Sounds like a good plan to me."

"These NCAA players mean business. Have you seen the size of some of these guys?"

"Yeah," Mike replied. "Some of them are fuckin' huge."

"And that's my point. I have to play against them, and most of them could kick my ass right now."

Nathan's honest analysis made Mike laugh.

"I have six weeks until our first game. I fully intend to be at my strongest and best condition by then."

On their way home, Mike started talking about Ashley. Her name seemed to pop up in their conversations quite often lately. Although Mike and Ashley were still in the incipient stage of their relationship, Nathan couldn't remember a time when Mike showed so much interest in a girl so early.

"Things have been getting pretty intense between Ashley and me," Mike said. "We kissed for a solid forty minutes the other night."

"Gabby and I do that sometimes."

"I think things are going to get more physical soon. Do you have any condoms?"

Nathan tried not to laugh. "Yes I do."

"Think I could have one?"

"You can have the whole box," Nathan offered. "I'll get them for you when we get home."

With their busy schedules, Nathan and Gabby didn't see each other as often as they hoped. Despite this, they made a conscious effort to spend at least one night a week together no matter what, and they did everything they could to make this precious time memorable.

"Gab and I are going out tonight," Nathan said, tossing a box of condoms to Mike. "You'll have the place to yourself for a while."

Mike caught the box and grinned. "Thanks, man."

He grabbed his keys and cellphone and put them in his pocket. "Good luck tonight."

Before Nathan picked up Gabby, he stopped at a nearby flower shop and bought a bouquet of red, yellow, and orange gladiolus, Gabby's favorite flowers. He had never bought flowers before, other than the corsage he gave her at Prom, so he was excited about presenting these to her.

When he arrived at Gabby's dorm room, he greeted her with a kiss. Trying to hide the flowers from her, he held them behind his back.

Gabby saw right through him. "What are you hiding back there?"

He presented her with the bouquet. "You mean these?"

She took the flowers from him and sniffed them. "Oh my god, these are beautiful. Thank you, Sweetie."

"You're welcome," he said.

She set them on her desk and grabbed her purse. "Where are we going tonight?"

"Salty's."

Salty's was Gabby's favorite seafood restaurant. They served fresh Alaskan salmon, local Pacific halibut, and Northwest oysters and clams. The salmon preparation was superb, and the halibut was always the freshest on the market. Aside from the exquisite cuisine, Salty's also had the best view in the city—a sweeping panorama of Elliott Bay and the Seattle city skyline.

"Tonight is all about you." He offered his hand to her. "You ready?"

"Absolutely."

Nathan parked downtown and they took a ferry from Pier 50 all the way across Elliott Bay to Salty's. The air was slightly crisp, and stars twinkled merrily in the beautiful nighttime sky. They stood on the bow of the ferry looking out at the water. Gabby stood in front of Nathan with his arms enveloped around her. She wasn't sure what was more romantic, the flowers and dinner Nathan offered or the ferry ride to get there.

"Thank you for doing this," she said.

"Anything for you, Babe."

She leaned against his chest and looked up at him. "I love you, Nathan."

"I love you too." The glow from the moon reflected in her eyes. Wanting to be closer to her, he slowly leaned in and kissed her.

After their date, they returned to Nathan's apartment. As he reached into his pocket to grab his keys, he noticed a sock tied around the doorknob, which made him chuckle.

"What is so funny?" Gabby asked.

Nathan pulled the sock off the doorknob and handed it to Gabby. "This."

She curled her lip and stared at it. "What am I supposed to do with a dirty sweat sock?"

"It's not a dirty sock, Gab. It's a do not disturb sign."

"What are you talking about?"

With a mischievous grin on his face, Nathan unlocked the door. "Mike's finally getting laid."

Gabby's jaw dropped. "Oh my god, I can't believe you said that."

"What? It's true. That's what the sock is for. When he ties the sock on the doorknob, I don't disturb him. He does the same for us."

"You hang a sock on the door to advertise to everyone that we're having sex?"

Obviously she misunderstood the purpose of the sock. "It's not an advertisement, it's our signal. The sock lets Mike know you're over here. It's common courtesy, Gab."

Gabby wasn't sure how she felt about this. She gave him a cockeyed sneer.

Nathan couldn't help but laugh. "We're roommates, Babe. We had to come up with something. Do you really want him walking in on us?"

"No," she admitted.

"Alright. Then what are you freaking out about?"

She held the sock between her thumb and forefinger. "A sweat sock? Really?" she teased. "You couldn't think of anything else?"

"It works, doesn't it?"

She shook her head. "You're crazy."

"Crazy about you." He reached his hand down to her waist and tickled her.

She screamed and tried to get away.

"Ssh," Nathan said. "You're disturbing my roommate."

She threw the sock at him and ran toward the bedroom with Nathan chasing close behind her.

In the morning, Nathan awoke with Gabby's naked body sprawled out across the bed. Somehow throughout the night she managed to confiscate most of the covers, leaving him with only the top sheet. He pulled back his share of the blanket and gently touched her arm. "Hey," he softly said.

She stretched and rolled over, moaning as she opened her eyes. "Good morning."

The soft flesh of her breast peeked out from under the sheet. Nathan found it enticing. He cupped his hand around the curvy flesh and gently grazed his fingertips across the nipple, making it perk up. "You're beautiful."

"You told me that last night."

"I know, and I'm telling you again." He rubbed his thumb across her lips then rolled over top of her and offered a slow, sensuous kiss. "Do you know what I'm craving?"

"What are you craving?"

"A big, juicy ham and cheese omelet smothered in sour cream."

Gabby giggled. "I take it you're hungry?"

"A little," he replied. "But do you know what I really want?"

"What?"

"You." He held her tighter in his arms and reclaimed her lips. Her soft skin felt smooth and silky in his hands. His eyes met her gaze and he slowly accessed her, experiencing a rush of pure pleasure. He maintained a purposeful, slow rhythm, never once taking his eyes off of hers. This physical intimacy was unlike anything they'd experienced together. He wanted nothing more than to be close to her, to love her intensely, to become a part of her.

Nathan held her tightly in his grasp, her naked breasts pressed against his chest. He felt her body heat radiate through him, and at that moment, he felt closer to her than he ever had before. Making love to her like this was the most powerful feeling in the world. It was his way of digging deep into the depths of her soul. Every emotion she felt, he felt too. Truly he had become one with her.

The smell of eggs cooking roused Mike from his slumber. He inhaled deeply, taking in the scent, and rolled over with a long stretch. "Can you smell that?"

Ashley also smelled the scrumptious aroma. "Mmm, that smells yummy."

"How much you wanna bet Nathan is making breakfast." Mike hopped out of bed and slipped on a pair of basketball shorts. "I'm gonna grab a drink. You want some water or something?"

"Sure," Ashley said. "Thanks."

Mike slinked into the kitchen where, indeed, Nathan was concocting what appeared to be omelets. "Good morning," he said, reaching into the refrigerator for two water bottles.

Nathan responded with a devilish smirk. "Well, good morning, Lothario."

Mike snorted at Nathan's reference to *Don Quixote*, a book they were forced to read in high school English class.

"You might want to avoid the bathroom for a while," Nathan said. "Gabby's in the shower."

"Duly noted." Feeling parched, Mike opened one of the water bottles and chugged down a huge gulp. "How was your night?"

"I think I should be asking you that question." Nathan flipped the omelet onto a plate and cracked two more eggs into a bowl, whisking them together.

Mike's lips slowly formed a smile. "My night was...exciting."

"Uh huh. And?"

Mike wasn't sure what Nathan expected him to say. "And what?"

"What did you think?"

Mike's face flushed slightly. "It's the most intense feeling I've ever experienced."

"Told ya." Nathan and Mike grinned at each other, and at that moment, they completely understood one another. "If you and Ashley want some eggs, you need to get dressed and come out here."

"We'll be out in a minute." Carrying both water bottles in his hand, Mike returned to the bedroom.

CHAPTER TWENTY-THREE

At the next practice session, the UW men finally received their game uniforms—white and gold for away games, purple and gold for home. This was also the day Coach Spoleda posted the list of starters and reserve players for their first game. There were some amazingly talented men on this team, most of whom had more experience than Nathan. Even though he felt confident, Nathan hoped he didn't have to spend his freshman year on the bench.

With bated breath, Nathan read the posted list:

Starting Team- Sorenson (PG), Ramirez (SG), Guenther (C), Ramusi (SF), Foster (PF).

Reserve Team 1- Hanson (PG), Garibay (SG), Kruz (C), Lockey (SF), Hoffman (PF)

Yes! He made the first reserve team, which meant he was backup for Brett. All that hard work paid off. Now that he had proven to himself, his coach, and the rest of the team that he had what it took to play college ball, he could rest easy and enjoy the game he loved.

Being on an NCAA team required Nathan to put one-hundred percent into every game, and he was more than willing to do that. His dedication on the court reflected in his game, and his teammates respected him for it. He couldn't wait to step on the court in a real game.

After an intense practice session, Nathan walked out of the gym with his athletic bag in his hand and his backpack over his shoulder. Trying to get Nathan's attention, his teammate, Andrew Garibay, ran behind him. "Hey, Hanson. Wait up."

Nathan slowed down, allowing Andrew time to catch up.

"What are you doing tonight?" Andrew asked.

"Studying."

On many occasions, Nathan had expressed to Andrew his desire to go to medical school, and although Andrew didn't fully comprehend Nathan's dedication, he was one of the few guys on the team who truly understood why he worked so hard. "Understandable."

Outside the arena, they ran into a petite blonde woman. Nathan smiled when he saw her. "What are you doing over here?"

"Thought we could grab some dinner together before we head over to the library," she suggested.

"Sounds good to me."

Although Nathan talked about Gabriella often, Andrew had never met her. By the way Nathan spoke to this woman, Andrew assumed she was his girlfriend. "You must be Gabby."

Gabby looked up. "Yes, and you are?"

Nathan cut in, "I'm sorry, Gab. I should have introduced you. This is Andrew Garibay."

Trying to be sociable, Gabby offered a friendly handshake. "Nice to meet you, Andrew. Would you like to join us for dinner?"

"No, thank you," Andrew chimed. "I'm meeting the guys at Eureka. Thanks for the invite though." Andrew threw his backpack over his shoulder and bumped knuckles with Nathan. "I'll see you at practice tomorrow."

"I'll be there." Nathan gripped Gabby's hand and headed toward the main campus. "Before we eat, I want to stop by the bookstore."

"What for?" she asked.

"I want to show you something."

A while back, the men had a team photo taken. The athletic department uploaded this photo onto the gohuskies website then had the image turned into a poster. They sold these posters at the bookstore and sometimes gave them away during games. As a team member, Nathan was given a free copy, but he wanted to pick up a few more to hand out to friends and family.

He grabbed four of them from the bin and took them up to the cashier.

"What is that?" Gabby asked.

"I'll show you in a minute." After paying for them, Nathan unrolled one and held it up so Gabby could see it. "Check this out."

On this poster, Nathan posed with his team, holding a basketball in his hand and looking like a badass in his purple uniform. They all had on serious game faces.

"What do you think?" he asked, wanting her honest opinion.

"Wow! You're on a poster. That is really neat."

"You can have this one." He rolled it back up and gave it to her.

"Are your parents coming to the game Saturday?"

"Of course. Lauren and Lacy are coming too. Oh," he said, remembering something he needed to tell her. "Coach put me on the reserve team."

Gabby hugged him in delight. "That's wonderful, Sweetie. Congratulations."

"Thanks. I worked my butt off for that spot. Can't wait to see court action on Saturday."

Saturday afternoon, as Nathan was about to head over to Alaska Airlines Arena for his first college basketball game, Gabby stopped him at the door. "Nathan?"

Her somber voice and woebegone expression told him something was bothering her. "What's the matter?"

"I wish I was on the court cheering for you."

"You will be cheering for me, Babe. I'll see your face in the stands. Knowing you're there supporting me is all I care about. You gonna get there early so you can sit up front?"

She nodded. "Yes."

"Good. My parents want to take us out to dinner after the game." He picked up his athletic bag and carried it over his shoulder. "I have to go."

"Good luck tonight."

"Thanks. I love you Babe." He gave her a kiss goodbye. "See you later."

The Huskies' first pre-season exhibition game was against Seton Hall, the Division II National Champions. Nathan watched them play last year and recalled how strong they were. Now he was going to be on the court playing against them.

As the men warmed up and stretched on the court, Nathan searched the arena for Gabby. He found her sitting with his parents in the front section, along his sisters and Mike and Ashley. The arena filled up quickly. Fans came dressed in UW shirts, carrying purple pompoms and noise makers. Coach Spoleda even donned a suit and a purple *Washington Basketball* tie, encouraging team spirit. Television cameras were set up all over the place and game announcers prepared for their commentary.

"Is he nervous?" Jane asked Gabby.

"He doesn't seem to be, but he usually hides it well," she answered. "He's more excited than anything else."

"He should be excited," Randy added. "He's wanted to play NCAA ball his whole life."

"He's been looking forward to this game all week," Mike interjected, expressing his take on the situation. "He's gonna kick ass. I can't wait to watch him play."

Jane observed her son on the court during shootarounds. Nathan was making shots, from both the key and three-point range. "He looks good," she remarked. "I hope he gets some court time tonight."

"I'm sure he will," Randy stated.

Nathan made his college debut in the first half, allowing Brett to take a breather. During the second half, he took over as point when Brett ran into foul trouble in the last ten minutes of the game. He was able to maintain their lead and finished the game with an 86-77 victory. He played a total of fourteen minutes, and within that time, he managed to rack up nine points, one steal, and two assists. This pre-season exhibition game not only showcased the Huskies' skills, it also gave Nathan the opportunity to show off his powerful presence on the court.

Nathan's family celebrated his season debut over dinner.

"I'm so proud of you," his mother said. "You held your ground and dominated the court tonight."

"Thanks, Mom," Nathan replied. "I can't believe Brett had so many fouls. That's not like him at all."

"It allowed you to display how effective you are on the court, so take it all in stride."

Nathan lifted his glass to his lips. "Oh, I am. I feel pretty good about my first game."

"And you should. You shined tonight. I bet you'll see more game time because of it."

"I hope so."

Along with action shots from the game, the Huskies' website posted a full synopsis: **The Huskies Surge Past Seton Hall to Take an 86-77 Victory!**

The article listed stats of each player and gave a play by play of each half. When Nathan came to the part that mentioned him, his whole world became brighter.

Sorenson's three fouls in the second half gave debuting freshman, Nathan Hanson, the opportunity to score six of his nine points, all of which were from three-point range. Hanson brazenly drove the lane, and at times shot over multiple defenders to score.

After reading this article, Nathan felt more confident that his performance during the game would make Coach Spoleda more willing to give him floor time.

No one really understood how truly time challenged NCAA basketball players were during the season. Gabby and Mike, however, witnessed this every day with Nathan. In a typical day, he woke up around 6:00 A.M. and immediately took physical inventory. This entailed making sure the inevitable in-season aches and pains did not manifest themselves into full-blown injuries overnight. Provided everything was in working order, some light stretching ensued. This fifteen-some-odd-minute ritual was necessary to get the body moving and the blood pumping in preparation for another physically demanding day. Most days, Nathan shared breakfast with Gabby. Unlike the rank and file student, sleeping late and skipping breakfast was not an option for the competitive basketball player. Doing so would risk physical meltdown and contribute toward unwanted weight loss. Nathan was doing all he could to maintain his body weight and even put on some solid muscle mass, so breakfast was a necessity.

Because of afternoon practice sessions, basketball players had to schedule the majority of their classes in the morning. Nathan's classes usually concluded between 12:00 and 1:00, at which time a hearty lunch ensued. All meals, including lunch, were required if Nathan hoped to perform at his best during practice later in the day, not to mention having energy left when it was time to study. Following lunch, it was on to life maintenance chores. On most days, Nathan reported to his father's clinic to work for a few hours before it was time to head over to the gym.

Basketball practice involved two to three hours of physically demanding court time, including arduous skill drills and shooting practice. Sometimes the team sat for film sessions or scouting reports and engaged in injury/recovery treatments. In addition to hours on the hardwood, the players had to go to and from the gym, warm up, cool down, and generally engaged in some sanity-promoting locker room banter, which tacked on another thirty to forty-five minutes.

Following the on-court action, Nathan hit the weight room to pump iron with Mike. A hot shower followed. He often met Gabby for dinner, where he consumed huge amounts of food to replenish his energy-depleted body. When the meal broke, usually around 8:00 P.M., it was time to hit the books, either at the library or in the privacy of his apartment. Needless to say, by the time he sat to study he was ultra-exhausted, and staying awake became a worthy challenge.

Nathan quickly discovered that game days were no less busy. Besides the game itself, which Nathan was required to report to a minimum of ninety minutes before tipoff, game day consisted of a physically necessary pre-game meal, stretching to loosen up muscles, and warming up with shootarounds. As physically draining as practice sessions could be, they didn't hold a candle to games in terms of wearing the body down. Playing in a fast-paced, physical basketball game left Nathan tired, dehydrated, and often bruised. The combination of the added intensity brought about by competition and the energy and excitement supplied by a noisy, crowd-filled arena encouraged the body to go the extra mile. The downside of going the mile was the aftermath, which came in the form of soreness.

Soreness was not the only byproduct of game play. The body and mind were in overdrive after competition, as adrenaline continued to pulse through the system. This heightened state did not abate quickly. It lingered well into the night. As such, sleep did not come easily. Nathan was the soundest of sleepers, but after a physically intense basketball game, he struggled to get a good night's rest. Periodically losing a night's sleep seemed trivial, especially considering he was a young, highly conditioned athlete.

However, fatigue that accumulated from a night of lost sleep wreaked havoc on the body over time.

While the average student had his or her weekends free, college basketball players, because of games, practice schedules, and travel time, did not have that luxury. Since Sundays were Nathan's only off days, at least until the team started traveling, he utilized this day to its full advantage.

This Sunday, he and Gabby planned to hang out at the apartment and share pizza and a movie with Mike and Ashley. But before spending an evening with his friends, Nathan went over to his parents' house to do some laundry. He put a load in the washer then plopped on the sofa and turned on the TV, hoping to catch a pre-season NBA game.

Randy stepped into the living room and sat in the chair beside him. "Who's playing?"

"Spurs and Blazers," Nathan replied.

"One of the better point guards in the league."

"He's decent," Nathan confirmed. "Twenty points per game, eight assists, eighty-five percent on the line, and as far as point guards go, he does well with steals. He isn't the greatest from three-point range, but he's up there in assists."

"And for a point guard, assists are important."

"Exactly," Nathan concurred. "The best point guard of all time, in my opinion, was Magic Johnson. That dude was an awesome athlete. He'd shove a ball down the defense's throat and carve them up in a drive. He was selfless on the court, and he made passing cool."

"Of course he did. That's because my Lakers dominate," Randy boasted, knowing he'd get a rise out of Nathan.

"I beg to differ," Nathan argued. "The 1995-96 Chicago Bulls shattered the record for most wins in a regular season. And the 1985-86 Celtics posted a 40-1 record at Boston Garden. They held on to a home winning percentage of ninety-seven percent. That's the best in NBA history."

Randy had to be the most diehard Lakers fan ever to exist. He had been a loyal follower since he was old enough to know what basketball was. "The Lakers have won the National Championship sixteen times. And historically, the Lakers have had better individual players."

"Why does that matter?" Nathan claimed. "Basketball isn't about being a big name player or gaining popularity points. It's about working as a team to win games."

"But you said Johnson was your favorite point guard."

Nathan didn't see his father's point. "So?"

"Johnson was a popular, big name player, and he was a Laker. When it comes to ultimate players and ultimate teams, the Lakers win hands down."

Nathan upheld his argument. "No, Johnson wins hands down, regardless of what team he was on."

With Randy being a diehard Lakers fan and Nathan a dedicated Spurs fan, they frequently had debates like this. When the Lakers and the Spurs played one another, the living room tended to get very loud.

Randy missed having these conversations with his son, but as he spoke with Nathan, he noticed how rundown he appeared. He had bruises on his arms and lacked his usual energy level. Concerned about his son's wellbeing, Randy asked, "How you doing?"

"I'm fine. Just tired."

Randy knew there was more to it than that. "You don't look fine. What's going on, Nate?"

Expressing his frustrations, Nathan poured it all out. "I'm in class all day, work all afternoon, and spend hours on end at practice, which leaves evenings for studying. But by the time I get home, it's close to 8:30, and because I read slowly, I'm up 'til midnight trying to get everything done. I rarely have time to hang out with Gabby, and I haven't been sleeping well."

Nathan desperately needed a pep talk, so Randy did his best to re-inspire his son. "You know, Nate, a friend of mine is on the admissions board for UW's School of Medicine. I was talking to him the other day and your name came up."

Nathan looked away from the game and directly at his father. "Why were you talking about me?"

"We were discussing basketball, and I was telling him how tough it is to be a college athlete. I happened to mention to him that you were a pre-med Biology major who was also on the basketball team. He was impressed with that, and he told me a few things I was not aware of."

"Like what?" Nathan asked.

Randy explained, "Being a college athlete with a competitive GPA is a huge advantage to getting into medical school."

Now interested in what his father had to say, Nathan sat up and paid attention. "He told you that?"

"He specifically noted that the admittance panel was most impressed with pre-med students who played college sports. They stood out over other applicants. He told me there weren't many college athletes who applied, but the ones who did were exceptional candidates and even better medical students because, with their involvement in sports training, they possessed the necessary discipline and perseverance to be successful in medical school. Their ability to handle responsibility and section off time was pretty sharp, so the demands they had while they were balancing pre-med requirements and college athletics far outweighed any demands medical school threw at them."

Recently some of the people Nathan encountered thought he was crazy for dedicating so much time and energy to both school and basketball. Despite this negativity, Nathan refused to give up on his dreams or lower his expectations. He remained committed to both medical school and his team. Hearing this information from his father boosted his spirits and made him feel that perhaps his dedication was worth it in the long run. "I'm glad you told me that," Nathan said.

"Why?"

"Because one of the guys on the team thinks I'm crazy for trying to pursue medical school while playing basketball. He pretty much told me it's impossible for a good college athlete to gain admittance into a professional graduate school. He thinks that if I dedicate my time and energy to the game, I'll have no hope of getting into medical school. But if my efforts go into gaining admittance into medical school, my game will suffer. He says there's no way I can be successful at both, that eventually something's gonna give."

"He doesn't know what he's talking about," Randy encouraged. "This is not an inconceivable dream you're pursuing, Nathan. It can be done, if you have the determination and dedication to do it. I've never seen you give up on anything, and you never go down without a fight. You are very capable of accomplishing your goals. Stay focused, balance your time, and prioritize. You can do this."

His father's encouraging words couldn't have come at a better time. "Thanks, Dad. That makes me feel a lot better."

"You're not in this alone," Randy reminded him. "You have our full support. Don't be too proud to ask for help if you need it. And if you want to vent, you know how to reach me. That's what your family is here for."

Upon returning to UW, Nathan put his laundry away then spent four hours studying, writing a research paper, and working on Pre-Calculus homework.

Since the very first day of school, Nathan put every ounce of energy he had into both basketball and his class load. Gabriella and Mike offered their support on multiple levels. One of the ways Mike helped out was by taking care of apartment needs and picking up necessary groceries so Nathan could focus on studying. While Mike was cleaning up the apartment, he glanced over at Nathan, who was sound asleep on the sofa. He had worked so diligently and dedicated so much time and energy to both basketball and school that sheer exhaustion set in and his body finally crashed.

Gabby and Ashley came over about 5:30, each carrying a box of pizza. When they knocked on the door, Mike rushed to answer it. "Ssh," he said, putting his finger over his lips.

"Why are we shushing?" Gabby asked.

Mike pointed to the couch. "He's been out for a little over an hour now."

Gabby's eyes shifted to Nathan. "Poor guy. He's exhausted."

Mike agreed. "He's working his ass off."

The girls tiptoed inside and set the pizza boxes on the kitchen island. "I have to say," Ashley added. "I have a whole new respect for college athletes. I never realized how much they go through."

"Especially him," Mike affirmed. "'Cause it's not just basketball, it's school and his job and the volunteer work he's doing. I don't know how he keeps this up."

"I'm really proud of him," Gabby said.

"So am I."

Their whispering wakened Nathan, who sat up, stretched, and combed his fingers through his hair.

"It's alive," Mike teased him.

When Nathan was a little more alert, he arose from the couch and joined them in the kitchen.

Gabby stood on her tiptoes and kissed him. "Hi, Sleepyhead."

He stretched gracefully and yawned. "How long was I out?"

"About an hour," Mike replied.

The aroma of pizza, something Nathan hadn't eaten in a while, permeated through the apartment. "Man, I'm starving."

Mike grabbed some paper plates then handed everyone a soda. They all dug in, making themselves comfortable in the living room while Nathan put on a movie.

Overjoyed with his performance at the game on Saturday, and encouraged by the conversation he had with his father, Nathan was re-inspired about his college career path. He felt blessed to have such a strong support system. Even though he was tired, he felt good about the direction his future was heading.

At the end of another hard-core practice session, Coach Spoleda offered critique to his team. "Ok men, good job. Tighter defense and much better on those rebounds today. I want to go over travel protocol tomorrow, so bring your game planner to practice. Shower up. And Hanson," Coach exclaimed, "See me in my office."

"Yes, Sir." On the way to the locker room, Nathan questioned Brett about his coach's request. "Any insights as to why coach wants to see me?"

"Nope," Brett replied. "Not a clue. I wouldn't worry about it though."

After a refreshing shower, Nathan proceeded to his coach's office. The door was open, so he peeked his head inside. "You wanted to see me, Coach?"

"Yes," Coach Spoleda said as he looked up from his paperwork. "Have a seat."

Nathan filled his lungs with air and sat in a chair across from his coach's desk. "Is everything alright?"

"Yes, everything is fine," Coach reassured him. "Your game is coming along nicely. I'm impressed with your progress."

"Thank you. I'm doing my best."

"You have keen situational awareness and strong ball handling skills, but I have a few things I'd like you to work on." Coach leaned forward in his chair. "Today during practice, two of your teammates were wide open, yet you chose to take the shot yourself. Was there a reason for that?"

Although Nathan was a bit flustered by this question, he did his best to justify his actions. "I saw a shot opportunity and took advantage of it."

"I see." Coach Spoleda tightened his jaw.

Nathan sensed his coach wasn't happy with his response. "Is that a problem, Sir?"

"You are a strong offensive player. You're effective on the court and powerful from three-point range, but your job is to make sure the ball gets to the right players at the right time. If one of your teammates has a better scoring opportunity, you need to get the ball to them."

Nathan gave a nod of acknowledgement. "I understand."

Coach sat back in his seat. A deep frown creased his brow. "Nathan, I know the transition from high school to college is difficult. The social adjustments, the demanding course requirements, trying to balance the various aspects of your life. The added pressure of fulfilling pre-med requirements doesn't make it any easier. I checked your current grades. Are you aware that you're failing your English class?"

Those words rang through Nathan's head like a cymbal crash. He shifted in his seat. "Yes, Sir, I am."

"What can I do to help you?"

Unsure what to say, Nathan scratched his head. "I don't know. Writing has always been problematic for me. My spelling is terrible, I don't have the best grammar skills, and I can't seem to organize my thoughts logically."

"Have you been to the writing labs?"

"The morning labs are only open while I'm in class, and in the afternoon, I simply don't have time. I honestly don't know how much good it would do though. After reading two or three chapters from a textbook every night and studying all my notes for several hours at a time, my dyslexia kicks in and I start seeing double. It's frustrating."

"Do you have a friend or family member who can look over your papers before you turn them in?" Coach Spoleda suggested.

"I could have my girlfriend check them. She's good at that kind of thing. But she has her own classes to worry about. I don't want to burden her with mine."

"What about family?"

Nathan contested this statement. "My dad's busy with his medical practice. He doesn't have time to look over every paper I write."

Nathan's pride had created a barrier that blocked him from getting the help he needed. Coach Spoleda had to intervene. "When I first met you, I also met your parents. They are incredible people who obviously support you and encourage you to do your best."

"Yes, Sir. They do. In fact, back in her prime, my mother was a pretty dominant force on the court. She's a good ball handler and an excellent shooter. I've learned a lot from her."

"Sounds like it."

"And my dad offered me a job in his clinic. He works around my schedule as much as he can, so I kinda come in whenever I have time. It's good experience for me when I start applying to medical schools."

"It most certainly is. Sounds like you have a pretty strong support system," his coach affirmed.

"Very much so, Sir."

"Good. Talk to your parents. Keep them up to date on how you're doing."

"I do," Nathan explained. "Medical school is something I've wanted for a long time. They've always been supportive of my career goals."

"I'm glad to hear that." Coach Spoleda looked his freshman point guard dead in the eye. "May I offer you a piece of advice?"

"I'll take whatever advice you have, Sir."

"As determined as you are, don't try to take on too much," Coach Spoleda warned. "Balance your time and break your studying into chunks. Take advantage of all the in-between times and use them to read a chapter or write a paragraph. That time can really add up. Utilize your summers to take care of time consuming things you don't have time for during the season—get your volunteer work out of the way, shadow in a hospital, and take more challenging classes. Sit down and plan it all out ahead of time. That way you won't have so much on your plate at one time. You have a challenging road ahead of you, and I will offer whatever assistance I can."

Nathan smiled gratefully. "Thank you, Sir. That means a lot to me."

"Don't give up on your dreams, Nathan. You have the determination and the aptitude to get there. Any time you have problems or need advice, feel free to talk to me. If I don't have the answers, we'll find someone who does. And when you get to the point where you are ready for recommendation letters, let me know. I will gladly write you one."

"Thanks, Coach. I appreciate that."

CHAPTER TWENTY-FOUR

For Nathan's first road trip, the team was set to travel to Maryland for a series of games in the Hall of Fame Classic Tipoff Tournament. His opponents were Loyola Maryland, a private Jesuit school, and Albany from the America East Conference.

Travel included packing, and subsequently making arrangements with professors ahead of time to get any work he would miss while on the road. To keep from falling behind, Nathan packed his backpack with books and spiral notebooks. He also filled his purple athletic bag with a practice jersey, extra basketball shorts, Under Armor shooting shirts, basketball shoes, and other miscellaneous personal items. All of this made up the bulk of his checked baggage.

"All packed," Nathan said, double checking his bags to make sure he hadn't forgotten anything.

"What time are you leaving tomorrow?" Gabby asked.

"Flight leaves at 10:30. We're meeting at the gym by 7:30 to catch our bus."

She stared at the packed athletic bag in the middle of the bedroom floor. "Wish I could go with you."

"Maybe you should consider trying out for the cheerleading squad again, then you could." He gently touched the tip of her nose.

"Who says I want to?"

"You know you miss it."

She sat down on the bed. "So? What's your point?"

"What's my point?" Nathan repeated, his voice thick with sarcasm. "My point is I know how much you love cheering. You live it, breathe it. Cheering has always been a big part of your life. You want to cheer, don't even tell me you don't."

"I'm not good enough to cheer with these women."

Although Nathan wasn't sure why, Gabby was full of self-doubt. "Yes you are," he argued persistently.

"Not according to them, I'm not. I didn't make the squad, Nathan. Obviously…"

"You're giving up?" he cut in. "Throwing in the towel when things get a little tough? Letting someone else dictate what you can and can't do? Giving in to defeat? That's not like you, Gab. You don't just give up because some person on a panel says you can't do something."

"This is different."

"No it's not," he contradicted.

"Yes it is," she pushed back.

"You know what I think? I think you're making excuses."

She denied this accusation. "I am not."

"Yes you are. Every time I bring up the Huskies cheering squad, you find some reason why you can't be a part of it."

"Why do you care so much?"

That comment offended him. "Excuse me?"

"I don't understand why you are so concerned about me cheering again."

He tried to reason with her. "Gabby, I know how important this is to you. I care about it because you care about it. Don't deny it either because I know better. I saw that heartbreaking look on your face when you didn't make the squad. You can't hide it from me. I know you too well."

He was right, but she felt defeated and her confidence bubble had been burst by this rejection, and talking about it was bringing her down.

Nathan sensed he had pushed the issue too far. He sat down next to her and held her hand in his. "Honey, I'm not trying to upset you. I'm trying to understand. Why are you giving up so easily?"

"I'm not giving up," she replied.

"Yes you are. You won't even consider trying again, and I don't agree with that. I know that if you tried out for the squad again you'd get in."

She shook her head. "It's not that easy."

At least he was coming down to the wire as to why she was feeling this way. It was going to be tough and it was going to take a lot of hard work on her part, but Nathan knew this was something she really wanted. If it wasn't, she wouldn't have gotten so upset when she didn't make the squad, and she wouldn't be crying about it now. Trying to get her to feel better, he offered his perspective. "I know it's not easy. Believe me, Babe, I totally understand that. Playing college basketball is the hardest, most demanding thing I've ever done. And it's frustrating sometimes because I feel the time I invest into it isn't worth it. But I keep doing it because it's important to me, it's something I've wanted my whole life. So I'm going to keep at it, I'm going to work my ass off for it, and I'm not going to give up. Bottom line is you need to ask yourself how badly you want this. Wanting something as much as I know you want cheering should make you work even harder to achieve it. If you want it bad enough, you'll make it happen."

Nathan knew her well. "I do want it, but the competition is tough."

"You can do it," he encouraged. "I have complete confidence in that. You need to get out there, work harder than you've ever worked before, and go for it. You're not a quitter, Gab. You never have been."

Cheering was her life, something she loved, something she had to do. She felt naked without it, but she had to overcome her own fears and apprehensions to make it happen.

In the morning, as bus loading time approached, Nathan hadn't shown up. Being late would not be a good way to begin his first college road trip. Brett checked the time, wondering what the hell was taking him so long. That's when a red Mustang pulled into the parking lot. Nathan stepped out carrying his purple athletic bag in his hand with his backpack over his shoulder.

Brett tapped his watch. "Cutting it a little close, aren't you, Hanson?"

"I was a bit pre-occupied." Nathan beeped his car alarm and slipped his car keys in his pocket.

"Pre-occupied with what?"

"Gabby." He slid his athletic bag into the storage compartment under the bus.

"You were having sex, in other words."

"Who was having sex?" Andrew asked as the men boarded the bus.

"Hanson," Brett replied, giving Nathan a hard time.

Andrew remarked, "I read somewhere that pre-game sex weakens muscles and decreases your performance."

"Dude," Brett contradicted, "There's no evidence anywhere to confirm that there are detrimental physical effects from having sex."

"I would think," another teammate, Julian Ramirez, added, "That sex would enhance performance because you're pumped up and the adrenaline is rushing." He turned to Nathan, who was sitting in the seat next to him. "That is, if you performed well in the first place."

"Shut up," Nathan retorted.

"Isn't your girlfriend a cheerleader, Hanson?" Julian asked.

"Yeah."

"Why isn't she traveling with us?"

"She tried out for the Huskies' squad last spring, but didn't make the team."

"Is she going to try again?"

"I think she should," Nathan said, "but convincing her of that is a different story."

"I can talk to her if you want," Julian shrewdly suggested.

"Um...no," Nathan declined. "I think I can handle talking to my girlfriend."

"I would love to see her in a purple cheering skirt."

"See, that's where I have the advantage," Nathan declared with a smirk on his face. "I get to see her in a skirt any time I want. Or I can just take it off of her and see her in nothing at all."

"Well, aren't you a lucky bastard."

"Leave him alone, Ramirez," Brett insisted. "Maybe if you'd find your own girlfriend, you wouldn't be lusting over Hanson's."

Nathan got comfortable in his seat, fiddling with his iPhone so he could listen to some tunes on their way to the airport.

The basketball team was sure to be met by a huge contingent of Huskies fans because the Dawg Pack, as the team quickly came to be known, was just that awesome. While all of the lucky fans treated road trips as a wallet-draining vacation, the chaotic excursion was all work for the members of the basketball program. College basketball road trips were a different monster than the basketball road trips in high school of which Nathan had been a part of. Preparation for NCAA trips began months in advance.

To ensure the team had a non-miserable traveling experience, it all came down to having a good Ops guy. With the basketball team, these duties fell to a man by the name of Tim Marshall, the assistant coach. Tim was responsible for planning and executing trips from the day the schedule was finalized until the team returned to Seattle. However, this was not an easy task. He had to make flight and hotel arrangements for twenty-five plus people and secure restaurant reservations. And finding gyms to practice in was no easy task. There were a lot of pieces to the road trip puzzle—and a lot of puzzles throughout the season.

Almost all of the teams in the Huskies athletic department flew commercially. This meant the buses typically left UW fairly early in the morning the day before the competition and drove forty-five minutes to the SEA-TAC airport. Once the team arrived at their destination, they dropped off their bags at the hotel then immediately left for practice. They returned to the hotel for dinner and study hall, which often included proctored tests, before a curfew was instilled. Under the watchful UW basketball coaching staff, partying and fornication didn't happen. That kind of behavior was not tolerated on road trips.

Nathan worked on a Chemistry lab report and read a couple chapters from his textbook, but quickly became distracted when someone texted him.

Nathan shared a room with Andrew Garibay, whom he had developed a close friendship with. Through this friendship, Nathan had told him about his and Gabby's history together. Knowing how much Gabriella meant to Nathan, Andrew assumed that's who he was messaging. "What's Gabby up to?"

Nathan replied, "She's hangin' with her roommate and getting some studying done."

"You know, my cousin is a Husky cheerleader."

"Is she?"

"Yes," Andrew said. "I can arrange for Gabby to meet her. Maybe Karla can give her some pointers."

Nathan set his phone down. "Gabby doesn't need advice, she needs confidence. She's the best cheerleader I know. She was excited about tryouts last spring, but something happened. I'm not sure what it was and she won't elaborate on it. I just know that when she came out, she looked really pissed off and didn't want to talk on the way home. She says it's because of the way the panel was set up, but I don't think that's what it was."

"Do you think she was nervous?" Andrew assumed.

Nathan lifted a shoulder. "I don't know. Maybe. I know she misses it. I'm trying to convince her to try out again. There's no reason why she shouldn't make the team. Gabby's better than most of the women I've seen at cheer practice. She can perform some unbelievable stunts, stuff I could never dream of doing." Nathan put his Chemistry book away and crossed his ankles.

"Is she one of those girls on the top of the pyramid?"

"Yes, she's a flyer," Nathan declared. "And it scares the crap out of me. They toss her up in the air and I cringe every time, praying they catch her on the way back down."

"I bet," Andrew concurred.

"And you should see her on the dance floor. Her squad used to do our halftime shows. Of course I never got to see them during basketball season, but during football season, they would do dance routines on the field. I loved watching those. Gabby has some moves."

"Have you ever watched the UW squad?" Andrew asked.

"I never really paid that much attention. Was always focused on the game. "

"Watch them sometime. Washington may be a bit up north and somewhat off the map when it comes to cheerleaders but damn, they should be given their own television show. The UW cheer squad is definitely one of the best in the country. I love watching them cheer."

"Really?" Nathan asked, curious now as to the caliber of this squad.

"Yeah. They have amazing cheer choreography and tumbling routines, and the girls, the ones on the top of the pyramid like Gabby, those girls can get some height on their flips. I'm not normally into that kind of thing, but that squad has extraordinary athleticism."

Nathan was even more interested in the cheering squad now. "That definitely sounds like Gabby's kind of cheering. No wonder she's so attracted to them."

In the morning, wakeup call rang twenty-five minutes prior to breakfast, followed by shootarounds at the arena and a walk-through of the scouting report. Four hours before the game, the team returned to the hotel for a lovely catered meal of chicken strips, mashed potatoes, and seasoned vegetables. Players then filed into the trainer's hotel room to get taped up. After necessary taping, the team piled onto the bus and left the hotel in time to arrive at the arena an hour and a half before game time.

The camaraderie on road trips was one thing Nathan could not replicate in any way. Many of his greatest friendships were formed during these trips. Waiting in airports or sharing pre-game meals gave him premier opportunities to bond with his teammates. An NCAA athletic road trip was the most chaotic and stressful work-related experience in Nathan's life, but there was no way he would trade that experience. The only thing that would have made it better was if Gabby would have been traveling with him.

Before Nathan knew it, the tournament was over and they were on an early morning flight back to Seattle. Bleary eyed and physically exhausted, he slept on the plane. After packing and re-packing, bus rides to the airport, early morning flights, dealing with delays, and exerting all of his energy in two physically aggressive basketball games, Nathan discovered that road trips contributed to raising his fatigue level. His body was ground down bit by bit, creating more physical wear and tear. He'd never been so exhausted.

When the plane finally landed in Seattle, Nathan couldn't wait to get home. As soon as he stepped on the bus back to UW, he called Gabby to let her know he was on his way.

She met him at his apartment, excited and anxious to see him. The minute he pulled up, Gabby ran to his car and threw her arms around him. "I missed you."

"I missed you too." Being in her presence made everything ok.

"How was your trip?" she asked.

"Draining." He gave her a kiss then popped the trunk and pulled his gear out of the car.

Gabby helped him unload. "You guys played well this weekend."

"We did alright. Wish my stats would have been a little better."

"You got six assists in the Loyola game. That's good," Gabby praised him.

"It's not good enough, and I didn't do very well in the field." Nathan closed the trunk and beeped the alarm.

"You scored nine points," Gabby reminded him, having watched the game on the ESPN college channel.

"But I missed one of my outside shots. Four guys were in double figures, and if I would have made that shot, I could have joined them."

"I thought you did well," Gabby encouraged him.

"We lost to Albany," he complained. "We could have won that game, if we would have started the right way. Casey sat on the bench for most of the first half, and we committed six turnovers in the first eight minutes. We were slow, and our defense sucked. Coach warned us too, that if we didn't tighten our defense, they were going to beat us. We should have put more pressure on the ball."

"You did turn up the pressure; you swarmed them. The way you came out in the second half, I thought you guys would beat them."

"Well, we didn't," Nathan griped. "And a lot of that was my fault. I tanked a three-pointer when I should have let Casey take the shot. In turn, Albany snagged the rebound and scored on us."

"It wasn't just you, Nathan. Ramirez missed his first six shot attempts and Ramusi got hit in the eye and had to get stitches. That game was pretty aggressive."

"Tell me about it." He rolled up his sleeve and showed Gabby the huge bruise on his shoulder.

She winced. "Ow. That looks painful."

"That guard from Albany was fuckin' mean. He battered the hell out of me. I'm pretty sore."

"You need a hot shower, and I'll give you a massage."

Her undying support was encouraging. "Thanks, Babe. That would be great."

As the season progressed, Nathan began to make quite a name for himself, not only around campus, but within the PAC-12 Conference. He had a huge hometown fan following. This contingent included family, friends of the family, high school friends, high school teachers and coaches, his father's colleagues, and basically the entire Kirkland community. His parents came to every game they could. The televised away games they couldn't attend, they watched from home. Gabby, Mike, and Ashley went to all the home games and screamed louder than anyone else there. Nathan definitely had a cheering section.

Well into their PAC-12 conference games, Nathan was getting more floor time. He was a strong backup point guard for Washington, which was part of the reason why Washington was currently holding an overall 14-2 record. They were undefeated in conference play and had an 8-0 record on their own territory. The Huskies didn't fare quite as well on the road though, holding a 6-2 away record. Despite this, they were still currently ranked first in the PAC-12 conference.

This week they traveled to Oregon. The University of Oregon was tough competition. Their starting point guard was ranked fifth in the league, was a first team all-conference selection the previous year, and was the top scorer in the Northwest Athletic Association. He was a powerful three-point shooter and was difficult to guard from the outside. He meant business and wasn't going to go down without a fight.

Brett was experienced against this team and had gone up against their point guard before. He felt confident about their upcoming game. However competing against Oregon was new to Nathan, so Brett offered him some advice. "Oregon is competitive in every way, and Barker's a pretty prolific shooter. Do not let him spring loose. We're going to have to trail him everywhere, get physical with him. We need to gain a foothold early. Your fast break game is going to be crucial."

Nathan listened attentively to every word Brett said. "Alright."

"Be aggressive and look for off screens. You need to be on your A game tonight."

The game started off intense and physical. It was fast-paced, and players were bumping into each other left and right. Fouls were being called and Nathan was convinced that blood was bound to be shed before the game was over.

He couldn't have been more right. Early in the first half, while attempting to steal the ball, Brett fell to the floor shaking his hand and wincing in pain. The team doctor rushed out to check on him. Immediately, Brett was taken off the court and brought to the locker room.

Coach Spoleda called on Nathan. "Hanson, you're in."

Nathan got off the bench and walked over to his coach.

"Be gritty and don't lose your composure," Coach Spoleda instructed. "Get the ball to the open man."

Nathan nodded in understanding. "Yes, Sir."

He was determined to play the game of his life and show his coach, his team, and all of the screaming fans in the arena that he had what it took to be a college point guard. His adrenaline overflowed and he was pumped up beyond belief.

Throughout the game, Nathan displayed some steel by making four consecutive jumpshots and firing a three pointer in the final minutes of the game to send the Huskies to a buoying 76-74 win.

On the bus back to the hotel, Nathan used the opportunity to call Gabby. "Hey, Babe. Did you watch the game?"

"Yes. I went over to your place because Mike had it on," she declared. "I wish I could have been there to see it in person."

He pulled the phone a little closer and ducked down in his seat so he could have more privacy. "What are you wearing?"

Gabby thought this was an odd question. "Why do you want to know what I'm wearing?"

"Because, I bet you are wearing something amazingly sexy, and I would love to take it off you right now."

Somewhat embarrassed by his bold comment, Gabby said, "Nathan."

"What?" he asked innocently. "I can't help it. You turn me on. Just hearing your voice gets me hot. When I get back, there are so many things I want to do to you."

She played along with his lustful mood. "Oh really? And what are you going to do to me?"

He proceeded to describe exactly what he wanted to do to her, however talking like this made him want her even more.

The next morning, Nathan went online to read up on NBA games he had missed from being on the road. As he browsed the internet, he came across an article on the gohuskies website: *Brett Sorenson left the Huskies' game against Oregon with a dislocated left index finger. Fortunately, the injury was on Sorenson's non-shooting hand. Sorenson hurt the finger early in the first half Thursday night while attempting to steal the ball from Oregon's center Roy Hiller when he fell to the floor shaking his hand and grimacing in pain. He immediately went to the locker room. A short time later, the Huskies said he would miss the rest of the game.*

At that point, freshman player, Nathan Hanson, took over as point guard for Washington and ended up finishing the game with a pretty solid line of nineteen points, two steals, and six assists. If Sorenson ends up missing some time, the Huskies are in good hands with Hanson as their point.

The article listed a few highlights from the game and posted an interview with Coach Spoleda, who gave his insights into the game.

"Hanson's not intimidated by circumstances," Coach Spoleda was quoted to say. *"He's scrappy and gritty. He's one of the guys on our team that brings toughness."*

Reading this article boosted Nathan's confidence. "What do you suppose that means?" he asked Andrew.

Andrew stepped out of the bathroom with a towel wrapped around his waist. "What does what mean?"

"In this article, Coach said I was scrappy and gritty. Makes me sound like a mangy dog in a dog fight."

Andrew expressed his interpretation. "Think it means you're a badass, but he can't say that in an interview."

Nathan laughed, "No, I suppose not."

Before the team headed to breakfast, Coach Spoleda posted the starting lineup for the Oregon State game: *Hanson (PG), Ramirez (SG), Guenther (C), Ramusi (SF), Foster (PF).* This would be Nathan's first opportunity to play starting position in NCAA competition.

The first thing he did when he saw this was text Gabby. *Good news. I'm starting tonight.*

Yay! she praised him. *You're going to be amazing.*

I hope.

You will be. You always are.

Although he felt confident, Gabby's words always uplifted him. She was always his biggest fan, and as much as he wanted to talk to her, he had to join his team. *Having breakfast w/ the team now, so I can't really talk. Just wanted to let you know.*

I love you, she typed followed by a string of x's and o's.

I love you too. Have a great day! He put a little heart emoji at the end of his message.

Texting Gabby was a daily occurrence for Nathan, especially when he was on the road.

Many of the guys on the team were involved in relationships. However, Nathan and Gabby seemed to be the couple that had been together the longest and were the most stable. Nathan was proud to be in a deep, committed relationship. He talked about Gabby often, and everyone knew how important she was to him.

Although the guys supported each other and offered advice as far as relationships and women were concerned, there was one guy on this team, Geoff Foster, who regularly gave the so called 'pussy whipped' men a hard time. He saw Nathan texting his girlfriend and couldn't let it go. "I really don't understand why you waste your time trying to maintain a relationship with one woman. Being single is way easier. Why are you so hung up on this chick?"

Unamused by Geoff's comment, Nathan replied, "My life wouldn't be complete without Gabby. She's my best friend. Haven't you ever had an emotional connection with someone?"

"Don't want to if it means I have to check in every hour and lose my freedom," Geoff complained. "As it stands now, I don't have to answer to a woman, I can do whatever I want, and I don't have to listen to her nag all the time."

Nathan snorted derisively. "You make it sound like being in a relationship is a prison sentence."

"I don't like being tied down. Relationships cramp my style. Don't get me wrong, I love women, but I need a woman who won't be a demanding little cunt."

Nathan wondered why Geoff was so bitter. "Have you ever been in a serious relationship?"

"Once, but never again. That bitch totally tried to control my life. She kept me from my friends and criticized everything I did. I couldn't stand being around her. She annoyed the crap out of me. Naggin' and complainin' non-stop."

"Why were you with her if you didn't like her?"

"She willingly put out."

This irrational logic baffled Nathan. "You stayed with her for sex?"

"She was annoying as hell, but every time she'd put out, she'd shut up. It made her a little more tolerable."

Nathan shook his head in disbelief. "If you didn't like the woman, you shouldn't have stayed with her. It shouldn't matter if the sex was good or not."

"When she stopped putting out, I stopped putting up with her crap and ditched her ass. You know, there are a lot of women out there who are totally into you. I hear them talking. They would die for you to take them to bed."

Nathan didn't care. "So?"

"So, maybe you should check out the greener grass."

"I'm already standing in the greenest pasture. It doesn't get any greener than this."

"How can you be so sure if you've never experienced life on the other side of the fence?"

Nathan maintained his argument. "I like my side of the fence."

"I know some chicks; I can hook you up. Your girlfriend will never know."

Nathan immediately refuted this ridiculous suggestion. "Not interested, Geoff. I'm in a relationship, a very happy relationship with a woman I care about."

"Suit yourself. That leaves more chicks for me."

Nathan never realized how shallow Geoff Foster was. He also didn't understand men who held that kind of mentality. Some of the athletes he had run across were so nonchalant about having affairs or cheating on their girlfriends. To them it was standard practice. Nathan refused to fall into that trap. He was with the woman he loved and wanted to keep it that way.

Nathan had the best game of his college career against Oregon State that night. He tallied twenty points and made UW history by scoring six three pointers in one game, making him tied for the seventh overall in that category. He felt pretty good about his performance.

His coach, however, wasn't nearly as impressed. The moment they returned to the hotel, Coach Spoleda gave Nathan a directive. "Hanson, may I speak with you please?"

"Yes, Sir."

Since his coach gave him no indication as to why he wanted to speak with him, Nathan wasn't sure what to expect when he reported to his coach's room.

"Have a seat," Coach said.

Nathan did as he was told.

With an intimidating stare, Coach Spoleda loomed over him with his arms crossed stiffly. "Apparently you've forgotten the conversation we had last week."

"I didn't forget."

"Then explain to me why you're still calling the shots instead of passing to the open man."

Unsure what to say, he leaned on his elbows and stared at his hands.

"You were worried about your stats, weren't you?"

Brooding, he chewed on his coach's words.

Coach sat across from him and cleared his throat. "Nathan, you are without a doubt a valuable asset to this team. You have strong defensive skills and you're a solid shooter, but I need you to focus more on the team as a whole. Your job on that court is to get the ball into the hands of the open man. You should not take the shot unless you have no other options."

"Yes, Sir. I understand."

Trying to get him to comprehend the seriousness of his actions, Coach said, "I put you in this position because during practice you showed me you were a team player. But what I'm seeing from you lately is a selfish player who's more interested in improving his stats than focusing on what's best for the team. This is high stakes game play, and there are four other men out there with you, all of whom have more court time than you do. For the benefit of this team, I suggest you figure out how to utilize their skills."

Feeling dejected, Nathan hung his head. "Yes, Sir."

"We get nowhere as a team if we don't work together." To help Nathan accomplish this task, Coach Spoleda offered a suggestion. "Next practice, I challenge you to lead the offense without taking any shot attempts."

Nathan raised an eyebrow. "None at all?"

"None."

He sputtered his breath, reluctant to accept this challenge. "I'll try."

"I think you'll see a difference in your ability to lead the team when you focus more on your passing game." He smiled at his freshman point guard, hoping he got his point across. "Get some rest. We have an early flight tomorrow."

On previous road trips, being away from Gabby didn't seem to get to him, but during this trip, he caught himself staring at her picture more often than usual and couldn't get her voice out of his head. He couldn't wait to get home. As soon as the plane landed in Seattle, he texted Gabby and told her he was on his way home. When the bus pulled into the parking lot of the arena, he didn't stick around to chit chat with his teammates like he usually did. Instead, he immediately loaded his bags in the car and headed back to the apartment.

Gabby was just walking up to his apartment complex when Nathan approached with his purple athletic bag in his hand and his backpack over his shoulder. The minute he saw Gabby, he dropped his bags on the ground and swept her into his arms. He covered her mouth with his, and held her close, never wanting to let her go.

When they made it to the front door of his apartment, Nathan struggled for his keys. Once the door was unlocked, he dropped his bags in front of the door and kicked off his shoes. He slid Gabby's jacket off her shoulders then unlatched his pants and untucked his shirt. They were so engrossed in each other that they didn't notice Mike and Ashley sitting on the couch in the living room. They passed right by them, leaving a trail of clothing from the front door to Nathan's room.

When Mike heard Nathan's door close, he looked at Ashley and laughed.

"They didn't see us, did they?" she asked.

"I don't think so." Mike put his arm around her and returned to the movie they were watching.

Panting and covered in sweat, Nathan pulled Gabby against his warm pulsing body. He held her for a moment, snuggled on top of the comforter with their legs intertwined. "You want something to drink?" Nathan asked, trying to catch his breath.

"Water would be great."

"Be right back." He kissed her softly and rolled out of bed. With nothing on but a pair of basketball shorts, he plodded out to the kitchen. Mike and Ashley were on the couch. Nathan grinned when he saw them. "Oh, hey guys. When did you get here?"

"We've been here the whole time," Mike teased with a smirk on his face.

Nathan didn't remember seeing them when he and Gabby walked in, but then again he wasn't really paying attention. "I'm sorry. I didn't see you."

"No worries. Looked like you were busy anyway."

With a smug grin on his face, he pulled a water bottle from the fridge. He unscrewed the lid and chugged down the entire thing then tossed the empty bottle in the recycling can. "Have you guys eaten yet?"

"No."

"You want to snag some tacos?"

"Sounds good to me."

Nathan grabbed two more bottles and brought them into the bedroom. He handed one to Gabby. "Did you know Mike and Ashley were out there?"

"No." She sat up to take a drink, her naked body fully exposed to him.

He leaned against the wall and stared at her, first fixating on her breasts then drifting his gaze up to her eyes. "Apparently they've been out there the whole time."

Which meant Mike and Ashley most likely heard everything that went on in that room over the last twenty minutes. "Are you serious?"

Nathan tried not to laugh. "Yup."

Her cheeks turned bright red. Attempting to hide from this embarrassment, she buried herself under the covers.

"It's not a big deal, Gab. Come out." He tried to pry the sheet from her hand, but she clung onto it with a death grip. "You can't stay under there all day."

"If you want me to come out, you have to come get me."

Playing along, he crawled under the covers, tickling her along the way.

CHAPTER TWENTY-FIVE

The Huskies had their rivalry game against Washington State University the following weekend. The UW-WSU game was the biggest competition of the year. Nathan's parents came to the game, along with his sisters, Mike and Ashley, Dr. Ryan and his wife, and Gabby, all of whom screamed and cheered right along with the rest of the crowd.

At this point in the season, Brett and Nathan shared floor time pretty equally. Nathan popped into the game midway through the first half, then Coach Spoleda put him in again during the last five minutes.

Tension was high. The score kept seesawing back and forth and the Huskies were down by two with a little over fifteen seconds left on the game clock. Washington had the ball.

As Nathan dribbled across the court, the only thing he could think about was 'get the ball to the open man.' He vocalized with his teammates, trying to get them to spread out. The ball exchanged hands a few times, but his teammates were double-teamed and unable to break through.

Eight seconds.

Nathan had to act quickly. He scanned the floor and found an open spot outside the three-point line. 'Don't take the shot unless you have no other options.' He had run out of options. With just over three seconds remaining, he pulled a desperation move. He made a shot attempt from three-point range. It easily cleared the net, giving Washington the win.

After the game, Nathan and Gabby went for a walk along the shoreline. The wind carried the sounds of a distant motor boat that passed by. "You made quite a name for yourself on the basketball court tonight, Nathan."

"I'm not in this for the glory, Gab. You know that."

"Some of your teammates are really full of themselves. Have you heard the things they say? I know it's easy to let the recognition and popularity get to your head, yet you've stayed so humble through all this."

"I told you I wouldn't let the game change me," he reminded her. "I intend to keep that promise." He brushed a gentle kiss across her forehead. "I know this hasn't been easy. Our schedules never seem to be in sync and we really don't spend as much time together as we should."

"It's ok. Right now basketball is your life. We'll be able to spend more time together when the season is over."

"Which reminds me. I was talking to one of the cheerleaders the other day and she told me about cheer clinics. They go over dance routines and the cheering material you'll need to know for tryouts, and they give you checklists of the tumbles and stunts you need to perform. She said they specifically look for women who know toss stunts. There's a clinic coming up next month. You should check it out."

Gabby had her doubts. "I don't know, Nathan."

"You are far more talented than many women on that squad, and none of them can do the stunts you do."

"You're just saying that to make me feel better."

"No, I'm saying it because it's true," he insisted. "You're one of the best, Gab."

"You really think so?"

"Hands down." Nathan always had confidence in her even if she didn't. He took both of her hands in his and did his best to encourage her. "You gonna check out the cheer clinic?"

She bobbed her head. "I think I will."

"That's my girl."

This month's Sports Illustrated featured college basketball's topped ranked NCAA teams. According to this article, Washington was ninth overall in the country. They were the top contender for the PAC-12 tournament and were the topic of talk when it came to NCAA playoffs.

Randy was especially intrigued by this particular story because the Huskies were one of the featured teams. He skipped the other articles and turned directly to the page where UW was featured. There, big as life, was a photo of Nathan and another teammate jumping up to the net trying to snag a rebound during the WSU game. The article included overall stats for each player and recapped highlights from each game. There was also a section featuring specific players. Nathan was one of them.

After losing several key players to graduation last year, the University of Washington was in need of some fresh young talent. Who better to fill a primary offensive role than freshman Nathan Hanson.

The article referred to Nathan as *a powerful presence on the court* and mentioned that he *meshed well with his teammates.* As Randy read this, the corners of his mouth curved upward. His son was making history, and the name Nathan Hanson had become nationally known.

Over a cup of coffee, Randy sat across from Jim with a cocky smirk on his face. He took a sip from his steaming cup then placed the article in Jim's hand. "Check this out."

The highlighted game photo immediately captured Jim's attention. "Is that Nathan?"

"Yup," Randy boasted. "My son is in Sports Illustrated. How cool is that?"

"I've been watchin' his games. He is a powerhouse on the court."

"I know," Randy replied. "His passing game has improved tremendously and he's getting stronger on the defensive end. Jane and I are proud of him."

"Can I borrow this magazine? I want to read that article."

"Sure, but I want it back. I get bragging rights on that one."

Jim couldn't argue with that. "For sure."

The success of the UW men's basketball team resulted in the players' names being talked about all over campus. Nathan was one of the more popular players on the team, especially with the women. Daily, it seemed, women were throwing themselves at him.

When Gabby met Nathan for lunch one afternoon, a group of women walked past them, giggling and giving Nathan the flirty eye. Not wanting to be rude, Nathan acknowledged them by flashing a sexy smile.

Gabby stared him down with an unpleasant scowl on her face. "Were you flirting with them?"

He scoffed at her assumption. "Of course not."

"It looked like they were hitting on you."

Nathan blew it off. "Women hit on me all the time."

She could see why. Nathan was a good looking, physically fit guy. And with his status on campus, his name and face were everywhere. However, he didn't seem to think that women flirting with him was a big deal. "So that makes it ok for you to flirt back?"

"I wasn't flirting with them," he denied. "I simply acknowledged their existence. Don't want to be rude to my fans."

Normally Nathan was humble and kept a pretty low profile, but right now he had a cocky attitude and an overinflated head. Gabby didn't like it one bit. "Your fans?"

"Look around, Gab." He quickly surveyed the room. "You know all these women are jealous of you, right?"

"Why would they be jealous of me?"

"Because you're with me," he bragged. "You should feel honored."

His overweening, patronizing mindset grated on her nerves. "What?"

He looked at her as if it was obvious. "I'm part of the Dawg Pack. We're bigshots around here. Every woman in this room would die to be in your shoes. They all see us together, holding hands and kissing. Every one of them would give anything to walk around campus on my arm."

Repulsed by the casual way he shot his mouth off, she turned her nose up. "Oh really? Well, maybe you should walk around campus with one of them then." She picked up her backpack and stormed off.

Not sure what he had said that made her angry, Nathan ran after her. "Gabby, wait!"

She held up her hand and refused to acknowledge him.

Nathan stood speechless, trying to figure out what went wrong. When it finally dawned on him, he scoffed at his own stupidity. "Smooth move, Asshole."

Later that evening, when Nathan walked into his apartment, he didn't even have time to put his athletic bag down before Mike swarmed him. "What the hell did you do to Gabby?"

Although Nathan knew exactly what Mike was referring to, he played dumb. "What do you mean?"

"Ashley called me a few minutes ago and said Gabby's been crying all afternoon. What happened?"

Nathan knew he had carelessly inserted his foot into his mouth, but didn't realize Gabby was so hurt by what he said. He dropped his bag on the floor and combed his fingers through his hair. "I let my ego get the best of me and said something incredibly stupid."

"You made your girlfriend cry."

"It wasn't intentional." Feeling flustered, Nathan knew what he had to do. "I'm going over there."

Mike shook his head, hoping it wasn't too late. "Good luck, man. You're gonna need it."

Nathan rushed over to Gabby's room and knocked on the door.

When Ashley answered, she glared at him, outraged by his actions. "What do you want?"

Defensively, he replied, "I know she's here, Ashley. Let me talk to her."

"No," she insisted.

Nathan peered over Ashley's head and saw Gabby sitting on her bed hugging her knees. Seeing her in misery made him feel even worse. Begging for a chance at redemption, Nathan pleaded, "Come on, Gab. Let's talk about this."

Ashley attempted to shoo him away. "I think you've done enough."

Gabby spoke up, "It's ok, Ashley. Let him in."

Ashley glanced over her shoulder. "Are you sure?"

With a sniffle, Gabby nodded.

Ashley moved aside and let him in, but as she did, she turned to Gabby and said, "I'll be down in the lobby if you need me."

When Ashley left the room, Gabby stared at Nathan with a sulky expression on her face. An awkward hush fell between them.

Nathan wasn't sure what to say. Gabby was hurt, and it was his fault. Breaking the silence, he said, "I'm sorry."

She wiped her eyes dolefully. "How could you say something like that?"

He reflected on what he said and the arrogant way he acted, not blaming her one bit for being upset over this. "What I said was selfish, extremely insensitive, and I was totally full of myself. I'm really sorry, Gab."

She laid her feelings out on the table. "You promised you wouldn't get like this. You told me you didn't care about the glory or the popularity, yet your head is so swollen right now, I don't even recognize you."

Trying to rectify his mistake, he offered an admission of guilt. "You're right. I let it go to my head, and I shouldn't have done that."

Tears welled her eyes again. "You broke a promise to me, Nathan."

Realizing now that this situation was far more serious than him recklessly inserting his foot in his mouth, he begged for forgiveness. "I'm sorry. It wasn't intentional."

"You acted like a jerk."

"I know I did, and there's no excuse for it."

She sniffled and wiped her eyes. "That isn't who you are. That has never been who you are. You've always been selfless and caring and considerate of other people. The man I love is humble and never says rude or hurtful things. But the man I saw today was not Nathan Hanson. I don't know who he was."

She was absolutely right, and there was no way he could justify his actions. "I had a moment of weakness. I was arrogant, and what I said was inappropriate and completely uncalled for. I totally betrayed your trust."

"I'm so mad at you."

"You have every right to be."

She turned her eyes away and wept.

His heart stuttered, and there was a falling, spinning-down feeling in the pit of his stomach. He reached for her hand, hoping she would acknowledge him. "Gab, look at me."

She didn't want to look at him. She was angry and hurt and didn't even want to be around him right now.

Nathan began to panic, fearing Gabby would never forgive him. "I'm sorry. I make a mistake. Give me a chance to make it up to you."

Feeling betrayed, she refused to respond.

His whole world was crumbling right before his eyes. Gabby was his life, and he couldn't survive without her. Trying to win her forgiveness, he offered any apologetic words he could think of. "Please talk to me. Say something."

But she wouldn't say a word. She wouldn't even look at him. She simply buried her face in her hands and sobbed.

CHAPTER TWENTY-SIX

Throughout his basketball career, Nathan's parents and coaches taught him the importance of humility. His mother told him once that humility was a psychological quality characterized by being more modest, down-to-earth, and respectful. This conception of humility implied that Nathan acknowledged his mistakes, realized his limits, and was never arrogant or egotistical.

Every top athlete in any particular sport had traits associated with humility. Those traits influenced everything he or she did, from the way they prepared for a game to how they conducted themselves during the game. As an athlete, it was important to be confident, but if Nathan didn't respect that the other team was at least as good as or better than he was, he probably wouldn't train as hard or prepare himself mentally to succeed. Humbleness allowed Nathan to be open to learning, which improved his skills on the court.

Aside from the many lessons learned about humility throughout his life, Nathan's parents also taught him that athletes who showed more humble traits achieved higher grades than those who were arrogant and vain. If a student athlete couldn't compete in the classroom, he couldn't compete on the court either. Nathan always extended his best effort with every play during every practice and on every assignment in every classroom.

But no matter how disciplined, how talented, how humble, or how competitive he was, he would never accomplish great achievement without support—support from his coaches, athletic trainers, professors, friends, and family. With the support offered by the people around him, namely Gabriella, Michael, and his parents, Nathan was able to follow his grueling daily routines, having faith in their purpose.

Sunday afternoon, Nathan came over to his parents' house to wash some laundry. When Jane saw him, the first thing she noticed was how much he had bulked up. He was in better shape than he had ever been in his life, and he had the look and attitude of a hard core basketball player.

Extremely proud of his reputation on the court, his mother gave him a huge hug. "I'm so proud of you, Honey. You are doing so well for your first year."

Nathan had recently checked his grades. Considering his many hours of basketball commitments and late nights of studying, he fared pretty well. He had A's and B's in all of his classes, except for English Composition. That class had caused him grief all semester. The work was time-consuming and the professor was extremely picky. Any tiny grammatical, spelling, or structural error instantly lowered his grade. "My English grade isn't very good."

"What's the problem?"

Nathan reached into his back pocket and pulled out a graded research paper. It had the letter *D* printed on the top in bright red ink. "Writing has never been my strong suit, but this professor makes it worse. He's nitpicky, and he criticizes everything I write. He's one of those professors who grades you down if he doesn't agree with your opinion. He gave me a D on this paper last week because he didn't agree with my take on health insurance." He handed the paper to his mother. "He said I had no evidence to back up my claim when I clearly stated my argument and gave research to support it. I even included a physician's point of view by getting Dad's opinion on the topic. But he said it wasn't enough. I'm convinced he has a personal vendetta against me."

"You could file a complaint with the university," Jane suggested.

"He's the head of his department. There's not a whole lot I can do. I need this class, but it's severely dropping my GPA. I'm worried it might hurt my chances of getting into med school."

Jane gave the paper back to him. "Talk to your dad, Honey. Maybe he can offer you some advice."

Most college athletes, who hoped for a chance at earning a million-dollar professional contract, used their degree as plan B. Nathan was different than most in this respect; his degree was his primary plan. He had no desire to be a professional athlete, so he had to stay disciplined and focus on school. Self-discipline was something his father was remarkably good at, and it rubbed off on Nathan, to a certain degree. College students were expected to study at least one hour per academic class if they expected to maintain good grades. Although Nathan did a pretty good job of juggling his study time, the act of studying was extremely stressful.

Nathan peeked into his father's home office, where Randy was concentrating on some kind of medical research. "Dad?"

Randy looked up. "Come in, Nathan."

Nathan crept inside and sat in a chair next to his father. "Whatcha doing?"

"Looking up information on an obscure case I have." He set the book down and turned his attention to his son. "What's up?"

Nathan handed his father the paper he wrote.

"What's this?"

"That research paper I wrote about health insurance."

Randy unfolded the document and saw the low grade on the top. "Ouch. That hurts."

"I'm failing this class," Nathan remarked. "I'm doing everything I can to rectify it, but nothing I do is good enough for this guy."

Randy skimmed through the paper. It had some grammar and sentence structure issues, but the information contained within it was sound. "Some professors are hard to please." Hoping his son wasn't feeling defeated, Randy asked, "How are you doing otherwise? You hanging in there?"

"I'm doing ok. Mike has been a big help. He takes care of the apartment and makes sure I have quiet time to study. And Dr. Hogan, my pre-med advisor, has helped me find ways to balance my academic requirements with basketball. Coach Spoleda told me he wanted to contribute to helping me get into med school and asked if there was anything he could do to help me. He even offered to write me a recommendation letter if I needed it," Nathan commented.

"That's good. I'm glad he's supporting you." Randy hadn't heard Nathan mention Gabby all day. This was unusual considering Nathan always talked about her. He hoped, with everything going on in Nathan's life, that things were alright between them. "How's Gabby?"

With the recent developments that occurred between him and Gabby, Nathan was reluctant to say anything. "She and I got into a fight last week."

Randy had never known a time when Nathan and Gabby had any kind of disagreement, so this news was surprising. "You did?"

"Yeah. I said something really stupid and now she's not speaking to me."

"That's not good."

"I tried talking to her, but I don't think she was in the mood to listen to me at the time," Nathan said sadly. "I decided to give her a few days to cool off."

"Sometimes that's the best thing you can do."

"With my busy practice schedule and studying, I'm not giving her the attention she deserves. We don't spend as much time together as we should, and I feel like I'm neglecting her."

"Have you talked to her about this?" Randy advised.

"I told her I felt bad about it, but at the time, she didn't seem to think it was a big deal."

Having experienced something similar when he was dating his wife, Randy offered some advice. "You know, your mother and I went through a time like that for a while when I was in med school. It was imperative that we communicated with each other. We utilized whatever time we had to its maximum potential. The time we spent together became more about quality rather than quantity."

"I want to do something special for her to show her how much I appreciate her patience and support. I need to make this up to her, but I don't know how."

"What is something she really loves that you haven't done together in a while?"

The perfect thought hit him. "Dancing. The last time she and I went dancing together was at Prom."

"Well," Randy laughed. "That won't do. You need to take her dancing. It will let her know you're thinking about her needs, and it's a great way to show her that you appreciate what she's doing for you. You'll get to be close to her and hold her in your arms all night, and it will give you two a chance to talk. Might even lead to something more intimate."

"Hopefully."

That night, Nathan took his father's advice. He bought a bouquet of flowers at a nearby flower shop and headed over to Gabby's dorm room.

When Gabby answered, Nathan's shoulders dropped. The pain he felt funneled into his heart. "Hey, Gab."

Her lips formed a hard line as she stared at the flowers in his hand. "Are you trying to suck up to me?"

"If you really must know, yes, I am." He handed her the bouquet. "Can I come in?"

With a reluctant nod, she showed him inside.

Nathan plopped down on the bed, and for a moment their eyes met. "Look, Gab. I know I screwed up. I said some very disrespectful things the other day and was totally full of myself. Those words never should have come out of my mouth."

Gabby wasn't sure what to say. She closed her eyes, fighting the heartache that had held her hostage for days.

On the verge of tears, Nathan held both of her hands and pulled her onto the bed with him. "I'm sorry, Honey. I never meant to hurt you." Begging for forgiveness, he nuzzled his forehead against hers. "Please tell me I haven't lost you over this."

Nathan sounded pitiful. His begging puppy dog eyes and pouty lip made Gabby giggle. "You sound pathetic."

"For you, I'll suffer through the humiliation." He breathed a sigh of relief, comforted by the fact that she was finally speaking to him. "Do you forgive me?"

"Yes." She scrunched up her forehead, causing angry wrinkles to form. "But I'm still mad at you. If you were trying to impress someone, you went about it the wrong way."

"I wasn't trying to impress anyone. I was just being a jerk."

She gave him a serious stare down. "You're a nice guy, Nathan. People like you and respect you because of who you are. Don't try to be the big man on campus."

"I won't. I promise this will never happen again." He gently touched her face with his hand and rubbed his thumb across her lips. Bringing their mouths within the same breathing space, he said, "I love you, Baby."

"I love you too."

He wrapped her in his arms and his lips entwined with hers.

The dance club Nathan found was located in Seattle's University District. The club featured exclusive DJs and local bands. There were several seating areas, including discreet private video booths and a VIP area with huge plasma TVs. The interior was expansive and open to accommodate the wall-to-wall sea of people that entered the crowd on weekend nights.

The minute they walked in the door, Gabby grabbed Nathan's hand and led him onto the dance floor. "Dance with me."

They spent several hours together, mingling among the crowd, sharing private conversations, and enjoying the festive atmosphere. Nathan even stole a few kisses throughout the evening.

When they'd had enough clubbing, Nathan drove them across the lake to Kirkland. They parked on the side of the road and trekked down a path about a half mile to a small beach surrounded by woodland. Nestled between the trees was an old abandoned fishing cabin. Nathan found this hidden gem many years ago. He showed it to Gabby the night they shared their first kiss. A year later, they lost their virginity together on a blanket inside the cabin.

Tonight, they sat on the dock side by side with their feet dangling over the edge. Nathan put his arm around Gabby, and she rested her head on his shoulder. Together, they enjoyed the clear star-painted sky and the moon glow that reflected off the water, making the water ripples shimmer in luminous splendor.

"You know what I was thinking about the other day?" Nathan said.

"What?"

"Do you remember that night, after the homecoming game, when we all went down to Dairy Queen?"

Gabby started to laugh. "Oh god. You and Mike were so hyper. Who puts pepper on ice cream?"

"It was better than the hot sauce Mike put on his. That was nasty. I can't believe he actually ate that." Sharing memories with Gabby always made him laugh. "We've had some good times, you and me."

"Yes we have."

He scooted closer and kissed the top of her head. "I'm sorry I haven't been myself lately. I've had a lot of things on my mind."

Gabby looked up at him. His face was tense and his eyes stared off into the distance, obvious signs that he was stressed. "Like what?"

He gathered his thoughts and began to empty the overstuffed file cabinet in his head. "Playoffs are coming up soon, which means my schedule is about to get worse, if that's even possible."

"We'll make it work, Nathan. We always have."

"I know we'll make it work, but I feel like I'm taking my stress out on you."

"What are you so stressed about?"

"I'm failing my English class."

She turned her body to face him. "Why didn't you say something?"

"I didn't want to burden you with it. You have enough on your plate."

"But I could have helped you. You spent all that time in high school helping me with Physics. The least I could have done was get you through English class."

Nathan wished now that he hadn't kept this from her. "I'm sorry. I should have told you." Trying to unleash some of his uncertainties, he said, "Coach has been calling me into his office a lot lately."

"Why?"

"He says I need to work on my passing game. During practice, he's forcing me to pass and won't let me make any shot attempts. It's driving me crazy."

Gabby stared at the water, disappointed. "How come you didn't come to me with any of this?"

"I don't know. I didn't want to push my problems on you." He took in a big breath and combed his fingers through his hair. "I'm just so overwhelmed right now. I'm inundated with homework, my nose is constantly buried in a textbook, and I have no time for myself. I feel like the Energizer Bunny, except my batteries are about to expire. I won't even get a break over the holidays because we have games and tournaments scheduled the entire time. If I'm lucky, I get one day a week off, but I have to spend the majority of that day studying so I don't fall behind. It hasn't even been a full year yet, and I'm already burned out."

Sympathizing with his plight, Gabby gently touched his cheek with her hand. "You can do this, Nathan. I know you can."

He chuckled mirthlessly. "I'm tired, Gab."

"Hang in there, Sweetie. Spring break is just around the corner."

CHAPTER TWENTY-SEVEN

"Oh man. You guys suck!" Nathan exclaimed when his SORRY game board piece got knocked back into the start circle, first by Mike, now by Gabby.

Gabby laughed at him. "You're not as good as you think, are you?"

"It doesn't help that you keep knocking me back in here and make me have to start all over," he complained.

"That's the way the game's played," Gabby reminded him.

"I know, but one of these days I'm actually going to beat you at this game." Nathan drew another card, hoping to get his game piece out. No such luck. "I think you rigged these cards."

Gabby gave him a hard time. "If you can't take the heat…"

"Who says I can't take the heat?" he asked.

"You're sure doing an awful lot of whining over there." Gabby got up and reached into the refrigerator to grab a soda. "You want a drink?" she asked.

"Sure." Nathan, Gabby, Mike, and Ashley took a break in their game, and Nathan pulled out his phone. "Anyone else hungry?"

"What'd you have in mind?" Mike asked.

"You guys up for Chinese food?"

"Ooh," Ashley declared. "That sounds yummy."

"I'm in," Mike said, pulling a ten dollar bill out of his wallet.

Over fried rice, egg rolls, and sodas, the four of them continued their game.

"I heard the PAC-12 tournament is gonna be in Vegas this year," Mike said, excited about this event.

"Yup," Nathan replied. "At the MGM Grand. ESPN and the PAC-12 Network have contracted with the league to broadcast the whole thing."

"Wow, they're really going all out, aren't they?" Mike stated.

"The league's had some poor attendance figures for the tournament in the past. Guess they figured the increase in national exposure would help."

"Smart move. How much are tickets?" Mike asked.

"Not sure," Nathan replied. "Anywhere from one-fifty to two-hundred a game I would guess."

"College kids can't afford that. No wonder they have attendance problems."

Nathan laughed. "No shit."

The Huskies were currently in first place in the PAC-12 conference. They won the conference tournament title last year and made an appearance in the national NCAA tournament sixteen times in the past, twice in the Final Four. They had yet to win a national championship.

"Are your parents going?" Mike asked.

"Of course they are." Nathan looked over at Gabby. "Wish you could be there."

"I can't afford tickets, Nathan. You know that."

He offered an alternative. "Maybe my parents can get tickets for you."

"I'm not asking them that."

"I'll talk to them. I really want you there, Gab."

At work the next day, when Randy had a break between patients, Nathan peeked his head into his father's office. "Dad, can I talk to you for a minute?"

Randy looked up from the lab results he was reading. "Sure. What's up?"

Nathan stepped inside and closed the door. "I don't like asking you and Mom for favors, but this is really important."

Randy set the paperwork on his desk. "What is it?"

"As you know, the PAC-12 tournament is in Vegas this year," Nathan began. "I know you and Mom were planning to attend, but I'd really like Gabby to be there. The only problem is, she doesn't have money for tickets or airfare."

Randy knew exactly what Nathan wanted. "You want us to get her there, don't you?"

"I know that's asking a lot."

Nathan rarely asked for money or help that involved material things, so when he did ask, Randy and Jane were more willing to offer their help. "Tell you what," Randy said. "Let me talk to your mother and we'll see what we can do."

"Thanks."

"Speaking of airfare, I'm making reservations for this summer. You don't have practice in June do you?"

"No," Nathan said. "But I was planning on taking some summer classes."

"When?"

"They start June sixteenth."

"So you're available the first two weeks of June?"

"Yes." Nathan anticipated another fabulous vacation at one of the exciting destinations his father always managed to find. "Where are we going?"

"The Mayan Riviera. Is Gabby available during that time? We'd like to invite her to come with us again."

Nathan grinned joyfully. "I'm sure she will be, but I'll ask her."

"Please do."

A week later, Nathan met Gabby for dinner after practice, as he often did. "The conference tournament is in two weeks," Nathan said.

"You excited?"

"I am," Nathan replied. "We're ranked first seed for this tournament, so I'm hoping all goes well. I'm gonna be honest though, I'm a little nervous."

"Why?"

"Sports channels from all over the country will be broadcasting the entire thing for millions of people to see. That's a little intimidating."

"I don't see what you're worried about. You've played in high-stakes tournaments before."

"But this is different," Nathan explained. "This is the NCAA. The competition is tougher and a lot more aggressive. You've seen the bruises I come home with every weekend. These are big name teams we're up against, nationally renowned teams full of potential NBA stars. People talk about these national tournaments for years. They bet thousands of dollars on these games. I'm not experienced at this level of competition. Brett is, but I'm not. I'm glad he's starting through all of this, because I don't know if I can handle that right now."

"Why are you doubting yourself?" she questioned.

"This is a different playing field, Gab. Higher stakes, stronger teams. National titles are on the line. That's a lot of pressure. Which is why I need you there. I'm a lot calmer and much more confident when I know you're there."

Gabby didn't understand why he was bringing this up again. He already knew she couldn't afford to attend. "We've already talked about this. As much as I would love to go, I just can't."

Nathan pulled an envelope out of his pocket and handed it to Gabby. "Here."

"What is this?"

"Open it," he insisted.

She ripped open the envelope and pulled out admission tickets to the PAC-12 tournament, round trip airline reservations to Las Vegas, and room accommodations at the MGM Grand hotel. "How did you do this?"

"I didn't. My parents did. You are in the room right next door to theirs, and all three of you are flying together on the same flight."

Gabby's eyes gleamed. "I can't believe they did this."

"My parents like you, Gab. And they know how much you wanted to go and how much I wanted you to be there, so they helped us out a bit."

Gabby didn't know what to say. "This is incredible. Thank you." She gave him a big bear hug.

"Don't thank me. Thank my parents."

The PAC-12 men's basketball tournament was a four day event, starting on Wednesday, ending on Saturday. Because they were ranked first in their league, the Huskies had a first round bye, which meant they weren't playing on Wednesday. They would meet their first opponent, the winner of the USC-Arizona game, Thursday night.

The fabulous neon lights on the Las Vegas Strip were in full view when the Huskies flew into Las Vegas Tuesday evening. Nathan had traveled with his family to many places, but he'd never been to Las Vegas before. Although he was here on team business, the experience was no doubt going to be a memorable one.

Their hotel, the MGM Grand, was the third largest hotel in the world and the largest resort complex in the United States. All two hundred ninety-three feet of this thirty-floor building were paneled with plates of emerald green glass. When they first pulled up to the hotel, Nathan felt like he was in the middle of movie. The entire building was lined with palm trees and illuminated with green lights. It was glitzy and full of Las Vegas flair.

MGM was known for its lions. The first one, a forty-five foot bronze statue, greeted them as soon as they walked through the golden doors. But of course, one lion was not enough. Upon entering the hotel, a larger-than-life gold statuesque lion stood proudly in the center of the rotunda. Raised on a pedestal of flowers, this golden lion acted as doorman and gave Nathan a glimpse into what was beyond the velvet ropes that lined the front desk. This elegant hotel lobby had an Art Deco theme and looked like something out of a classic Hollywood movie. Use of gold was prominent throughout the hotel. Glimmering on the ceiling were thousands of tiny gold stars. The lobby even had gold light fixtures, gold-patterned flooring, and tons of gold lions.

Enthralled by it all, Nathan circled the entire lobby to get the full effect. "Dude, look at this place. I've stayed in nice four and five-star hotels before, but this is over the top."

Andrew doubted the sincerity of Nathan's statement. "When have you ever been in a five-star hotel?"

"On vacation with my parents. My dad won't stay in any hotel that has less than four-stars. He's anal about that kind of thing."

Nathan had mentioned once that his father made good money in his medical practice, but Nathan didn't act like a spoiled rich kid and wasn't in the habit of bragging about his lifestyle. "I bet your parents own a big ass mansion."

"No, but they do own lakefront property. When basketball season is over and the weather warms up a bit, we'll take the boat out and go skiing," Nathan offered. "Do you waterski?"

"A little," Andrew said. "Haven't been in a long time though."

"We can grill up some burgers, crank some tunes, and relax on the water. It'll be fun. I'll introduce you to Mike."

Nathan and Andrew never really spent much time together off the court, other than hotel stays during road trips. Staying in hotels together was where the majority of their conversations, connections, and friendship building occurred. Although they enjoyed their hotel bonding time, hanging out in a pressure-free environment was something they both looked forward to. "Why isn't Mike playing basketball?"

"He didn't get any recruitment calls, and quite frankly I'm not sure he wants to play college ball, especially after seeing everything I had to do this year."

Much to their joy, Nathan and Andrew shared a room on this trip. With sleek, modern furnishings, a remote-controlled television, and access to free Wi-Fi, their spacious hotel room was full of wide-open possibilities.

Andrew set his athletic bag on the bed and looked out the window at the fabulous view of the city. "They definitely have us staying in style, don't they?"

Nathan leaned back on the mattress. "This is so comfortable. I'm gonna sleep like a rock here."

"That's a good thing," Andrew said. "We're going to need all the sleep we can get."

In the morning, after a hearty breakfast, a scheduled practice session ensued, proceeded by attending the USC-Arizona game at the Grand Garden Arena. During this game, both Randy and Gabby texted Nathan to inform him they had landed in Las Vegas, which meant they would be arriving at the hotel soon.

While riding the bus back to the hotel, Nathan hobbled across the aisle and sat next to his coach. "Hey, Coach."

Coach Spoleda looked away from the scouting report he was reading. "Hello, Nathan."

"What are we doing when we get back to the hotel?"

"Nothing planned until dinner. Why?"

"My parents just checked into their room. I was wondering if I could go down and visit with them for a while before we meet for dinner. They're two floors down from us."

"I don't see a problem with that," his coach proclaimed. "Just make sure you're back by 6:30. We need to talk about tomorrow's game plan."

"I'll be back by then," Nathan promised.

"Keep your phone on in case I need to reach you."

"I will. Thanks, Coach."

As soon as the bus pulled up to the hotel, Nathan headed to the fifteenth floor. Before he greeted his parents, he knocked on Gabby's door.

She answered with a huge smile on her face. "Hey you!"

"Hey!" He held her in his arms and kissed her intensely on the lips. "I have an hour and a half before I have to meet my team for dinner. Between now and then, I'm all yours." They maneuvered into the room, and Nathan closed the door with his foot.

Randy checked the time on his phone. "Didn't Nathan say he was going to stop by before dinner?"

"Maybe he got tied up with his team," Jane replied. "It does happen, Randy. He's not here on vacation you know."

"I know, but it would be nice if we could see our son while we're down here."

"We have until Saturday. It's not like any of us are going anywhere."

"True." He snuck up behind her and nibbled on her neck. "I'm thinking later tonight, after dinner, you and I need to check out the Jacuzzi, maybe order a bottle of wine."

Her whole body tingled. "Are you getting fresh with me, Doctor?"

"Maybe."

"You certainly know how to please, don't you?"

"That's my job." He leaned forward and slowly descended his lips to meet hers.

In the room next door, Nathan glanced at the clock. "Forty-five minutes to spare."

Gabby laughed at him. "Why are you so obsessed with the time?"

"Because I'm on a tight schedule. It won't look good if I'm late for our team dinner."

"You would have some explaining to do, wouldn't you?"

"Just a bit." He stroked Gabby's hair and moved it off her face. "I'm glad I got to spend a little time with you tonight. I never get to see you when we travel. Next year that will be different. Are you ready for tryouts?"

"Yup," she stated. "I feel confident. Jayden has been working with me on lifts and stunts."

Nathan had never heard that name before. "Who's Jayden?"

"A guy who's been coming to the cheer clinics. I have to have a stunt partner to try out for the coed team. He's really good. He and the other guys are experienced bases, which is good when when we do toss stunts."

Although the thought of another man looking up her cheer skirt when she stood on his shoulders made him uneasy, he felt better knowing strong, experienced men were catching her. "You're spending all of your practice time with this Jayden guy?"

Gabby knew what he was thinking. "Nathan, relax. He's just my lift partner, that's all. The only man who holds my heart is you," she reassured him. "If I make the team, I'll be doing lifts with men all the time. That's the way a coed team work."

"I know that," he stated. "And I prefer men catching you over women. It scares the hell out of me when you fly through the air like that. I cringe every time."

"And that's my point. He's good, Nathan, and I trust him."

"If you trust him then I trust him. Can I meet him?"

"Sure," Gabby said. "In fact, he and I were talking about you yesterday."

"You were?"

"Yes, and he was so excited when he found out that the Huskies' own Nathan Hanson was my boyfriend. He watches all the games and has been following you all season." Gabby giggled. "I had to laugh at him the other day when he asked if I could get you to sign a tee-shirt for him."

Nathan thought that was funny. "He acts like I'm some kind of superstar."

"He just knows you're good." She lifted her head and kissed him. "And I know you're good in many other ways."

"Oh really?" Nathan raised his eyebrows. "How good?"

She gave him a frisky smile. "The best."

He drew her a bit closer and kissed her tenderly on the lips. "I would like to see my parents before dinner."

"Can I shower first?"

He hopped to his feet and held out his hands to lift her up. "I'll shower with you."

When Nathan's mother answered the door, she greeted him with a hug. "Hi, Sweetheart."

"Hi, Mom. How was your flight?"

"Crowded," she answered.

"I'm not surprised." Giving his father an update on the tournament, Nathan said, "We're playing Arizona tomorrow."

"What time?"

"10:00 A.M."

"We'll be there."

Thursday's game against Arizona was the first in a series of challenges the Huskies had to overcome to defend their championship title. Many Huskies' players were seasoned in conference play. Some even had National Tournament experience. Brett Sorenson was one of them. He was on the PAC-12 Champion team last year team and also played for Washington when they made it into the Final Four two years prior. Although Brett was the more experienced point guard, Nathan was getting ample game time during this tournament.

He went off on Arizona Thursday night to the tune of fifteen points, then followed up by scoring twelve points in the semifinals against UCLA. The game was physically demanding, but ended with a victory for Washington, which moved them forward to face Colorado in the final game Saturday night.

When the post-season tournament began, only two PAC-12 teams had legitimate hopes of landing a bid into the big dance. One of them was Washington, the other was UCLA. With UCLA out of contention now, Colorado was part of the dance. The winner of the Washington-Colorado game would be crowned PAC-12 Champion and automatically move on to play in the Nationals during March Madness. Both teams were fighting for their NCAA Tournament lives.

The Colorado game contained all the desperation of a major title bout, and Nathan was smack in the middle of it. He went in several times throughout the first half, racking up twelve points and five assists for Washington. He got bumped by other players, poked in the eye by the opposing point guard, and almost injured himself when he ran into a foldable chair on the sidelines trying to retrieve a loose ball.

He pounded the court again at the end of the second half. Colorado attempted a scoring run, which was quickly diverted when Julian Ramirez, one of the veteran players for Washington, stole the ball. He immediately passed it across court to Geoff Foster. Geoff received the pass and tossed it to Nathan, who was all alone under the net. This ordinary play became spectacular when Nathan performed a move no one had ever seen him do before. He jumped up to the rim and slammed the ball into the net. Nathan was not a dunker, so watching him pull this off shocked not only the Husky fans in the arena, but the announcers as well.

Jane rose to her feet, awed over what she just witnessed her son do. "Oh my god, Randy. Did you see that?"

"Yes I did," he teased with a chuckle. "Damn. He is out for blood tonight."

Nathan's aggressiveness on the court continued as he took charge in another offensive run. Vocalizing and signaling to his team, Nathan and his teammates shuffled around the court. He pumped faked a pass then spun around 180 degrees, dribbling behind him to get the ball to a wide open shooter. Once in the paint, the shooter jumped up for two points. Bam! Another assist to add to his stats, and one more bucket tacked on to their now five point lead.

With under a minute left in the game, Nathan worked his magic on defense, trying to keep Colorado's point guard from affectively leading his team. In the middle of a run across the half court, Nathan fell backwards onto the hardwood, drawing a charging foul against the offense.

This brought him to the free-throw line.

Nathan was deadly accurate on the line. But in a high stakes situation like this, with millions of people watching him, his nerves were shaky. He took the ball in his hand and puffed air through his cheeks, relieving some tension. Then he dribbled twice, focused his eyes on the net, and released. Swish! He followed the same ritual on his second shot. It too went in smoothly. Two more points to add to his stats. Now, with only forty seconds left on the clock, Colorado had no hope of making up a seven point deficit. Nathan's free throws sealed the win for Washington.

This game was far from aesthetically pleasing, but Washington, who led the PAC-12 all season, maintained their championship title and snagged their slot in the NCAA National Tournament.

CHAPTER TWENTY-EIGHT

The Huskies managed to make it through the first two rounds of the NCAA Basketball Tournament, but lost to Kentucky in the Sweet Sixteen. They ended their season with a 26-6 record.

Nathan was disappointed to see the season end with a tough loss, but thrilled he would finally get to rest his battered body and spend some quality time with Gabby.

He awoke in the morning so stiff and sore he could barely move. "As much as I love basketball, I'm actually glad the season is over. My muscles are seriously fatigued, and my entire body is bruised. I need time to recuperate."

"You played hard this season," Gabby told him.

"I got my ass kicked is what happened," Nathan joked, rubbing his sore arm and showing her the brush burn on his elbow. "Some of these guys show no mercy. I've been banged around and bruised more this season than I have my whole life. I'm not sure if I was playing basketball or fighting in a boxing match."

Coach Spoleda closed out the season with a final team meeting. He gave the players a heads up on when to prepare for next year and let them take a look at the stats and bios of the new recruits who were coming in. Before they left the arena, they all cleaned out their athletic lockers.

Nathan stopped by his coach's office on the way out, at which time Coach Spoleda handed his freshman superstar a *PAC-12 Men's Basketball Champions* tee-shirt. "This was well deserved," he said. "I was very impressed with your progress this year. You jumped right in and proved to everyone that you are definitely a college caliber player. You grew tremendously both as a player and a person. You're a Husky through and through. I'm very proud of you."

"Thanks."

"It's been an honor working with you this year. I look forward to seeing what you are capable of next season."

Nathan was truly flattered by his coach's compliment. "I'm looking forward to playing for you again, Sir. I learned a lot this year. My offensive game has improved substantially."

"Yes it has. I'm glad I was able to teach you a thing or two."

"I think you're a wonderful coach. You insist we work hard, you push us to improve, and to me, you are approachable and easy to talk to," Nathan declared. "Thank you for all your help this year."

"You're very welcome. And I meant what I said about helping you in your endeavor to get into medical school. If there's anything I can do, please do not hesitate to ask."

"I will," Nathan smiled. "Thanks, Coach."

"Enjoy your off time and have a great summer, Nathan."

"You too."

As Nathan left the locker room, he ran into Andrew. They greeted each other with a knuckle bump. "Hey, man. Some of the guys are going to party it up tonight," Andrew said. "You wanna come?"

Nathan declined the invitation. "No thanks. Gabby has her second round of tryouts tonight and I want to be there to support her. I'm heading over there now."

"Mind if I join you?" Andrew asked, hoping he could catch a peek at the Huskies cheerleaders.

"Not at all."

The competitors were nervous enough without having other people watching them, so Nathan and Andrew did their best to make an unobtrusive entrance. Nathan found a seat far enough back that he was virtually unnoticeable, but in a good enough position that Gabby would know he was there.

When Gabby looked up at the stands, she acknowledged that she saw him.

"How's she doing?" Andrew asked.

"She made it through the first round yesterday, which boosted her confidence quite a bit. She's still nervous, but if she can overcome her fear long enough to show off how good she is, she'll impress the judges."

Nathan and Andrew watched as Gabby performed several dance and cheer routines to the fight song, jazz music, and the Husky drum chorale. The judges seemed impressed, and they hadn't even seen her at her best yet. Her lifts and toss stunts were next, and that is where Gabby truly shined.

As Andrew watched Gabriella perform, he became increasingly aware of her talent. "She's good."

"I told you she was," Nathan bragged. "Wait until you see her stunt routines. I don't know how she twists around like that. I get edgy watching her, though."

"Why?"

"The stunts she performs scare the hell out of me. When you see the height she gets, you'll understand why."

While Gabby and her partner prepared for their sequence of lifts and toss stunts, two other male cheerleaders formed a blanket around them. As uneasy as Gabby's toss stunts made him, Nathan couldn't help but be impressed by the level of difficulty and sheer athleticism it took to pull them off. He watched in nervous anticipation as Gabby's partner lifted her above his head, preparing to toss her into the air. "Come on, Baby. Nail this," Nathan said to himself, hoping Gabby would somehow feel his urgency.

The men formed a tighter blanket and Jayden threw her into the air. Gabby performed a double twist with a flip and ended with the splits in midair before landing safely into the arms of the three men who had committed to catching her.

"God damn, Dude," Andrew announced, a little too excitedly. "What the hell kind of acrobatic shit was that? She had to have been at least twenty feet in the air. That was some crazy height."

"See why it scares the crap out of me when she does that?" Nathan reiterated.

"It scared the hell out of me too."

At the end of tryouts, a bright smile decorated Gabby's face. Nathan could tell she felt good about her performance. She bolted over to him and threw her arms around his neck.

He squeezed her tightly. "Awesome, awesome job, Baby. You were outstanding!"

"You think so?" she asked, wanting reassurance.

"Absolutely. You totally nailed that toss."

Gabby's cheer partner strode over to them and congratulated her. "Nice job, Gabriella. I think you are a shoe in for this."

"Thanks, Jayden." Gabby used this opportunity to introduce him to Nathan.

But Jayden didn't have to be introduced. He knew the face standing in front of him all too well. "You're Nathan Hanson."

Nathan offered a firm handshake. "Yes I am."

"That dunk you knocked out in the tournament was badass."

Nathan chuckled at Jayden's flattery. "Thank you. And thank you for catching Gabby. I always worry when she's in the air like that, but she seems to trust you."

"You don't need to worry. I'm not going to let her fall."

"Oh, I'll worry," Nathan corrected, not putting as much trust into Jayden as Gabby seemed to. "I don't want her to get hurt."

"Neither do I. Trust me, she's in good hands." Before he departed, Jayden said, "Good luck, Gabriella. I'll see you tomorrow for the final list."

"Good luck to you too. Thanks again, Jayden."

Jayden flashed Gabby a flirty smile and winked at her as he left the gym.

Nathan eyed their interaction like a hawk, and he didn't like what he saw. When Jayden was out of sight, he questioned Gabby about Jayden's behavior. "He was totally sizing you up."

Gabby couldn't contain her laughter. "No, he most definitely was not."

"Yes he was. He had some serious fuck me eyes going on there."

"I'm sensing a bit of jealousy."

"Maybe I'm just not comfortable knowing he's peeking up at places he shouldn't have his eyes. I don't want to imagine the inappropriate things he's thinking about you when he's holding you above his head like that."

Gabby laughed even harder at Nathan's jealous accusation. "I promise you that is not what's he's thinking."

"Gabby, he's a guy, and you are a beautiful woman with an incredible body. I'm not stupid. I know what guys think."

She gently placed her hand on his chest. "I guarantee that isn't what he's thinking. He's not that kind of guy."

"He was ogling all over you. I saw him, Gab."

"You are completely overreacting." She tried desperately not to laugh at him. "It's nothing at all like that."

"I'm glad you find this funny," he said, frustrated with the humor she found in this.

"I'm only laughing because you are way off base. He's gay, Nathan," she boldly announced. "He's not attracted to girls, least of all me."

That remark took him by surprise. "What?"

"He's gay. He told me. And he has a boyfriend."

Nathan felt kind of foolish now for jumping to conclusions. "Why didn't you tell me this before?"

"I didn't think it mattered. I can't believe you were jealous of him. Why are you so insecure?"

"I'm not insecure," he denied. "I just don't like all these guys gawking at you with their lustful eyes. It makes me uncomfortable."

"Why?"

"I know damn well what men think when they see you, Gab. I know what they want."

"I don't care what they want. My heart belongs to you."

"And I feel extremely lucky for that. I don't deserve you," he blurted out rather recklessly.

His self-doubting demeanor disturbed her. "Why would you say that?"

"Because, I totally neglected you during the season. I acted like an arrogant jerk, and I didn't give you the attention you deserve."

She put her arms around him, trying to make him feel more secure. "Sweetie, you gave me all the attention I needed. You have things going on in your life that require you to give one hundred percent. Don't ever think you don't afford me enough attention. I'm not going to be demanding of your time. I'll take what I can get."

"But you deserve more than that."

"So do you, but we are going to make the most of this, and I am going to support you every step of the way. If that means giving you space and time to get done what you need to get done for school, then that is my gift to you. Please let me offer that to you."

"What about you?" he asked. "I want to support you too."

"You do. You came out here tonight to cheer me on, didn't you?" Gabby reminded him.

"Yes."

"You talked to your parents so I could get tickets to the tournament."

He refused to take credit for that. "But they're the ones who bought them for you."

"But they wouldn't have done it if you hadn't asked them to. Why are you making such a fuss over this?"

"I guess I got a little insecure thinking that another man might have been trying to steal you away from me."

She shook her head at his absurd assumption. "That is never going to happen. I love you."

"I love you too," he declared. "I always have." He took both of her hands in his and kissed her in the middle of the basketball court. When he was satisfied, he picked up his bag and offered his hand. "Come on. I'll buy you dinner."

She grabbed her belongings, and together they walked out of Alaska Airlines Arena.

People loved to watch the Husky cheerleaders perform. Many even suggested they create their own TV show, showing off their Husky kicks and stretches. But Nathan didn't need to attend a game or sneak in on a practice session to get a show. He received a personal Husky Kick and Stretch Show in his bedroom several times a week.

Panting from the physical exertion, Nathan rolled onto his back. His chest heaved, and a smile of complete satisfaction filled his face.

Feeling frisky, Gabby crawled on top of him, straddling his lap.

"What are you doing?" Nathan asked.

"Who says we're finished?"

"Really? You want more?"

"Always." When she leaned over to kiss him, her hair fell in his face.

He pulled it back and joined his lips to hers, sitting up so he was propped against the headboard. His hands moved gently down the length of her back then bracketed her waist, rubbing the arc of her hip bones with this thumb. Instinctively, she arched her body toward him and threw her hair back, exposing her bare breasts to him. His lips brushed her nipples as he dug his fingers into her hips, surrendering to her masterful power of seduction.

The sensation of her feminine curves intertwined with his drove him mad with want. His breath left him and a moan of ecstasy slipped through his lips. Covered in sweat, his heart pounded.

"When are they posting the list?" he panted, glancing over at the alarm clock.

"Around 1:00."

It was currently 12:27. "We should probably head over there soon."

"I want to shower first."

"So do I." He gently touched the tip of her nose with his fingertip. "But you need to get off me."

"Oh, that's charming," she said. "Whatever happened to being a gentleman?"

"My gentlemanly ways went out the window the minute you took your panties off." He stroked his fingers through her hair and touched his lips to her forehead. "Neither one of us can shower if you're sitting on me."

"You're gonna have to make me move then."

He raised an eyebrow at her. "Is that a challenge?"

"Maybe."

He tickled her waist, and she kicked and screamed trying to escape. When she was finally able to break free, she scurried toward the door. He intervened by wrapping an arm around her and pulling her onto his lap. Flesh on flesh, with almost no space between them, he could feel her heartbeat. Her body heat flowed onto him, and for a moment, he gazed at her in loving adoration.

"What?" she asked, wondering why he was staring at her.

"I love your eyes." He flattered her by kissing her eyelids. Then he slowly moved his kisses down her neck, across her collarbone, to the side of her breast. He eventually reclaimed her lips and leaned back, dragging her onto the mattress with him.

When Nathan and Gabby arrived at the gym, Jayden was just leaving. "Are you in?" Gabby asked, getting straight to the point.

"I am," Jayden boasted. "Thanks to you."

"Congratulations."

"Thank you."

Shaky with nerves, Gabby looked up at Nathan. "What if I don't make it?"

"You got this, Babe. I have no doubts." Feeling anxious, Gabby squeezed his hand. Nathan squeezed back, offering reassurance. "Come on. Let's take a look."

They stepped up to the posted list together. Gabby couldn't look. She closed her eyes and summoned a deep breath, holding it in. Turning her head a fraction, she peeked at the names on the list.

Nathan pointed to the name on the very top. "There you are, Gab. First on the list."

Her mouth dropped open and her breath became heavy. She stood in shock for a minute, letting the actuality sink in. "I did it!"

He grinned proudly. "Of course you did. I knew you would."

She threw her arms around him and he lifted her off the ground. "Thank you so much for encouraging me to do this, Nathan."

"You never should have doubted yourself."

Gabby was about to engage in a schedule very similar to Nathan's. UW cheer was a full-fledged, year-round sport, without the scholarships and abundant publicity all other sports seemed to get. On top of regularly-scheduled practices, the members of the cheerleading squad put in hours upon hours of work simply because they were dedicated to the team. Besides getting the crowd pumped up during games, they were expected to be at fundraisers, parades, and other extracurricular events.

Fall was football and volleyball season, which consisted of twelve-hour game days, a full week of homecoming activities, and several spirit events to kick off the semester. Late fall and winter, the cheerleaders were occupied with basketball games, battle of the bands, and preparing for nationals. Since the squad had no teams to cheer for in the spring, April was the time to prepare for tryouts. Summers were a big commitment with six-hour practices each day, but according to Gabby, the time commitment was the only downside of cheer.

She had always cheered courtside for Nathan when he played basketball, and not being able to do that this year made her feel like a part of her life was missing. Now that she was on the Huskies' cheer squad, she would get the opportunity to not only support the amazing Husky athletes, but to once again cheer for Nathan on the sidelines.

Monday evening, the new cheer squad met for an informal get-together and practice session. Since Nathan didn't have basketball practice, he decided to meet Gabby at the gym. When he got there, the squad members were taking turns tumbling across the floor. Nathan leaned against the wall with his hands in his pockets and watched while he waited for Gabby.

Several cheerleaders greeted him when they walked by. He acknowledged each one with a pleasant smile. While he and one of the male cheerleaders talked about basketball,

Gabby carried on a friendly conversation with a woman wearing a purple *Washington Cheer* tee-shirt. Curious to find out who this woman was, he politely excused himself and joined them on the opposite side of the gym.

The minute Gabby saw him, she reached for his hand. "We were just talking about you."

"You were?"

"Uh huh. I want you to meet someone."

Before Nathan could respond, an unknown woman jetted her hip out and lifted the corner of her mouth. "Well, if it isn't the infamous Nathan Hanson. The last time I saw you was at the high school state championship tournament in Tacoma. I was on the sidelines while you were on the court."

Nathan lowered his gaze in confusion. He had never seen this woman before, yet she acted like they were old friends. She didn't cheer with Gabby back in high school, in fact he didn't recognize her from Lake Washington High School at all. He tried to put the pieces together, thinking maybe she was a sister or a girlfriend of one of his former teammates, but nothing rang a bell. Feeling like an idiot for not knowing who she was, he said, "I'm sorry, you seem to know who I am, but I don't have the first clue who you are."

"Nathan," Gabby cut in, "This is Lizzie. She cheered for Rainier Beach."

He stared at this woman with a crooked grin. "Seriously?"

"Yes," Lizzie replied. "While Gabby was cheering for you, I was on the opposite end of the court cheering for your rivals."

Nathan cocked his head. "You don't hold any kind of grudge because we beat you guys, do you?"

Lizzie laughed. "No hard feelings at all. I couldn't believe it when Gabby told me you were her boyfriend. It is a pleasure to finally meet you."

Nathan offered a friendly handshake. "Nice meeting you too."

"I invited her to join us for dinner," Gabby said. "I hope that's ok."

"Of course it is. It will give us a chance to become better acquainted."

CHAPTER TWENTY-NINE

Nathan and Gabby were sound asleep, wrapped in each other's arms, when their slumber was disrupted by Nathan's annoyingly loud ringtone. Gabby rolled over and groaned, covering her head with a pillow.

Wearily, Nathan reached for his phone. "Hello?"

Gabby opened her drowsy eyes, wondering why someone was calling him at one o-clock in the morning. "Who is it?"

Listening closely, his eyebrows turned downward. "Where are you?"

Getting no indication from Nathan as to who he was talking to or what was happening, Gabby asked, "What's going on?"

Nathan held up his hand to shush her for a minute so he could hear the person on the other end. "What the hell are you doing there?"

Gabby may not have known what was going on, but whatever it was, Nathan was worried because he shot out of bed and rushed to get dressed.

"Stay put," he said into the phone. "I'll be there in a bit." He hung up, shoved his phone in his back pocket, then fumbled around for his wallet.

"Who was that?" Gabby asked.

"Mike. I need to go pick him up."

"Pick him up from where?"

"He's at a party at one of the frat houses. He's drunk off his ass and has no idea where his keys are, which is probably a good thing because he has no business driving in his condition."

This behavior didn't sound at all like something Mike would do. "A frat party? I thought he was with Ashley tonight."

"So did I."

Mike was one of the most laidback, down to earth people Gabby had ever known. Partying and going wild was not his style. "Since when does Mike hang out at frat parties and get drunk?"

"He doesn't." And that was Nathan's concern. "I have to go. I'll be back in a little while." He grabbed his keys and kissed her before he left.

Since Michael had no idea where he was, Nathan had to drive around Greek Row for a while before he found the right fraternity. Loud music thumped through the entire house and college students staggered around in every direction. Several people stood around with beer bottles and red plastic cups in their hands, and one person was throwing up by a nearby tree. Mike sat on the front lawn hugging his knees.

Worried about his friend, Nathan muttered, "Michael, what the hell did you do?" He got out of his car and cautiously strode onto the grass, taking a seat next to his best friend. "Hey."

Mike turned his head. "What are you doing here?"

His eyes were red and bloodshot, and his speech was slurred and incoherent. "I'm taking you home."

Nathan tried to help Mike up, but he had lost all muscle coordination. His balance was severely impaired and he stumbled over his own feet. Once Nathan was able to get him to his feet, his body began to sway from side to side. Nathan guided him to the car and buckled him in the passenger's seat. As soon as they were secure, he pulled away from the house and drove Mike home.

When Gabby heard Nathan come in, she got out of bed, slipped on some clothes, and went out to the living room to see what she could do to help.

Nathan led Mike inside the apartment, which turned out to be much more challenging than he anticipated simply because Mike was several inches taller than he was and wasn't able to stand on his own.

"Is he ok?" Gabby asked, closing the front door.

Nathan eased Mike onto the couch, placing a pillow under his head. "Get his shoes."

Gabby removed Mike's sneakers and lifted his feet onto the sofa.

"Can you go in his room and grab a blanket, please?"

"Sure."

While Gabby went to fetch a blanket, Nathan grabbed a wastebasket and set it beside the couch in case Mike felt the urge to throw up.

Michael groaned and rolled over.

"Lie down," Nathan said, encouraging him to rest. "Just relax."

Gabby returned to the room and handed Nathan the blanket. Nathan, in turn, covered Mike up, making sure he was comfortable, and left him there to rest. Genuinely concerned about his friend, he exhaled with a thick sigh. "What the hell did he get himself into? And where is Ashley?"

"I have no idea," Gabby replied. "She told me she and Mike were going out tonight, but she never said they were going to a frat party."

Nathan shook his head, appalled by this erratic behavior from his best friend. "Has Ashley been to parties like this before?"

Gabby shrugged. "I don't know. She's never said anything to me about it."

Nathan pondered for a moment. "I wonder what possessed him to go there tonight? That's not something he would normally do."

Several times throughout the night, Nathan crawled out of bed to check on Mike, who remained sound asleep on the couch. He didn't really show any signs of life until about 10:00 A.M.. "Gab?" Nathan called to her.

Gabby emerged from the bedroom. "Yes?"

"Do me a favor. Go over to your place and see if Ashley is over there."

"Alright." She looked over at Mike, worried about his wellbeing. "Is he gonna be ok?"

"I think so. He's not going to feel very well when he finally wakes up though."

"No, probably not." She slipped on her shoes and gave Nathan a kiss. "I'll call you in a bit."

"Thanks."

After Gabby left, Nathan poured a glass of orange juice for himself. As he was about to take a drink, Mike rolled over and opened his eyes. "Good morning," Nathan said.

Holding his throbbing head in his hands, Mike groaned in agony. "Son of a bitch. My fucking head is killing me." His tongue was extremely dry, and the bright light from the kitchen made his eyes burn. "What the hell happened last night?"

"I was hoping you could tell me." Nathan grabbed a water bottle out of the fridge and brought it into the living room.

Mike slowly sat up, trying to keep the room from spinning. "I have got to get this nasty taste out of my mouth."

Nathan handed the bottle to Mike, who immediately chugged down half of it.

"Do you remember anything?" Nathan asked, hoping to gain some insights about Mike's physical condition.

"Ashley and I planned to go to a movie last night, but she decided she wanted to check out this party instead. When we got there, we both drank a few beers, but all I remember after that was her hanging all over some guy in a

Seahawks shirt. About ten minutes later, the two of them went upstairs. I didn't see her for the rest of the night." Mike felt around his pockets. "Shit. Where the hell are my keys?"

"You lost them last night."

"And where the fuck is my phone?"

"It's sitting on the kitchen counter," Nathan assured him. "How did you get yourself stuck in the middle of a frat party? And why in god's name were you drinking like that?"

Mike tried to explain, "It was Ashley, man. She promised we'd only stop by for a little while. I couldn't very well tell her no, could I?"

"Yes, and you should have. She doesn't control you, Mike." Nathan's phone rang. It was Gabby.

"Ashley's not over here," Gabby declared. "It looks like she's been gone all night."

"Have you heard from her? Has anyone seen her?"

"I talked to a few people, but no one has seen her since yesterday afternoon."

Nathan pursed his lips together. "Alright, come back over here. We'll figure something out." He hung up his phone and tried to get more information from Mike. "Have you heard from Ashley?"

"No, and I don't know where she is," he said, carrying a bitter tone. "She ditched me last night. She begged me to take her to this frat party, got me drunk, then took off with some dude."

"You know what she was doing when she went upstairs with him, don't you?"

Mike snickered cynically. "Of course I do. I'm not stupid. That bitch is fuckin' history."

Mike spent the majority of the day battling fatigue and drinking so much water and Gatorade, Nathan thought he was going to start seeping orange sport drink out his pores. He slept most of the afternoon and couldn't even look at food without throwing up.

While Mike slept, Nathan went back over to the frat house to see if he could recover Mike's missing keys. Gabby went with him.

Nathan pulled up to the curb and took a moment to examine his surroundings. This place looked much different today than it did last night. It actually looked like a civilized domicile instead of a chaotic congregation of drunken college students roaming aimlessly across the front yard. Several cars were parked out front, including Mike's. Now all Nathan needed was the keys. "I'll be right back," he said to Gabby.

"Please be careful."

He stepped out of the car and walked up to the front porch. When he knocked, a very large man, probably only a year or two older than him, stood in the doorway. He stared at Nathan for a minute, trying to figure out who this person on his front porch was.

But before Nathan could say anything, this gargantuan man grinned stupidly and said, "Dude! You're that dude!"

Nathan had no idea what this guy was talking about. "Excuse me?"

"You're that basketball player who made that badass dunk in the playoffs. You should have been at our party last night, man. It was totally awesome!"

Obviously, this guy was not the sharpest tool in the shed. Nathan wondered if he was normally this apish or if he still had alcohol in his system which made him sound like a total moron. "I wasn't, but a friend of mine was. His car is parked out front, but he seems to have misplaced his keys. Did you guys find any lying around?"

"We have five sets. Wanna come in and check them out? I'll shoot you a brew."

Nathan refused. "I'll wait out here, thank you."

"You sure?"

"Yes." Nathan waited on the front porch until this man returned with a plastic bowl full of keys. He reached for a set with a basketball dangling off the key ring. "These are his. Thank you."

"You sure you don't wanna come in and have a brewskie, Dude?" the man insisted.

"No, thank you. I'm good. But thanks for your help."

"No problem." As Nathan walked away, this man yelled, "The Dawg Pack rules!"

This guy was incredibly loud and obnoxious. He reminded Nathan of those idiots in movies or TV sitcoms who dance around with bulging bellies sucking beer from beer bong hats. Nathan laughed as he returned to the car.

"What is so funny?" Gabby asked, seeing the smug grin Nathan wore.

"That guy has lost a few brain cells."

"Who?"

"The dumbass standing on the porch."

Gabby looked over at the guy, who was pumping his fists and shouting, "Woot, woot. Go Huskies!" She laughed at his ridiculous behavior.

Nathan handed Gabby his car keys. "Let's get the hell out of here."

"Why are you giving me your keys?"

"Because you are driving the Mustang back. I'm going to take Mike's car."

"I get to drive your car?"

"Yup." He leaned over and kissed her. "I'll see you back at the apartment."

Mike awoke the next morning feeling better physically, but worn emotionally. In the last two years he had been involved in five semi-serious relationships, all of which ended badly. His first girlfriend, Victoria, faulted him for getting too serious and ended their relationship only two months after it began. The next girl he dated, Jackie, told him she didn't like his smartass attitude, didn't think he was funny, and picked a huge fight with him in front of all of his friends, all because he was lovingly teasing her. His relationship with Rachel, the longest he'd had to date, ended with her saying she needed to expand her horizons and find someone more intellectual. That one ripped his heart out and seriously bruised his ego. The next girl, Emily, accused him of neglecting her when he failed to text her one day because his phone died. And Ashley just flat out cheated on him. Mike had always been on the receiving end of a break up, but this time he was the one ending the relationship.

When Gabby came over that night, Mike asked, "Is Ashley over at your place?"

"Yes," Gabby replied.

Mike picked up his keys and shoved them in his pocket. "I'm going to head over there. I won't be long."

"Good luck," Nathan said.

As Mike stepped out the door, Gabby asked, "What's going on?"

Nathan shook his head. "I'm not sure I should tell you. I think we should wait until Mike gets back and let him tell you."

But Gabby didn't have to wait. She put the pieces together and figured it out herself. "He's breaking up with her, isn't he?"

"He needs to, Gab. She's not good for him, and he knows that. As much as he may like her, she's dragging him into situations he otherwise would never be a part of. And the cold hard truth is she cheated on him. That's really the bottom line…and the last straw for him. He'd been contemplating breaking up with her for a while. This weekend sealed that fate."

"You never told me this," Gabby complained.

"It wasn't my place to tell you. There are certain things Mike and I talk about that stay between us, Gab. Don't take it personally."

"I don't. I am kinda surprised it's taken him this long though. She's really not his type."

Nathan chuckled. "No she is not. Not at all."

Knowing Ashley was alone, Mike headed upstairs to her room. Dreading this encounter, he took a big breath to calm himself before he knocked on the door.

Ashley answered, surprised to see him. "I wasn't expecting you tonight. What are you doing here?"

"I need to talk to you."

She opened the door and invited him inside. "Do you want to sit down?"

Mike stood stiffly, declining her invitation. "No thank you. I'm not staying long."

Ashley sat down instead. "What's up?"

He bluntly stated what was on his mind. "I don't think we should see each other anymore."

"Why not?"

Mike spelled it out for her. "Because when I'm with you, I always seem to end up in compromising situations. You drug my to a party this weekend then took off with another guy. I can't be with someone who one, expects me to constantly satisfy her lust for excitement. And two, thinks it is perfectly ok to sleep around while she's involved with me."

Ashley looked at him with begging eyes. "I was drunk, Mike. It meant nothing."

"It wasn't just that. It's our whole relationship. It's dragging me down, and quite frankly, I don't trust you." Mike looked her in the eye and said, "We're done. Please don't call me, don't text me, don't come over to my apartment, and do not drag Nathan or Gabriella into this."

"Gabby's my roommate," Ashley argued with snippiness in her tone.

"She's also my best friend's girlfriend, and someone I have known a hell of lot longer than you have. I have the upmost respect for Gabby. I will not have her caught in the middle of this."

Ashley glared at him with a snarl on her face. "Get out of my room."

Mike didn't hesitate. He left the building and never looked back.

When Mike returned to the apartment, Gabby offered her sympathies. "You alright?"

"I'll be alright." Mike sat on a stool at the kitchen island. "I wasn't happy with her. I felt used and abused. Can't stay in a relationship when I feel like that."

"I agree," Nathan said. "And honestly, Mike, you two really didn't have anything in common."

"I know," Mike chuckled a little. "Her idea of a good time is drinking beer and eating chili dogs at Monster Truck races. Guess that's the only entertainment they have in small town Utah."

Trying to cheer Mike up, Gabby teased, "That and watching the salt flats get salty."

After talking to Nathan and Gabby, Mike felt much better about this situation. "You guys wanna catch a movie or something?"

"Sure," Nathan replied. "Let me grab my keys."

CHAPTER THIRTY

Mike popped the top on his soda. "How do you and Gabby do it?" he asked Nathan. "You two genuinely love each other and no matter what, you always manage to make things work out between you. Your closeness and commitment to one another is absolute and unconditional. I want a relationship like that."

"It's not that hard," Nathan proclaimed.

"For you, maybe. But I can't seem to figure it out."

"Relationships build from trust and a genuine understanding of one another. That isn't something you can develop overnight. It takes time."

Frustrated with the whole dating scene, Mike plopped down on the couch and flipped on the TV. "Seems like girls don't want to take the time for that."

"The right girl will. It's all about communication. You have to talk to each other and develop a trusting friendship. How long did Gabby and I know each other before we started dating?"

"Three years," Mike replied.

"Exactly. It all starts there. You have to be friends before a romantic relationship can develop." Nathan reached into the refrigerator and pulled out a Pepsi, joining Mike in the living room. "Speaking of which, there's someone Gabby and I want you to meet."

"Female?"

"Yes," Nathan confirmed

Mike shook his head, skeptical about the whole thing. "I don't know, man."

"She's Gabby's friend. Gab wants to invite her to my parents' house next weekend." Nathan already made plans for Mike and Andrew to join them for waterskiing, barbecue, and to hang out on the beach. He hoped Gabby's friend would come too. More so, Nathan wanted Michael to be open about meeting this girl. "I think you'll really like her."

Mike had already planned on coming, but knowing now that Nathan was trying to set him up gave him a different attitude about their weekend plans. "I'm not sure I want to throw my heart out there again."

"You have nothing to lose here. She's nice, she's easy to talk to, and she's fun. You don't have to jump into anything romantic. Just hang out with her, be her friend. You never know, something more may develop."

"And it may not," Mike claimed, not quite as enthusiastic as Nathan was.

"No, it might not. But you don't have to be romantically involved with every woman you meet," Nathan explained. "If you don't like her, you don't ever have to see her again. But you may gain a friend out of it. Regardless, you've lost nothing."

Mike still wasn't convinced.

Trying to persuade him, Nathan said, "She really wants to meet you."

Nathan was certainly persistent. "What's her name?"

"Elizabeth, but everyone calls her Lizzie."

"She a cheerleader?"

"Yup. She's on the squad with Gabby." Nathan grinned, trying to read Mike's thoughts. "So, what do you think?"

He decided to be more open-minded and give it a shot. "Alright."

"Sweet," Nathan said excitedly. "Next weekend is gonna be awesome!"

Anticipating the arrival of his friends, Nathan gathered ski equipment on the beach behind his parents' house and prepared the boat for a day on the water.

His father came out to offer assistance. "Hey, Nate"

"Hey, Dad," Nathan replied, trying to untangle the ski rope.

Randy grabbed the other end to help disentangle it. "Who's coming over today?"

"Gabby, Mike, one of Gabby's friends, and one of my teammates."

"Haven't seen Mike in a while. How's he doing?"

"He's doing ok," Nathan stated. "His grades aren't that great, and his dad's been giving him a hard time about it. He likes his job though. The hours are pretty flexible and the pay is decent."

"That's good."

"He's a little bummed about the whole relationship thing," Nathan declared.

"Why?" Randy asked curiously. "What's going on?"

"He just broke up with another girlfriend."

Michael had many girlfriends in high school, but had trouble sustaining meaningful relationships with any of them. The fact that he had been through yet another break up really wasn't surprising. "Again?" Randy questioned.

"This one totally cheated on him. She took him to a party, got drunk, then ditched him for another guy. I didn't think she was good for him anyway. She was a drama queen and tried to make him into her personal party toy."

"Wow! He doesn't seem to have much luck with girls does he?" Randy asked.

"He has a problem with jumping in too fast. He commits to a relationship before he even gets to know the girl and usually ends up drowning because of it."

"Well, that's not gonna work," Randy said. "Gotta be friends before you jump onto the love boat."

"That's what I told him. He needs to understand that just because she's a female doesn't mean he has to be romantically involved with her. It is possible to be friends with girls. I have a lot of friends who are women."

"As do I," Randy added. "Having a friend who is a girl is a lot different than having a girlfriend." He rolled up the rope and handed it to Nathan. "Speaking of which, how's Gabby?"

"Couldn't be better. She's excited about cheering again. She's missed it."

"I bet she has."

"That spark is back in her eyes. She denies it ever left, but I know better. She's happier when she's cheering. I can't wait to see her in that Washington cheering uniform."

Nathan's lustful, dream-like gaze made Randy laugh. "Why does that not surprise me?"

"I can't help it," Nathan argued. "Gabby is a beautiful woman, and she looks hot in a cheering uniform. She turns me on in many ways."

"Most guys your age have a different girlfriend every month, but you and Gabby have been together for several years now. I didn't even have a girlfriend when I was your age. I was totally into the dating scene, but didn't want a commitment of any kind."

This information kind of surprised him. "Really?"

"Oh hell no. I was too involved with myself and striving towards my goals to worry about maintaining a relationship. I was not at all interested in that."

"What about Mom?" Nathan wondered.

"I didn't meet your mom until I was twenty-three, and I wasn't planning on having a serious relationship with her."

"What do you mean?"

"I'm going to confess something about myself that I'm not particularly proud of," Randy admitted. "In college, I was the king of one night stands."

Nathan didn't believe him. "No way."

"Ask Jim if you don't believe me. I dated so many women, and most of them ended up in my apartment afterwards. Honestly, Nathan, I don't even remember their names now."

Nathan gawked at his father, a bit ashamed of him. "Dad!"

"I know. I told you I wasn't proud of it." Randy paused for a minute and grinned. "Then I met your mother. She was different. She hit me like a ton of bricks, and no matter how hard I tried, I couldn't fight the way I felt about her. I knew I was in love with her, I just didn't want to admit it."

"Why not?"

Randy shrugged. "I don't know. At the time I wasn't sure I was ready to make that kind of commitment. I was too wrapped up in medical school and really didn't want to be distracted by a relationship. But one night, when your mom and I went to a dance club, I held her in my arms and looked into her eyes. Her lips were so enticing, and with that smile of hers, she drove me crazy. That night was the first time I kissed her. There was no turning back for me after that. I was hooked. We've been together ever since."

"You never told me that story before," Nathan said.

"Didn't seem relevant at the time. But on a similar note, I've witnessed yours and Gabby's relationship grow over the last few years. There's no doubt in my mind that you love her, Nathan."

Grinning blissfully, Nathan explained, "I've always loved her, Dad."

The spark in their relationship continued to grow every day. Today was no exception. "How far away are you?" Nathan asked Gabby over the phone.

"Probably about fifteen minutes. Do you need us to pick up anything?" she asked.

"Can you grab a bag of ice for the cooler?"

"Sure," Gabby replied.

"Thanks. Love you, Gab. See you soon." Nathan put his phone back in his pocket and continued to prep the boat. He placed ski vests in the back storage compartment, put a cooler full of sodas by the stern, and had tunes plugged into the dash so they could rock out while they enjoyed the warm spring weather.

When Mike showed up, he and Nathan greeted each other with a knuckle bump. "What's going on?"

Nathan tossed some towels into the boat and stuck the orange flag next to one of the seats. "Looking forward to chillin' today."

"Me too," Mike concurred.

"Andrew just texted me; he's on his way. And Gabby and Lizzie will be here in about fifteen minutes."

"Cool," Mike said, tossing his athletic bag into the back of the boat. "Has Andrew ever been skiing before?"

"Yes, but it's been a while," Nathan replied. "He's looking forward to meeting you, by the way. But with our basketball schedule, finding time to do that was kind of difficult."

"True." Mike helped Nathan load skis into the boat then sat in the sand waiting for the girls. "Tell me more about this Lizzie chick."

"She already knows who you are."

Mike cocked his head. "How is that possible?"

"She was a cheerleader for Rainer Beach and, believe it or not, she was at the state tournament cheering for them during the finals."

This made Michael laugh. "No shit?"

"Yup. Small world, isn't it?"

"Yeah it is."

"Gabby and I were talking about you the other day, and she kinda got a funny look on her face. She called you the guy who stole the trophy away from them and blamed you for their loss."

Mike rolled his eyes. "Oh, great."

"It's cool. That was high school. She's on our team now. Proud and true purple and gold. Anyway, when I first met Lizzie, she immediately knew who I was. When she found out you were my best friend, she thought it was funny how a year ago she was cheering against us."

"That is kinda crazy."

Just as Mike said that, Gabby and Lizzie trotted down to the beach dressed in bikini tops and shorts, each carrying a bag of ice. "Well, look who's here," Nathan declared, greeting Gabby with a kiss.

Gabby handed the bag to Nathan "This ice is really cold."

"Thanks for picking it up." He opened the bag and dumped it inside the cooler atop soda cans and water bottles.

Mike glanced over at Lizzie, sizing her up from head to toe. She was pretty, had a fit, curvy figure, and a smile that could brighten any room even on the darkest of days. "You must be Lizzie."

"And you, Sir, are the man who jumpshot your way to the most upsetting victory in high school basketball history," Lizzie stated boldly.

"I suppose you could put it that way. Although Hanson is to blame too. He passed me the ball."

"I know, and it was a tremendous play." She held out an open palm. "Pleased to meet you, Michael Lynott."

Mike gladly gripped her hand. "Well, this hardly seems fair. You know my full name, but I don't know yours."

"It's Magnusen," she replied. "Lizzie Magnusen."

Mike smiled at her. "It's a pleasure to meet you, Lizzie Magnusen."

Mike was a nice person with a courteous, friendly nature. He had a lighter side to his personality that she hadn't seen on the basketball court over a year ago.

Anxious to get in the water, Nathan announced, "We have tunes, we have ski gear, we have a boat, we have a cooler full of provisions. The only thing missing is

Andrew." He checked the time on his watch. "Where is he?"

"Yo!" Andrew called out, checking out the stellar view and spectacular elegance of the Hanson's home. "This is a nice pad." He spotted Mike and offered a friendly handshake. "Andrew Garibay. I've heard a lot about you."

"Don't believe everything Nathan tells you."

"I don't believe a damn thing he tells me."

This comment made Mike laugh.

"So," Nathan cut in. "Who wants to go skiing?"

Everyone hopped in the boat and caked sunscreen on their winter-induced ghostly white bodies while Nathan revved up the motor. The engine buzzed and the propeller churned the water below. He carefully backed the boat away from the dock and sped off across the lake.

The five of them took turns skiing, starting from the water. They shared spotting responsibilities, and every time Nathan took a run, Mike took over the throttle. The friends had the best time together, laughing, sharing stories, and blasting their favorite songs. They took a break from skiing for a while and parked the boat in the middle of the lake.

"Are you serious?" Mike asked, thinking Nathan's story was hilarious.

"Yeah, I'm serious. He beat the crap out of him," Nathan added.

"Who beats up a mascot, especially since he's just a dude in an oversized fluff suit?" Mike asked. "Jackass must have been high or something."

Andrew interjected, "The mascot wasn't even the team we were playing against that day. The stupid idiot was punching the wrong team's mascot."

"Did he get fined or something?" Mike asked.

"He got his ass escorted out of the arena by security."

"And the guy in the mascot suit ended up in the hospital with a fractured jaw and a broken nose," Nathan clarified.

Thinking this was the oddest, most ridiculous thing he'd ever heard, Mike said, "There's an extreme fan for you."

"That's not extreme," Gabby stated. "That's just stupid."

"Some people really take college basketball too seriously, don't they?" Lizzie remarked.

"I guess so," Mike concluded.

"I understand serious fans, but that guy was a psycho," Andrew concluded.

Nathan agreed. "If he wouldn't have been kicked out, I think the fans would have turned on him."

When her favorite song came on, Lizzie hopped to her feet and reached for the volume control on the stereo. "I love this song!" She turned it way up and sang at the top of her lungs.

Gabby joined her.

Nathan always enjoyed hanging out with Gabby. Even before they started dating, he made excuses to spend time with her simply because he loved her lighthearted and playful nature. She was spunky and spirited and fun to be around. She often let her 'fun side' come out, yet at the same time she could be serious when he needed her to be. Seeing Gabby acting silly, shaking her booty to the music, and singing in a loud, off-key yelp made Nathan smile. He absolutely adored her.

After expressing herself unflinchingly, Lizzie plopped herself down on the seat right next to Michael. "We need to go dancing," she suggested.

Mike started laughing. "Evidently you have never seen me dance. That sight would get you to change your mind real quick."

"You're not any worse than I am," Nathan said.

Gabby begged to differ. "You're not that bad, Nathan."

Nathan almost rolled out of his seat. "Do you pay attention when we go dancing? I'm like a fish out of water, flopping around on the floor while you're smokin' up the dance floor. I don't hold a candle next to you out there."

"You're not that bad," she repeated. "You also haven't taken all the dance classes I have."

"You know who's a good dancer?" Nathan remarked, shifting the conversation. "My sister. Lacy totally rocks on the dance floor."

"Yeah she does," Mike concurred.

"You never told me your sister was a dancer," Andrew said.

"Lacy is," Nathan explained. "And she's a badass. Lauren is talented too. She's an actress and has a hell of a voice. That girl can sing."

Gabby offered her opinion. "I tried to talk Lacy into joining the cheer squad, but she said she wasn't interested."

"That's because she's a dancer, Gab, not a gymnast. You, on the other hand, are an acrobat."

"Dude!" Andrew exclaimed, directing his attention to Gabby. "You get some mad height on your tosses. I watched you at your tryout. You rocked it!"

Gabby tittered at his flattery. "Thank you. Nathan doesn't like it when I do toss stunts."

"The only reason I don't like it is because I fear you will be dropped," Nathan said. "I don't want you to get hurt."

She leaned over to kiss him. "Thank you for your concern."

"We do need to go dancing though," Lizzie reiterated. "It'll be fun."

"I'm in." Gabby turned to Mike wanting his opinion. "What about you?"

Mike chuckled. "I'm in if Nathan is."

Everyone waited for Nathan's response. "I'm in, only because I want to mess with Mike on the dance floor."

"Good," Gabby said. "Next weekend is covered."

When the friends returned to shore, Andrew headed home for the night, but Nathan, Gabby, Michael, and Lizzie stoked up the barbecue and prepared burgers to appease their hunger-laden bodies. As the sun began to set, the four friends relaxed on the beach with sodas and water bottles. The lights of Seattle reflected off the lake and a distant motorboat gracefully slid over the water. Since the air was a little chilly, they all slipped on sweats and sweatshirts to stay warm. They arranged lawn chairs in a circle and leaned back to chat.

"We definitely need to do this more often," Mike declared.

Nathan couldn't have agreed more. "I am totally with you on that. This is a nice break from school and basketball."

Lizzie sat upright in her lawn chair and crossed her legs. "Speaking of basketball," she directed at Mike. "How come you aren't playing for UW?"

Mike had made the choice not to pursue college basketball. His SAT scores were only mediocre, and he didn't have the best grade point average in high school. Maintaining the required GPA to remain in athletics was always something he struggled with. Now that he was accepted into college, he wanted to focus on his classes and not worry about the added stress of basketball. "Playing NCAA was always Nathan's thing, not mine. Besides, trying to play while in college would be too much to deal with. It's a lot of work and takes a lot more dedication than I'm willing to put in to it. I don't know how Nathan keeps up with it all."

"How long have you two known each other?" Lizzie asked, curious about the friendship Nathan and Mike had.

Mike looked over at Nathan. "Since we were, what, six?"

"Yup," Nathan answered. "We met through peewee basketball."

"His mom was our coach," Mike added with a slight chuckle.

Lizzie asked, "Your mom is a basketball coach?"

"She was," Nathan explained. "Now she's focusing on her sports psychology practice."

She turned her attention to Mike again. "You should be a basketball coach. You'd be good at something like that."

"Coaching basketball?" Mike asked.

"Yes. You have the type of personality that is ideal for coaching. You're even-tempered, competitive, easy to talk to. Athletes need a coach who is approachable, but one will also push them to win."

"Actually, it's interesting you said that, because although my dad doesn't agree with me, I've considered taking this Health degree I'm pursuing into the education domain and get my high school teaching certificate and coaching credentials."

"I think you should." Lizzie casually took a sip of her water, glancing at Mike over the lip of her bottle.

It was cute to watch the interaction between Mike and Lizzie. They were playful with each other, had a lot to talk about, and their personalities meshed well. They'd been laughing and joking around together all day and seemed to really enjoy each other's company. Nathan hoped something more than friendship would develop between them. His only concern was that Mike had a tendency to jump in too quickly. Maybe this time he would take it slow and let the relationship develop naturally.

CHAPTER THIRTY-ONE

This year Dr. Randal Hanson was celebrating his fiftieth birthday. His family had many things planned for this event. Among these was a surprise party in which Jane arranged for family members and all of his closest friends to attend. His children designed a birthday cake for him, which, in order to prevent Randy from seeing it, Nathan agreed to pick up from the bakery on the way to his parents' house Friday afternoon.

Greg was off that day, therefore Randy was the only doctor in the clinic. He was exceptionally busy, and by noon, he was running about twenty minutes behind. With Randy swamped at work, Jane spent the afternoon hanging decorations, preparing food, making a pitcher of iced tea, and purchasing cases of soda and six packs of Corona for the hordes of people who were about to invade her home. With everything she had to do, she needed a bit more time to prepare. Somehow, she had to stall Randy. To accomplish this, she instilled the help of his parents.

Randy's father had been coming down with an illness for a few days now. He was about ready to pick up some medications for it, but instead, Randy's mother used this as a diversion.

When Randy saw he had missed a call from his mother, the first available break he had, he called her back. "Hey, Mom. You rang?"

"Hi, Honey. I need you to come over here and take a look at your father."

"Why? What's wrong?"

"He's coming down with something, and he refuses to see a doctor."

This was not unusual behavior from his father. Dr. Mark Hanson was extremely stubborn when it came to necessary doctor visits. "That figures. I'm with patients right now, but I'll stop by on my way home."

"Thanks, Sweetheart."

Randy's sister, Stephanie, was finishing up last minute paperwork and shutting down the clinic when Randy stepped out to the lobby. "What a busy day," he said.

"Some days are like that."

"Some days?" he scoffed. "Most days are." He glanced at the clock. 5:28 P.M., which meant he'd be stuck in rush hour traffic on his drive home. "I'm gonna run over to Mom and Dad's house. Mom says Dad's coming down with something."

Stephanie was in on the plan to stall her brother, so she played along. "I hope he's ok."

"From what Mom told me, it doesn't sound too serious. I'll keep you posted." He removed his stethoscope from around his neck and pulled his car keys out of his pocket. "Have a good weekend, Steph. Thanks for all of your help today."

"No problem," she smiled. "Drive safely."

"Will do." Randy had to fight his way through stop-and-go traffic over the Evergreen Bridge and across the lake to Kirkland, where both he and his parents lived. He drove straight to his parents' house, pulled the Jaguar into the driveway, and shut off the ignition. He picked up his stethoscope from the passenger seat and stepped out of the car. Whistling cheerfully, he beeped his car alarm and made his way to his parents' front door, knocking with a rhythmic rap.

His mother greeted him with a hug. "Thank you for coming, Honey."

"It's no problem." Randy stepped inside. "Where's Dad?"

"He's in the kitchen."

Randy headed that direction. He found his father sitting at the kitchen table sipping on a cup of coffee with a newspaper in his hand. "I hope that's decaffeinated you're drinking, Dr. Hanson," Randy teased.

His father looked up. "Hello, Randal."

Randy sat in the chair across from him. "You know coffee isn't good for you, especially if you're sick."

Mark Hanson found his son's comment amusing. "That's a hypocritical thing for you to say. You are the biggest coffee addict I know."

"Yes, but I'm not sick," Randy tried to justify. "Mom tells me you are."

Downgrading the situation, Mark shook his head. "I'm fine." He coughed slightly and grabbed a tissue to blow his nose.

"You're stuffed up."

"It's just a cold."

"Sounds like more than a cold to me." Randy rose to his feet and washed his hands at the kitchen sink.

"You came all the way over here for a little sniffle?"

"No. I came over here because I'm concerned about you, and so is Mom. She wouldn't have called if she thought all you had was a cold." Randy dried his hands with a paper towel and turned off the water. Knowing his parents' house well, he reached into a drawer in the kitchen where his mother stored the thermometer and brought it to his father. "For my own reassurance, put this under your tongue. If there's nothing wrong with you, you can rub it in my face and say I told you so."

Mark chuckled at his son's persistence. "I'm not sure who's more stubborn about this, you or your mother."

"We care about you, Dad. Now humor me please." While the thermometer was under his father's tongue, Randy placed the bell of his stethoscope on his father's chest. His lungs sounded clear. When the thermometer beeped, Randy checked his temperature. He had a slight fever. "Nothing a little Mucinex can't cure."

"I told you I was fine."

Randy wrapped up his stethoscope, put the thermometer back in the drawer, and re-sanitized his hands. "You need to get some rest."

"In case you have forgotten, my boy, I was a doctor well before you were even conceived. I think I know what my body needs."

"But just because you know what your body needs doesn't mean you'll take your own advice. Are you going to get some rest, or am I going to have to force you to?"

Mark burst out laughing. "That I would like to see. Now go home. I'm fine."

Randy grinned at his father. "Alright. But take care of yourself, and drink something other than coffee, please."

He blew off his son's comment and shooed him toward the door. "Go home."

"Love ya, Dad."

"Love you too, Son."

Randy left his parents' house and headed home. When he pulled into his driveway, several cars, many of which he recognized, were parked by the curb in front of his house. He didn't recall having any plans tonight, but then again, Jane sometimes invited people over on a whim. He gathered his belongings and walked into the house. Several of his friends, his wife, and his kids were all gathered in his living room. Wondering what all the hype was about, Randy asked, "What's all this?"

All of the people in the house spontaneously shouted, "Happy birthday!"

This was not at all what Randy expected. How his family managed to pull this off without him knowing about it took strategic planning and cunning sneakiness. "Wow! Thank you."

A layered cake, decorated with fondant images of a pill box, dentures, hemorrhoid cream, and a handicapped parking sign, sat in the center of the table ready to be sliced. Printed on the top were the words *Happy Birthday, Dad*. Black and silver balloons and streamers were strung throughout the house and his dearest friends stood in a huddle around the table. Among them were two of his best friends from medical school, Bruce and Amanda Buckman.

Randy grinned when he saw them. They exchanged pleasantries, greeting each other with hugs, before Randy asked, "What's new?"

Bruce updated him. "Mandy's practice is growing nicely. She's pretty much the busiest and most talked about pediatrician in Santa Monica."

Amanda didn't share his enthusiasm. "It's not that big of a deal."

Bruce laughed at her modest analysis. "It is a big deal. You're just too modest to admit it."

Jim, having also been a part of this social group during their medical school years, joined in the conversation. "How's life in the land of neurosurgery?"

"Performed a craniotomy and clipped off an aneurism yesterday," Bruce replied. "How's the ER treating you?"

"Busier than hell."

Bruce snorted derisively. "Story of my life."

Around midnight, guests began to head home. Since Bruce and Mandy were staying in Randy's guestroom for the weekend, the two men made themselves comfortable in the living room. Besides being close friends who triumphed over medical school together, Randy Hanson and Bruce Buckman had a history. They were once brother-in-laws, back when Bruce was married to Randy's sister, and two of Randy's nieces shared Bruce's last name. To Randy, Bruce was more like a brother.

Enjoying a moment of peace, Randy sat in the recliner with a cup of coffee in his hand. "Has your schedule settled down at all?"

Bruce kicked off his shoes, and leaned back. "No. I worked ninety hours last week and had to beg, borrow, and steal to get a few days off to come up here. When I'm one of the only neurosurgeons within a hundred mile radius, the head of surgery is reluctant to let me leave."

"Bet the money is nice though," Randy assumed.

"It is," Bruce replied. "But with two kids in college next year, Mandy and I will need every penny."

"I hear ya. Nathan has a full ride, so we aren't really paying for much as far as he's concerned, but I'm gonna have two girls in college while Nathan is in medical school. That's gonna clean out the bank account, especially since Lauren is seriously looking at Juilliard."

"Juilliard, huh?" Bruce arched his eyebrows. "Good for her."

"Yes, good for her," Randy said. "But not so good for the pocketbook. And Lacy wants Columbia's dance program. I'm gonna go bankrupt paying for school for the kids."

Bruce had to laugh.

"Where's Nikki this weekend?" Nicole Buckman was Bruce and Mandy's daughter. She was the youngest of their three girls.

"She's with Mandy's parents, which she loves because they spoil her."

"I bet they do," Randy chuckled. "You gonna see Alyssa this weekend?" Alyssa Buckman was the middle child. She lived with Stephanie in Seattle most of the year, with the exception of summer months, Spring break, and every other Christmas. During that time, she was in Santa Monica with Bruce and Mandy.

"Yup. I've already made arrangements with Stephanie to spend the day with her tomorrow. Alyssa loves artsy stuff, so Mandy and I are going to pick her up for lunch, walk around Olympic Sculpture Park, and check out the Seattle Art Museum."

Being a local resident who grew up in Seattle, Randy was well acquainted with the culture, cuisine, and natural beauty of the emerald city. "You need to take her to Chihuly Garden and Glass. It's a huge showroom for a local glassmaker, and there's a great restaurant there to have lunch. It's pretty cool."

Grateful for the suggestion, Bruce replied, "Thanks. She'll love that."

"Sounds like you guys are going to have fun tomorrow."

"Yup. We're looking forward to it."

Before the Buckmans reported to the airport for their return flight to Santa Monica, Randy, Jim, and Bruce got together for a game of basketball. They invited Nathan and Mike to join them. The two young men came over Sunday morning wearing basketball attire; Nathan even brought his ball. Together, the five men made their way to Peter Kirk Park.

From the serene vitality of wetlands to the constant vibrancy of downtown, Peter Kirk Park provided something for everyone—gleaming waterfronts, a public pool, and outdoor picnic areas. The park also had tennis courts and basketball hoops for that afternoon game and a skate park for those who felt a little more adventurous. But on this particular day, all the men cared about was the basketball court.

Nathan took position in the center of the court and dribbled the ball. "Are you sure you wanna do this, Dad?"

Randy shot him a questionable look. "Why wouldn't I?"

Nathan tried to explain. "First off, we're younger than you guys. Secondly, I have some pretty solid experience on the court. We're gonna kick your butts."

Randy didn't agree with him. "Evidently you don't know the golden rule of basketball, do you?"

"What golden rule?"

"Age and treachery will always triumph over youth and skill."

"Treachery?" Nathan asked with wide eyes. "Are you planning on cheating?"

"I never cheat."

Even though the teams were unbalanced with three versus two, Nathan felt confident. "Alright, old man." He tossed the ball to his father. "Let's see what you got."

Bruce and Jim laughed as Randy took the ball to the side of the court.

"Kid's cocky, isn't he?" Jim said.

"Well, he *is* good," Randy defended. "He's aggressive, and fast, and has some pretty good offensive moves." Randy considered this situation carefully. He realized three fifty-year-old men were going up against two young sprouts, one of whom played NCAA basketball. "Come to think of it, we're probably going to get our asses kicked."

Nathan grew impatient. "Come on, Dad. Quit stalling. Get on the court and take your punishment."

Randy passed the ball to Bruce, who began dribbling across the court with Mike moving in to block him. The older, distinguished men hadn't played a game of basketball together in years, and they were feeling their age. As they took on these two young, athletic men, all three of them realized that youth and skill was stomping them into the ground. Nathan alone was no match for any of them. He was quick, and he was virtually impossible to block. And Michael was so tall, none of them could shoot over him. He easily defended against their shots.

Panting, Randy and his teammates huddled on the side of the court. Randy peered over his shoulder at his son and Michael, both of whom stared them down, cross-armed.

"Dude," Jim declared, out of breath and feeling like he was about to collapse. "Nathan is kickin' my ass. I can't block him. He shoots right over me then runs the other direction like a jackrabbit in heat."

"I know," Randy said. "We need to come up with another plan. Bruce, hold Mike back while I grab Nathan's arm. Jim will snatch the ball and run to the hoop."

"That's cheating," Bruce declared.

Jim thought it was funny as hell and was perfectly willing to go along with this conniving plan. "Sweet. I'm all over it."

"What's the hold up?" Nathan asked, wanting to move the game along. "We don't have all day."

Randy, Jim, and Bruce took their position on the court. Even though the three men executed their shifty plan perfectly, Randy failed to take into consideration the fact that Nathan had been working out regularly and was a lot stronger now than he was. Thus, their plan backfired in their faces. While Bruce fought to hold Mike back, Nathan escaped his father's grip and easily maintained possession of the ball by knocking it out of Randy's hands. He quickly dribbled across the court and made an impressive reverse layup.

Jim stood in the middle of the court laughing hysterically. "Nice plan, Dude. Totally in your face."

Nathan held the ball under his arm. "That move is illegal, Dad. You would get so many fouls called for that."

"That's why it's called treachery, Son."

"It's called cheating," Nathan corrected. "Which brings me to the line. But I'm not even going attempt the shots, because I already know I'll sink them both, and I wouldn't want to humiliate you further by rubbing this in your face. You can't even win by cheating."

Randy drew back a bit, shocked by his son's cockiness. "Wow! You are really sure of yourself, aren't you?"

"Just admit we schooled you so you can go home and Icy Hot yourself, because I guarantee you are going to feel this in the morning, and no amount of coffee is going to ease your pain."

Jim desperately tried to maintain a straight face while he waited for Randy to come up with a good comeback line. But Randy didn't seem to have any energy left to formulate one. "Dude, I'm starvin'," Jim declared.

Satiating Jim's request, Randy and Nathan looked at each at the exact same time and simultaneously said, "Wing Dome!"

Everyone piled into Jim's Jeep and headed down the street to grab some lunch.

The Wing Dome was one of the Hanson's favorite hangout spots. The wings were served hot, the brew was served ice cold, and the game was always on. Feeling brave and in a competitive mood, Nathan dared his father to something called a Seven Deadly Wings Challenge. Locals that stopped at Wing Dome had surely noticed The Wall of Flame. This wall held photo bragging rights for those brave enough to attempt and succeed at the famous wing challenge.

"Think you've got what it takes to be added to the wall?" Nathan challenged his father. "Let's decide once and for all if you can handle the heat." He slapped a twenty dollar bill on the table.

Randy, fueled by pride, would rather burn the shit out of his mouth than admit to his son he was a pussy. With sloth-like determination, Randy pulled out his wallet and placed a twenty on top of Nathan's. Together, they would face the merciless wrath of the Seven Deadly Wings Challenge.

The rules were simple. First, they each had to sign a waiver admitting they were ignorant of personal danger, swollen lips, dry tear ducts, explosive bodily functions, and overall unpleasantness. They each had seven minutes to eat seven ultra-hot wings to the bone, but they could not drink anything during the seven minutes. No napkins were allowed during the challenge. They had to lick clean any sauce off their hands before the seven minutes were up.

Before the clock started, Nathan eyed his father cunningly. "You ready to throw down the gauntlet and cough up some dough?"

Randy knew he was going to regret this, and probably end up with killer heartburn later, but he boldly went where he had never gone before.

"Dude," Jim shook his head. "You are fuckin' crazy. Just admit to the kid you're a wuss."

Standing his ground and protecting his pride, Randy replied, "No way. That cocky kid needs someone to put him in his place."

Bruce mocked Randy's comment. "And you're stupid enough to do it, aren't you?"

"Can't let my son show me up." Randy turned to Nathan and said, "Alright, you cocky little shit, you ready to put your mouth where your ego is?"

"You are a glutton for punishment, aren't you?" Nathan teased.

"Bring it on."

All was going well, for the first few minutes. Randy's mouth was on fire, but he could tell by the look on his son's face that Nathan wasn't fairing much better. He desperately wanted a beer, a glass of water, or even a bottle of Ranch salad dressing, anything to take this torrential burning sensation off his tongue. His eyes started to water, but he wasn't going to quit. He couldn't lose to his son twice in one day.

By now the entire place was watching this contest of father versus son. Some were rooting for Nathan, others rooted for Randy. Both of them were thinking this was the longest seven minutes of their lives.

As the seven minutes slowly came to a close, Randy and Nathan both had one more wing to go. They glared at each other impudently and dug in. The entire Wing Dome cheered as the clock ticked down. When all was said and done, they both successfully completed the challenge. Randy immediately grabbed his bottle of Corona off the table and chugged it down, putting out the infernal flames inside his mouth. Nathan was right behind him with the entire pitcher of water.

"Holy crap that's hot," Nathan sighed in relief. "I'm impressed, Dad. Apparently you can handle the heat."

Randy took his twenty back and shoved it in his pocket. "You wanna bring on the heat? I'll take it." He winked at his son then headed to the bathroom to wash his hands.

Mike couldn't believe Dr. Hanson actually managed to meet this challenge. "Dude, your dad is a badass."

Nathan chugged down another gulp of water. "Yeah, he's a cool guy."

Randy didn't feel very well the next day. He was suffering from massive heartburn and chewed down antacid tablets like they were going out of style. Greg noticed this unusual behavior from his partner and asked him about it. "Have a little too much birthday fun over the weekend?"

With a grunt of defeat, Randy replied, "My son challenged me to that seven-alarm hot wing thing at Wing Dome yesterday, and I'm regretting it today."

Greg found this amusing. "Were you the wing master?"

"Let's put it this way. My portrait is now officially on the wall of flame."

"Another recognition to add to the others you possess," Greg teased.

"That's right. One I claim proudly."

Stephanie interrupted their conversation, "Dr. Hutchins, you have a phone call on line one."

"Alright. I'll take it in my office." Greg laughed as he stepped into the office to take the call.

Later that afternoon, Randy stopped by Swedish Medical Center to meet Jim for a cup of coffee.

When Jim saw him, he developed an impish smirk. "How's my favorite wingman?"

Randy took a seat. "Man, those damn hot wings are doing a number on my stomach today."

Jim had to laugh. "Not nineteen anymore, are ya buddy?"

"Hell no." He rubbed his hand across his chest in extreme discomfort.

"I have something that might make your suffering a little more bearable." Jim handed him a package wrapped in red tissue paper with a black curly ribbon tied around it.

"What's this?"

"Consider it a late birthday gift."

Randy untied the ribbon and ripped the tissue paper off. Inside was a bright red tee-shirt with an imprint of the devil holding a basket of hot wings. In large white letters across the top were the words *Come to the Dark Side, We Have Hot Wings*. "Oh my god, Jim. That is great."

"Thought you'd get a kick out of that. It will go nicely with your collection of crazy ass tee-shirts."

"Yes it will. Thanks." Randy folded the tee-shirt and took a sip of his coffee.

"I talked to Chris last night," Jim proclaimed.

"How's he doing?"

"He gave me some interesting information."

Randy peeked over the rim of his cup. "And what's that?"

"Guess who's gonna to be a grandfather?"

A mischievous grin slowly developed on Randy's face. "You?"

"Yup. He and that girlfriend of his are gonna have a baby."

Randy had to laugh. "Grandpa Jim. Wow, you really are an old fart, aren't you?"

"Speak for yourself," Jim replied, unamused by Randy's mocking. "Just wait 'til it happens to you, Bro."

"It better not happen for a long time. None of my kids are old enough or mature enough to handle that."

"Not so sure Chris is either."

Unable to read Jim feelings about this, Randy asked, "Should I be congratulating you?"

"It hasn't quite sunk in yet. Give me a few days."

"You got it."

CHAPTER THIRTY-TWO

College students all around campus were finishing up final exams and packing up boxes to go back home for the summer. Because Nathan signed up for summer classes, and since he and Mike lived in apartment style housing, UW allowed them to sign a three month extended contract on their apartment, with the stipulation that they paid rent during the summer months. They decided to take the university up on this offer. This arrangement was convenient for both of them because they wouldn't have to give up their domicile or worry about searching for housing elsewhere. Residing on campus during the summer also meant Nathan could easily get to his summer classes without the added expense of commuting.

Gabby, on the other hand, was forced to move out of the dorms for the summer. She was in her room packing when Nathan came over to offer assistance. "How's it going in here?"

Gabby sat on the bed with a frown on her face. "It's going ok."

"What's with the pouty face?"

"I can't go back and live with my mother," she declared. "I just can't, but I really don't have the money to get an apartment on my own. With cheer practice and work, I need to be able to get to campus easily, but I don't have a car. I could take the bus, but that's a really long commute, and paying for bus fare all the time is going to be expensive." She begged him for advice. "What am I supposed to do?"

He thought about her predicament and offered an alternative. "Mike and I just signed a three month extension on our apartment. What if you stayed with me?"

Her eyes widened at his suggestion. "You?"

"Yeah," Nathan confirmed. "It's only temporary. You come and go all the time anyway, so it won't be anything unusual. I'm sure if I talk to Mike about the situation, he'll be cool with it."

"What about all of my stuff?" she asked, taking into account the numerous boxes of dorm gear and décor she had managed to accumulate.

"Only bring over what you need. We'll store the rest at my parents' house."

She was concerned that his parents might get the wrong impression. "Are you sure they won't mind?"

"Let me talk to my dad. You know he's cool about stuff like that. As long as we are honest with him, I'm sure he'll work with us."

"I'll pay my own way," she assured him.

"I know you will. I'm not concerned about that, but I do agree that moving back in with your mother is a very bad idea."

She eyed him pitifully, hoping she wasn't imposing on him and Mike. "Are you sure it's ok?"

Nathan laughed at the pathetic look on her face. "It's not a problem, Babe. I'll talk to Mike." To offer reassurance, he leaned over and kissed her. "Now, let's finish getting you packed."

Part of the packing process involved loading suitcases for Mexico. Nathan had already packed his bag, but since Gabby hadn't yet, Nathan helped her. As soon as the task was complete, he brought both suitcases over to his parents' house, at which time he moved Gabby's stuff into Randy and Jane's garage.

"Thanks, Dad," Nathan proclaimed as he and his father neatly stacked the last box.

"This is not to be a permanent arrangement, Nathan," Randy stipulated.

"I know. It's not. She just needs a place to stay over the summer. When school starts again, she'll go back into the dorms."

Although Randy wasn't happy about this arrangement, he knew it was probably the best situation for Gabby at this point in time. "You better be responsible about this. You cannot let her become a distraction," Randy insisted. "Remember, you are trying to get some of your pre-med requirements out of the way this summer."

"I know, and I will," Nathan assured. "Gabby's going to be busy with work and cheer practice anyway. With my classes and more hours at the clinic, neither one of us is going to have a whole lot of free time on our hands."

For the most part, Nathan was trustworthy and responsible, so Randy supported his son's decision. "Alright. I'm trusting you."

"Thank you."

Randy stepped out of the garage and walked around the perimeter of his yard, making sure the house was up to his standards. "You and Gabby need to be over here no later than 6:00 A.M. tomorrow. We need to get the SUV loaded up and be on our way early enough to stop and get breakfast before we head to the airport."

Nathan replied with a nod. "We'll be ready."

"Uncle Jim will keep an eye on the house, so I would suggest you park the Mustang in the garage. You can leave your keys in the bowl on the dining room table if you want."

"Thanks. I will probably do that."

That evening, Randy popped by Jim's house to drop off the keys. Jim opened the door barefoot, wearing bright orange baggies and a grey tee-shirt that read, *I'd Rather Be Surfing.*

Randy greeted him with their secret handshake. "Hey, Gramps."

"Fuck you, Loser." Jim invited him inside. "Want some coffee?"

"Of course, but it better be strong coffee tonight. It's been one of those days." Randy knew Jim's house well; the two of them always made themselves at home in each other's place of residence. He reached into the cupboard and pulled out a coffee mug. "I like my coffee how I like my Death Star: gigantic, on the dark side, and powerful enough to destroy a planet."

"It'll do," Jim followed Randy into the kitchen. "You all ready for your trip?"

"Yup. Looking forward to it." Randy syphoned coffee from the coffee pot and dumped two heaping spoonfuls of sugar into it. "You and Jill need to come with us."

"Can't this year, Bro. This new position is keepin' me mondo busy. When I'm not appeasin' the executive suit gods, I'm swamped with scheduling." Jim had recently been promoted to head of the ER at Swedish Medical Center. Acquiring this position meant he was responsible for directing the staff in efficient use of emergency medical services, overseeing staff operations, training and hiring new staff members, scheduling, and ensuring all Emergency Room services were in compliance with professional standards. All of this, along with his normal ER physician responsibilities, kept him exceptionally busy.

"But this is what you wanted," Randy reminded him.

"And I love it, but when the hospital director offered me this position, I told him I wanted floor time. That was one of the provisos of me taking this job."

"You getting any?" Randy asked, sipping from his steaming mug.

"I'm scheduling myself into the rotation. It just blows right now because I'm tryin' to set everything up the way I want it done, and that takes time. Once I get it all organized, it should run pretty smoothly."

"How's Jill feel about all of this?"

"She's happy about it. She knows how I operate, so working under my direction will be an easy adjustment for her. She puts up with my bullshit all day long anyway."

"And you definitely have a lot of that," Randy added, teasing his best friend.

Jim sat on a stool across from his best friend. "What time are you guys leavin' tomorrow?"

"Hopefully by six. I want to try to dodge downtown traffic and feed the hordes before the long flight." Randy reached into his pocket and handed Jim an extra set of house keys. "Nate's gonna leave the Mustang in the garage along with the Jag. And my neighbors know you're housesitting for us, so hopefully we won't have any issues like we did last time."

Jim recollected the last time he housesat for them—when he went around to check the back of the house, the neighbors called the police. It took him nearly an hour and several phone calls to convince them he wasn't there to burglarize the property. "It's good to know your neighbors are on the lookout for suspicious behavior."

"Sometimes they get a little too involved with what goes on at my house."

"Nosey nellies?" Jim questioned.

"On occasion."

Jim slid the keys in his pocket. "Anything I need to know?"

"Yes," Randy said. "No more broccoli for Fingers. Last time he ate it he had excruciating gas for a week." Randy had been a long-time owner of an African Grey parrot. This particular bird, named Mr. Fingers, generally had a gentle disposition and lively intelligence. He loved to serenade the family with of one of the many songs he knew and was able to speak over eight-hundred words. But he didn't just speak, he also imitated almost any sound, which could be a nuisance if a fire truck or helicopter happened to pass by.

Although Jim wasn't particularly fond of this bird, only because it often bit him, he willingly accepted the responsibility of looking after him while Randy was out of town. "No broccoli." Jim laughed. "Good tip."

While the Hansons were traveling and getting settled into their Mexican paradise, Jim had to deal with issues in the ER. Since Jim was an ER physician in a teaching hospital, he often worked with medical students and resident doctors. Wondering if Dr. Martin, his newbie partner for the evening, was going to be late again, he looked at his watch. "Dammit. He's late again. This is the third time this week."

Jill gently placed her hand on Jim's shoulder. "He'll be here."

Dr. Martin had been in the residency program for less than a week, and he had a lot on his plate right now, however schedule juggling shouldn't have been one of them. "He better get his ass here soon or he's getting pit duty tonight." Although Jim did his part to educate new doctors, he tried to keep Dr. Martin away from complicated cases, mainly because he had a tendency to buckle under pressure.

The ER was packed with awaiting patients. Already Jim had to deal with several broken appendages from a man who fell out a second story window, a nail gun incident, a major burn on the arm and upper torso from a gas explosion, injuries from multiple automobile accidents, and just fifteen minutes ago, he sent a gunshot victim into the OR to have a bullet removed and tissue damage repaired.

"Well, this shift is starting out with a bang," he said to himself, then smiled at his own dark humor. Emergency Room physicians were like that sometimes. Occasionally, Jim had to make light of the situation or he would go crazy—and crazy was something he couldn't afford to be. Despite the blood and horror he walked into every day, he needed to keep his cool and know instantly what to do, which wasn't always easy.

Besides the overabundance of severe cases in the ER, Jim had to deal with family members that night. Friends and family always wanted to help, but since they couldn't really help, they ran around, cried a lot, and asked stupid questions. But Jim wouldn't have it any other way. It only meant they cared.

As if things weren't chaotic enough, Jim heard one of the ER nurses call out, "Code blue coming in." The staff busily set up for the incoming emergency and rushed over to meet the ambulance at the receiving door.

Right at that moment Dr. Martin showed up. Jim looked at the clock. "You're five minutes late."

"Only five? That's not so..."

Before this resident doctor could finish his statement, Jim gave him a cold, hard stare. "There are a thousand ways to die in less than a minute. Get here on time."

Martin dropped his jaw, then he dropped his head.

Jim could tell he was profoundly embarrassed, but that was good. He should have been. Huffing to let him know how displeased he was, Jim wasn't about to let him off easily. "If you're late one more time, I'm taking you off the criticals list. Do I make myself clear?"

"Yes, Sir." He sat down, feeling totally deflated.

Jim let him stew for a while, which allowed time for his own anger to ebb before he spoke again. "Martin, you have a good academic record, one of the better ones I've seen, but all the head knowledge in the world won't help if you're not at the scene in time to use it. Remember the Golden Hour rule. If severe injury or illness doesn't kill a victim within the first five minutes, chances are, he has about an hour before irreversible shock sets in. One hour. That's all. If you can't pull it together by then, you might as well call the coroner. Time is everything."

"I'm sorry, Dr. Ryan," Dr. Martin mumbled. "I didn't think I would be needed for anything important this evening."

"But that's just it," Jim snapped. "That's the nature of this business. Boring, boring, boring, interspersed with sharp bursts of barely organized chaos. You have to be ready at all times."

When the ambulance arrived, all the color drained from Martin's face. This was a real call, and the chaos was about to begin.

Jim jumped out to help unload the gurney from the back of the ambulance and wheeled it to the closest exam room. Martin turned away and began to freeze up. Jim had to give him a reality check. "Move it, Martin! Time is critical!"

Blood was splattered across the gurney and the victim was about to go into cardiac arrest. Martin's face grew pale. Jim shot him a quick 'calm down' look, but instead of reacting, Dr. Martin froze.

Jim did his best to encourage him. "Focus. Follow my lead and do exactly what I tell you to do."

Martin cracked his knuckles before attending to the blood-covered victim.

"Start an IV," Jim said calmly, but Martin was already pulling the intravenous equipment and attaching it to the victim. Thank god he hadn't fallen apart completely. "Jill!" Jim hollered to get her attention.

He didn't have to say another word. She knew exactly what he wanted. She grabbed the blood pressure cuff and slapped it on the patient before reaching for the oxygen mask, strapping it to the patient's face.

Jim examined the victim's broken body looking for signs to tell him what was wrong. All he saw was blood, and there was way too much of it covering this woman's body. There were no signs of external injury, only rectal/vaginal bleeding and blood seeping from the mouth, which indicated internal bleeding.

"Grab a Co-Ag compress and put pressure on the abdomen," Jim told Dr. Martin.

Dr. Martin followed Jim's instructions and took necessary steps to suppress the bleeding.

"What are we reading?" Jim inquired, demanding vitals, and Jill posed a CO_2 number that was way too high. The patient was going into carbon dioxide acidosis because of her depressed breathing. If they couldn't get her blood ph back to normal, it could trigger cardiac arrest. Jim glanced at the defibrillator paddles, but quickly looked away, hoping he didn't have to use them. "Sodium bicarb. Full ampoule," he ordered.

Martin shot the bicarbonate into the IV line then grabbed the shock drug kit.

"O_2 is low as well," Jill called out.

In a situation like this, time was essential. Jim saw Martin glancing over his shoulder staring at the clock instead of focusing on the situation. He was still slightly shaky, so Jim shot him a quick nod of reassurance as if to say, *Just keep it together. We'll pull her through.*

Jim reached for the FleurOx, a clear fluorocarbon-based blood replacement fluid that could transport oxygen better than real blood. But keeping the oxygen level up wasn't the only thing they needed to do. They had to increase the blood volume. That's what kept the blood pressure up. All the oxygen in the world wouldn't help if there wasn't enough pressure in the system to push it where it needed to go.

Jill carefully watched the BP monitor. "Eighty over forty, Doctor, and dropping. PR of one-seventy."

The patient was going into shock. Their Golden Hour was ticking away quickly. "Push the FleurOx," he instructed.

The resident doctor clamped his hand around the IV bag, squeezing it to make it flow faster. As he did, nurses and ER staff zipped the victim's legs and lower abdomen into the trauma suit and began inflating it. External pressure applied to the legs and belly from the ballooning suit slowed the bleeding and forced blood from the lower body into the upper trunk and head, hopefully raising the blood pressure. Sure enough, the BP started to inch its way back up.

Jim quickly started a second IV line pushing gluco-saline.

"The O_2 levels are still low," Jill stated, diligently watching the monitors.

"How's her breathing?" Jim asked, waiting for a response from Dr. Martin.

Martin watched the blood-soaked upper body. Her chest was barely moving. "Not good," he replied.

"Then we need to intubate."

Martin stared at Jim as if he didn't know what that meant.

"Martin, did you hear me?" Jim barked.

Martin came out of his temporary trance and immediately began tearing open the intubation kit.

Intubation involved sticking a tube down the throat and into the windpipe. A bulb on the end of the tube was then inflated to seal it in the trachea and a respirator would then take over the breathing. If the procedure was not performed properly, permanent damage could occur. But if not performed at all, this patient would be lost.

Jim grabbed the laryngoscope and quickly tilted the head back. As he peered in, he saw blood bubbling up from the esophagus. No wonder the patient was having trouble breathing; she was aspirating blood clots. Using a gloved finger to scoop the mess out of the way, Jim cleared the throat and pulled the scope up to expose the larynx. Now all he needed to do was thread the respirator tube past the vocal chords. "Watch how this is done," he told his protégé. He quickly and carefully slipped the tube into the trachea and inflated the bulb. Turning the respirator on, he heard the click and whoosh of the machine starting up. There were no leaks in the trachea;

the seal was good, so he pulled the scope out. Slowly, the patient began to respond.

As the patient stabilized, Jim eyed the cardiac paddles. He was glad it didn't come to that. In cases involving deep shock, the defibrillator was a last resort, and most of the time it didn't work. When the patient was stable enough for surgery, they moved her to the OR. Their job here was done.

Jim removed his latex gloves and went to the sink to wash his hands, prepping himself for the next patient. "The patient in exam room two needs sutures," he said to Dr. Martin. "Take care of that please."

Martin stared at him, wondering why Dr. Ryan wanted him to engage in such a mundane task after the action he was just involved with.

"Is there a problem?" Jim asked, drying off his hands.

"No, Sir, there's not."

"Then get on it."

Around midnight, an obscure case came into the ER. "What the hell?" Jim said, sifting through data trying to make sense of it. Seven different patients in seven different exam rooms all had the exact same symptoms—rapid heart rate, bright blue-colored urine, and the skin around their foreskin and groin area was not only breaking out in a rash, but was also turning blue. Jim had never seen anything like this before. "Dr. Martin, come here and look at this."

The young doctor came over to investigate. "All seven of them? Is this some kind of epidemic?"

Jim was completely stumped. "Hell if I know."

He ran some tests to get more definitive answers. After interviewing all seven patients, Jim learned that all of them were at the same party where they drank what they called 'purple punch', which was basically grape juice and any kind of alcohol they could get their hands on. But neither one of those substances led to symptoms like this when consumed. So he took urine samples and had them analyzed for other substances.

When Jill brought the lab results back, Jim tried not to laugh. "Are you serious?"

"That's what the report says," she confirmed.

Apparently this 'purple punch' had been spiked with methylene blue, which at room temperature was a solid odorless green powder. However, when mixed with water, such as in grape juice, it yielded a blue solution when dissolved. Methylene blue was a relatively harmless substance used as a medical dye to better see internal tissues during scans or to examine RNA or DNA under the microscope. In low doses, it had been known to have antioxidant qualities and could even improve memory consolidation and protect the brain from disease, but the side effects of it could sometimes be severe if used in excess—hives, rapid heart rate, blue skin, and blue-tinged urine. This explained the symptoms. "Smurf juice," Jim joked. "Wow! Now I've seen everything."

Wondering how to treat this, Jill asked, "What do we do?"

"Monitor their heart rates and give them an ointment for the rash. The remaining side effects will subside as it leaves their system."

Jill took Jim's advice and retrieved a rash ointment from the pharmacy for these seven young men then continued to monitor their heart rates until they were back to normal.

For the rest of the night, this obscure incident became known as the 'Smurf Juice Epidemic'. Jim, being the smartass he was, used this as a prime opportunity to express some much needed humor in the chaotic world of the ER. He somehow managed to scrape up a red gnome hat. He put it on his head then popped over to the nurse's station and addressed everyone. "Hello my fellow Smurficans. How's it smurfin'?"

This unusual greeting turned everyone's heads. When the ER technicians, nurses, and medical residents saw him in blue scrubs with this ridiculous hat on his head, they all busted out laughing.

Dr. Ryan was always the comic relief in the madness of the Emergency Room. Everyone loved him for that reason alone, and the fact that he was the best damn ER doctor any of them had the privilege to work with. He was serious when he needed to be, but could always shatter the ice in stressful or tense situations.

Jill rolled her eyes. "Oh god, Jim. Where did you find that?"

"What? You don't like it?" He reached up and touched his hat, posing for her. "I think it's rather smurfy myself."

"You're nuts."

He offered her a friendly smile then removed the silly hat he was wearing before he checked on his next patient.

By morning, the ER was pretty slow. Jim left the floor and reported to his office to catch up on paperwork.

After working a twelve-hour shift, Dr. Martin felt pretty confident with his skills. He was pushing staff members around and speaking to people with a brash tone. On several occasions he made derogatory comments toward some of the nurses, speaking to them as if they were peons in the ranks of the ER. Jill was tending to a patient in an exam room when Dr. Martin barged in and tried to take over. Even though Jill assured him that she had the situation under control, he leered at her and unashamedly said, "Move your pretty ass out of my way and let this doctor do his job."

Already several nurses had come to her complaining about inappropriate comments this resident doctor had made to them throughout the shift. Now he was being rude to her. Being the shift lead nurse on staff, Jill felt it necessary to report him to the head of the ER. She stormed into Jim's office. "You need to do something about that son-of-a-bitch!"

Her bold entrance took him by surprise.

"He is a rude, inconsiderate, chauvinistic pig."

Jim got up and closed the door, wondering why his wife was causing such a stink. "Who are you talking about?"

"Dr. Martin."

"The new resident?" he asked for clarification.

"Yes, the new resident. How many Dr. Martins are there in this hospital?"

Trying to get her to calm down, he put his hands on her shoulders and forced her to sit in the chair.

"Do you know what he just did? He barged into my exam room and told me to move my pretty ass out of *his* way so *he* could do *his* job."

Jim found this hard to believe. "He said that?"

"Yes, but that's not the only issue. He's been making rude, inappropriate comments all night and has made sexual advances toward several nurses. I'm going to file a grievance against him, and there are four other nurses out on the floor who are right there with me, James!"

His wife was about to blow a gasket. "Calm down."

"That behavior is completely inappropriate," she argued.

"I agree with you, but before you resort to that, let's see if we can deal with this in a diplomatic manner."

"How?" She crossed her arms and glared at him, waiting for a reasonable answer.

"Let me talk to him."

"What good is that going to do? The guy is a total…"

Jim stopped her. "Let me handle this."

"Fine." She stood up and stormed out of his office.

Great. Now his wife was angry. What else could possibly happen on this shift? This day just kept getting better and better. Jim took a deep breath to retain his composure before he headed out to the ER. "Dr. Martin, may I speak with you in my office for minute, please?"

"Yeah, sure."

When Dr. Martin stepped into the room, Jim closed the door behind them. "Sit down," he demanded.

Martin obeyed.

Jim sat on the edge of his desk and folded his arms across his chest. "I've been pretty patient with you as far as showing up on time is concerned. According to protocol, I should have restricted your duty and pulled you from criticals for noncompliance. Instead, I offered forgiveness and gave you another chance. But that wasn't enough for you, was it?"

Dr. Martin leaned back, baffled. "What are you talking about?"

"I have five extremely irate women out there who are ready to file sexual harassment grievances against you."

When the significance of this complaint sank in, the smug grin on Martin's face quickly faded.

"You see what I'm getting at, don't you?"

"Yes, I do."

"The nursing staff in the ER works harder and does more to save the lives of patients than you ever will. If it wasn't for them, this department would be dysfunctional and nothing would ever get done. Patients would die, the waiting room would back up beyond repair, and all of us would go crazy in the process. The men and women who wear nursing scrubs deserve your respect, and I will not tolerate anything less than that. Do you understand?"

Dr. Martin nodded. "Yes, Sir."

"Do you really want a sexual harassment charge in your file?"

"No. Not at all."

"These women are probably going to file complaints about you, and there is nothing I can do to stop them, in fact I will back them up. But you might, and I emphasize might, be able to resolve this issue by offering them an apology. And you can start with my wife."

He stared at Jim with hawk-like eyes. "Your wife?"

"Yes. The blonde nurse whom you told, and let me see if I can get these words right, to move her pretty ass out of your way." Jim shot him an evil glare.

Dr. Martin's cheeks turned bright red. "That's your wife?"

"Yes she is, and her name is Jill. But it shouldn't matter whose wife she is. She's a damn good nurse with a lot more ER experience than you have, and she knows how to get the job done. She, as well as all the other nurses on this ward, *will* get respect from you. They deserve it and they demand it. I demand it. To keep a bad situation from potentially becoming far worse for yourself, I strongly suggest you take whatever action is necessary to rectify this situation."

"Yes, Dr. Ryan." Dr. Martin immediately returned to the ER and offered apologies to all the nurses he had offended, starting with Jill.

Jim observed these interactions, making sure this doctor complied with his request. Jill, in her own subtle way, showed her appreciation by mouthing the words 'thank you.' He winked at her then returned to his office to close out paperwork so he and Jill could go home.

Jim did not realize that Jill had been standing close enough to his office door to overhear the entire conversation he had with Dr. Martin. As they settled into bed that night, Jill looked at him with a wide smile on her face.

Her staring him down with that wolf-like grin made him uneasy. "What did I do that's makin' you eye me like that?"

"I overheard what you said to Dr. Martin today, how you complimented ER nurses and told him how hard we work."

"Just tellin' him the truth," Jim justified.

"Well, it meant a lot to me. Thank you, James."

"It's no problem. I wasn't about to let him talk to my babe like that. The kid is brash and totally overconfident.

Besides, he was bein' an assmunch and needed to be knocked down a notch. He's one of those dudes who thinks he's invincible, but if he's not careful, the undertow is gonna drag him under and give him a beatdown."

Jill giggled at him.

Jim sat up and supported his body weight on his elbow. "What's so funny?"

"It is so cute when you do that," she told him.

"Do what?"

"How you can switch from serious doctor mode to silly surfer at the drop of a hat. It's almost as if you come to work wearing scrubs, but underneath you have on your baggies and Oakleys. It's adorable."

"That's who I am, Babe."

Lately Jim had been rundown and lacking his usual enthusiasm. Offering support, she gently touched his face with her hand. "I know you've been stressed with this new job."

He denied this accusation, "Nah, just busy."

"James," she corrected. "You can't hide it from me."

He closed his eyes and drifted into his fantasy world of sand and surf. "I need some time to chillax and unwind."

She knew exactly what he needed. "You're off tomorrow. Go surfing."

Surfing always calmed him. It reenergized his spirit and helped him refocus. But he felt guilty leaving her alone on their day off so he could go surfing. "But I wanted to spend the day with you."

"We can spend time together on Thursday. Tomorrow you need to load up the Jeep and go to Westport."

"Are you sure?"

"Yes. Go," she insisted.

Grinning from ear to ear, Jim leaned over and tenderly kissed her on the lips. "You're awesome! Thank you for understanding."

She moved her lips to his ear and whispered, "I love you, James."

He placed his hands around her pretty cheek and gazed into her eyes. "Love you, Honeybun." He kissed her again, drawing her closer this time.

CHAPTER THIRTY-THREE

"Honey," Randy yelled from the kitchen. "Have you seen my keys?" In a rush to get out the door, he quickly chowed down half a bagel while he syphoned coffee directly from the brewer.

Jane trotted down the stairs with not only Randy's keys, but his wallet and cellphone as well, handing him all three. "You left them on the dresser."

"Thanks, Babe." He put his wallet in his back pocket and slipped his cellphone in the other. When he turned his head, his travel coffee cup was about to overflow. In a panic, he set his keys on the counter and rushed to pull the mug out of the stream, replacing it with the pot instead. Some of it flowed onto him, burning his skin. "Dammit!"

"Sweetie, be careful," Jane advised. "You won't do your patients any good in surgery today if you burn yourself."

He reached for a paper towel to dry his hands then attempted to clean the counter where coffee had spilled.

Jane took the paper towel from him. "I'll get it."

He dumped some contents from his overflowing cup down the sink then drowned it in sugar and creamer before he tightened the lid.

It wasn't like Randy to be disoriented, unorganized, or misplacing things. Jane questioned this unusual behavior. "Why are you in such a rush this morning?"

Randy sipped from his cup and tapped on his watch. "I'm running late." With coffee cup in hand, he picked up his keys and gave his wife a kiss. "I have to go."

Concerned that he was going to race down the freeway to get to work, Jane cautioned her husband. "Randy, please drive safely."

He grabbed his stethoscope off the coffee table. "I will. I love you, Babe."

"I love you. Have a good day."

He got in the car and peeled out of the driveway.

Freeway traffic on Highway 520 moved at snail speed. But because the 520 crossed Lake Washington on a 7,578 ft. floating bridge, he had no other place else to go. "Great," he scoffed. "Just great." He probably shouldn't have complained, because on exceptionally stormy, windy days, the bridge was closed due to high waves hitting the road. At least he didn't have to go out of his way to take a longer alternative route.

After being trapped on the bridge for nearly thirty-five minutes, Randy finally made it to Montlake Boulevard. Turning right would take him to the University of Washington. Turning left took him down 24th Street, through Interlaken Park, to East Cherry Street, where both the physician's entrance to Swedish Medical Center and his clinic were located.

Everyone at the hospital and clinic recognized Randy's cherry red Jaguar. This particular vehicle had a four-hundred ninety-five horsepower V8 Supercharged engine and could go zero to sixty in 4.2 seconds. It had black leather sport seats and chrome exterior trim finish. Randy loved this car.

He pulled into his parking space at the clinic with the radio blasting. Ready to start his day, he shut off the engine, grabbed his stethoscope and coffee cup, then exited the car.

When he walked into the clinic, Stephanie looked up at the clock. "You're late," she declared. "You are aware that you have a surgery scheduled in fifteen minutes, aren't you?"

Randy skimmed through the appointment schedule. "I love how you haven't seen me in a week, but instead of saying 'Good morning, Randy. How was your trip?' you start hounding me about the time."

"I'm sorry. How was your trip?" she corrected herself.

"Very good. Thank you for asking." He scanned the area for Greg. He wasn't in the clinic, and he couldn't remember seeing his car in the parking lot. "Is Greg here yet?"

"He got called in for a delivery early this morning, but should be back before his first appointment," Stephanie explained.

"Already swamped and the day hasn't even started yet." He checked the time on his watch. "I'm gonna head over to the hospital."

"Welcome home, Randy."

"Thanks." He walked briskly over to Swedish Medical Center to prepare for a series of scheduled surgeries he had that morning.

Following his morning surgical procedure, Randy met Jim at Starbucks. Sipping on a cup of coffee, Jim handed Randy the key to his house. "Enjoy your trip?" he asked

"Oh yeah. I love Mexico. You and Jill need to come with us next year."

"Hopefully things will slow down enough in the ER for me to take a vacation. We're shorthanded right now, and quite honestly this resident I have is more of a hindrance than a help."

"Why is that?" Randy asked.

"The assmunch always shows up late for his shift. He tends to freak out in life-threatening situations, but is over-confident with simple calls so he doesn't pay attention to details. And, get this," Jim said. "Five nurses have now filed sexual harassment complaints against him, my wife included."

Randy chuckled. "Do I dare ask what he did?"

"He messed with the wrong woman is what he did. You know as well as I do that Jill isn't gonna put up with that crap."

"Jane wouldn't either."

"He's gonna get kicked out of the program if he's not careful, and I'm not gonna bend over backwards to save his ass," Jim warned.

"I don't blame you. If the guy can't handle the heat..."

Jim finished his sentence, "He needs to get the hell out of the fire."

"Speaking of fire," Randy gulped down his latte, "Any problems with the neighbors this time?"

"Nah, but that damn loud-mouthed bird of yours..." Jim shook his head in disgust. "Fuckin' thing bit my finger then crapped all over my arm."

Randy knew Jim didn't care much for his bird. It seemed like every time Jim bird-sat, Mr. Fingers would bite him. "Man, he really hates you," Randy teased with a laugh. "What'd you do to piss off my bird?"

"I didn't do a damn thing to him," Jim defended. "That cracker muncher has never liked me."

"You didn't feed him broccoli, did you?"

"Hell no," Jim assured. "It was gnarly enough that he crapped on me. I wasn't about to deal with bird fart."

This made Randy laugh.

"It's not fuckin' funny, Dude. I think he does that on purpose."

"He's a bird, Jim. I seriously doubt he holds a vengeance." Still chuckling, Randy said, "Thank you for taking care of him and keeping an eye on the house for us."

"No problem. You know I'll hold down the fort for you any time you need me too."

"I know. I appreciate that." They sat and chatted over coffee for about ten more minutes before they both had to report back to their doctorly duties.

CHAPTER THIRTY-FOUR

Even though Gabby had cheer practice and Nathan was scheduled to work in his father's clinic that day, they both slept in. With a big stretch and a yawn, Nathan awoke feeling jet-lagged and hungry. He placed his hand on his rumbling stomach. "Man, I'm starving."

Gabby rolled over and groaned. "You are always hungry. Don't you think about anything other than food?"

"Sure I do. I think about basketball. I think about school. I think about beaches and sunsets and fishing." He grazed his lips across her ear. "I think about sex."

"Pervert."

"You know you love it." He hopped out of bed and slipped on a pair of basketball shorts. "What shall we do about breakfast?"

Gabby hid her face in the pillow.

Nathan tried to coax her out of bed. "Come on, lazy bones. Get up."

With a groan of disapproval, she hid under the covers.

"Oh no you don't," he chuckled, taking the covers off of her.

Kicking and squirming, trying to fight him off, she wrestled with him in a battle of blanket tug-of-war. When he was able to pull the covers from her grasp, he picked her up and carried her over his shoulder.

She struggled to get loose. "Put me down!"

"You can't spend the entire day in bed," he argued.

"Why not?"

"Because you can't. We have things to do today."
Nathan gently set her down on the floor then gripped her
hand in his. Drawing her nearer, he wrapped one arm
around her waist. He gazed deep into her eyes, making his
intentions clear. Slowly, he moved his gaze to her lips then
back up to her eyes again. Tilting his head slightly, he
kissed her—a gentle, lingering touch of the lips, as if both
were taking the time to memorize the feeling. He offered
her light nibbles while his wandering hand pressed their
bodies closer. Sensuously, he moved his tongue across her
lip. She responded with the same. The kiss they shared was
mutual, deliberate, and purposeful.

Nathan pulled back slightly and nuzzled his forehead
to hers, maintaining constant eye contact. At that moment,
they were completely in sync with one another. He
exchanged a smile with her while she wrapped her arms
around his neck. She kissed him, a deep, sensuous kiss that
slowly increased in intensity. As they alternated taking the
lead, he cradled her face with his hand. Kissing her was the
simplest act of affection, yet it was the most erotic and
loving feeling shared between them.

When he finally came up for air, he took her hand and
led her toward the door. "Come on."

"Where are we going?"

"Shower with me."

She knew exactly what he was implying.

Nathan and Gabby had a lot of variety in their sex life,
exploring new positions or trying different locations
frequently. But sex in the shower was something they had
never tried before.

As soon as they were in the bathroom, Nathan locked
the door. He reached into the shower stall and turned on
the hot water. As they waited for the water to heat up, he
swept Gabby into his arms. When the bathroom mirror
became foggy, he drug her into the shower with him. The
steamy water running down her sleek body aroused his
senses. Gabby was beautiful from head to toe—her face,

breasts, tummy, legs—every inch of her simply stunned him. Using a soft washcloth, Nathan lathered her up, taking his time to caress sensitive areas and sneak in a finger now and then. Her body tingled from the contact. This intimate and seductive act, combined with the tender kisses and steaming water, helped put them both in the mood.

Gabby pressed her naked body against his and wrapped her left leg around his waist. To keep her steady, Nathan placed his right hand under her thigh. This left his other hand free to caress her body and run his fingers through her hair. Gabby knew how to stretch sexual boundaries, and seeing this display of sexuality along with her extreme flexibility drove Nathan mad with want.

As the feeling intensified, he picked her up entirely. She wrapped both legs around him and he pushed her backside against the wall. His fingertips dug into the fleshiness of her buttocks as he repeatedly thrust into her, varying the rhythm from quick and deep to slow and sensuous. Hearing her moan and feeling her breath on his skin aroused every sense. He gazed into her eyes, further boosting the intimacy factor.

Gabriella was someone he truly loved, and sharing this closeness with her was the most intense feeling in the world. She was the one person he felt safe with. The one he could share his deepest emotions with. The one he felt dedicated to protect 'til the end of days. When they were interlocked together like this, the two became one.

When they stepped out of the shower, Nathan peeked into Mike's room. His bed hadn't been slept in. "Hmm," he said to Gabby. "Mike didn't come home last night."

"Maybe he spent the night at his dad's house."

"That is possible, but unlikely." He checked his phone to see if Mike left him a message. Nothing. "I wonder where he is."

About an hour later, Mike walked in the door.

"Where have you been," Nathan asked.

"Spent the night with Lizzie."

"Really?" Nathan teased. "I go to Mexico for a week and you guys share a bed. Interesting."

"We didn't share a bed. I fell asleep on her couch. I was over there watching a movie last night, and the next thing I know, it's 7:00 A.M." He reached into the fridge and chugged milk straight from the carton. "How was your trip?"

"Had a blast. We saw some cool Mayan history, and my dad and I went Marlin fishing."

"Catch anything?"

"Caught a twenty-five pounder."

"Nice." He placed the carton back on the shelf. "Lizzie and I are going to that dance club tonight. You and Gabby want to come?"

"Sure. Sounds like fun."

Gabby met Nathan at his apartment that evening, accompanied by Lizzie. As the ladies approached the door, they heard music coming from inside the apartment. Nathan had left the door unlocked, so Gabby let herself in. When she and Lizzie stepped inside, Nathan was bopping around the kitchen singing. Luckily, Nathan hadn't seen them walk in, which made it easy to sneak up on him.

"Ssh," Gabby whispered, placing her index finger up to her lip.

Lizzie covered her mouth with her hand, trying to suppress her giggles.

Together they tiptoed into the living room, where they sat on the couch and watched Nathan for several minutes. He was completely oblivious to their presence, until he turned around and saw them staring at him.

"Nice moves, Sweetie," Gabby said between giggles.

Nathan grinned bashfully. Considering he didn't dance very well, watching him must have been quite amusing. "I didn't think anyone was here."

Gabby got up and placed her hand on his chest, teasing him, "Maybe you should be on the pom squad."

"I think that would be a bad idea," Nathan laughed. "You stick with the pompoms. I'll keep to the court." It was nearly 7:00 P.M. and Mike hadn't reported home from work yet. The four of them planned to leave in thirty minutes. Nathan wondered what was keeping him.

"Where's Mike?" Lizzie asked.

"I don't know. He was scheduled to be off almost an hour ago."

"He remembered about tonight, didn't he?"

"Yeah. He and I were talking about it this morning."

Five minutes later, Michael swaggered into the apartment with a grin plastered on his face. "Hola, mi amigo. Cómo estás?"

Responding to Mike's obvious blissful mood, Nathan said, "Buenos noches, compadre. Qué pasa?"

"Stupid inventory," Mike complained. "Boss wouldn't let anyone leave until we finished."

"That sucks."

"Yes it does. I'm gonna change so we can get outta here."

At the club, the four of them let loose. They sipped on sodas, joked around together, and spent the evening stress free.

While on the dance floor, Nathan pulled Gabby's hand to his chest, tucking it between them. He drew her body closer so they were intimately face to face. In her ear, he whispered, "Do you remember the first time we danced together?"

"Uh huh," Gabby confirmed. "It was the eighth grade dance. Scott wanted to dance with me, but I chose you instead."

Nathan chuckled a bit. "He should have known you'd pick me. Everybody knew we liked each other."

Wanting to be closer to him, she rested her head on his chest.

Nathan took in the flowery scent of her hair. "I need you, Gab, more than you can possibly imagine." Slowly, he tilted his head so they were brushing noses. Smiling at her, he moved his mouth closer to hers and kissed her. While they kissed, he pressed the hand he was holding against his chest and gently brushed his fingertips up Gabby's neck. Her hair felt soft under his fingers.

Midway through the evening, Nathan lost track of Mike and Lizzie. He assumed they left together. So he and Gabby left as well.

In the morning Nathan went into the kitchen to make breakfast. While cracking an egg into a bowl, a girl he had never seen before came out of Mike's room with a handbag and a pair of shoes in her hand. Trying to be polite, Nathan acknowledged her. "Good morning."

She stared at him momentarily, but didn't reply. In a rush to leave, she snuck out the front door.

Shortly afterwards, Mike emerged dressed in a pair of boxer shorts. His hair was all mussed up and he needed to shave.

Nathan pointed to the front door. "Who the hell was that?"

Mike tactlessly scratched himself and yawned. "Amber."

"Who's Amber?"

"Some chick I met at the club last night."

Nathan cocked his head, surprised by this outcome. "Did you sleep with her?"

"Yeah."

Many times Mike had mentioned how much he liked Lizzie and how he felt more than just friendship towards her. He even told Nathan he wanted to bump their relationship to a more romantic level. If that was indeed the case, why in the world was Mike sharing his bed with a woman he barely knew? "You cheated on Lizzie?"

Mike denied this accusation. "Kinda hard to cheat on someone when you aren't involved in a relationship with them. She's not my girlfriend. We have no commitment."

"I thought you said you wanted to kick things up a notch?"

Mike's entire posture sagged. "Doesn't mean she wants to."

Something must have happened between Mike and Lizzie that made him react this way. "Did she say that?"

"Not in those exact words, but that's pretty much what she implied." Mike grabbed a glass out of the cupboard and filled it with milk. "We were having a great time together, until I tried to kiss her." He slipped the gallon of milk back into the fridge and sat on the stool at the kitchen island.

"You tried to kiss her?"

"Yup," Mike replied. "Things kinda went downhill from there."

"What happened?" Nathan whisked his egg with a fork and dumped it into a skillet.

"She turned her head away, told me she didn't want to ruin our friendship by complicating things, then walked out the door. All I could do was stand there and watch the only woman I've ever really cared about walk away." Mike's eyes became misty.

Nathan furrowed his brow, puzzled by this turn of events. "That doesn't make sense. Gabby told me she talks about you all the time."

"Well, apparently not in the way she thought. So seeing as the woman I love wants nothing to do with me, I said fuck it and decided I'd get myself laid." Mike slammed down the rest of his milk.

Nathan shook his head, scoffing at Mike's illogical solution. "Do you feel better now?"

"No. I feel worse," Mike admitted. "Not only did my heart get kicked around, but now I feel guilty as hell. One night stands suck."

Almost every night that week, Mike had a sock hanging on the apartment doorknob, but in the morning, the woman who walked out of the apartment was not the same person Nathan had seen the day before. Mike was not the kind of guy to sleep around with random women. The fact that he was doing this raised red flags. To make matters worse, Mike seemed to be slipping into some kind of depressive state. He disappeared for hours on end, and when he finally came home, he was intoxicated. He hadn't reported to work in days, and anytime Gabby came over, he either left the apartment or locked himself in his room. He was miserable and wallowing in his own self-pity. This impetuous behavior worried Nathan.

Monday morning, after watching another woman walk out of his apartment, Nathan decided to confront Mike about this bazaar behavior. "You've brought a different woman home every night this week."

To Mike, this was insignificant. "So?"

"Do you even know these women?"

Mike snapped defensively, "Who I choose to bring into my bed is none of your business."

"Did you go out and get drunk again last night?"

"Who are you, my father?"

Trying to get Mike to admit that what he was doing was self-destructive and only bringing him more misery, Nathan explained, "Sleep with whoever you want, and drink yourself to oblivion if that's what you want to do, but keep in mind that you're the one who told me alcohol makes you feel like crap and meaningless sex gives you a guilt trip. Why the hell are you torturing yourself like this?"

"Why do you care?" Mike snapped.

Offended and hurt by Mike's comment, Nathan replied, "You and I have been friends for thirteen years. I care about you, and this isn't who you are." No one knew Michael Lynott better than Nathan did, in fact he probably knew Mike better than anyone else on Earth. His best friend was suffering from a heartache and Nathan saw right through him. But rather than speculating about the situation, he asked, "It's Lizzie, isn't it?"

With pain written all over his face, Mike closed his eyes and shook his head in defeat. "I can't..." He couldn't finish his sentence. The heartache ran through his body and up to his head, where traces of it leaked out through his eyes.

Mike was about to break down and let loose of the emotional state he was in. Nathan tried to intervene. "It's alright. You know you can talk to me."

He was able to compose himself long enough to finish his sentence. "I can't shake this."

Hoping Mike would reconsider his recent actions, Nathan asked, "And you think getting drunk and having sex with random women is the solution?"

Mike hung his head in disgrace, feeling horribly guilty and ashamed of the way he'd been acting. "I know she thinks that getting romantically involved will ruin our friendship, but dammit, I love her and she totally shot me down. Do you know how humiliating and painful that is?"

Trying to help his friend deal with this, Nathan offered a suggestion, "Have you talked to her since Friday night?"

Mike shook his head. "I can't."

"Why not?"

"She totally ripped my heart out."

"Which is why you need to call her," Nathan argued.

Mike stared at Nathan thinking that idea was ludicrous. "What the hell am I supposed to say to her?"

"Maybe she needs to hear that you care about her."

Mike disagreed. "Lizzie knows I care about her. I love her."

"Did you ever tell her that?"

"No."

"She won't know how you feel if you don't tell her," Nathan advised.

Pondering this situation, Mike let out a discouraged sigh. "Relationships give me nothing but heartache. I'll never have what you and Gabby have."

"Things aren't always perfect between Gabby and I. We've had our share of problems just like any other couple."

Mike peered down the hall at Nathan's closed bedroom door. "Is she here?"

"No, she had to work this morning, and I have a class I need to get ready for. But I suggest you talk to Lizzie. Tell her how you feel."

Mike came home that evening bleary-eyed and sick to his stomach. He hobbled in the door and almost ran into the wall. Before Nathan had a chance to say anything to him, he rushed to the bathroom and threw up.

This erratic, reckless behavior was really getting out of control. Mike needed an intervention before he slipped into an irreversible downward spiral. Although he didn't want to get Lizzie involved, Nathan felt she might be able to talk some sense into him.

"Why did you come to me?" Lizzie asked.

"Because you're the reason he's acting like this."

She immediately disputed that accusation. "How is this my fault?"

"He told me what happened at the club."

Lizzie's face stiffened sternly. "Did he tell you he came onto me and tried to back me into a corner?"

Nathan drew back. This was not at all the story he heard. "What?"

"Yeah." Lizzie tightened her stance. "He fed me some stupid line about how I'm the only girl he ever cared about then backed me against the wall and tried to kiss me. When I refused, he became aggressive."

His charcoal-spoked eyes widened in surprise. "That doesn't sound like something Mike would do."

"Well he did, and I was just as surprised as you are."

Nathan scratched his head, baffled by this behavior.

"I don't know what you want me to do, Nathan. I haven't heard from him since that night at the club, and quite frankly, I don't know what I'd say to him if I saw him. When I refused to let him kiss me, he made it pretty obvious he never want to talk to me again."

When Nathan came home, Mike was passed out on the couch. Desperate to find out what was going on, Nathan woke him up.

Michael buried his head under a pillow and groaned. "Dude, I'm sleeping. Go away."

"Did you go to work today?"

"No. They got tired of me calling in and fired me."

"We have rent due next week. Do you have your half?"

"I'll get it."

"How?" Nathan asked. "You're not working, and you spend all your money on booze."

"I didn't ask for your opinion."

Outraged by Mike's recent behavior, Nathan stood his ground. "This behavior is bullshit. Why are you letting a girl tear you apart like this?"

Mike sat up, offended that his best friend questioned his judgement. "Do I tell you how to live your life? No I don't, so I'd appreciate it if you wouldn't tell me how to live mine."

"I don't give a crap what you do, until it starts affecting who you are. What the hell is going on, Mike?"

Mike rose to his feet. "You know what? I'm done. I don't have to explain myself to you or anyone else. If I choose to go out all night and share my bed with a pretty girl, that's my business, not yours." He grabbed his car keys and stormed out the door.

Lately, everything seemed to set Mike off, but he'd never gone off on Nathan before. Alarmed by this aggressiveness, Nathan trailed after him. "Mike, come on. I'm sorry."

Mike stuck his middle finger in the air and kept walking.

CHAPTER THIRTY-FIVE

Summer classes and work schedules kept both Nathan and Gabby busy. Nathan had class for four and half hours a day then went to work in his father's clinic all afternoon, saving his evenings for studying. Gabby worked at the daycare center in the morning and had cheer practice for three to four hours every afternoon. Despite this, they made time every night to share dinner together.

Concerned about the latest developments with Mike, Nathan reached out to Gabby. "I wish I knew what was going on with him, but he won't talk to me."

"Maybe it has something to do with his parents. You know he's never really gotten along with either of them."

"He rarely talks to his parents. And none of this started until that night at the club with Lizzie."

Gabby poked a fork into her salad. "She told me about that."

Nathan slumped over. "I'm worried about him. When I came home last night, he was passed out on the couch. He told me he lost his job. When I asked him about it, he got all defensive and walked out. Mike's never spoken to me like that before."

"Maybe he was just having a bad day."

"Every day for the last two weeks has been a bad day. He never did come home last night, and I haven't heard from him all day."

"Sounds to me like he's crying for help."

"But he should be coming to me. We've been best friends since grade school."

"You've been busy with classes and basketball, Nathan."

In retrospect, she had a good point. As kids, he and Michael always hung out together, but since they started college, even though they shared an apartment, the time they spent together had slowly dwindled. "So this is his outcry to me to pay more attention to him?"

"He doesn't have any brothers or sisters, and he doesn't like his parents. You're pretty much the only family he has."

Nathan felt a knot in the pit of his stomach. Gut instinct told him his friend was on the verge of a tragic meltdown. "Shit."

He tried texting Mike several times throughout the night, but he never responded. Not knowing where his friend was or what he was doing, Nathan's fingers tensed. "Why isn't he answering me?"

"Did you try calling him?" Gabby suggested.

Nathan dialed Mike's number again. His phone went straight to voicemail. "Come on, Mike. Talk to me."

When Mike didn't come home that night, Nathan's fears escalated. He paced around the living room calling anyone he could think of to see if they'd seen or heard from him. No one had.

At 8:30 A.M., Nathan received a phone call from his father. "Nathan, you might want to sit down."

"Why?"

"Just sit down."

Nathan did as his father asked.

Randy's voice shook, struggling for the right words. "Mike's father called me this morning."

The brittle tone in his father's voice brushed fear over Nathan's features. "What's going on?"

Randy's breathing become shallow, as if someone struck him in the chest. "They found Mike's car parked by the side of the road at 2:00 A.M. this morning."

A deafening silence fell between them. "Is he ok?"

"He um…" Randy choked over his words. "He was leaned over the steering wheel holding his dad's pistol in his hand."

Nathan's heart sank to the floor. "What was he doing with a gun?"

Randy hesitated to tell him. "Nathan. Mike took his own life last night."

Nathan's chest squeezed in anguish. Shock held him immobile. "What? That can't be. I just saw him two days ago. How can…" A sensation of intense sickness and desolation overcame him. His hands began to shake, and his throat seemed to close up. "Oh god, no!" He covered his face with his hands and gave vent to the agony of his loss.

Worried about his son's overwhelming sorrow, Randy asked, "Is Gabby there with you?"

Smothering a sob, he drew in a few deep breaths until he was strong enough to answer. "She's at work."

"Do you want me to come over?"

He closed his eyes, reliving the last conversation he had with Mike. His body shuddered at the thought. "No. I'll call Gabby."

"Are you sure?"

Choking through tears, he swallowed hard. "Yeah."

"I'm so sorry, Nathan," Randy said, offering support. "Your mother and I are here for you, you know that."

With a moan of distress, he wept aloud. The torment of the last few weeks gnawed at him, stabbing at his very soul. He couldn't bear the thought of life without Michael Lynott.

"If you need me, just call. I'll be here."

Nathan sniffled through sobs. "Thanks, Dad."

"Love you, Nate."

"Love you too." Feeling sick to his stomach, he tore himself away from the phone. He wasn't up to coping with this right now. He needed Gabby. With a choking cry, he dialed her number.

"Hi, Sweetie," she answered. "I can't talk right now. I'm at work." She heard his voice shudder as he drew a sharp breath. "What's wrong?"

"I need you."

Deep sobs racked his insides. It wasn't like Nathan to openly cry like this. Something was seriously wrong. "Nathan, what is it?"

"Gabby, please," he implored. "Is there any way you can leave work and come over here?"

The pain in his heart gnawed at her soul. "Give me a few minutes. Let me see what I can do."

"Hurry."

The longer it took Gabby to get there, the more the heartache tore Nathan apart. When she finally walked in the door, a glazed look of despair spread over his face. He held his arms out to her, begging for consolation.

She rushed to his side, sinking into his arms. "What happened?"

His chest rose and fell with labored breathing. "Michael."

Based on Nathan's reaction, Gabby assumed the worst. "What about him?"

"They found his body...he had a gun and he..." Nathan couldn't continue. His misery was so acute, he was in physical pain.

Gabby's mouth opened in dismay. "Oh god."

He wept aloud, rocking her back and forth. "Don't leave me," he wailed. "Please don't leave me."

It took Nathan several hours to regain his composure. Concerned about his state of mind, Gabby didn't want to leave him alone. She called her cheer coach and told her there was a family emergency and she wouldn't make it to practice. Her coach fully understood, which gave Gabby much needed time with Nathan.

The next several days sent Nathan plummeting down an emotional rollercoaster. Almost everything brought him to tears. When he saw Mike's parents at the memorial service, a surge of despair swept over him. He buried his face in Gabby's shoulder and cried. The eulogy, the photograph of Mike staring at them from atop the casket, the funeral precession—it was all too much for Nathan to handle. He didn't speak to anyone all day and spent the majority of his time seeking comfort in Gabby.

Following the service, Nathan and Gabby reported to his parents' house. Gripping a cup of coffee, Randy placed his hand on Nathan's shoulder. "Come out on the deck with me."

Nathan jammed his hands in his pockets and joined his father.

Randy grabbed two lawn chairs and positioned them on the deck facing the lake. He sat in one. Nathan sat in the other. "How you doing?"

Nathan hung his head. Overcome with grief and guilt, he tried not to cry.

"I understand your pain, Nathan. He was your best friend."

Breathing hard, he huffed a few times then tightened his hands into fists. "I don't understand this," he said. "If he was having problems, why didn't he come talk to me?"

"Was he having problems?"

"His grades weren't that great, and his dad was giving him a hard time about school. He also recently got rejected by a girl he fell in love with. I really don't know what else was going on because he became reclusive and shut me out, and it's my fault."

Randy didn't agree with Nathan's logic. "How could that have been your fault?"

"Because I wasn't available when he needed me. He spent all that time supporting me and helping me when my basketball schedule was nuts, but I wasn't there when he needed me. I was his family, Dad. We were like brothers, and I was so busy with my own life that I failed to acknowledge his." He squeezed his eyes shut and wrapped his arms around himself.

"This isn't your fault, Nate."

"You don't understand. The last words we said to each other were spoken in anger. He was drunk and depressed, and I gave him a hard time about rent money. He pretty much told me to leave him alone then flipped me off on his way out the door. I never should have let him get in the car. I should have gone after him."

"And what would you have done then?"

"I don't know." He looked heavenward; his vision clouded with tears. "I should have done something, said something, gotten someone else involved, someone who might have been able to help him."

Seeing his son in this much misery broke Randy's heart. "Nathan."

"He was my best friend, my brother." A steady stream flowed from his eyes. "I should have been there for him, and I wasn't."

Randy's heart ached. Nathan was miserable, and there was nothing he could do about it. He offered comfort the only way he knew how—he gave Nathan a hug and let him cry. "This will take time, Son. Healing takes time."

Over the next few days, Gabby helped Nathan box up all of Mike's belongings. He had to pause every ten minutes or so to recompose himself, but eventually he was able to get most of the boxes packed. When they got to the closet and Nathan saw Mike's high school letter jacket, the pain was too much for him to bear. He gripped the jacket in his hands and sobbed.

Gabby crawled over to him and wrapped her arms around his shoulders.

Desperately seeking comfort, he clung to her, releasing a torment of bereavement.

CHAPTER THIRTY-SIX

The most impressive and challenging moves in cheerleading were the stunts in which flyers were lifted up and tossed in the air by their teammates. Even though Gabby had a lot of experience with stunts, it still made Nathan nervous every time she performed them. He was fortunate Gabby had someone she trusted who was a good base to support her.

Gabby's partner, Jayden, was exceptionally strong. His upper body strength superseded that of most men. Not only was he powerfully strong, he also had many years of experience as a base, which made Nathan feel a little more comfortable about Gabby doing stunts with him.

Stunts required communication between those performing the stunt. Gabby and Jayden spent several months practicing together and had become exceptionally good at communicating using non-verbal cues. With their coach's guidance, Gabby and Jayden developed amazing stunt routines. They were considered the best coed pair in the stunt department. As they performed their lifts and stunts, extra bases were devoted to act as spotters in case, god forbid, Gabby lost her footing or became unsteady and fell.

For most lifts, getting down was just as difficult as getting up. Dismounts had to be smooth, but also exciting for the crowd. Nathan, however, was more concerned about the safety aspects involved. Gabby trusted Jayden, but Nathan wanted to extend that trust to himself. To accomplish this, he made it a priority to get to know Jayden on a more personal level.

After work, Nathan popped in to see the end of cheer practice. When he walked into the gym, Jayden was steadily holding Gabby above his head with one hand. This task required amazing strength and balance on behalf of both parties. Nathan marveled at the incredible power and coordination it took to pull off a stunt like that. He couldn't do it. Then, in one quick motion, Jayden tossed Gabby up in the air, just high enough for her to jack-knife and touch her toes, before he caught her and set her down on the gym floor.

"Nice one," Nathan applauded, gaining the attention of the cheer squad. They all knew him from basketball, but seeing Nathan Hanson off the court was a rare treat for most of them.

Gabby smiled at him. "Hi, Sweetie."

"Hey." He greeted her with a kiss then acknowledged Jayden. "You know, I hold Gabby in my arms every night, but I would never be able to hold her above my head like that. It takes amazing strength to do that. That's pretty badass."

A big name athlete complimenting his athletic ability boosted Jayden's confidence. "Gabby is a good partner. Makes it easier for me."

"I appreciate you keeping her safe."

"That's my job." As Jayden left the gym, he waved at Gabby. "I'll see you tomorrow, Gabby."

She waved back. "Bye, Jayden."

Nathan planned to meet Mike's parents tonight to drop off all the boxes he packed. He'd been avoiding this task for days, but could no longer put it off. Gabby knew how emotionally difficult this was going to be for him. Offering her support, she reached out and touched his arm. "How you doing?"

His breath quickened. "I don't want to do this."

"I know." She rose to her tiptoes and kissed him. "It'll be ok. I'll be there with you."

Drawing in a long breath, he took her hand and escorted her out of the gym.

Carrying a box in his arms, Nathan hesitated before he knocked on the door. "I can't do this. I can't look his mother in the eye."

"It's gonna be ok."

He took a deep breath and puffed out his cheeks. "What am I supposed to say to them?"

"We'll figure it out together." She gently rubbed his back and inched him toward the door.

When Nathan knocked, Mike's father answered. He peered at Nathan with glossy eyes then wavered for a minute before giving him a hug. "Nathan. It's good to see you."

"You too, Sir."

He and Gabby stayed and chatted for about an hour, trying to ease each other's pain during this difficult time. Before Nathan left, Mr. Lynott handed him Mike's letter jacket. "Mike would have wanted you to have this."

With shaky hands, Nathan reached for the jacket.

"You were a good friend to him, Nathan. He looked up to you and would have gladly given you the shirt off his back if he could have."

Nathan stared down at the jacket. He heard a roaring in his ears and the whole world seemed to be moving in slow motion. He felt like he was trapped in a dream world; a horrific, nightmarish dream world. "Thank you, Sir. This means a lot to me."

"Don't be a stranger, okay? Stop by and visit once in a while."

Nathan disguised his sadness with a smile. "I will, Sir."

When Mike's father closed the door, Nathan had to take a minute to compose himself.

"You ok?" Gabby asked.

"Yeah." He slipped Mike's jacket over his shoulders and held Gabby's hand on the way to the car.

Temperatures in Seattle during the summer usually hovered around a pleasant seventy-five. But in recent weeks, bleak, overcast skies engulfed the city, matching Nathan's dismal mood. On several occasions, skies remained cloudy all day and often brought bouts of rain. Other days, the sun broke through the clouds, bringing partly sunny skies for a while. But it usually wasn't long before the dark clouds reappeared and rain once again spilled out over the city.

According to the latest weather report, the foray into warm weather was expected over the weekend. Brighter days were in store. Nathan just needed to hang in there a bit longer to find them.

He peeked out the window at the gloomy grey sky. "It's going to rain again. We haven't had a day of sunshine in weeks."

"It's supposed to be nice this weekend," Gabby told him.

"I hope so, because this weather sucks. I want to go water skiing." With high hopes, Nathan had his sunglasses on standby.

After two weeks of below normal temperatures and above average rainfall, summer finally decided to get serious. The Fourth of July weekend was on the toasty side, reaching eighty-six degrees. The flag flew high amidst clear skies on Independence Day. Nathan and his family spent the weekend outside, enjoying the beautiful weather, joined by Gabby and the Ryan family.

Throughout the day, they took the boat out waterskiing, lounged on the beach, and splashed around in the lake. While Randy stoked up the barbecue, Nathan and Gabby set up the volleyball net.

Jim watched them for a few minutes before he took a sip of his Corona. "How's Nathan doing?" he asked, knowing Nathan was having a hard time adjusting to life without his childhood friend.

"As good as can be expected, I guess. It's been a rough couple of weeks." Randy's eyelids were droopy, and his energy level was well below normal.

"You look like hell, Dude. You goin' for a new zombie style?"

Randy rubbed the back of his neck. "I didn't get much sleep last night."

Teasing his friend, Jim said, "Too much hanky-panky in the bedroom?"

"No, it was just a long ass night."

"What happened?" Jim asked.

Randy proceeded to tell him. "A chorus of infant cries flooded L&D all night. For some reason every pregnant woman in Seattle went into labor, and most of them were my patients."

"That sucks," Jim declared.

"Yes it did. My day was pretty chaotic, and unexpected deliveries went well into the night. I didn't make it home until around midnight. However, enjoying my peaceful slumber was short-lived because three hours later, I got a call that another one of my patients checked in, in latent stages of labor. Mind you, it was three o'clock in the morning, and after less than three hours of sleep, fatigue had kicked in. Somehow I managed to drive into Seattle. I pulled into the hospital groggy beyond belief and felt like a wad of gum squished on the asphalt, baked in the sun, and stuck on a motorcycle tire burning rubber on a gravel trail."

Jim found Randy's account of the whole thing hilarious. "That's bad."

"That's just the beginning. I headed up to L&D, desperately chugging down a cup of coffee, and walked into my patient's room only to find her kicking and screaming at my nurses because apparently no amount of Demerol was relieving her agony."

"A lot of women in labor scream obscenities and yell."

"Yes, they do, and some even call their husbands horrible names. But this woman didn't. In fact, she didn't say a damn thing to him. Instead, she punched him in the face and threw up on him."

Jim broke into hysterical laughter. "Bet he wasn't expecting that."

"No he wasn't. But the excitement wasn't over yet. Upon seeing a pool of blood, acquired from the steady stream that was now gushing from his nose, his face turned ghostly white. He followed her in a vomit fest then passed out in the middle of the floor. By this time, the baby's head was crowning, but the nurses were occupied with trying to revive the guy, leaving me to carry on unassisted. To make matters worse, halfway through the delivery, I had to stop her from pushing because the baby's shoulder was pinching the umbilical cord and cutting the oxygen supply from his not-quite-yet-born brain. Luckily I was able to remedy this situation and the baby only suffered a brachial plexus injury."

"That's good," Jim said.

"Her husband finally came to, completely missing the show, and ended up being treated for a head contusion and a posterior nosebleed."

Jim chuckled. "Sounds like you had a crazy night."

"Crazy doesn't even come close."

"I too had an interesting day yesterday."

"Why is that?" Randy asked as he sipped from his bottle of Corona.

"I taught a snot-nosed resident doctor lesson 101 on how to piss off the ER Director."

"Uh oh. What happened?"

"I had this patient who needed a procedure done, so I called the cardiology department, only I didn't recognize the voice on the other line. Turns out the guy was the surgical resident on call. Anyway, I told him I had a patient who went to his PMD a few days ago for weakness and was found to have a benign rhabdomyoma on the tricuspid valve of his right ventricle. Dr. Snotnose then proceeded to develop an attitude with me and rudely interrupted by saying, 'And how then can I help you?' I answered the douchebag by telling him he could start by lettin' me finish. I then proceeded to ask him if he actually held a medical degree."

Randy laughed loudly. "You didn't really ask him that, did you?"

"Hell yeah, I did," Jim admitted. "Why the fuck did he think I was callin'? To chat about the weather? Obviously I needed a surgical excision done, but of course he's too busy to be concerned about petty things like that."

"Cardiac rhabdomyoma can be fatal if not treated," Randy declared.

"I know that and you know that, but apparently Dr. Know-It-All neglected to recognize the seriousness of this condition and blew me off."

"He figured out the severity of the situation I hope," Randy replied.

"Only after I explained to him what a rhabdomyoma was. Dumbass."

CHAPTER THIRTY-SEVEN

One thing that was vital to the success of Huskies men's basketball was working as a team, which meant getting to know one another and learning each other's strengths. Coach Spoleda accomplished this vital socialization in several ways. One way he did this was by encouraging the team members who were still in town during the summer to meet informally to grab lunch together or play casual basketball games in the gym or at a park. He even organized a barbecue at his house toward the end of summer to bring all of his players together and get them to start communicating with each other. This was something he insisted on. The men were like a brotherhood.

Five new members were joining the team this season. Two sophomores and three freshmen—Joaquin Santiago, Mikel Kingsley, Keeton Sullivan, Creshaun Damir, and Devonte Williams. One of these new teammates, Joaquin Santiago, was from Argentina. Santiago was a sophomore like Nathan. He played basketball for a year at a university in Argentina, where some scouts watched him play and sent his name to Coach Spoleda. After viewing basketball footage of Santiago and reviewing his stats, recruiters were sent down to talk to him, offering a scholarship at UW. Santiago longed for adventure at an American university, so he gladly signed on.

Andre Giraldi was also from Argentina. He had played for the Huskies for the last two years. Nathan knew him well and loved sharing the court with him. He was a strong defensive player who excelled at blocking shots. He was good at pulling the rebound, racking up double-figures almost every game.

In an attempt to create more tightness among his players, Coach Spoleda arranged for the entire Dawg Pack to spend a week in Mendoza, Argentina on a team bonding trip. Since this was a place Nathan had never been to before, he was excited about this adventure.

Mendoza was spread across the wide valley of the Río Mendoza, over one-thousand kilometers west of Buenos Aires, on the eastern side of the Andes. Because Argentina was in the Southern hemisphere, it was winter when the players arrived, and the temperature was between fifty-five and sixty-five degrees. The mountain air was cool, and the sky was a beautiful bright blue.

Nathan's initial impression of Mendoza was that it was largely a pedestrian city full of outdoor cafés. People freely strolled the streets. Outdoor sports like mountain climbing, horseback riding, hiking, and paragliding were popular, and since it was winter, an influx of skiers flooded the area.

Another striking feature was that every street was lined with bushy sycamore trees, allowing Nathan and his teammates many opportunities to wander around the leafy avenues and parks to soak up the atmosphere. In the heart of the city was the main plaza, where much of the daily action took place. Plaza de España, as it was called, had Spanish tiled benches and shady trees to sit under. The central wall depicted a mosaic of images and texts of the Spanish colonization. It was crowned by a gorgeous statue.

The men got a taste of Argentinian culture when they visited The National History Museum. This particular museum dealt with every aspect of Argentina's past, taking them right up to date with modern day life. Nathan ate up every aspect of this small city, from the history to all the stunning scenery. It was quite different from any other place he had visited before.

Nathan and his teammates took a day trip to the Parque Provincial Aconcagua. This day tour offered breathtaking views along a scenic two hour drive. The park itself had an inclined gravel walking trail that took them to a viewpoint, where Nathan was able to capture several pictures of the river ravine below. From there, they took a hike up Cerro Arco, the looming mountain to Mendoza's northwest. This pleasant half-day hike offered spectacular views of both the Andean foothills and the vast expanse of Mendoza's plains.

As Nathan looked out on the gorgeous scene, he spoke to his new team member, Joaquin Santiago. Although Joaquin was from Mendoza, he could speak English. He occasionally had grammar issues, such as leaving off articles or misconjugating verbs, but he had a large vocabulary and was quite fluent when he spoke.

Nathan looked forward to using his Spanish skills with his new teammate. But since Joaquin was going to be attending an American university, he asked Nathan to speak in English so he could polish his skills.

Nathan granted his request. "It is absolutely gorgeous here."

In an Argentine accent, Joaquin replied, "Seattle is also beautiful city. The Lake…what is the name of it?"

"Lake Washington," Nathan stated.

"Yes, Lake Washington. And you have very pretty mountain."

"Mt. Rainier," Nathan added. "My family and I go skiing on that mountain every winter."

"My family and I visit Andes often as well."

"You know, my parents have a house on the lake. Maybe you could come out for a visit. We can take the boat out and go waterskiing. Have you ever been waterskiing?" Nathan asked.

"Long time ago," Joaquin replied.

"We will have to get you out on the water then," Nathan offered with a smile. "I think you'll like Seattle. I'll show you around when we get back."

"That would be very nice."

The men visited Cacheuta, located about an hour outside of Mendoza. This area had a large network of natural hot springs, giving the men time to unwind and relax. Lounging in the steaming water, Nathan and his teammates shared stories about their families and talked about their girlfriends. Anytime Nathan had the opportunity to talk about Gabby, he ate it up.

"You have girlfriend?" Santiago asked Nathan.

Nathan grinned widely. "Yes I do."

"What is her name?"

"Gabby. She's a cheerleader for Washington."

This captured Joaquin's attention. "She cheers at basketball games?"

"Yes," Nathan replied. "And football games, and pretty much any other opportunity she can squeeze in the chance to cheer."

Joaquin openly laughed. "She must really enjoy cheering."

"Loves it. Definitely one of her favorite things."

"How long has she been girlfriend of yours?"

Nathan explained, "We've known each other for six years, but have officially been a couple for three."

Joaquin raised an eyebrow, impressed that Nathan had managed to maintain a relationship with the same girl for so long. "You are a lucky man."

Nathan beamed with pride. "I am. She's an incredible woman."

After some chill time at the hot springs, the men reported back to their hotel. Nathan loved his time in Argentina. This vacation gave him an opportunity to spend quality time with his teammates off the basketball court.

But he missed Gabby.

As soon as Nathan landed in Seattle, he sent her a text. She agreed to meet him with the car at Alaska Airlines Arena. Leaning against the Mustang, she anxiously waited for the bus to pull up. The second Nathan stepped off the bus, Gabby jumped into his arms, almost knocking him over. "I missed you."

Nathan was so happy to see her. He dropped his bag on the ground and held her in his arms, soaking in her tender kiss. "I missed you too. There's someone I want you to meet."

"Who?" she asked.

"Joaquin Santiago, our new forward."

Gabby held Nathan's hand and joyfully pranced over to meet Joaquin. "The guy from Argentina?"

"Yes." Trying to gain his friend's attention, Nathan called out, "Joaquin."

Joaquin turned around. "Sí?"

"This is my girlfriend, Gabriella."

He held out his hand to her. "Hola, Gabby. Mucho gusto."

Gabby had no clue what that meant. "What?"

Nathan translated for her. "He said it's nice to meet you."

"Pleasure to meet you too, Joaquin."

"Nathan speaks of you often," Joaquin remarked.

She looked up at Nathan with a smile. "Does he?"

"Yes." Switching back to Spanish, he said, "Ella es una mucha hermosa."

Nathan eyed Gabby with loving eyes. "Sí, estoy de acuerdo."

Gabby wrinkled her forehead, wondering what they were saying. "Are you guys talking about me?"

Nathan told her what they said. "He said he thinks you're pretty. I told him I agreed with him."

Gabby bowed gracefully. "Gracias."

Nathan figured that being in a new country, transferring to a different university, and just overall adjusting to a completely different cultural setting must have been shocking for Joaquin. Wanting to offer assistance, he asked. "Do you know where your room is? Can you find your way around campus?"

"Andre said he would help me find my way."

"If you'd like, we can get together next weekend. I'll show you around Seattle."

"That will be great. Thank you so much for your kindness. Enjoy your weekend, my friend."

"I'll see you on Monday. Adios, mi amigo."

Joaquin waved goodbye then made his way toward campus.

Holding Gabby's hand, Nathan picked up his bag.

"He seems nice," Gabby commented.

"He's a good guy. Gonna need a little support getting adjusted."

Gabby popped the trunk and Nathan tossed his bag inside. "It's good you invited him to hang with us next weekend. That will help."

"Gotta make him feel welcome." He took the keys from Gabby. "You ready?"

She nodded. "Uh huh."

"Good. Let's go home."

With Gabby in his arms, Nathan peered over the edge of the bed. Gabby's purple canvas shoes were on the floor right next to him. She wore slip-on shoes almost every day, and she owned several pairs in many different colors. While Nathan was down in South America, he purchased a pair of Espadrilles, a pair of cotton canvas shoes with jute soles that were handmade in Argentina. "I got you something." He hung over the side, stretching for his athletic bag. He pulled out a box wrapped in purple metallic paper and handed it to Gabby. "Here. I found these and thought you'd like them."

She opened the box to reveal a pair of fuchsia canvas slip-on shoes. "Ooh. These are pretty."

He dug around in his bag for a smaller box. This one wasn't wrapped. "I got this for you too."

She gave him an enquiring eye. "Another one?"

"Yup."

A delightful smile raced across her face. She opened the second box to find a string of beautifully handcrafted pink gems embedded between silver links. "Oh my god, this is gorgeous."

"I had that custom made for you. Those gems are called Inca Rose, and they're pretty rare. They're only found in Argentina." He reached into the box and carefully pulled out the bracelet, latching it around her wrist.

Gabby marveled at the crystalline rose-colored gems. She'd never seen anything like them before. "This is beautiful, Nathan. I love it!" She thanked him with a kiss. "Thank you."

He gazed upon her with loving eyes. "You're welcome."

Another Argentinian product Nathan purchased was a small tub of Dulce de Leche, a rich and decadent sweet syrup used to flavor candies, bananas, or other sweet foods, such as cookies and ice cream. It was also a popular spread on pancakes or a dip for pretzels. Randy often ordered Dulce de Leche flavored coffee products from Starbucks, so Nathan gave the tub to his father.

"Thanks, Nate."

"You're welcome. And let me tell you, no one makes Dulce de Leche like the Argentinians. That stuff is tasty."

Randy set the tub on the kitchen counter. "How was your trip?"

"The trip was great. Argentina is beautiful, and I loved the bonding time we all had."

Randy leaned against the counter and took a sip of his coffee. "How are you doing? Are you feeling any better? Were you able to get your mind off things and relax a bit?"

"A little. Michael was a huge part of my life. Without him, I feel like a part of me is missing." He slouched on a barstool at the kitchen island. "I had a conversation with my coach while we were in Argentina. He arranged to have Andrew room with me." Nathan's eyes grew misty. "It's gonna be hard, you know, having Andrew in Mike's room. It's going to take some time to adjust."

"Take all the time you need," Randy said. "I know this has been hard for you. But please remember that you're not alone. Your family and friends are here for you, Nate. You can talk to me any time you need to."

"I know. And I'm sure I will."

Randy walked past Nathan and mussed up his hair. "Come on. Let's go for a ride."

Nathan watched his father grab his car keys and head toward the door. "Where are we going?"

"I wanna hang out with my son. Let's enjoy some scenery and talk."

"Alright." He combed his fingers through his hair and followed his father out to the garage.

It wasn't uncommon for Randy to leave the confines of the city to get some fresh air and let his sports car breathe. With its proximity to three major freeways and countless highways, exploring Washington was incredibly easy, and they had the whole afternoon at their disposal.

Randy put the top down on the Jaguar, and they made their way out of Kirkland. As they drove through the countryside, they witnessed some of the most gorgeous scenery in the country. They passed a broad span of Washington farmland, with fields and fences in every direction, and stopped at the occasional fruit or espresso stand. They headed east on old Highway 2, driving along Steven's Pass Highway, where they followed the Skykomish River. The scenery was especially pretty through here. They passed through three historic towns—Sultan, Goldbar, and Startup—where they saw a tiny roadside chapel that looked like a white outhouse at first.

Upon second look, they noticed the prim cross on the tiny steeple roof. The sign outside the chapel said, *Stop. Rest. Worship.* So that is exactly what Nathan and his father did.

After a brief side stop to take in a moment of reverence, the winding highway took them through misty fields and mountains with thick green foliage. Randy hit the turnoff to Iron Goat trailhead, one of Washington's greatest trail ways in the Stevens Pass historic area. Not only did they see lovely forests of ferns, alders, and evergreens from this trail, they also saw history. The Great Northern Railway used to run along this trail. There were remnants of rail tunnels, snow shed coverings, and machinery grown over with plants and moss as wilderness reclaimed the area. Walking through this wilderness history museum was a unique experience for the two of them, and it gave them the opportunity to spend quality father-son bonding time together.

After an hour or so of exploring the old railroad, they got back in the car and returned to the highway, which took them through the Wenatchee National Forest and eventually to Leavenworth. Driving into Leavenworth was a bit of a shock because one minute they were in the middle of wilderness then all of a sudden they were in a Bavarian village. Everything in this riverside town was built in Bavarian style architecture—even the gas station where they stopped to refill the car. Walking around the tourist-friendly town was fun, especially in the summer. There were some cute little shops, and the town had the most brightly colored hanging flower pots they'd ever seen. They grabbed lunch at the München Haus, where they got a taste of authentic German charbroiled sausages, ciderkraut, and specialty mustards.

Just outside of the town, they drove through rolling vineyards and checked out some of the local fruit stands to sample some scrumptiously juicy watermelon. By midafternoon, they decided to head back home. Knowing

Nathan had been going through a rough time, Randy held the keys out to him. "You're driving home."

Nathan's eyes widened in surprise. Randy was always extraordinarily protective of his treasured sports cars. He had never let Nathan drive the Jaguar before. "Seriously?"

"Yes." Randy placed the keys in Nathan's hand. "Take the wheel. Enjoy the open road."

With great delight, Nathan sat behind the wheel of the Jag and revved up the engine. The primal power of this high-performance sports car was nothing but sensual. This car was relaxed and comfortable, yet at the same time was capable of achieving a sub-eight-minute lap on the Nürburgring course. This car piloted so smoothly, and it was fast. The adrenaline rush was intense. Nathan was in driving heaven.

Nathan drove across the old Skykomish River Bridge and returned to civilization. When they got to the city of Monroe, he turned down Highway 522, which led them back to the freeway and home. It was late evening by the time they returned.

Curiously questioning where her boys had been all day, Jane asked, "Where'd you guys go?"

Randy placed his car keys in the glass bowl on the dining room table. "We went for a drive up Stevens Pass."

"Ooh, it's pretty back there."

"Yes it is."

Jane looked over at her son. "Gabby called looking for you."

Nathan was surprised to hear this. "She did?"

"Yes. She seemed a bit frazzled. Did you tell her you were coming over here?"

"I told her where I was. Didn't know I was going on a scenic drive through the mountains, but I'm glad we did." Nathan grinned, overjoyed that he and his father shared this special time together. "Thanks, Dad. It was fun hanging out with you today. I really needed that."

"I enjoyed it too."

Nathan hugged both of his parents before he hopped in the Mustang and headed back to UW. He called Gabby on the way.

"Oh my god, Nathan, where have you been?" Her tone was urgent and panicky.

Nathan laughed at her. "What do you mean, where have I been? I told you I was going over to my parents' house today."

"I tried calling you," she argued.

"I was out of cell coverage for a while," he explained. "My dad and I went for a drive."

"I was worried. I thought something had happened. And then I called your mom and she didn't know where you guys were either. You scared the crap out of me, Nathan. Don't ever do that again!" she insisted.

"Do what? Hang out with my dad?" he questioned, thinking that was an outlandish and irrational request.

"No. Take off like that and not tell me where you are."

"I did tell you where I was," he justified with a jesting quip. "Quit freaking out, Gab."

"You scared me half to death. I thought the worst when I didn't hear from you. Why didn't you at least text me and tell me what was going on?"

After recent events, he realized that yes, he probably should have tried to contact her and let her know he would be gone for several hours. Recognizing his error, he apologized. "I'm sorry. I didn't think I was going to be gone that long. I didn't mean to scare you."

"Are you on your way?" she asked.

"Yes. I'm about to hit the freeway. I need to go so I can focus on driving."

She agreed that was a good idea. "Please be careful."

"I will."

Feeling calmer now, she proclaimed, "I love you."

"I love you, too. I'll see you in a bit." He hung up his cellphone and focused on the road, carefully merging onto the freeway to make his way to the other side of Lake Washington.

CHAPTER THIRTY-EIGHT

The new academic year was right around the corner. Although Nathan was still recuperating from the loss of his best friend, he looked forward to kicking off his sophomore year. Gabby had recently moved into her new dorm room, so Nathan stopped by after work to check it out.

He always loved Gabby's taste in décor and her keen sense of interior decorating. She had subtle ways of expressing herself and had the ability to make the room inviting without being overbearing. Nathan was glad her new roommate, Karina, had better taste than her previous roommate did. Together, Gabby and Karina made the room blend nicely, incorporating both of their tastes and purchasing matching accessories so the entire room flowed and was quite pleasant.

"Wow," Nathan declared as he looked around. "Looks nice in here. I could sleep here." He sat on Gabby's bed and leaned back on the pillow. Getting more comfortable, he kicked off his shoes and clasped his hands behind his head.

"You look comfy."

"I am very comfortable. But you know what would make me more comfortable?"

"What?" she asked.

He took her hand in his and pulled her on top of him. "This." He kissed her tenderly on the lips, slowly at first.

Gradually, he extended each kiss a bit longer than the last one, increasing the intensity each time.

In the middle of their makeout session, the door flew opened. Nathan immediately sat up and looked over at their intruder.

Walking in on Gabby and Nathan turned Karina's face a bright shade of red. "I am so sorry. I did not mean to barge in on you."

Nathan didn't think it was a big deal. "No worries. You must be Karina."

She stared at him for a minute. His face was surprisingly familiar, but she couldn't recall where she had seen him before. "I know you from somewhere."

"Do you?" Nathan asked, flashing a warm smile.

Gabby repositioned herself so she was sitting by Nathan's side. "I'm sorry, Karina. I didn't introduce you. This is Nathan Hanson."

Karina knew that name. She followed Huskies sports teams diligently and was a huge basketball fan. With a curious expression, she asked, "Nathan Hanson? Like point guard on the basketball team Hanson?"

"Yours truly," Nathan boasted.

Karina slapped her hand over her mouth. She had never seen him up close and personal like this before, in fact she had never seen him off the court at all. The only time she saw his face was in news articles, game photographs, or pounding the hardwood with a basketball in his hand. "That's where I've seen you before."

"Most likely," Nathan declared.

"Gabby said your name was Nathan, but you didn't tell me it was you."

"Surprise," Nathan joked. "But seriously, it's a pleasure to meet you." He take a quick peek at his watch. It was almost 7:00 P.M. "I didn't realize how late it was. No wonder I'm hungry. You wanna grab some dinner, Gab?"

She laughed at his constant lust for food. "Why am I not surprised you want to eat?"

"Am I not allowed to eat?" he asked innocently, acting like he was going to starve to death if he didn't get nourishment soon.

"You are always hungry," she teased him.

"I'm starving." He slipped his shoes back on then stood up and took Gabby by the hand. Being cordial, he invited Karina to come with them. "You wanna join us?"

Karina shook her head. "I wouldn't want to intrude on you guys."

"You won't," Nathan assured. "Come with us."

Karina agreed, and the three of them went to the Local Point to grab a bite to eat.

When Nathan returned to his apartment that night, Andrew was on the couch watching ESPN. "Hey," Nathan said, setting his keys on the counter. "I see you got settled in."

"I did."

Nathan occupied the chair across from him.

Sensing Nathan's overwhelming apprehension with this situation, Andrew offered his sympathies. "I know how close you and Mike were, and I know how hard this is, but I appreciate you opening up to me and giving me a chance to help you get through this."

Nathan choked back tears. "I appreciate your willingness to try."

"So," Andrew shifted in his seat, "where you been?"

"Checking out Gabby's dorm room."

"And?"

"It looks nice. I should probably warn you."

"About?"

"Gabby comes and goes a lot. She pretty much has free range of the apartment, so don't be surprised if you wake up in the morning and she's in the shower or invading the refrigerator. She basically lives here."

"It's cool, man. I kinda figured that was the case."

"Which reminds me," Nathan added. "Mike and I had a signal we used to signify when we had a girl over, you know, just in case."

"Alright. What'd you have in mind?"

Nathan didn't want to use the same sock signal he and Mike used. He wanted something unique, but nothing that would stir up memories of Michael. Doing so often resulted in an emotional meltdown. "I don't know."

"What about the porch light? If things heat up, we turn it on."

A glowing lightbulb was far more subtle than a sock tied to the doorknob. "That'll work."

Along with the new academic year came the first football game of the season, which was bound to be packed with avid Huskies fans. Dressed in her cheerleading uniform, Gabby painted a purple glitter W on her right cheek and tied her hair back into a ponytail with a big purple bow. The Husky cheerleading uniforms were skin-tight. The white cheer shirts had a low V-cut neck with a purple and gold W across the chest. A matching purple and gold stripe ran across the bottom edge of her white cheer skirt.

When she bent over to pick up her shoes, Nathan could see the purple leotard bottom she had on. He stared at her behind. "You look hot."

Gabby plopped on the bed and slid on her shoes. "You're just saying that."

"No I am not," he insisted. "Those cheer uniforms are sexy, Babe. Much better than the ones you wore in high school." He took her hands in his and pulled her to her feet. Feeling frisky, he snuck his hands down to her backside, where he squeezed suggestively. "You are amazingly sexy, and you're going to make it difficult for me to focus on the game tonight."

She rolled her eyes at his shameless flattery. "Whatever."

"I'm serious," he decreed. "I'm not sure what will be more exciting, seeing you cheer or watching the game."

"Where are you guys sitting?"

"Gonna try to get within the first five rows if we can," he replied. "But I have a feeling those seats are going to fill up quickly."

"They usually do," she concurred. "Might want to head over there early."

"Why don't I just take you over there," he suggested. "I'll stay and snag some seats for everyone."

"If you want." After tying her shoes, Gabby grabbed her metallic purple and gold pompoms.

Nathan pulled his car keys out of his pocket. "You ready?"

"You don't have to drive me over there, Nathan. I can walk." Gabby shoved her pompoms into an athletic bag and zipped it.

"I want to." He picked up her bag and carried it over his shoulder, and together they walked out to the car.

When they were in high school, Nathan watched Gabby cheer hundreds of times. But the Husky cheer and dance squad was far more entertaining than anything he had ever seen as far as cheering was concerned. Nathan loved watching Gabby stretch her foot above her head, perform a high kick, or shake her booty on the sidelines. And even though it made him nervous, he enjoyed watching her do flips and stunts. She was definitely a crowd pleaser and knew how to get the huge pack of Husky football fans pumped up. Watching the cheerleaders became a new spectator sport for Nathan, now that Gabby was involved.

The entire time Gabby stood on the sidelines cheering and shaking her pompoms, Nathan had a huge grin on his face. She spotted him in the stands and waved. He winked at her and waved back. "Damn, she looks hot."

Acknowledging Nathan's cheerful mood, Andrew laughed at him. "You haven't taken your eyes off her since kickoff. There's saliva dripping off your fangs. You look like a wolf in heat."

Nathan denied that accusation. "I do not."

"Have you even been watching the game?"

"Yes, I've been watching the game. We're ahead by a touchdown."

Andrew snorted under his breath. "Why do I have the feeling our porchlight is going to be on tonight?"

Being a smartass, Nathan countered, "Just to indulge you, I'm going to turn on every damn light in the apartment."

But despite Nathan's retort, Andrew wasn't wrong in his assumption. Lying in bed together, Gabby rested her head on Nathan's chest. His arm went around her shoulders and he lovingly ran his fingers through her hair. As a token of his adoration and love for her, he kissed the top of her head.

"Nathan?" She gently placed her hand between the pecks of his chest and relaxed more comfortably in his arms. "Did you mean what you said?"

Hoping she would refresh his memory, he asked, "What did I say?"

"When you told me you were going to marry me someday."

The corner of his lips tugged up in an inviting smile. "Of course I meant it. Wouldn't have said it if I didn't." He stroked her bare shoulder, feeling her soft skin under his hand. "I need you more than you can possibly imagine, Gab. I know I've been a bear to be around lately. I haven't been sleeping well, I can't think straight, I've been an emotional wreck."

"That's to be expected, but you're working through it the best you can."

He rubbed his temple with his fingers. "I feel like I'm losing my mind."

"Just take it one day at a time, Sweetie. We'll get through it together."

He moved his lips closer to her ear and whispered, "Thank you for being here when I needed you."

Gabby turned her head so their lips were almost touching. "I'll always be here for you, Nathan."

"And knowing that means the world to me."

He softly kissed her on the lips then snuggled in to get more comfortable. They were now lying on their sides facing the same direction. They had full body contact, which was perfect for cuddling.

Nathan reached his arm around her and gently cupped the soft skin of her breast while he nibbled at her neck. Gabby closed her eyes, taking in his loving touch. He rubbed his hands across her tummy and hips then slowly made his way to her inner thigh. While he fondled and explored with his hands, his lips offered loving pecks across on her shoulder. This physical, intimate contact easily turned him on. Raising her leg, Gabby reached her hand around and helped guide him at the right angle. He gripped her thigh with his hand and drew her closer to him. The slow, low intensity was deeply satisfying, and at that moment their hearts beat in perfect sync.

When they were finished, he reached over and clicked off the bedside table lamp. The influx of emotions, constant stress, and endless sleepless nights of the last few weeks finally caught up to him. He closed his weary eyes and drifted off to sleep.

Football season was in full swing, but basketball season was just beginning. The Huskies had a diverse team this year, representing many countries, including Argentina, Jamaica, Kenya, and England. Many areas around the United States were represented as well, from Anchorage, Alaska all the way to Chicago, Illinois.

The varying skills of this particular team was what made them so talented. They all worked well together and were learning each other's strengths on the court. Since Brett Sorenson was no longer with them, Nathan was the point guard who had the most NCAA game experience, including the March Madness National Tournament. Being the veteran point guard, Coach Spoleda relied on him to lead the offense during most of their practice sessions. This gave the prospective starting team a chance to get used to playing together and gave the newer members the opportunity to learn Nathan's signals and communication strategies.

Even though he was only a sophomore, Nathan was good at leading his team. He was superior at reading the court, and his teammates all respected him. However, this did not mean Coach Spoleda was going to hand him the starting position; he had to work to earn it. They had a new guy on the team, a freshman from Surrey, England by the name of Keeton Sullivan, who was also fighting for that slot. Keeton had some skills, but Nathan was determined to show him what being a PAC-12 NCAA Huskies point guard was all about.

During a practice game, Coach Spoleda had Nathan play point against Sullivan to see how the new freshman performed under pressure. Keeton was good at handing off the ball to the open man, but seemed reluctant to take a shot under pressure. Nathan didn't hold back against him as far as defense was concerned. He was able to block one of his outside shot attempts and stole the ball from him twice. Nathan didn't go easy on him offensively either. He busted through Sullivan's defensive attempts to lay one out on the rim then turned around a minute later and shot over him to make a three pointer.

Sullivan had the skills, but he lacked grittiness and confidence on the court, two things Nathan had that he was not afraid to show off.

After practice, Coach Spoleda called out, "Hanson. Meet me in my office."

"Yes, Sir."

As the team proceeded to the locker room to shower, Andrew walked over to Nathan. "Why does Coach wanna see you? Do you think it has something to do with Sullivan?"

Nathan shrugged. "I don't know. Maybe."

"You were kinda hard on him today."

"I'm not gonna go easy on the guy just because he's new," Nathan defended. "Better he learn from me how the big boys play than from the other team when they smack him down."

"True." Andrew picked up a towel and wiped sweat off his brow. "Well, good luck. Hopefully it's not a big deal."

"Hopefully not."

Despite his nervous concerns, Nathan reported to his coach's office as directed. When he got there, the door was wide open, and Spoleda was concentrating on some sort of file. Nathan knocked on the door frame, hoping he wasn't keeping his coach from something important. "You wanted to see me, Coach?"

"Yes, Nathan. Come in. Have a seat."

Nathan sat in the chair across from his coach feeling a bit apprehensive. The last time Coach called him into his office like this, he lectured him about being a ball hog. "Is there something wrong, Sir?"

Nathan's tense and nervous posture made him laugh. "Relax. I just want to talk to you."

Nathan leaned back, relieving some tension.

"First off, I wanted to tell you how sorry I am."

Even though his coach meant well, Nathan was tired of people telling him how sorry they were. Every time someone talked about Mike or offered sympathy, Nathan felt a knot in his stomach. Why couldn't they just leave him alone and let him deal with this in peace?

"I know the last two months have been tough. If you ever need to talk, my door is always open."

"Thanks, Coach. I appreciate that."

"I'm sure you know that you are the most experienced point guard on this team right now," Coach Spoleda explained. "Which means the team is counting on you to lead them on the court."

"Yes, Sir. I am aware of that."

"We have some new faces, some that aren't as seasoned as you are in high-stakes competition. You have tournament experience, through both high school championships and NCAA playoffs. But we are a different team this year with different players and a different dynamic. We are going to have to push ourselves to the limits."

Nathan confidently assented, "You know I'll work hard for you, Sir."

"I know you will. You've already proven that. But what I need is for you to show your new teammates the ropes. You have an intense level of passion when you play. If we are going to make it into the National Championships again, the whole team has to play with that same passion. As the team's most experienced point guard, I'm counting on you to push the others to play at that level."

"I'll do my best."

Coach Spoleda leaned back in his chair. "I saw a different side of you today, an aggressive side I haven't seen before. You were a little rough with Sullivan."

Nathan was quick to apologize, "I'm sorry, Coach. But at some point he has to learn that the Huskies play hardball on the court. You definitely didn't train us to be pussies."

He chuckled at Nathan's humorously honest apology. "It's ok. I like to see that aggression on the court. But you have to keep it under control. Don't let your emotions effect your game."

"I won't."

Coach looked his point guard in the eye and plainly stated, "Sullivan is going to need your guidance. He seems to be having a hard time transitioning, which is causing him to be apprehensive on the court. He needs a bit of encouragement. I want you to mentor him, both on and off the court."

Feeling better and more confident about this situation, Nathan asked, "What would you like me to do?"

"Make him feel welcome. Make him feel like he's an important part of the team."

"He is an important part of the team. All of the guys are. If one of us is missing, we aren't a team. We all contribute in some way to our overall success. Not one of us is more important than the others. It's the brotherhood we have that makes us who we are, Sir."

Coach Spoleda beamed proudly at his young point guard. "That's the team spirit I'm looking for. Do you think you can get some of your grit to rub off on Sullivan?"

"I'll certainly try, Sir."

Coach Spoleda sat up a little. "There's one more thing. I saw your class schedule. You have several challenging science and math courses lined up this semester."

That was an odd thing for him to say, considering Nathan was a Biology major. "Yes, Sir, I do."

"I'm a bit concerned you might be trying to take on too much, especially after all the emotional turmoil you've had to deal with lately."

"Science and Math courses are easy for me," Nathan claimed. "They'll boost my GPA."

"I don't want you to overwhelm yourself. I need my point guard on target this season."

"I'll be fine, Sir. Finding time to study seems to be my biggest challenge, but I've developed a routine that works for me." Nathan searched for the right words. "I'm dedicated to the game, and while I'm on the court I will give you one-hundred percent and play my heart out for this team, but I have goals that go beyond the hardwood. Medical school is my pursuit of passion."

"Yes, Nathan. I know that. And you are very ambitious in that pursuit, I must say."

Nathan added more to his argument, "I've decided on a specialty, something that combines two things I love most."

"And what's that?" Coach asked.

"Sports Medicine and Orthopedics. I'd like to help injured athletes recover."

This sparked Spoleda's interest. "Well then, perhaps after you graduate from medical school you can come back and work with some of our athletes."

"I would love that. Do you think Dr. Whittier would mind giving me some insights on athletic training?"

"Certainly won't hurt to ask him." Coach Spoleda was proud of the dedication and hard work Nathan put into not only the game, but also his dreams of medical school. "If there's anything I can do to help you, please don't hesitate to ask. I'm here to support my athletes."

"I know, and I appreciate that."

Adhering to his coach's directive, Nathan counseled Keeton and offered him advice about the game. Throughout the week, he tried to get to know him better by having conversations with him outside of practice. Nathan sat on the sidelines with a textbook in his lap sipping down a Gatorade while he waited for Gabby to finish cheer practice. Periodically, while he was reading and highlighting in this book, he glanced up to watch the cheerleaders.

Keeton came out of the locker room and joined him. In his thick Cockney accent, he said, "'Ello Nathan."

Nathan looked up from studying. "Oh, hey."

Keeton set his athletic bag on the floor and took a seat. "Diligent I see."

"Try to take advantage of every minute I have." Nathan again stopped to watch the cheerleaders, paying particular attention to Gabby.

"You know," Keeton declared. "Over the last several days I've learned more about you, but I must say, you 'ave me a bit...baffled."

Uncertain about Keeton's meaning behind that statement, Nathan rebutted, "What makes you say that?"

"You are a walking contradiction, my friend."

Completely confused, Nathan asked for clarification. "Care to elaborate?"

"Take, for example, what you are doing now."

"Studying?" Nathan questioned, not following Sullivan's logic.

"Yes. You are a serious athlete, yet such a brilliant scholar. And you 'ave got to be one of the most laidback mates I 'ave ever gotten the privilege to know. Yet on the court, you are ruthless and quite aggressive."

Keeton's analysis made Nathan laugh. "I take my game seriously."

"I 'ave noticed." Once again Nathan looked over at the cheerleaders, giving a pretty blonde a flirtatious smile. "And you are a man who speaks about his girlfriend so favorably and claims to be faithful and loyal, yet you are a trifle bit flirty."

Obviously Keeton was confused. "What are you talking about?"

"That blonde over there," Keeton pointed to Gabriella. "It's obvious you fancy her. You've been eyeing her all afternoon. In fact, you flirt with her every time the cheerleaders practice out 'ere. What would your girlfriend say?"

Nathan now understood why Keeton was confused. He had never met Gabby or seen a picture of her. And every time Nathan spoke to Keeton about her, he failed to mention that she was on the cheerleading squad. "I really don't think she'll mind."

Keeton looked puzzled. "Why is that?"

"That cheerleader *is* my girlfriend."

Keeton peered at Gabby, who was wrapping up her practice session. "Blimey. My apologies, Mate."

"No worries." Now that cheering practice was over, Nathan called out to Gabby, signaling for her to come join him. "Come here for a sec."

Gabby took a swig of water and ambled over to greet him. She was slightly out of breath from tumbling across the gym, and her ponytail was starting to fall out. "Hi, Sweetie. What's up?"

"Want you to meet someone." He gently put his hand on her back. "This is Keeton Sullivan."

She waved at him. "Hello."

"Pleasure," he responded in his British accent.

Hearing him talk like that made Gabby grin. "Ooh, you're going to get a lot of women with that accent of yours."

Gabby's comment left him red-faced.

"I'm gonna shower," she said to Nathan. "I won't be long."

"I'll be out here waiting."

As she headed for the showers, Keeton chuckled, "Friendly girl."

Nathan couldn't have agreed more. "That she is."

When Nathan met Gabby outside the locker room, Lizzie was giving one of his teammates a flirty eye and giggling at his stupid jokes. Although he was happy the two of them seemed to be hitting it off, seeing Lizzie with someone other than Mike sent Nathan into a frenzy.

He gripped Gabby's hand and earnestly escorted her out of the gym.

Gabby couldn't figure out what was so pressing that Nathan felt it necessary to sprint out of there. She'd never seen him dash out of the gym with such haste before. "Why are you in such a hurry?"

"Isn't it obvious?"

"No."

"Lizzie was totally flirting with him."

"So?"

"So maybe she should stay away from my friends and be more selective about the guys she dates."

Nathan's unmerited hostility toward Lizzie made Gabby a bit defensive. "Why would you care who she dates?"

"That girl is toxic. She flirts with every guy she meets, then as soon as he gets attached to her, she rips his heart out and bails. I feel like I should warn him before she breaks his heart."

She couldn't believe he said that. "That's not nice."

"Do you not remember what she did to Mike?"

"Of course I remember," she said, scoffing him. "But that was an isolated incident."

He tried not to laugh at her cluelessness. "Oh my god, Gabby, do you pay attention to things that go on around you?"

"Of course I do. I'm not stupid, Nathan."

In his defense, he replied, "I didn't say you were stupid. I'm just trying to figure out why you don't see a problem with this."

Getting a bit snippy, she complained, "Stop picking on me."

"I'm not picking on you. I just find it hard to believe that you don't see her for what she really is."

"I don't know what you're talking about."

Gabby was around Lizzie every day. How could she not see it? "Wow, you are not a very good judge of character, are you? You can't honestly stand here and tell me you don't see it."

The cross look she shot him led him to believe she was mad at him.

"What's that look for?" he asked.

"You're being mean."

"I'm not being mean. I'm telling it like it is."

She let go of his hand and walked a bit faster, trying to distance herself from him.

He called out to her, "Oh, come on. Don't be pissed."

She turned around and gave him a stare down. "Why are you being so judgmental toward Lizzie? And why are you picking on me?"

"I was teasing you. I think your random moments of blonde oblivion are cute."

She put her hands on her hips and snarled. "That's not funny."

"You know I find you irresistible." Even though she fought him, he swept her into his arms.

But she wasn't in the mood to snuggle. She wanted to be mad. "Stop it."

Her angry face was cute, even if it was directed at him. "You're adorable when you're angry."

"No I'm not," she pouted.

"Yes you are." Despite his efforts to uplift her spirits, Gabby kept her pouty lip. He tried a different approach. "You know, if you keep your lower lip popped out like that a little birdie is gonna come poop on it."

Nathan's absurd comment made her giggle. "That's gross!"

"Got you to smile though, didn't it?"

Her smile grew a bit wider.

Trying to redeem himself, Nathan said. "I'm sorry. I wasn't trying to be mean. I only tease you because I love you."

"I know."

Giving her puppy dog eyes, he begged, "Are you still mad at me?"

"No."

He kissed the top of her head. "Good. Then let's go home and eat."

At his apartment, Nathan reached into his wallet. When he couldn't find what he was looking for, he frantically dumped all the contents on the kitchen counter.

Gabby tried to ease his frazzled state. "Did you lose something?"

"Yes. A piece of paper with an address on it. I had it in my wallet and now it's not here." He searched the pockets of his jeans and dug through his athletic bag. Still no signs of it.

"Can't you look it up?"

"No, I can't look it up. It has coordinates, directions to the location where Mike and I…" He clenched his fists and pounded on the counter.

Gabby had witnessed Nathan go through a gamut of emotions during his grieving process—shock, confusion, countless tears, denial, and depression—but she had yet to see him get angry, until today. "Sweetie, calm down."

"Gabby, you don't understand. I have to have that address. Mike and I made a deal. We pinky swore on it." In a state of panic, he raised his hand to his forehead and began to breathe erratically.

"You're going to hyperventilate," she warned.

He dug through every drawer and cabinet in the kitchen and searched every closet, tearing the apartment apart. Gabby didn't even know what was written on it or why it was significant, but obviously it was important to Nathan.

"This would be a lot easier if I knew what I was looking for," Gabby said.

"I told you, it's a light blue sticky note with coordinates printed on it. It has directions that lead to the secret cave."

Gabby had no idea what he was babbling about. "What secret cave?"

"The cave where Mike and I used to hide our most prized possessions. Our time capsule is in there."

Ok. Nathan's radical behavior was starting to scare her. "What are you talking about?"

"When Mike and I were kids, we kept objects, pictures, artifacts in a weather-proof box and buried it inside this cave. We swore when we were grown, we'd dig it up and open it together. But now I can't because I've lost the fucking coordinates and Mike had to go and leave me." Nathan plopped down on the sofa, buried his face in his hands, and cried.

Gabby's heart ached. Since Mike's death, Nathan had good days and bad days. Today was one of his bad days. He was overly sensitive, had a very short fuse, and was super critical of everyone and everything he saw. The tiniest things set him off. His emotions juggled back and forth like a ping-pong match, and he didn't seem to know what he wanted. She wished there was something she could do to take this pain and confusion away from him. Trying to offer some form of comfort, she joined him on the sofa and gently rubbed his back. "Sweetie, we'll find it, ok? And I'll go to the cave with you and we'll open your time capsule together."

"It's not the same. You're not Mike."

"I know that, but let me help you."

"You can't help me. No one can help me, unless you have some sort of magical powers that can bring him back." Nathan couldn't suppress his sorrow no matter how hard he tried. He squeezed Gabby into his arms and cried into her shoulder.

CHAPTER THIRTY-NINE

The first exhibition basketball game of the season was Wednesday night. This would be Gabby's first time cheering alongside Nathan on an NCAA court. The Huskies' cheer uniforms that the women wore on the basketball court were purple. They exposed Gabby's curvy, sexy midriff and bellybutton. A gold and white W was sewn across the front of her chest and a gold and white stripe ran across the seam under her breasts. The super short mini skirt with a slit up each side showed off the amazing shape of her legs. Nathan liked this purple uniform. It exposed more skin than the one she wore during football season, and it showed off Gabby's amazing figure.

When Gabby came out of the bathroom, Nathan did a double take. "Wow," he said, ogling over her. "Looking sexy there, Babe."

She redirected him. "Focus on the game."

He stuffed a pair of socks into his athletic bag. "UConn is a tough team. They're gonna give us a run for our money."

"You need to be careful," Gabby insisted. "I know how aggressive you can get on the court, Nathan."

"I'm not gonna hold back in a game, Gab. You, of all people, should know that."

Coach Spoleda put Nathan in as starting point guard for this game, just like Nathan hoped he would. This position would require a lot of responsibility from him, but his coach wouldn't have given him the opportunity to lead the team if he didn't think he could handle it.

The reserve team this year was just as strong as the starting team. Both teams had high average field goal percentages, but the starters tended to be a little more solid defensively. The biggest difference was the experience level of the players. The starters had more conference league game play minutes on the court and more tournament experience.

The first game of the season was an exciting one. UConn's offense was explosive and it was difficult to defend against them, but the Dawg Pack held on. On offensive, Nathan was able to hold the team together, getting the ball to the open man. If no one was open, Nathan took the pressure shot himself. He was making more baskets than he was missing, which was good for Washington. The Huskies were able to maintain a pretty even score throughout the game.

With two minutes left, Coach Spoleda called a timeout. He went over the game plan with his team then they all returned to the court. UConn had the ball. They missed their shot attempt, leaving the Huskies an open opportunity to score.

Nathan took charge. He passed the ball around a couple times, but because the defense was tight, passing wasn't getting them very far. Somehow they had to get the ball to the net. In a desperation move, Nathan pushed his way through the defense to the paint. When he jumped in to make a layup, he and two other players knocked into each other, resulting in a pileup, which caused Nathan to land on another player's foot on the way down. His ankle rolled outward while his foot turned inward. He felt the pain right away and collapsed to the floor.

With an agonizing wince on his face, Nathan leaned forward and gripped his ankle.

Gabby witnessed this horror from the sidelines. Her hand went over her mouth, gasping. "Oh my god."

Leaving her cheer formation, she crawled over to his side. "Nathan?"

Gritting his teeth, trying to suppress the excruciating pain he was in, he looked over at Gabby. But before he could answer, Dr. Whittier, the Husky basketball athletic trainer, rushed out to the court.

Jane and Randy saw this whole incident from five seats back. Worried about her son, Jane asked, "Is he alright?"

Randy squinted, trying to get a closer look at what the doctor was doing. "The trainer's checking him now."

"Can you see anything?" Jane asked. "It's not broken is it?"

"I don't know. Too far away to determine much of anything." Randy stood up and stepped into the aisle.

"Where are you going?" Jane asked.

"I wanna see what's going on."

The area around Nathan's ankle was tender and it hurt to move it. Dr. Whittier figured it was probably sprained, but he wanted to examine it further to be certain. Checking for more serious injuries, Dr. Whittier and the assistant coach helped Nathan off the floor. They supported him on their shoulders while he hobbled on one foot to the locker room.

Feeling helpless, all Gabby could do was watch.

Randy pushed his way through the mobs and tried to get into the locker room, but a man in armed uniform stopped him at the entrance. "Sir, you can't come in here."

"That's my son," Randy said, trying to justify entry into this restricted area.

When Nathan heard his father's voice, he sat up on the exam table. "Hi Dad."

The security guard let Randy through.

Randy rushed over to Nathan's side. "You alright?"

Nathan wiggled his foot slightly, which made him cringe. "It hurts to move it."

Randy immediately saw that the ankle was swollen and beginning to bruise. "That doesn't look good, Nate."

Directing his attention to Randy, Dr. Whittier asked, "Nathan tells me you're a physician."

"Yes I am." Randy was concerned about the seriousness of this injury. He hoped Dr. Whittier was being thorough in his examination. "Did you run x-rays?"

"It's not broken," Dr. Whittier explained while he put ice on Nathan's ankle and wrapped it in place with an ACE bandage. "It's a mild inversion ankle sprain. The lateral ligaments were stretched too far. He's got some pain and swelling on the outside, but he's not complaining of pain on the inside of the joint at all."

"That's good," Randy replied.

Dr. Whittier checked the wrap job he did then gave Nathan some Advil and a bottle of water. "For at least the first twenty-four to seventy-two hours you need to keep ice on this," he instructed. "Remember to always keep a thin cloth between the ice and your skin, and press the ice pack firmly against all the curves of the affected area. Keep it elevated, and take Advil. It will reduce swelling and pain."

Nathan bobbed his head. "Yes, Sir. I know how to ice an injury."

"And you're out the rest of the game."

Looking down at the enormous bag of ice on his ankle, Nathan laughed humorlessly. "I kinda figured that. Am I gonna be able to play Saturday?"

"Depends," Dr. Whittier replied. "We'll go day to day and see how you're doing."

"Thanks, Dr. Whittier."

The athletic trainer returned to the court, leaving Nathan and his father alone in the locker room.

Randy looked Nathan in the eye. "You need to let this heal."

"I will." He took a sip of water and popped two Advil in his mouth.

"Properly, Nathan," Randy insisted. "Don't be so quick to bounce around on that ankle or you're going to cause further injury."

Wishing his father would let it go, Nathan replied, "I can handle this."

Nathan rested his ankle that night and all the next day, keeping it iced and wrapped in an ACE bandage to bring the swelling down. He felt ridiculous hobbling around campus carrying a cooler so he could apply an ice pack every ten to twenty minutes, but if he wanted to return to the court, he needed to comply with his athletic trainer's request.

During practice Thursday afternoon, Nathan sat on the sidelines, his ankle elevated with an icepack. He wished he could get up and play, but Dr. Whittier hadn't cleared him yet.

When practice was over, the doctor approached Nathan and said, "Come into the locker room with me. Let's see how you're doing."

Nathan hobbled out of his seat and followed the doctor into the locker room.

Dr. Whittier took the ACE bandage off and poked around at Nathan's ankle. "Swelling's down." He examined further for evidence of injury. "It's still bruised a little, but it looks good. How's it feel?"

Nathan wiggled his foot around freely. "Loose."

"Can you stand on it?"

"Been walking on it all day," Nathan declared.

"With an ACE?" Dr. Whittier asked.

"Yes."

"Ok. Let's try it without."

Nathan bounded to his feet.

"Slowly," the doctor ordered. "Don't put added stress on it. Stop if it feels painful."

Nathan gradually put his body weight on his injured ankle. It felt stable.

"Any pain?" Dr. Whittier asked.

"No."

"Can you walk on it?"

Nathan was able to walk with no pain. "Feels good. Strong."

"Good. Before I clear you to play, I wanna wait until you can hop on your ankle with no pain."

Nathan tried to hop.

"Don't push it," Dr. Whittier demanded. "Take it easy."

Nathan started off by moving up and down on the ball of his foot to see if his ankle could hold the weight. Stable with no pain. Then he took a few baby hops, which made him wince a little.

Dr. Whittier's head dipped with a quick nod. "That's what I thought. You need to keep it wrapped and iced for another twenty-four hours."

Nathan hopped back on the table so Dr. Whittier could rewrap his ankle. "Alright."

The doctor handed him an ankle brace. "You'll need this to protect your ankle on the court. Wear it to every practice session and every game for at least the next two weeks."

This sounded hopeful. If Dr. Whittier was saying he needed a brace for games perhaps that meant he was able to get back on the court. "So am I clear?"

"I'm not going to clear you to play quite yet, but you're clear to travel with the team this weekend. I think by Saturday you'll be fine."

Nathan grinned. "Awesome."

CHAPTER FORTY

Nathan and Gabby were invited over to Randy and Jane's house for dinner that night. Concerned about the injury his son had sustained, Randy examined Nathan's ankle. It was slightly bruised, but was no longer swollen. And didn't seem to be bothering Nathan. Even though Nathan's athletic trainer had cleared him to travel with the team, Randy didn't want his son running around on the court injured. He thought Nathan needed to sit out and let his ankle fully heal.

"Dad, I'm fine. It's not that bad. I've had it wrapped and have been icing it," Nathan argued. "Dr. Whittier gave me a brace to wear to keep it stabilized."

Randy poked around the injury to make sure no further damage had accrued. "I still don't think you should play this weekend."

"But it's not bothering me," Nathan proclaimed. "Doc checked it today. He thinks I'll be fine by Saturday."

"And I'm telling you that you need to let it heal completely before you do more damage."

Jane interjected her opinion, "Randy, Sweetie, these athletic trainers won't clear athletes if they don't feel they are healed enough to be safe on the court. If Dr. Whittier clears him for Saturday's game, then we should support Nathan's decision to play."

Randy glared at his wife, not at all pleased about the comment she just made.

"He's a professional, Randy," she added. "He's not going to put Nathan in jeopardy or risk him getting further injury. These athletic trainers care about their athletes."

"And I care about my son."

Nathan tried to reason with his father. "If Dr. Whittier clears me and Coach wants me in the game, I'm going to play. My team needs me, Dad."

Randy stopped messing with Nathan's ankle and abruptly stood up. "Fine. But I don't agree with this decision."

Nathan thought his father was overreacting. "I'll be fine."

After Nathan and Gabby left, Randy stood in the middle of the living room with a cross expression on his face. "I need to talk to you," he snarled at Jane.

"What do you want to talk about?"

"In private." He headed up to their bedroom. What he wanted to say did not need to be expressed in front of the girls.

Sensing there was something bothering him, Jane followed her husband up to the bedroom. Concerned about Randy's less than cheerful disposition tonight, she closed the door and asked, "What is wrong with you?"

"Me?" he bellowed. "What the hell was that?"

"What was what?"

"You outwardly undermined my authority in front of Nathan."

Jane looked at her husband as if he were crazy. "You were being irrational."

"I was being a concerned father, and I was expressing my professional medical opinion. You totally disregarded my judgement."

Frustrated by Randy's pompous attitude, she replied, "Did you ever stop to think that there are other doctors in this world besides you who know what they're doing?"

"What is that supposed to mean?"

"You don't always have to be right, Randy. Other doctors' opinions matter just as much as yours does."

"So you're saying I'm wrong?" he assumed.

"No, I'm not saying that. I'm just saying that other doctors might be right. You treat other doctors' opinions as if they hold no merit. Dr. Whittier is trained to deal with athletic injuries. You're not."

He glared at her with burning, reproachful eyes. "Don't push this, Jane."

"Push what? The fact that Nathan is justified in his argument? That fact that I disagree with you?"

"No!" he raised his voice. "The fact that you deliberately undermined me."

"I wasn't trying to undermine you. I was trying to get you to see this from a different perspective."

Being completely illogical now, he blurted out, "Makes me wonder what else you've said to Nathan to undermine my authority."

She shook her head at him and his nonsensicality. "What are you talking about?"

"Is negating my authority a common practice for you? Are there other times when you've said yes to the kids when I specifically told them no?" He stared at her, seething.

"That's ridiculous. This has nothing to do with you. It has to do with Nathan. I was trying to help our son."

"By subjecting him to further injury? By questioning my medical judgment? The last time I looked, I was the one in this house with a medical degree, not you!"

His stubborn condescension made her mad. "Just because you have a medical degree doesn't make you Mr. Know-it-all when it comes to the kids."

"When medical issues are involved, yes it does."

She rolled her eyes and huffed. "Do you really think you are that high and mighty? That no one else's opinion matters? You are being extremely big-headed, Jonathan Randal! You can't possibly be that arrogant!"

She was calling him by his full name. That was never a good sign; it usually meant she was mad at him. But he wasn't budging on this one. He felt violated and dishonored. "So I'm arrogant now? Why? Because I'm concerned?"

"No, because you have a holier-than-thou attitude and think you are always right."

Reasoning with her was impossible. Randy was to the point where he didn't even want to talk to her anymore. He bit his tongue, fuming from the inside out. "Don't undermine my authority or question my medical judgment in front of Nathan or the girls ever again."

She pushed back, "Then don't be irrationally superior to everyone else around you."

Damn that woman was stubborn. He took a deep breath to keep from blowing up at her. "You are impossible sometimes, you know that?"

"But I'm also right, and that must really piss you off."

Randy had enough of this conversation. He turned his back to her and stormed out of the room.

She simply shook her head, disgusted by his egotistical viewpoint.

Jane and Randy Hanson didn't speak to each other for the rest of the night. In fact, he was so angry that he slept in the guestroom that night.

In the morning, after showering and dressing, Randy came downstairs ready for work, but he didn't greet his wife with a kiss like he usually did. In fact, he didn't acknowledge her existence at all. He simply sat at the dining room table and buried his nose in the newspaper.

Wanting to make peace, Jane prepared a cup of coffee for him. She set it on the table, hoping to shatter the ice between them. "I made you some coffee."

Randy loved Jane's coffee. A cup of her coffee energized him. It gave him that boost he needed and always put him in a good mood. But this morning, just to make a point, he refused to drink it. "I'll stop at

Starbucks." Without another word, he grabbed his keys, his cellphone, and his stethoscope and marched out the door.

All weekend long, the tension between Randy and Jane was extremely high. They spent the entire weekend not speaking to each other, and every night Randy slept in the guestroom. Both were equally stubborn, and neither was giving in. The distance between them grew and friction intensified daily.

Jane loved the man, but he was the most stubborn person she knew. He was deliberately being cold and distant and refused to offer conciliation. An impenetrable wall had developed between them. She hoped it wasn't too late for them to reconcile this situation and demolish the coldness that had escalated to an almost irreparable level.

Feeling like there was nothing she could say or do to break the barrier between them, Jane sat on the couch and cried.

Lacy came home from school and found her mother on the couch with her face buried in her hands. "Mom?"

Jane quickly wiped her eyes. "Hi Sweetie," she sniffled. "How was your day?"

But Lacy didn't let her mother off the hook. "You're crying."

Not wanting her daughter to worry, Jane faked a smile. "I'm fine, Honey."

Lacy knew better. She sat on the couch and put her arm around her mother. "I know something is going on with you and Dad. He avoided being home all weekend, he's sleeping in the other room, and you two haven't spoken to each other since last week."

Jane hid behind her silent tears. "We'll be okay. We're just having a disagreement."

When Randy got home that night, around 10:30 P.M., he went straight into his home office and closed the door without saying a word to his wife. Tormented by Randy's coldness, she plodded up to her room. She wished he would talk to her, or simply acknowledge her existence, but his pigheaded pride was getting the best of him.

Lauren and Lacy tried to carry on with their usual daily activities, but with their parents acting like this, maintaining normalcy was difficult. Randy and Jane hadn't said a word to each other in days, weren't showing any kind of affection toward one another, and avoided being in the same room. The tension in the house was thick, and neither Lauren nor Lacy could stand it any longer. As soon as Nathan was back from his weekend road trip, Lacy called him to express her concerns.

"What do you mean, they're not speaking to each other?" Nathan questioned, not believing what his sister told him.

"Dad hasn't been coming home until after ten o'clock every night, and when he does come home, he and Mom don't talk," Lacy said. "He just goes into his office and closes the door. And he's been sleeping in the guestroom."

Nathan released a disheartened sigh. "This is bad."

"Mom was sitting on the couch crying when I came home from school today," Lacy added. "Something is seriously wrong, Nathan. You have to talk to Dad."

"And what do you suggest I say to him?"

"I don't know," Lacy responded. "But you need to say something."

"I'll try. Don't know if it will do any good though."

"Anything you say will help."

Nathan hung up his phone and shoved it in his pocket. "This is just fabulous. Like I don't have enough to deal with right now."

Andrew overheard Nathan's cynical tone and looked up to see what was wrong. "What's up?"

"Apparently my parents aren't speaking to one another."

"Is that normal?"

"Not at all. They argue on rare occasions, but have never gotten into a full blown fight before. According to my sister, they haven't spoken in four days."

"That doesn't sound good."

"No, it's not good at all."

While Nathan was at work the next day, he confronted his father about the phone call he had with his sister. He wasn't quite sure how he was going to address the issue, but he knew he had to say something. When Randy stepped into his office to grab a sip of coffee, Nathan followed him inside and closed the door.

Randy looked up. "Why did you close the door?"

"Because we need to talk."

Randy chuckled. "Oh really?"

"Yeah." Nathan sat in Randy's desk chair and looked his father dead in the eye. "What's going on with you and Mom?"

Randy dumped sugar in his coffee cup, completely ignoring the question.

"I know you heard me."

"What makes you think there is something going on with your mother and me?"

"Lacy called me last night," Nathan explained. "She said you've been sleeping in the guestroom. And why haven't you been getting home until after ten o'clock every night? I know for a fact you don't schedule appointments on weekends, and there's no way you could possibly be at the hospital that late every night."

Apparently Nathan was lecturing him. Randy wasn't sure if he should laugh at this role reversal or be angry at his son for cocking attitude with him.

"Mom was crying when Lacy got home from school yesterday," Nathan added.

The thought of his wife crying made Randy uneasy. He dropped his stirring spoon and stared at his son with a blank expression. "She was?"

"Yes, she was. How could you not know that?"

"We're just having a little spat."

"Sounds like more than a spat to me."

Trying to explain the situation, Randy uttered, "This is something your mother and I need to work out. It doesn't concern you."

Nathan took offense to that remark. "She's my mother, and she was crying. Of course I'm concerned."

"Lower your voice," Randy insisted, hoping no one in the clinic heard them.

Nathan ignored his father's request. "Fix it!"

"It's not that simple."

"What do you mean it's not that simple? Just talk to her."

"Sometimes marriages have problems that are complicated."

"You don't have to tell me about relationships and problems. All relationships have problems once in a while, but that's why you talk to each other and find a way to work it out."

Randy wasn't so sure he liked his son's tenacious tone. "I am well aware of that, Nathan."

"Do you love her?" Nathan insisted on knowing.

Perturbed with his son's pushiness, he countered, "What kind of a question is that?"

"Do you?" Nathan asked again, not giving in until he got an answer.

In silent contemplation, Randy twirled his wedding ring around his finger.

His father's lack of response made Nathan anxious. "Dad?"

With certainty, Randy replied, "Yes. I love her very much."

"Then tell her."

Closing his eyes, Randy replayed the events that had occurred over the last few days. He couldn't believe he was acting so stubborn and egotistical. "I'm such an ass," he concluded. "Why do I do that to her?"

For once, Nathan offered his father advice. "It's not too late to fix it. Just talk to her."

After his last appointment that evening, Randy rushed home. As soon as he walked in the door, he went straight into his home office without saying a word to anyone. He rummaged through the bookshelves and pulled down the wedding scrapbook, thumbing through the pages until he found what he was looking for. Very carefully, he pulled out the vows he had written for Jane, rubbing his thumb across them. When he exited the room, he saw his girls on the sofa braiding each other's hair. "Is Mom upstairs?"

"I think so."

Randy traipsed up to his bedroom and quietly entered the room, relieved to see his wife's face.

Jane stared at him sadly.

With a heavy heart, Randy closed the door, giving them more privacy. He held his vows in his hand and read the words out loud. "I love you, not only for what you are, but also for what I am when I am with you. I love you, not only for what you have made of yourself, but for what you are making of me. I love you for the part of me you bring out. I love you for passing over all those foolish things, weak things that are seen within me. I love you for drawing into the light all the inner belongings that no one else had looked far enough to find..." As Randy read the rest of the words to his wife, he desperately fought to contain his emotions. When he was finished, he set the notecard on the dresser and sat on the edge of the bed, taking Jane's hand in his. "You're my sunshine, Jane. I can't breathe without you. I can't sleep without you. I can't live without you. I need you every day of my life." By now his breathing became shallow and he struggled to maintain his composure.

But it was too late for Jane. She buried her face in his shoulder and released the pain that had been dragging her down for days.

Randy pulled her into his arms and drew her as close to him as he possibly could. "Janey, I love you. And these vows I said to you on the altar still hold true. But lately, everything I said and everything I promised I would do, I have neglected in every way. I have not been a good husband to you." Realizing how much he had hurt her, he closed his eyes and kissed her head. "I'm so sorry, Honey. I blew things out of proportion, made a mountain out of a molehill. I was stubborn, selfish, and completely lacking in understanding. I said some terrible things in anger. You did not deserve that. Nobody deserves that."

They sat on the bed for several minutes just letting their emotions flow.

When they regained their composure, Randy lifted her chin with his finger and looked into her eyes. "You're getting tears all over your pretty face."

She managed to muster a smile. Wiping her eyes, she sniffled through her tears. "I'm sorry I made you mad."

He shook his head in denial. "You have no reason to be sorry. You have put up with so much crap from me over the years, much more than any woman should have to endure. Spouts of arrogance, unbearable stubbornness, and me just flat out being an asshole. Yet despite it all you've always been loyal, supportive, and faithful. And you've always believed in me, even when I haven't deserved it. I'm the one who should be apologizing, Jane. Not you."

"I don't want to fight anymore," she whimpered.

"I don't want to fight either. This isn't who we are. This isn't what our marriage is about." He lovingly rubbed his thumb across her lips. "Can you find it your heart to forgive a pig-headed, arrogant jerk?"

Jane giggled and mustered a smile.

He cradled his hands around her face and kissed her then wrapped her up tightly in his arms and leaned back on the bed, taking her with him. Within minutes, the heat level turned up several notches.

When they finally came up for air, Randy moved the hair off her face and looked into her emerald green eyes. "I haven't been eating worth a crap. This liquid coffee diet and lack of decent nourishment is making me edgy. I need real food."

"Do you want me to make dinner?"

"No," he refuted. "Let's go out to eat."

"Where do you want to go?"

"One of your favorite places." To jog her memory, he offered hints. "Italian wine. Almond Gnocchi. Vanilla Panna Cotta."

The corners of her mouth slowly curved upward. She knew exactly what he was talking about. "Juanitas?"

"Yes, Ma'am."

She bit her lip and gave Randy a huge hug. "Thank you, Sweetheart. I love that place."

"I know you do. That's why we're going." He held her tightly and gave her another kiss. "Have the girls get ready. I'll be right down."

When Jane reported downstairs, Lauren and Lacy were in the living room watching their favorite TV show. "Get up, girls," Jane ordered. "Get your shoes on and grab a jacket."

Based on the recent happenings between her parents, Lauren thought something was wrong. "Why? What's going on?"

Randy trotted down the stairs. "I am taking my gorgeous girls out to dinner." He grabbed Jane by the waist and kissed her with a hunger that had built up for days.

Lauren and Lacy looked at each other and smiled. Things were finally back to normal.

Randy broke away from Jane and gave his daughters a directive. "You heard your mother. Get your shoes and jackets."

The twins stared at him, but didn't move.

He chuckled. "What are you waiting for? Let's go."

They both bounced off the couch and rushed upstairs.

"Should we call Nathan and see if he and Gabby want to join us?" Jane suggested.

"That's a good idea." He reached into his pocket and pulled out his cellphone, dialing Nathan's number.

CHAPTER FORTY-ONE

Nathan chugged down a can of V8 juice while he waited at the airport terminal with his team. They had a two-game series in Arizona this weekend, one against University of Arizona and one against Arizona State. The cheerleaders booked the same flight, which meant Nathan was traveling with Gabby.

With a textbook on his lap and a highlighter in his hand, Nathan somehow managed to tune everything out around him. Joaquin sat to the left of Nathan and looked down at the textbook he was reading. The section Nathan was highlighting said something about cell membranes and molecules. Above the words was a complicated diagram and some chemical formulas Joaquin didn't understand. "What is this you are reading?" he asked.

Nathan momentarily looked away from his textbook. "I'm sorry. Did you ask me something?"

"Yes. What are you reading?" Joaquin repeated.

He placed an index card in the page to mark where he left off. "It's Biochem."

Joaquin had never heard that English word before. "What is Biochem?"

Nathan explained, "The study of chemical processes in living organisms. It deals with the structures, functions, and interactions of biological macromolecules. How living things obtain energy from food, the chemical basis of heredity, fundamental changes that occur in disease, things like that."

"Ah, I see," Joaquin declared, still not fully understanding. "Is this one of your pre-med classes?"

"No. It's for my Biology degree."

"Chemistry I do not understand," Joaquin said. "Very complicated. One must really have a knack for science to grasp the complexities of that discipline."

"Science has always been my thing. I have my father to thank for that."

"He is a doctor. I imagine he would instill that in you."

"Among other things."

Joaquin peeked over his shoulder to see Gabby chatting and laughing with one of her fellow cheerleaders, a pretty Latino woman. "Who is that woman your Gabby is talking to?"

Nathan looked behind him. "Anna Suarez?"

"Yes," Joaquin confirmed with a grin the size of California. "She is very pretty, and seems to be a friendly person."

"She's very friendly," Nathan chuckled. "Sometimes a little too friendly."

"You know her?"

"Not personally, no. But Gabby does."

"Perhaps she can introduce us?" Joaquin suggested.

Nathan was more than happy to help. "I bet we can arrange that.

When their boarding call was announced, Gabby took her seat, which was closer to the front of the plane than Nathan's was. Although the basketball team and the cheerleaders traveled together, they didn't always sit in the same section of the plane. For this particular flight, Nathan sat six rows behind Gabby, with Joaquin on one side of him and Andrew on the other. Developing a sly plan, Nathan looked over at Joaquin. "You said you wanted to meet Anna, right?"

"Yes," Joaquin confirmed. "I would like that very much."

"I think I'm about to make that happen for you. Hold on a minute." He squeezed between the aisles and made his way to Gabby's row. Bargaining with Anna, who sat in the window seat next to Gabby, Nathan offered, "I'll pay you twenty bucks if you'll switch seats with me."

Anna laughed at Nathan's ridiculous suggestion. "And why should I?"

"So I can sit by my girlfriend during this flight."

"Where are you sitting?" Anna asked, hoping he didn't have a crappy seat.

Nathan pointed six rows back. "Back there with Garibay and Santiago."

Joaquin waved his hand in the air, acknowledging where Nathan was sitting.

She considered his proposal. "Santiago, huh?"

In desperation, Nathan pulled his wallet out of his pocket and whipped out a twenty dollar bill. "Come on, Anna. Switch seats with me."

Anna pushed his hand away. "I don't want your money, Hanson. You can have my seat."

"Thank you. I owe you one."

As Anna made her way six rows back, Nathan eyed Joaquin with a shrewd grin on his face.

Joaquin responded with a thumbs up.

"What was that all about?" Gabby asked, leering at Nathan.

Nathan took his seat by the window. "What do you mean?"

She cocked her head at him. "What are you up to?"

"What makes you think I'm up to something?"

"That cocky grin on your face. You are up to something, Nathan James Hanson."

Nathan was slightly dazed by this comment. Gabby had never called him by his full name before. "Nathan James? You're calling me by my full name now? What's up with that?"

"You have some ulterior motive up your sleeve. I can tell by that smirk on your face."

"I'm not up to anything," he denied. "I just wanted to enjoy this flight with my beautiful girlfriend." He leaned over and kissed her. "And Santiago wanted to meet Anna."

"Aha!" she exclaimed. "I knew it. This whole display was to set him up with her, wasn't it?"

"Not completely, no," he denied. "I was helping him out, but I also wanted to sit by you."

"You are cunning, aren't you?" Gabby said, poking fun at Nathan's boyish antics. "Cunning and cute."

Nathan lovingly touched the tip of her nose. "Not as cute as you."

During the game against Arizona State, the ball got loose on a steal. Nathan and another player fought for possession, playing tug-of-war while they piled on top of each other. In the commotion, Gabby heard the squeal of flesh on hardwood as Nathan slid across the floor. Despite his efforts to gain possession, the ball got away from him and flew out of bounds to the sidelines, hitting Gabby smack in the face. She held her hand over her nose, hoping there wasn't any blood.

The referee blew the whistle and called Nathan on a foul. Nathan immediately rose to his feet and stormed to the center of the court, challenging the call. "What the fuck? That guy was all over me. You should have called the foul on him."

Gabby gasped, shocked to hear those words come out of Nathan's mouth.

Questioning a ref's decision was considered unsportsmanlike conduct. As a result, the referee held one hand upright with the other crossed perpendicularly above it, forming a T.

Nathan protested loudly. "You're calling me on a technical? This is bullshit."

Taking his frustrations out on the other team, Nathan shoved the opposing player on his way to the bench. Nathan's foul language and backtalk from a player was bad enough, but showing physical aggression toward another player was more than the ref was willing to tolerate. He pointed to the locker room, ejecting Nathan from the game.

Seething with mounted rage, Nathan threw his hands in the air. "You've got to be shitting me. You can't eject me for that."

Before this situation escalated out of control, Coach Spoleda rose to his feet and stood between Nathan and the referee. "Hit the showers," he demanded.

But Nathan wouldn't back down. "He can't throw me out of the game like that."

"He can do whatever the hell he wants. Hit the showers now, Hanson."

The downright serious look Coach Spoleda shot him told Nathan he wasn't playing around. In the face of his anger, he stormed off the court and into the locker room.

Gabby wasn't sure what to think. She'd never witnessed violent outbursts from Nathan before. This aggressive, argumentative behavior was definitely cause for concern.

Trying to cool off, Nathan stripped and stood under a steaming shower. He stared blankly up at the ceiling, reflecting on his actions. Not only did he disappoint his coach, he also let down his team. Easing some tension, he let the water massage his body, slowly soothing him.

When the team piled into the locker room, after being humiliated by Arizona State and losing by thirteen points, Geoff Foster started in on Nathan, getting in his face for throwing the game away. "If you wouldn't have cocked attitude with the ref, this wouldn't have happened," Geoff complained, shoving him into a locker. "We lost this game because of you."

Nathan retaliated, placing his hands on Geoff's shoulders and pushing him right back. "It's not my fault you guys can't keep it together on the court."

"If you would have just taken the damn call instead of throwing a fit about it…"

Defending his friend and fellow teammate, Andrew intervened by stepping between them. "Back off, Foster. He made a mistake. We all make mistakes."

Coach Spoleda heard this squabbling among his players and immediately put a stop to it. "That's enough. I will not tolerate this childish bickering. We are a team, and we damn well better get our act together and start acting like one. Shower, change, and get your asses out to the bus. I want us out of here in less than forty-five minutes."

Nathan zipped up his bag and marched out of the locker room, waiting alone on the bus while the rest of the team showered.

When they returned to the hotel, Coach Spoleda gave his players an hour of cool down time before he called a mandatory team meeting. Nathan reported straight to his room, not speaking to anyone on the way. He grabbed his headphones out of his carryon, hooked them up to his iPhone, and leaned against the headboard of the bed. He crossed his ankles and stared vacantly out the window, zoning out of the world.

Nathan was having a hard time adjusting to life without his best friend, and even though Andrew tried to offer as much support as he could, Nathan wasn't always open to assistance. He struggled to deal with the emotions he felt and often keep them bottled up like a ticking time bomb. Trying to get him to talk, Andrew pulled a chair up next to him. "Whatcha listening to?"

Nathan removed his headphones and peeled his eyes away from the window. "Did you say something?"

"What are you listening to?"

"Linkin Park. It helps clear my head."

"Did I ever tell you about my friend Shawn?"

"No." Nathan shifted on the bed, sitting up with his legs crossed.

"Shawn and I met in sixth grade. We were best buds all through junior high and high school. We did everything together. One night, he and I were chillin' out on the front porch of my house when a car drove by and opened fire."

Nathan's jaw slackened.

"I ducked under the railing trying to dodge bullets. All I heard was gunfire, squealing tires, and Momma screaming. The whole thing lasted maybe ten seconds, but it seemed like a lifetime to me. The next thing I remember, Shawn was lying on the porch covered in blood."

Nathan covered his mouth with his hand. He'd never heard anything so horrific in his life. "Oh my god."

"We called 9-1-1, but he was already dead by the time they got there. That was the worst night of my life. I watched my best friend die."

Nathan's stomach felt a bit queasy. He closed his eyes attempting to get the horrifying image out of his head.

Trying to make a point, Andrew said, "I understand what you're going through, Nathan. I've been there. I know what it's like to lose a friend. I know how angry and confused you are, and I know how much this hurts. But you can't deal with the pain by lashing out at people or withdrawing from the world. Believe me, I tried. After Shawn died, I wallowed in my own anger and misery for a while. Almost lost my basketball scholarship because of it. You can't hold this in. It'll eat you up inside. Talk about it, get it off your chest. I'm here to listen, and I'll understand."

Nathan always liked Andrew, but after hearing this story he had a new level of respect for him. It eased his mind knowing he had a friend he could turn to who truly understood his grief. Sharing a common tragedy brought them closer together. "Thanks. That means a lot." Nathan bumped knuckles with him. "I'm gonna run downstairs and grab a soda. You want one?"

"No, thanks. I'm good."

"I'll be right back."

Down by the soda machine, Nathan ran into Gabby. "Hey you," he said, trying to get her attention.

She turned around. "Hey."

Gazing at her apologetically, he declared, "I'm sorry I hit you with the ball. Are you alright?"

She was more concerned about his emotional outburst during the game than her nose. "Are you?"

He sat on the floor and leaned against the wall. Releasing a heavy sigh, he rested his elbows on his bent knees. "I don't know what happened." He put his hand on his forehead, searching his thoughts. "I lost control."

Gabby sat next to him, hoping he would talk to her. "Nathan, I know you've been going through a lot. You're sad and angry and confused, and I understand that. But you're scaring me. You were cursing at a ref and pushed another player on the court. That's not like you at all. You're not an aggressive person or the kind of player to throw a fit like that. I was shocked by what I witnessed from you today." To express her support, she extended her hand and touched his arm. "What's going on, Sweetie?"

"I'm tired of people offering sympathy and telling me they're sorry. I'm tired of being angry and dealing with the pressure and the pain and..." His head felt like it was going to explode. "All the emotions I've felt over the last few months piled up until they were so big I couldn't hold them in any longer."

"Why were you trying to hold them in? Why didn't you talk to me?"

He stumbled over his words. "I didn't know what to say. I don't know what I'm feeling, and I don't know how to handle this."

"You know I'm here if you need to talk, Nathan. And you have friends, your coach, and teammates who want to support you. Don't try to take this on by yourself."

He massaged his temple and took a cleansing breath. "I feel cheated, dejected, and sometimes I feel so alone."

"You're not alone. Mike was my friend too. I know I wasn't as close to him as you were, but I still feel his loss. I understand that you're hurting and I know you're angry, but you're crumbling right in front of me, and that scares me."

Nathan hung his head.

Offering encouragement, Gabby said, "Sweetie, don't try to be Mr. Tough Guy. You can't keep it all locked up. You're losing control and forgetting who you are. Talk to me or your dad or whoever else you want to talk to. But don't shut us out. We're here to help you."

He lifted his chin and gazed at her. "I'm sorry, Gab. I should have come to you. I should've expressed my feelings instead of trying to hide from all this. From now on, I promise I'll open up."

She moved his arm a bit to look at the brush burn on his elbow. "That looks painful."

He glanced at his elbow. It was red and raw. "It's a little sore, but nothing Neosporin and a Band-Aid can't fix." He rubbed the red spot on her nose where the ball had hit her. Hoping she wasn't seriously injured, he asked, "Are you sure you're ok?"

Reassuring him, she smiled sweetly. "I'm fine."

With a slight chuckle, he said, "Looks like we both got war wounds from this game."

"Yeah."

Overwhelmed by her love and devotion, Nathan's eyes shifted from her pretty blue eyes to her soft lips. He raised his hand and gently curved it around her cheek. "I love you."

"I love you too, Sweetie."

"I want to be alone with you." Fornicating on road trips was strictly forbidden, but right now Nathan didn't care. He leaned closer and whispered, "Let's find someplace where we can be alone."

"Nathan, you know we can't do that."

"We need to find a way." He rose to his feet, took her by the hand, and lifted her off the floor. As discreetly as possible, they snuck down a corridor.

"What are we doing down here?" Gabby asked.

"There has to be a custodial closet around here somewhere."

She crinkled her nose, gawking at him as if he'd lost his mind. "You want to have sex in a closet?"

"I want to have sex anyplace we can. Closet, restroom, empty stairwell."

"If either of our coaches find out, we're both going to get in trouble."

"It will be worth it."

They found an empty laundry room with a couple of chairs in it—perfect for Gabby to straddle his lap. They checked to make sure no one was coming then barricaded the door.

While Nathan and Gabby were hidden in the laundry facility, Coach Spoleda knocked on Nathan's hotel room door.

Andrew peeked his head out. "Hey, Coach."

"Hello, Andrew. Is Nathan in there with you?"

Nathan told Andrew he was going to the lobby to get a soda, but that was over twenty minutes ago. Doing his best to cover for Nathan, Andrew lied to his coach. "He's in the shower right now."

Taking into consideration the emotional stress Nathan was under, Coach Spoleda believed him. "When he's done, please tell him I'd like to speak with him."

"Yes, Sir. I will do that."

About ten minutes later, Nathan returned to the room. Andrew hopped off the bed and greeted him at the door. "Where the hell have you been?"

"I was with Gabby."

Andrew knew exactly what that implied. "Coach came over here looking for you. I told him you were in the shower. You're lucky he fell for it."

"Thanks for covering for me."

Andrew shook his head and snickered. "You are ballsy, man. If you get caught, Coach is gonna bench your ass."

"After the way I acted today, he's probably going to bench me anyway."

"Speaking of which, he said he wants to talk to you."

Nathan figured he was about to get chewed out. "Is he in his room?"

"I think so. You might want to head over there."

Without hesitation, Nathan headed down the hall to his coach's room.

When he knocked, Coach Spoleda greeted him with a hard expression. "Come in and have a seat."

"Yes, Sir." Nathan stepped inside and sat down.

Worried about his point guard, Coach Spoleda said, "Nathan, I know you've been through a lot over the last few months. But you absolutely cannot let the emotional state you're in affect your performance."

"I know, Coach. I'm sorry. I don't know what happened."

"You lost control, is what happened. You buckled under the pressure, and that is something that can never happen on the court. You have got to pull it together. You're a better player than that. You are much more disciplined and much tighter than what I saw today."

"I know that, Sir. Today was definitely not my best game."

"No it was not. That kind of conduct will not be tolerated from me or from the NCAA. You need to get your head back in the game, because we cannot have another outburst like that. Do you understand?"

"Yes, Sir. I do."

"Good. Now pull yourself together and be the leader I know you're capable of being."

"Yes, Coach."

Nathan returned to his room and reflected on his coach's comments. He needed to snap out of this funk he was in or his life was going to fall apart and all of his goals and dreams would shatter.

CHAPTER FORTY-TWO

December and January were busy months for the Hansons for many reasons. Aside from preparing for Christmas, every winter Lake Washington High School held an event for seniors called A Daughter's Heart. This was a father-daughter dinner dance. Randy arranged not to be on-call that night so he could dedicate his full attention to his girls.

The night of the event, Randy slipped his grey silk dress shirt over his shoulders and buttoned it. "Honey, can you find me a tie to wear with this?" he asked his wife.

Jane searched his side of the closet for the perfect necktie. "The girls are excited."

"I'm looking forward to it too," he admitted. "Haven't quite figured out yet how I'm going to dance with both of them at the same time, but I'm hoping something will come to me." He buttoned his sleeves then tucked his shirt tail into his black dress pants.

Jane handed him a red, black, and grey patterned tie. "It's not every day they get a special date with their dad."

Randy draped the tie over the back of his neck and tied it into a Windsor knot. "Both of them should demand nothing less than complete respect from any man. And tonight I want to set the standard on how they should expect to be treated."

"And you are the perfect man to show them," Jane said, helping him straighten his tie. "You certainly know how to charm and romance a woman."

"Well, you make it easy, my dear."

Jane folded his collar over. "You look very handsome."

"Thanks, Babe." Randy softly kissed her. "Are the girls ready?"

"Almost. They're doing last minute things with their hair and makeup."

Randy openly protested. "Why do either one of them bother wearing makeup? They are beautiful girls, Jane. They shouldn't hide their pretty faces behind all that cosmetic crap."

"They're teenagers."

"So? Is there some bylaw that requires young women between the ages of thirteen and nineteen to cake unnecessary powder and paint on their faces?" he stated bluntly. "They're pretty the way they are."

"I'm sure they would be flattered to hear you say that."

"I've already told them that."

Jane gently placed her hand on his chest. "I'll get their corsages."

"Thank you." He grabbed his suitcoat and stepped into the hallway.

The bathroom upstairs bustled with the blissful sound of teenage girl giggles. Randy peeked his head inside to see what they were doing. "Hello, ladies."

The twins simultaneously responded, "Hi, Daddy."

His girls looked elegant in their formal gowns. Lauren had on a glittery strapless blue gown and Lacy's was a lively shade of red. Both of them had their hair in updos and each selected their own taste of jewelry to top off their individual look. "Wow, look at my gorgeous girls. I am one lucky dad. I get the privilege of accompanying two lovely ladies tonight."

"Daddy," Lauren said, blushing.

He gave each one a kiss on the cheek. "I'll be downstairs when you're ready. Don't take too long."

Randy headed to the kitchen to get the corsages he bought for each of them. "Damn, Jane," he said to his wife. "Where did the time go?" He felt a little heartbroken that his girls were all grown up, and they were some serious beauties, certain to attract many men in the not-so-distant future.

"They look nice don't they?"

"They're gorgeous, just like their mother."

Randy's night out with Lauren and Lacy was a memorable experience. The best part of their evening was when they were dancing. Lauren stood on one of Randy's feet and Lacy stood on the other while Randy held an arm around each one. Their ingenuity turned many heads.

Randy had a closer relationship with Lauren than he did with Lacy, but it wasn't from his lack of trying to bond with her. Lacy fought him more and questioned pretty much everything he said, expecting justification for his rules. She had a strong personality and was not afraid to stand up for herself or for Lauren. She was more risqué than her twin and far more spontaneous, often taking unnecessary risks. She was a bright girl with definitive goals in life, and nothing was going to stand in her way of reaching them. Lacy was definitely not timid and had no qualms about speaking her mind.

Lauren was more mature and sensible. She was much more cautious and modest in both personality and style than Lacy was. She carefully planned things out and stuck to her schedule, diligently. Lauren was the girl with class, and she had exclusive taste, just like her father. She was a conflict avoider and always obeyed rules without question. Although Lacy wasn't timid, Lauren was the more charismatic twin. She was slightly shy when she was one-on-one with unfamiliar people, but you would never know this once she stood on a stage. The stage was where she shined. Lauren was a born entertainer and loved an audience.

Even though they were identical twins, their personalities were anything but identical. Each was unique, with her own likes, dislikes, and life goals and dreams. However both girls were excellent students and had very caring natures about them. Randy was proud of them for that.

Throughout the evening, the great relationship Randy had with Lauren was deepened and an unspeakable connection was ignited between him and Lacy. He thoroughly enjoyed this bonding time with his daughters.

Christmas had always been a major event in the Hanson house. Every year, they hiked through the woods together searching for the perfect tree. Once they found it, they took turns with the saw then tied it to the top of the four-wheel drive. Once they had it home, they set the tree up in the living room. While Jane and the girls worked on decorating the tree, Randy sorted through the boxes of lights he had, deciding which ones he was going to use to illuminate his home in holiday cheer. Before he grabbed the ladder, he called Nathan. "Ok, Nate. Grab your Santa hat and come over here and help me."

"What are we doing?" Nathan asked.

"Climbing on the roof."

"That sounds unnecessarily hazardous, and I think my coach would frown upon the entire situation if I fell off the roof and broke a leg, hence becoming incapacitated for Wednesday's game."

"You're not gonna fall off the roof. Come help me hang up these Christmas lights," Randy requested.

"Can I bring Gabby?"

"Of course. She can help your mom and sisters with the tree. And maybe we'll get lucky and they'll be freshly baked cookies for us when we're finished."

That grabbed Nathan's attention. "Ooh. Yum! You have to share the chocolate chip ones this time though."

"Hey," Randy argued. "I shared last time."

"I got one," Nathan complained.

"You snooze, you lose."

"That's not fair. You live there. You get free access to Mom's chocolate chip cookies anytime you want."

Randy reiterated, "As I said, you snooze, you lose."

"Maybe Mom can share her recipe with Gabby." Nathan got all bright-eyed and bushy-tailed thinking about it. "Then I can have chocolate chip cookies too."

"Maybe you should learn how to bake," Randy teased.

"I can cook. It's just that cookie batter and I haven't quite connected on the molecular level yet. They don't turn out as chewy as Mom's when I make them. They're hard, brittle, and kinda cardboardish," Nathan admitted.

Randy laughed at his son's description. "Well then. Do me a favor and spare me the torture of eating one of yours."

"Will do," Nathan said with a chuckle. "Gab and I will be over in a bit. You gonna feed us?"

"Yes. You can stay for dinner."

"Woohoo!"

"Drive carefully. The roads are slick. Which reminds me, have you put snow tires on your car yet?"

"Yes, I have," Nathan assured his father.

"Good. The bridge is especially bad, and we're supposed to get more snow tonight."

"I'll be careful."

Randy was fanatical when it came to decorating for Christmas. His house was usually the brightest in his neighborhood and could be seen from boats passing by on the lake, which added a nice snippet of holiday cheer for the local fishermen.

Randy and his son spent the entire afternoon and early evening putting up Christmas lights. When they were finally finished, Nathan stood back to admire their handiwork. Colored lights hung on the eaves of the roof, around every window, and brightened the perimeter of the garage door. They wrapped lights around the trees, lined the front walkway with glowing candy canes, and placed an inflatable snowman and reindeer in the front yard.

An illuminated Santa Claus, with his rear-end sticking out, looked like he was stuck in the chimney. On the front door, Randy hung a hand-painted sign that said, *Get your hands off my cookies, Santa!* Nathan found his father's sick sense of humor amusing. "Why is Santa's ass sticking out of the chimney?"

"That's what happens when he eats all those cookies then tries to squeeze into a tight space," Randy explained. "Lesson learned, Santa! Don't eat my cookies."

Nathan shook his head and laughed. "Mom's going to think you've finally lost your mind."

"Mom is going to love it," Randy declared, proud of his unique Christmas décor. "I'm starving. Let's snag some dinner, then I'll fight you for some of those cookies."

"First one inside gets first dibs." Nathan ran toward the front door with Randy chasing right behind him.

The Hanson family equated Christmas with the holiday that came before the family ski trip. Every winter, Randy bought season passes for everyone. And every year, on December twenty-sixth, he, his wife, Gabby, Nathan, and the twins loaded the four-wheel drive with six pairs of skis, poles, boots, and other essential ski gear and made the two-hour drive to Mt. Rainier's Crystal Mountain ski resort.

Riding Mt. Rainier's gondola took ten minutes from base to summit. Perched at the top, at 6,872 feet, was the Summit House Restaurant. The restaurant served Northwest cuisine in an elegant alpine setting with unbelievable mountain views out every window. This was the perfect place to grab a quick meal following a full morning of ski runs.

Nathan removed his hat and gloves and placed them in a pile on the table. Getting more comfortable, he took a seat between Gabby and his mother. "Oh man. The skiing is awesome today!" he said to his father, who sat in the chair opposite him.

"Yes it is," Randy concurred.

Nathan unzipped his insulated jacket and hung it on the back of his chair. "Where are Lauren and Lacy?"

"They're coming," Randy said. "They're on the ski lift."

While they waited for the twins to show up, Randy ordered a cup of coffee. He was about to take a sip when he glanced out the window and saw something that made him look twice. Lauren and Lacy were removing their skis when a young man, whom Lacy seemed to know, started a conversation with them. At first, Lacy seemed happy to see him. But after a minute or two, their conversation became confrontational. Randy was about to intervene, but before he even made it out of his seat, Lacy kneed this kid in the groin. The young man fell to the ground, doubled over in pain.

Both Randy and Nathan cringed.

"Holy crap. Did you see that?" Nathan exclaimed.

Randy probably should have been upset with his daughter for getting aggressive with this kid, but instead he found himself laughing. "Yeah. I saw."

She yelled some sort of obscenity at this young man, threw a snowball at him, then marched the other direction.

Nathan thought this entire situation was hilarious. "What did he do to piss her off?"

"I don't know."

One thing was certain, Lacy definitely knew how to handle herself. She strolled into the lodge as if nothing happened. "Hi, Daddy."

Nathan couldn't let this incident go unnoticed. "Who is that guy?"

"Oh, you mean jerk face?" she corrected. "The guy keeps harassing me, trying to get me to go out with him. But he's a total loser. He's a liar and a cheat, I don't want anything to do with him."

Nathan chuckled, "You could have just told him no."

Lacy defended herself, "I already tried that, but he won't listen to me. He finally got the message, I think."

After a nut shot like that, Nathan certainly hoped so.

CHAPTER FORTY-THREE

When the Hanson family returned from their ski trip, Nathan and Randy went to the plasma center to donate blood. On the way, a car, traveling at an exceedingly high speed, rammed into the van in front of them. Randy slammed on his brakes and turned the wheel to the side of the road, trying to avoid being part of the accident. The van in front of him didn't fare as well. The entire back fender was smashed in and it spun a complete three-sixty before it stopped in the middle of the lane. The car that hit it flipped upside down and skidded several feet across the road before it finally came to a stop. Randy immediately grabbed his emergency kit and ran over to the flipped vehicle.

"Nathan," he hollered. "Check on the other car and call 9-1-1!"

Nathan pulled out his phone and dialed as he hurried over to the van. The driver stepped out of the vehicle, which meant she wasn't severely injured. After confirming EMS was on the way and ensuring the driver was ok, Nathan returned to help his father.

By now, there were three bystanders who stopped to assist, two of which tried to direct traffic away from the scene. The other knelt over the victim, who wasn't wearing a seatbelt and had been thrown several feet out the window. While Randy tended to his injuries in the middle of the road, the bystander held the man steady.

"What can I do to help?" Nathan asked. That's when he saw the extent of this man's injuries. He had gashing wounds on his arm and head, and his leg was bent out of place, most likely broken

"There's another pair of gloves in my bag," Randy said. "Put those on before you do anything."

"Alright."

Randy grabbed a gauze pad from his bag and applied it to the man's head. "How's the other driver?"

"She's a little shaken up, but she doesn't appear to be seriously injured."

"Did you get an ETA on the ambulance?"

"No. They just said they were on the way."

"Reach into my bag and grab the scissors."

Nathan pulled out the scissors and handed them to his father.

But Randy wouldn't take them. "Bring those over here. I need your help," he instructed

Nathan moved to the opposite side and squatted down next to the victim.

"Cut the shirt and see if you can get his pants loosened up a little."

Nathan held the scissors in his hand and loosened the man's clothing.

"Good. Now come apply pressure to this wound so I can check for injuries."

Nathan pressed the gauze down firmly with his hand, trying to stop the bleeding.

Randy felt around the chest, stomach, and groin region for tenderness. He didn't see any signs of internal injury.

The thoughtful bystander who was helping him had a dreadful frown on her face. Concerned about this man, the woman asked, "Is he going to be alright?"

Randy reassured her, "He has a few cuts and bruises." He glanced down at the man's mangled leg. "And probably a broken bone, but he'll recover. We need another pad on that head wound."

The woman ripped another gauze pad open and handed it to Nathan.

Nathan applied it on top of the others, being careful not to move the man's neck.

Randy heard sirens drawing near. "Good. EMS is here." He looked at Nathan and the helpful bystander and said, "When the paramedics get here, move out of their way and let them take over."

"What are you gonna do?" Nathan asked.

"Make sure the other driver isn't injured and ensure she has a way to get home."

Police officers, the fire department, and an ambulance all showed up at about the same time. As instructed, Nathan and the woman moved out of the way. Randy showed the EMT's his hospital badge and identified himself as a doctor. He told them what he had already done and gave a detailed account of what he witnessed with the accident. While EMT personnel continued to work on the victim, Randy grabbed his emergency kit and checked on the driver of the van.

"You alright?" Randy asked her.

The woman twirled her hair around her finger. "I think so. I'm not bleeding anywhere."

Randy introduced himself. "I'm Dr. Randy Hanson. I was in the vehicle right behind you."

"You're a doctor?" she asked, shaken and dazed.

"Yes, Ma'am." This woman seemed a little disoriented. Although she said she was alright, Randy wanted to ensure she didn't have any injuries. "Are you sure you're ok? I can do a quick workup on you."

This woman declined his offer. "I'm alright. I'm waiting for my husband to get here."

Ethically, Randy had to grant the woman's request. "You took a pretty big hit. You really should see a doctor."

"My husband is on his way. I'll have him take me." This woman shook Randy's hand, grateful for his compassion. "Thank you, Doctor."

Randy headed back to the car where Nathan stood waiting for him. "Is she alright?"

"She wouldn't let me examine her, but I think she'll be alright." Randy popped the trunk of his car and placed his medical bag in the back. "You did well, Son. You were calm and in control. Good job."

"It felt good to help that man."

Randy agreed. "One of the benefits of this profession. You get the satisfaction of knowing you can help people. Which reminds me, I have something for you." He pulled out a boxed set of Kaplan MCAT study guides. "Thought you could use these."

Nathan flashed a smile of gratitude. "Thanks."

"The more you practice, the higher you'll score. And I'd start sooner than later if I were you."

"I will." Worried about the man lying on the ground, Nathan took one last glance.

"He's in good hands, Nate." Randy patted his son's shoulder. "Let's go."

Nathan looked away from the scene and got back in the car with his father.

CHAPTER FORTY-FOUR

It was that time of the year again. The culmination of basketball season that Hoop Heads hung out for—March Madness. The University of Washington men's basketball team was once again involved in the PAC-12 tournament. Randy and Jane flew down to Las Vegas to offer Nathan support during the playoffs. After several rounds of intense competition, the Huskies qualified for the NCAA National Championship Tournament.

They made it further into the tournament this year than they did the previous year. Some tough first round wins and a tight game against Kentucky brought Coach Erik Spoleda and his Dawg Pack into the eliteness of the Final Four.

Although Nathan's season started out a bit rough, the bio they posted in the Final Four synopsis portrayed him in a positive light. They claimed he was *an athletic point guard with superior ball control.* He was a *strong defender* who had *mastered the three-point shot* and *excelled at finishing.* One of his teammates was quoted to say, *When the game is on the line, there is no one better to hand the ball to than Hanson.*

Jim was beyond excited, not only because it was college playoff season but also because Nathan and the Huskies were in the Final Four. He met Randy for coffee, anxious to hear his friend's insights about the tournament. "How's Nathan feelin' about all of this?"

Randy took a sip of his coffee. "He feels pretty good, but Syracuse is a fierce team and has been brutalizing opponents throughout this tournament."

"But Washington protects the ring effectively," Jim defended. "They can disrupt the rhythm of an offense better than any squad in America. And they know how to sink buckets. They're a great all-around basketball team, and I think they have a good shot at winnin' this thing."

Randy admired Jim's loyalty. "They have a decent chance. Depends on how badly they want it. Nathan has to stay focused and can't afford to have an off night."

"That son of yours is a damn good basketball player. He knocks up huge numbers and is virtually unguardable on the drive. He's a powerful run-and-gun. In my opinion, he's one of the best college point guards in the country. You have a future All-American on your hands, Bro."

"He certainly has the will to win."

Jim didn't think Randy was describing Nathan's skills adequately. "Dude, he has more skill, more drive, and more heart than most NCAA players out there."

Jim's comment made Randy think. "The kid was stuffing a basketball into a hoop before he could walk. His first word was ball. When he was a toddler, he'd pick up anything even remotely round and dunk into any open container he could find. I still remember the basketball hoop we got for him when he was just a little guy. He could barely reach it, and he couldn't dribble to save his life, but he was determined to get that ball into the hoop. Nate has always been obsessed with the game. How the hell did he go from being a little kid who loved to throw things into a basket to a dominant force on the court in one of the most important games of the year?"

Jim grinned pretentiously. "Pretty damn exciting, isn't it?"

"Pretty damn scary," Randy retorted.

"Your son is a powerhouse point guard," Jim boasted. "He is the leader of a team with Final Four demands on its hands. I would be damn proud of that."

"I am," Randy explained. "This has been a tough year for him. He had a few meltdowns earlier this season, but he pulled himself together."

Coming through the brackets, the Huskies were ranked as the number five seed. Washington had some confident veterans on their squad, and they were a well-rounded team, which made them unpredictable. As the widely overused term stated, you've got to be in it to win it. Unlike some of their more highly fancied opponents, the Huskies were still in it.

So far, they'd defeated some top-seeded teams in this NCAA tournament. The next team they were up against was Syracuse. UW's fight song boldly declared, 'Bow Down to Washington,' and although Nathan felt confident, the Vegas odds makers pegged Syracuse to win the national title. If Nathan and his teammates could keep up their momentum, Washington might have a chance to pull off the upset against Syracuse. If one underdog could make a run in this tournament, Washington was the one to do it.

The afternoon before the big game, Nathan leaned against the wall in the hallway outside his hotel room with his legs bent and his forearms resting on his knees. He tilted his head back and closed his eyes, listening to songs from his playlist, completely tuning out everything around him.

The cheerleading squad was staying in the same hotel as the basketball team, and Gabby's room was only a few doors down from Nathan's. She peeked her head out into the hall and saw him sitting on the floor in zone-out mode. "Poor guy," Gabby said. "He's so stressed."

"Who is?" Gabby's roommate asked.

"Nathan."

"How do you know?"

"Because he's totally zoned out," Gabby observed.

"Maybe he's just trying to focus."

Gabby shook her head. She knew better. "No. He only does that when he feels overwhelmed." She wanted to talk to him, but knew Coach Spoleda didn't like his players mingling with the cheerleaders or anyone else right before a big game. He wanted them to stay focused. Gabby understood this rationale, but right now Nathan needed her. Hearing her voice and seeing her face would help him relax. "I wish I could talk to him."

"Maybe you should."

The outcome of this game would greatly depend on Nathan's state of mind. For the sake of the game and the entire Huskies team, she ignored regulations and heeded her roommate's advice. She took a few strides down the hallway and sat on the floor next to Nathan. Trying to get his attention, he reached out and gently touched his arm.

Nathan opened his eyes, smiling when he saw her pretty face. He removed his ear buds so he could devote his attention to her. "Hey."

He was definitely tense. The troubled expression on his face and the tautness of his posture gave it away. "How you doing?"

"We watched a video of Syracuse last night. They're brutal, and they rarely miss shots inside the paint. This is a high stakes game against the number one ranked team in the country. That's a lot of pressure. I don't have as much experience as the other guys do in a high stakes situation like this, and I really wish Brett was here right now."

Gabby tried to ease his fears. "You are perfectly capable of leading this team to the finals. You're a strong player, Nathan. You guys work well together, and your teammates trust you."

"I know they do, but Syracuse's point is powerful. He's nearly impossible to stop offensively. He's strong and he's fast. If he gets loose, he'll charge the hoop and shoot right over me. I can't afford to make a mistake against him."

"You're doubting yourself," she warned.

But Nathan had every reason to feel doubtful. "Gabby, people have already said Syracuse is going to win this. They've bet money on it. We've pretty much been written out of this tournament."

"Who cares what they say?" Gabby declared. "You can't let some guy who sits around all day making up stupid game odds dictate to you who will or will not win this thing." She reached over and squeezed his hand. "I know you can do this, and I know you won't go down without a fight. You're going to get on that court tonight and make a serious impact. Syracuse is going to learn that the Huskies are not a force unseen."

He took both of her hands in his and looked into her eyes. Even on his worst days, Gabby was there to offer encouraging words and enduring support. "You've always believed in me, even when I haven't."

She lovingly cradled his face with her hand. "No matter what the outcome is tonight, you'll always be my hero."

Eyeing her lovingly, he leaned a bit closer. Nathan knew he wasn't supposed to fraternize with the cheerleaders, but right now he didn't care about rules and regulations. He pulled Gabby into his arms and kissed her.

Coach Spoleda and the assistant coach were gathered near the area. When the assistant coach looked up and saw Nathan and Gabby kissing, he hopped to his feet, ready to put an immediate end to this unacceptable behavior.

Coach Spoleda stopped him. "Tim, don't."

Appalled that Nathan would dare break the coach's very explicit rules, Tim replied, "He's kissing that cheerleader."

"That cheerleader is his girlfriend and has been for many years. This has been a tough season for him, and you know how worried he's been about this tournament. She might be the only person on this planet who can get his mind back in this game."

Nathan and Gabby were now sitting face to face carrying on a conversation. He was much more relaxed in her presence.

"That woman calms him," Spoleda said. "Let her work her magic."

Nathan and the Dawg Pack played their hearts out that night. Despite their valiant effort, they lost to Syracuse, which pulled them out of the tournament. But they were happy with their national Final Four finish, the furthest Washington had ever gone in the National Championships.

Because of their remarkable season, they were given a huge welcome home party, where each team member received a *NCAA Final Four, PAC-12 Champions* tee-shirt to commemorate the occasion. Many celebratory events were held in their honor. Even if they didn't come out on top, in Seattle, the Huskies were hometown champions.

As part of March Madness, the NCAA held the College Slam Dunk and Three Point Championship. Because Nathan had one of the highest three-point percentages in the entire NCAA, he was invited to compete. Gabby and Jane traveled with him.

Twenty-four of the biggest names in college hoops took to Georgia Tech's court in the men's three-point shooting competition. Each competitor had sixty seconds to shoot twenty-five balls from five racks spread throughout various three-point range positions around the court. There were several rounds. The top four from the first round would advance to the second. Then the top two from that round would compete for the title of College Three Point Shooting Champion.

Nathan watched as other worthy men took their attempts at the hoop, racking up nineteen or twenty points each. When it was his turn, he took position by the first rack and took a few deep breaths, waiting for the go-ahead to start.

The buzzer sounded.

He grasped the first ball in his hand and torched the nylon, sinking seventeen of twenty-five buckets, two of which were money balls, worth two points instead of one. He finished the first round with nineteen points, enough to move him to round two.

During the second round, he favored just as well, scoring twenty-one points. This qualified him for the final round. He and the shooting guard from Indiana were going head to head. The guard from Indiana went first. Nathan carefully watched his stroke, his rhythm, and his ball count so he knew what number he had to beat. The Hoosier scored a solid twenty-four points. He was going to be tough to overtake.

But Nathan didn't falter. In fact, he was on fire. He cleared his first rack completely, giving him six points right off the bat. Quickly, he moved on to the second rack, where he hit all but one, bringing his score to eleven. On the third rack, he sank three out of five, bringing his total to fourteen. He had two more racks to go and would have to be dead on to have a chance to win. He refocused and moved to rack four. He nailed all five shots, giving him a solid twenty points. On to the fifth and final rack. The first shot bounced off the rim, but he didn't let it faze him. He nailed the next three, bringing him within one point and one last ball to victory—the money ball. He grabbed the ball, focused his aim on the net, and let it fly. Time ceased as he watched the ball. It seemed to move in slow motion. In one fell swoop, it cleared the rim and swished through the net. Twenty-five total points, staking his claim to victory.

Jane and Gabby burst out of their seats, hugging each other and hopping around in the stands. The Huskies might not have won the National Championship, but

Nathan was the king of the three-pointer. He proved it here tonight.

The excitement didn't stop there. The event continued with the three-point Battle of the Champions. This event posed the winners of the men's and women's competitions against each other. The women had bested the men in the last six competitions. Nathan vowed to end that streak tonight.

Wearing a cocky grin, he strutted up to his competitor, a center from Georgetown. "You think you can take me?"

She laughed at him. "That sounds like a challenge."

"You do realize, don't you, that the women can't walk away with this every year. Gotta give it up sometime."

She raised an eyebrow. "And you think you are the one to do that?"

"I don't know. Do you?"

She extended her arm and shook his hand. "I'm Rebecca."

"Nathan Hanson. Good luck."

"Same to you."

"May the best man…" teasing her, he corrected, "or woman, win."

As Nathan promised he would, he indeed ended the women's winning streak. With the Battle of the Champions trophy in his hand, he grinned at Rebecca cunningly. She gave him a thumbs up, congratulating him for his dissonant success.

CHAPTER FORTY-FIVE

Basketball was officially over for the year, however the Huskies cheerleading squad had one last hoorah before the close of the season—the College Cheerleading and Dance Team Championships in Orlando, Florida. Some of the most talented collegiate teams in the country participated in this event. The weekend competition included cheer and dance teams, mascots, partner stunt, and coed partner stunt. Gabby and her cheerleading squad were competing in the coed team category, and she and Jayden were one of the top-ranked teams in the coed partner stunt competition.

Fortunately, this event coincided with their spring break. They reserved lodging accommodations at Disney's All-Star Sports Resort which included express bus transportation to all competition venues. Nathan arranged to go to Florida with Gabby to offer his support and cheer her on for a change. He wasn't able to get a flight with her team, but he was able to book a room at the same resort.

Although Nathan had been to Disney World with his family several times when he was young, he'd never stayed at this resort before. The moment he saw it, he beamed in excitement. It was decorated with bright, colorful pop art icons, such as a four-story football helmet, giant-sized surfboards that lined a sprawling pool area, and megaphone-shaped stairwells. The main building was called Stadium Hall and housed the End Zone Food Court, Game Point Arcade, and a gift shop named Sport

Goofy Gifts & Sundries. This hotel offered Nathan the best of both worlds—sports and Disney.

The resort's ten buildings were divided into five sports-themed sections: football, tennis, baseball, basketball, and surfing. When Nathan checked in, he was pleased to discover that he was staying in the Hoops Hotel Building. This basketball-themed building was lined with huge pennants of various sports teams. Seventy giant basketballs, approximately five feet in diameter, hung from the courtyard side of the building. Nathan's room was located right under a giant basketball hoop, which made his day even better. In addition to the regular hotel accommodations, this particular building had several basketball hoops available for guests to use.

As soon as Nathan settled in, he texted Gabby. She was about to head to practice with her team, so to kill time, Nathan snagged a basketball from the front desk and headed out to the courtyard. Everywhere he looked, college cheerleaders were tumbling and practicing routines. This hotel was definitely not a quiet, relaxing place, but Nathan didn't mind. He wasn't here to relax. He was here to support his cheerleader.

The first day of competition, the Washington cheer squad finished fifth overall, which was a pretty respectable position. Gabby and Jayden weren't scheduled to compete in the partner stunt competition until the following morning.

To help them relax, they took a dip in the pool. Nathan decided to join them. "Did I tell you that I ran into Brett last week?"

Gabby hopped out of the water and sat on the edge of the pool. "Where did you see him?"

"Over at the Husky Grind. I met Andrew for lunch, and right as we sat down to eat, Brett walked in the door. We invited him to join us, and the three of us spent about two hours catching up. I told him I was coming out here to watch your competition, and he wanted me to wish you luck. He said he'd wear his Huskies shirt tomorrow and cheer you guys on."

This was the sweetest thing she'd ever heard. "Aw. What a kind gesture. Next time you talk to him, tell him I said thank you."

"Will do."

After soaking in the pool for an hour, Gabby decided to turn in for the night, at which time Nathan went back to his room to get some studying done.

Two hours into studying, a rap on the door broke his concentration. He peeked out his curtain to see Gabby standing at his door. He invited her inside. "I thought you were going to bed?"

"I was, but I can't sleep." With a sulky frown, she sat on the end of his bed. "Your parents always come out to support you for things like this. How come mine don't?"

Even though this was a huge event in Gabby's life, neither of her parents bothered to attend. Her mother argued it was because she didn't have the funds to fly to Florida or pay for a hotel. Gabby's father claimed he couldn't take time off work. It bothered Nathan that Gabriella's mother never watched her cheer. He also felt it unacceptable that her father made promises about paying for school and claimed he wanted to be a part of his life, yet never delivered on either promise. "I don't know, Honey. They should both be here."

"I mean, I understand Mom is struggling with finances right now, and I know my dad is busy…"

"Those are excuses, Gab," Nathan contested. "Your mom knows how important this it to you. She should have found a way to get here. And as far as your dad is concerned, I'm disappointed. The man claimed he wanted to support you, but his actions sure speak otherwise."

Gabby eyes glossed over. "This isn't fair. What did I do to…"

"You didn't do anything," he cut in, not giving her a chance to say what was on her mind. "This is not your fault, and at no time are you to blame yourself because your parents choose not to take part in the joys and celebrations of your life. I don't want to hear that from you."

She sniffled through her silent tears. "I don't understand why."

"I don't either, Honey. I wish I had answers for you." He tenderly kissed her forehead. "I'll always be here to support you no matter what. And you know my parents offer their support as well."

"I know, and I appreciate that your parents do that, but it's not the same."

"I know it's not."

She fell into his arms, where she felt safe and comfortable.

"If you ever need anything, all you have to do is ask. There's nothing I wouldn't do for you." He lifted her chin and gazed at her pretty face. "It's late. You need to get some sleep so you can kick ass tomorrow."

She bobbed her head in agreement.

"I'll walk you back to your room." He held her hand and they made their way back to her section of the hotel. When they got to her door, Nathan kissed her goodnight. "Now go to bed. You need rest."

"I will," she smiled at him. "I love you, Nathan."

"I love you too, Gab. I'll see you in the morning."

Slowly, she released his hand. Nathan stood watch until she was safely inside.

Bright and early, at 5:30 in the morning, Nathan heard a group of cheerleaders practicing their routine right outside his window. He glared at the clock, unimpressed with this obnoxious awakening. With a groan, he rolled over onto his tummy and buried his head under the pillow. With all the rah-rah-rah's and go-team-go's, any attempt at trying to sleep was completely pointless. He stretched, combed his fingers through his hair, and sat up on the edge of the bed with his feet dangling over the side. He wasn't much of a coffee drinker, but this morning he needed a cup. Still groggy, he climbed out of bed and slipped on a pair of basketball shorts and a tee-shirt. Then, with room key in hand, he headed to the lobby to snag a cup of coffee.

Everywhere Nathan looked, he was surrounded by happy-go-lucky cheerleaders, and they were far too cheerful for his liking. He plodded into the lobby area and ran into more of them.

Gabby was having breakfast with Jayden. When she saw Nathan's cranky face, she had a hard time containing her giggles. "Someone woke up on the wrong side of the bed."

"Who?" Jayden asked.

"Nathan."

Jayden pivoted around to look. "Well, good morning," he sang out gleefully.

Grouchy from his rude awakening, Nathan plopped down in a chair. "Was it really necessary for those overly enthusiastic cheerleaders to practice right outside my window this morning? They seriously couldn't have found any other place to do that?"

"Did they wake you up?" Gabby asked.

"Yes, they woke me up." Gabby was wide awake and already dressed in her cheering attire, and she was just as cheerful as the other pom-pom people who swarmed the hotel. "Why are you up so early?"

"Check in for the competition is 7:30," she explained. "We wanted to grab some breakfast before we left."

He groaned and headed to the coffee pot.

Gabby laughed at him. "Wow, Nathan. You are crabby this morning."

"I don't appreciate being awakened by cheering chants at five o'clock in the morning. Rah rah red, go back to bed!" he grumbled, seriously lacking any kind of enthusiasm as he poured coffee in a cup and dumped in a ton of sugar.

Jayden thought this was hilarious.

Nathan didn't share his sentiments. "It's not funny, man. They didn't even consider that some hotel patrons might not be cheerleaders who had to be up at this god awful hour. They might as well have blown a damn trumpet outside my door."

"Maybe you should go back to bed," Gabby suggested.

Nathan glared at her. "And how the hell am I supposed to sleep with all this damn cheering and clapping going on?"

"You're being a Grinch," she told him.

"You guys…" he pointed to both of them, "are far too peppy at five o'clock in the morning." He grabbed his coffee and trudged back to his room.

Somewhat shocked by what he thought was an overreaction, Jayden asked, "Is he always that cranky in the morning?"

"Only when he wakes up tired," Gabby explained. "A warm shower will quickly cure that."

During the coed stunt contest, Gabby and Jayden had under a minute to complete as many lifts, tosses, and tumbling stunts as possible. The entire time they were performing, Nathan sat on the edge of his seat. Even though he trusted Jayden, he still feared the worst—that somehow Jayden would lose his footing and Gabby would come crashing to the ground sustaining serious injuries. Luckily, that didn't happen. Jayden held strong, and Gabby was the graceful, flexible, and powerful tumbler she always was.

Their biggest and final stunt combination was coming up next. It was a stunt they had struggled to stick during practices. Watching Gabby set up for this, Nathan mumbled to himself, "Come on, Baby. You can do this." As she performed a tumbling run across the stage, he held his breath. Once she got to a designated point, she pushed off from a handspring, flying into the air with a twist and turn. Jayden caught her then immediately balanced her above his head with one hand while she stretched into a bow and arrow position. It was a very difficult move that required a lot of strength and balance from both of them. This was something Nathan couldn't dream of doing, and wouldn't even want to attempt with Gabby; he would drop her for sure. Yet Jayden nailed it without a falter.

For their final hoorah, Jayden tossed Gabby in the air. She did a front flip and cleanly landed her dismount.

As long as Nathan had known her, Gabby protested, quite loudly, about cheerleading not being recognized as a legitimate sport. Nathan upheld her plight. He would gladly challenge any football quarterback, basketball superstar, golf virtuoso, tennis ace, or track speedster to attempt what Gabby and Jayden just did. None of them would be able to do it.

University of Washington's cheering partners, Gabriella Pervis and Jayden Lamb, were officially crowned as Coed Partner Stunt Champions. When the competition was over, and Gabby and Jayden took claim to their trophy, Gabby ran to Nathan and jumped into his arms.

He lifted her off the ground. "Awesome, awesome job, Babe! I'm so proud of you." He kissed her and gently set her down. Then he offered Jayden a congratulatory handshake. "Well done! I don't know how you do that, man. Your strength amazes me."

"Thank you."

"I'm proud of you guys. Way to put Washington on the map."

With competition complete, presentation of the trophies concluded, and the celebratory party over and done with, Gabby and Nathan could finally spend the day together at Disney World, something they had both anticipated for weeks.

Nathan brought a pair of khaki cargo shorts, a green tee-shirt with a picture of Goofy on it, sunglasses, and comfortable walking shoes just for this occasion. He was ready for a day of Disney. "Gabby, hurry up!" he demanded as he watched her put her hair up in a ponytail.

"Didn't your mother teach you not to rush a woman?"

"Depends on what I'm rushing her for. To achieve orgasm, you can take all the time you need. But when Disney is on the line, you need to hurry up."

She huffed at his off-color remark. "You have sex on the brain today."

"Maybe because we haven't had any since we've been down here. But as soon as we get home, you are in serious trouble." He grabbed her into his arms and drug her onto the bed with him. "Or we could do it now."

"I thought you were in a hurry to catch the shuttle?"

"For sex, I'll wait for the next one."

"You are so bad," she accused playfully.

"Bad?" he questioned. "That's not what you said last weekend. You were begging me not to stop."

Her mouth gaped open at his bold comment. "Nathan Hanson!"

"You liked it and you know it." Trying to get a rise out of her, he pressed his pelvis against hers.

Appalled by his serious lack of discretion, she retorted, "Oh my god."

He continued to goad her. "Yup. You've said that before too, especially when I'm deep inside you."

All of his sexual quips only meant one thing. "You want a quickie before we go?"

"Is that what you want?"

"I know what I want," she enticed him. "But I want to know what you want."

"No you don't."

"Yes I do." She reached down and unbuttoned his shorts. Once they were loose, she slid her hand into his pants.

Nathan closed his eyes, fighting back intense desire. It became increasingly more difficult for him to control his impulses. He stared at her in lustful delight as she stripped off her clothes, exposing her sexy, curvy, lusciously feminine body to him.

Then she surprised him by scooting to the end of the bed and spreading her legs wide open. With her index finger, she signaled for him to join her. Giving in to her insistent suggestion, he wasted no time stripping naked.

Gabby and Nathan felt so comfortable with each other that their chemistry together was erotically hot. They switched positions often and had a blast from kickoff to the final whistle. Feeling Gabby's body against his skin was sensuous and incredibly bonding.

Also bonding was their time together at Disney World. They were able to spend quality time together with no commitments or responsibilities. They conquered mountains, cruised down an exotic jungle river, braved a ghostly mansion, and got soaked to the skin with Brer Rabbit.

They popped into a gift shop, and Nathan saw something he had to have—a huge plush Goofy head hat with long, floppy ears dangling down the sides. "Check this out, Gab. This is the best hat ever. I'm so getting this."

"You're such a dork."

Disney was definitely bringing out his inner child. Proud of his find, Nathan put the hat on his head. "The Goofster is my hero."

"And now you can look like him," she teased.

"For sure. Who doesn't love Goofy?"

"I know you do."

He certainly did. The tall and lanky anthropomorphic dog was by far his favorite Disney character for many reasons. He was extremely clumsy and had little intelligence, yet he was also known to be intuitive and clever, albeit in his own unique, eccentric way. Nathan was a little goofy himself so he related to the character quite well.

Nathan looked ridiculous with that hat on his head. "You're goofy."

After making their purchases, they decided to find something to eat. They ended up at Gaston's Tavern where they chomped on mixed vegetable cups with dip and warm cinnamon rolls. They each enjoyed LeFou's Brew—the restaurant's signature non-alcoholic drink of frozen apple juice with a hint of toasted marshmallow topped with passion fruit and mango foam served in a souvenir goblet. It definitely hit the spot.

They concluded their day with a spectacular fireworks show, after which they returned to the hotel. The day was exhausting, but full of great memories and several pictures, including one taken with the two of them standing in front of a Mickey Mouse shaped flowerbed at the park's front entrance.

Nathan reclined on the bed and released a relaxed sigh. "Ok, today definitely ranks as one of my best days."

"I agree," Gabby said. "That incident with Goofy was hilarious. I can't believe he dumped water on your head."

Nathan laughed. "He went after my woman. Couldn't let him get away with that. That made an awesome picture though. It'll definitely be one to frame and put next to my bed."

Gabby joined him on the bed, lying on her tummy with her feet up in the air. "Thank you for coming down here with me."

"Of course." He reached over and touched her arm. "I wouldn't have missed this for the world. You definitely deserve the recognition you got. You're a talented woman, Gabby."

"I love you," she said.

"I love you more," he teased.

"I said it first," she concluded. "No backsies."

He looked at her adoringly, drew her closer to him, and wrapped her up tightly in his arms, indulging himself in her sweet kiss.

Monday afternoon, after returning to Seattle, Nathan waited outside by the courtyard for Gabby to get out of class. He had about a half an hour, so he sat on a bench and pulled some books and notes out of his backpack. He was so engrossed in studying that he didn't see Gabby approach him.

"Hey, Sweetie," she said.

He didn't respond. In fact, he acted like he didn't even hear her. Whatever he was reading had his full attention. Trying to divert his attention, she snuck up behind him, leaned over his shoulder, and laid a big, wet kiss on him.

This broke his concentration. "Hey, Babe."

"What are you reading that has you so absorbed?"

"It's an MCAT study guide my dad got for me. I'm actually doing pretty well."

"MCAT? You're prepping for that already?" she asked.

"I have to take that next year. I'm certainly not going to walk into it blindly. The more prep I have, the better. It's not a given that I'm going to get into medical school, Gab. I have to apply and go through the screening process just like everybody else."

Gabby thought that was a ridiculous thing for him to say. Of course he was going to get into medical school. He'd been working too hard not to. "You'll get in."

He wasn't as confident. "My grades are far from spectacular. In order to make myself a better candidate, higher MCAT scores are a necessity."

"Your grade point average isn't bad, and you're a dedicated college athlete. Everyone knows that's not easy to do."

Nathan tried to explain, "There's a lot more to it than that. Certainly a strong overall grade point average and competitive test scores will be big contributing factors, but to be a strong candidate I need to be well-rounded. Basketball will help considerably, but I also need to have quality volunteer experiences, notable leadership qualities, and strong letters of recommendation. I need to stand out above the others."

"You always stand out above everyone else. The problem is you don't think you do," Gabby stated.

"I'm trying to be realistic about this," Nathan clarified. "I don't want to be one of those people who applies year after year and can't get it because there's something I overlooked or some personal weakness I failed to address. I'm going to do this right and get in the first time."

"It really is ok if you don't finish first, Nathan."

"I have to come in first," he insisted. "In this case, coming in second means not getting in. Applying for medical school is not something I can half-ass my way through. I thought you were supporting me on this?"

"I am. I just think you are too hard on yourself."

"I have to be," he stated. "Do you really want me to neglect all of this and risk not getting in?"

"No. I want you to accept the fact that you're not perfect," Gabby contended. "Even the best doctors in the world make mistakes and have weaknesses."

Nathan had been very careful about documenting all of his volunteer and paid experiences in health care. He had done community service and teaching in the area of First Aid, CPR, and AED usage. He shadowed Jim in the ER and did some volunteer work in triage. He worked the last two years in his father's clinic and was an active member of The American Medical Student Association. All of these experiences were valuable ways to clarify his personal beliefs and display his dedication to the medical field. Nathan had the necessary knowledge, self-discipline, passion, and innate compassion to be a successful medical student, but he had to convince a panel of medical school admittance board members who didn't know anything about him.

"I have to prove myself on paper," he explained to Gabby. "The admissions officers who screen these applications know nothing about me other than what my file says or how my recommendation letters portray me. I need them to look beyond my stats and see who I really am."

"You'll get in," she said confidently. "I know you will."

CHAPTER FORTY-SIX

For her high school's spring production, Lauren was cast as the female lead in *Phantom of the Opera*. This particular production involved intense singing and emotional acting, which Lauren was extremely good at. She loved being on stage and particularly enjoyed singing in musicals. Being a part of this show carried many emotions for her, not only because it was one of her favorite musicals but also because it was her final high school stage performance.

Randy, Jane, Lacy, and Nathan had seen Lauren perform in musicals and plays many times before. Aside from her involvement in high school theatre, Lauren had also performed in regional and local theatre and was part of the Seattle Shakespearean Festival. She had extraordinary talent and was always a crowd favorite. As Nathan watched his sister on stage, he realized how truly skilled she was in the performing arts. Her voice resonated through the entire auditorium, and she made an emotional connection with the audience. When her character, Christine Daaé, stood in front of her father's grave marker and belted out 'Wishing You Were Somehow Here Again', images of Mike's face flashed through Nathan's head. It brought tears to his eyes.

Gabby squeezed his hand, offering condolence. Her eyes met his, and for the first time since Mike's death, he found peace of mind.

When Lauren took her bow at the curtain call, the audience stood in ovation. She was a class act, and Randy was convinced he had the most talented daughter in the world.

After the performance, the family met Lauren outside the auditorium. Randy presented her with a dozen red roses, congratulating her on a job well done. "Wonderful job, Baby." He gave her a huge bear hug. "You were the star of the show. I'm very proud of you."

"Thank you, Daddy."

Musicals were Lauren's passion. Ever since she was a little girl, she had taken voice lessons and was an active member of the Seattle Musical Playhouse, where she performed many times in front of crowds. She played a major role in every theater production Lake Washington High School put on, often being cast as the lead. Her parents put her in the Fifth Avenue Theatre summer program for youth, where she learned from professionals and acquired the necessary skills to be a true triple threat. These summer classes helped her build confidence over the years in a fun and supportive environment. She studied dance, improvisation, vocal technique, and song interpretation. She also learned audition techniques, makeup, stage presence, and participated in special panel discussions with professionals who revealed insights about the life of a working theater artist.

Lauren dreamed of performing on a Broadway stage. To help fulfill her Broadway visions, one of the things Lauren hoped for was to get into the Juilliard School. Some of the best performers in the world had gotten formal training from that school, but the admission process was grueling and time consuming. Lauren spent the entirety of her senior year preparing a resume, learning all she could about the school, and planning for one moment—her Juilliard audition.

Audition guidelines required her to present two memorized monologues—one classical and one contemporary—of contrasting natures, each approximately two minutes in length. The classical selection had to be from a Shakespearean play. She had two remaining monologues in reserve, in the event the panel needed to see additional material.

When she walked into the audition studio, all of the auditionees were gathered in a large group, warming up and improvising with one another. Lauren decided to join them. This helped calm her nerves and refocus her energy. After the orientation and warmup session, she was assigned a specific audition time.

When her name was called, she stepped into the audition room where a panel of several instructors from the acting, voice/speech, and movement disciplines were seated behind a long table. Lauren confidently stood in the center of the room, facing them. They asked her pertinent information and why she wanted to attend Juilliard. Next, she recited her classical monologue followed by her contemporary one. Aside from the monologue audition, she had to answer questions about the entire play from which her selection was chosen. She also had to prepare sixteen bars of a song to be sung a cappella. She chose 'Memories' from the musical *Cats*. This gave the faculty the opportunity to find out about her vocal range and instrument.

They then asked her to mime a kickball game with someone who was much better than she was. She ran around the room for a bit, making the faculty laugh. After presenting the panel with a copy of her resume, which included plays and performances she had been in as well all the vocal and theatre training she had, she was thanked, and went back out to the hallway nervously waiting. After a while, a list of callbacks was posted. Only five names were on the list. Lauren's was one of them. She made it through the first round, which was exciting news; it meant she was being considered for admission.

Her callback took place that evening. During this process, she was asked to participate in group exercises, present two additional monologues, do improvisations and cold readings, and sing a cappella. She was also asked to interview with the faculty.

Only forty individuals were selected to come to New York for two days for the final callback round. Lauren was overjoyed to be invited. Her mother made airline reservations and the two of them flew to New York together. During this final process, Lauren worked intensively with faculty, and had the opportunity to speak to current students and learn more about The Juilliard School. The incoming class of approximately twenty students would be selected from this final callback session.

Lauren anxiously awaited her letter from Juilliard. When the letter finally arrived, she was too nervous to open it. "I can't," she said, shoving the envelope toward Lacy. "You do it."

Lacy took the envelope in her hand and ripped it open. While she read, Lauren nervously bit her lip. "Oh my god! Oh my god! Oh my god!" Lacy rushed over and hugged her sister. "You did it! You got in!"

Lauren grabbed the letter and read it for herself.

The celebratory screaming brought Randy into Lacy's room. "What is going on up here?"

Lacy jumped up and down in excitement. "Lauren got into Juilliard!"

Randy grinned at his daughter proudly. "Is that right?"

Lauren ran across the room and threw her arms around her father. "I made it."

"Great job, Baby. I'm very proud of you. You have worked really hard for this."

"Thank you for all your support, Daddy."

"You're welcome. Now go tell your mother."

Lauren held the letter in her hand and ran downstairs to show her mom.

Both of Nathan's sisters were exceptionally talented, and he loved to watch them perform. Because Nathan was out of town on a road trip series, he missed Lacy's dance team competition this year. They came home with the first place trophy. Luckily, it had been recorded and put on DVD. When Nathan went to his parents' house Sunday, Lacy put the DVD in for him so he could see her dance team's winning routine.

As Nathan watched, he couldn't help but notice that one of the girls on the dance team had a much larger bosom than the others. Her dance uniform was tight fitting and her cleavage showed prominently. He fixated on this particular girl and started to snicker.

Lacy didn't understand why her brother was laughing at their dance routine. It wasn't funny at all. "What are you laughing about?"

"Who is that?" he asked.

"Who?" Lacy questioned, having no clue what he was talking about.

Nathan took the remote from her and paused the frame, deliberately exposing a still shot of this girl's cleavage. "That!" he said. "Who is that?"

"Don't pause right there."

He grinned devilishly. "That is the perfect place to pause. That chick has really nice boobs."

Lacy smacked her brother on the arm. "Oh my god! What a chauvinistic thing for you to say!"

"Hey, I know a hot chick when I see one."

"You don't say things like that about Gabby, do you?"

"Are you kidding? Gabby knows I think she's hot. In fact, she is super-hot. Her boobs aren't as big as this chicks, but yeah," he grinned lustfully. "Gabby definitely has nice boobs."

Disgusted by her brother's sexist attitude, Lacy scowled at him. "You're a jerk."

Nathan simply laughed at her.

Randy overheard this discussion, but instead of being upset with his son for making inappropriate sexual comments, he found himself chuckling under his breath.

Lacy heard her father's snickering and turned her nose up, appalled that he was encouraging this behavior. "Daddy!"

"Sorry." Randy wiped the grin off his face and cleared his throat. Faking a scowl, he looked his son in the eye, and scolded, "Nathan, you really shouldn't make derogatory comments about Lacy's friends like that."

Lacy could tell he didn't really mean it. "Mom!" she hollered.

Jane had been in the adjacent room and heard this entire conversation. Ashamed that her husband was fostering this ill behavior, she said to him, "Randy, don't encourage him, please."

A few weeks later, Lacy got her own letter in the mail from Columbia University. She had been accepted into the dance program. It looked like the Hanson twins were going to pursue their performing arts interests together in New York City. Although Randy couldn't have been more proud of them, he had his fatherly concerns.

To close out her senior year, Lauren was involved in the Fifth Avenue Theatre Awards, which was the high school version of the Tony Awards. Lake Washington High School received five nominations this year, two of which went to Lauren for her portrayal of Christine Daaé in *Phantom of the Opera*. The entire family attended this event.

The theater was packed with teenagers in costume, representing their schools' musical productions. Lake Washington High School had received several nominations in the past but had only won three times. This year, however, they took home top honors at The Annual Fifth Avenue Awards, including Best Outstanding Overall Musical Production. Lauren was surprised, yet honored, when she and her co-star both won in their respective categories. Lauren also walked away with the win for Outstanding Solo Performance after singing

'Wishing You Were Somehow Here Again' on stage during the excerpt expedition.

When Lauren got home from the awards ceremony that night, she had two Fifth Avenue Awards in her possession. She carefully displayed them on her dresser, claiming bragging rights to her final performance at Lake Washington High School.

Randy walked into her room and gave her a huge hug. "Congratulations, Honey. You are a talented young woman, and I'm very proud of you."

"Thank you, Daddy."

"The first two of many future recognitions you are bound to receive. Next time it will be a Tony." He held up his hands as if framing a theatre marque. "Now starring the beautiful and talented Lauren Hanson. And the crowd goes wild."

"Daddy, stop it," Lauren said with a bashful smile.

Affectionately, he kissed her forehead. "You'll see. Your name will be up in lights someday."

"I hope so."

CHAPTER FORTY-SEVEN

For their twenty-fifth anniversary, Jane and Randy renewed their wedding vows. They wanted to keep this event private so they only invited their kids and the Ryan family to attend, and they performed the ceremony on the beach in their backyard. The fact that his parents not only liked each other, but were still very much in love made Nathan's heart leap. It seemed like so many married couples these days were splitting up over derisory things, yet his parents always managed to find a way to work things out and keep the fire burning in their marriage.

Over the years, Nathan's father offered advice about relationships, and he learned many things from observing his parents' together. Communication seemed to be the key. They took time every day to talk and set aside private time to discuss and reach agreements on serious matters. Neither one expected the other to be a mind reader. Although they had been guilty of this, Randy advocated to never go to bed angry, that anger shouldn't simmer, but be dealt with as quickly as possible.

By watching his parents, Nathan learned there was a different kind of compromise that sometimes required a complete reversal in thinking. Sometimes his father would let his mother have her way, even without fully understanding the rationale for her request or decision. They made reasonable requests of each other but never pressured one another or made irrational demands. Neither one was afraid to give something up, if necessary, to reach a mutual goal. They advocated for each other. Sometimes Randy had to protect or defend Jane, and she did the same for him.

Just because Randy and Jane were married didn't mean they always acted like grownups. They still played together and weren't afraid to indulge. They went on dates and took family vacations to the Caribbean or Mexico at least once a year. The fun they had together helped bond them as a couple. Randy loved to make his wife laugh. Nathan still remembered, many years ago, when his father started singing 'Macho Man' when they all saw a shirtless guy running up the road. His mother couldn't stop laughing.

Jane and Randy were flexible in their marriage. They adapted to changing circumstances and encouraged each other to develop their talents, offering support in the process. Most importantly, they were loyal and faithful. When they promised they would stay married forever, they both truly believed it.

Nathan stood on the beach with Gabby and his sisters watching his parents renew their commitment to one another. As they sealed their promise with a kiss, Nathan felt blessed to have such strong role models who exemplified what love and marriage longevity was all about. He put his arm around Gabby and hoped that someday they would have a marriage as strong as his parents had.

As an anniversary gift to one another, Jane and Randy planned a trip to Bermuda, where they had spent their honeymoon. Going on this trip meant Lauren and Lacy would be staying home alone for an extended period of time. The twins were both eighteen now and were perfectly capable of taking care of themselves and the house in their parents' absence, but that didn't make Randy any less worried.

"No one is allowed in the house while we're gone," Randy told his daughters. "And no parties."

"Daddy," Lauren said. "When have we ever tried to do that?"

"When have you ever been left alone for this long with the whole house at your disposal?" Being the firm father he was, he reiterated his expectations. "I mean it. No parties and no boys."

Jane took a more nurturing approach. "The fridge and pantry are fully stocked. If you need anything, you have Grandma's number."

Randy pulled a wad of cash out of his wallet. He handed $100 to Lacy and $100 to Lauren. "Here's some money in case you need it," he offered. "You can use the SUV, but be responsible. No texting and no making or answering phone calls while you're driving. And if you use the gas, refill the tank."

"We will," Lacy replied.

"Make sure you lock the house and set the alarm any time you leave," he instructed.

"We know, Daddy," Lacy stated. "We will."

He exhaled with a worried sigh, hoping they were going to be ok. "Call if you need anything, and if you really run into a bind, Nathan said he'd be available."

"We'll be ok," Lauren maintained. "When are you going to stop worrying about us?"

"Never," he averred. "I'm your father. It's my job to worry about you."

Jane hugged both of her girls and gave them a kiss on the cheek. "Be careful, please."

"And don't do anything you don't want to have to explain when we get home," Randy reminded them. He gave them each a hug and kissed them on the forehead. "I love you, my princesses. We'll call you when we get there."

"Have a safe trip, and have fun," the girls said in perfect sync.

Jane and Randy got into the Jaguar and backed out of the driveway. Jane waved to the girls as they pulled away. "Finally, some time to ourselves to relax and unwind," she said. Then she saw the expression on Randy's face. He looked tense. "Which is obviously something you need."

Randy drove for a while, not saying anything, before his fatherly concerns finally came out. "Should we have gotten my parents to stay with them? I can still call my mom and have her go over there."

"They're going to be fine."

"Are you sure?"

Jane tried to reassure him. "They're both responsible. I really don't think we need to worry."

But he *was* worried. "I can't help it. They are young women alone on their own for an entire week."

"They can handle it. What are you going to do when they both go off to college without you?"

"Go out of my fuckin' mind," he plainly stated. "I'm really not sure I like the idea of sending both of them off to New York on their own."

Jane laughed at his incessant worrying. "What are you going to do? Pack yourself in a box and ship yourself to New York so you can look out for them? At some point you have to let them grow up and be independent young women."

"I know that, but why the hell did they have to grow up so damn fast? My little girls are women now, Jane."

"Yes," she agreed. "Very responsible women. They're going to fine."

Randy and Jane were staying in a one-bedroom ocean suite at the Fairmont Southampton Resort. The minute they walked into the room, Jane set her purse on the dresser and stepped onto the covered private balcony to soak in the sweeping ocean view. "Ooh, this is nice."

Randy sat on the bed and bounced to check the firmness of the mattress. "This is nice too. We can sink right into this. No squeaky springs or banging headboard either. Perfect!" He winked suggestively.

"There you go again," Jane said. "You have a dirty mind, Dr. Hanson."

"Hey," he defended. "I'm in Bermuda with my wife. This is the place we spent our honeymoon. I have every intention of making love as often as possible while we're here."

The website said this hotel offered a Keurig coffeemaker in every room, so one of the first things Randy did was search for it. When he confirmed his find, he said, "Sweet, and it even comes with K-cups."

Jane chuckled at his caffeine addiction. "What would you do without coffee?"

"I really don't think you want to know."

"Oh, I've seen you without caffeine in your system, and I wouldn't want you anywhere near a scalpel in that condition."

Her comment made him laugh because it was true.

Feeling jet lagged, Jane leaned back on the bed. "I can't believe it's been twenty-five years."

"Twenty-five wonderful years with the most beautiful woman in the world," Randy added, lying on the bed beside her.

"Twenty-five years of love and laughs with the most wonderful husband I could ever ask for."

"And I wouldn't trade any of the experiences we've shared for anything. We have so many memories, Janey." His lips brushed against hers as he spoke. "I'm ready for twenty-five more years of memories with you."

She bit her lip and smiled.

"God I love it when you do that. It's so sexy." He kissed her on the lips then leaned forward and whispered in her ear, "Twenty-five years of marriage and you still make me horny as hell."

She gave him a seductive eye, anticipating his obvious intentions.

They spent the rest of the day exploring the crystal blue waters and lounging on the warm pink sand. When the sun went down, they held hands and strolled along the beach with the waves lapping at their feet.

"We seriously need to retire here," Randy claimed. "I could spend every day of my life here with you. No hustle and bustle of the city. No traffic, no cellphones, no emergency calls, no deliveries at three o'clock in the morning. Not a care in the world. Just you and me."

She snuggled in closer. "It hasn't been just you and me for twenty years."

"I know."

"Do you remember life before the kids?" Jane teased.

Randy had to laugh. "Vaguely."

"We didn't have to worry about dance class or basketball camps or voice lessons."

"Or playing chauffer to seven giggling teenage girls during a sleepover," Randy added. "Shopping for leotards and dresses and a ridiculous quantity of shoes."

"And don't forget to include Nathan's basketball shoes in that mix," Jane added.

"For sure." Randy smiled thinking about it. "Or taking the girls to get their hair done. Manicures, pedicures, and makeup. Teddy bears and tea parties. Fuzzy pink bunny slippers. Tinkerbell." As he reminisced about all the experiences he had with his girls, his eyes brimmed with tears. "Hello Kitty stickers on my stethoscope. Little flowers made of tissue paper and pipe cleaners that they would sneak into the pockets of my lab coat before I'd leave for the hospital in the morning. The time they bedazzled my cellphone with pink and purple sparkly gems." Randy heaved a heavy sigh. "Dammit, Jane, I'm gonna miss them."

"I am too, but this is a once in a lifetime opportunity for both of them. They each have a chance to pursue their dreams. With Lauren's acting and singing talent and Lacy's passion for choreography, what better place for them to be than in the performing arts capital of the world. We have to let them embrace that."

"I know. I just…" Randy felt like crying. The thought of losing his girls broke his heart. "It's going to be hard to let them go."

Jane gently touched his face. "The quality time you spent with them and the special things you did, neither one of them will ever forget that." She could see he wasn't eased by that. "The girls love you, Randy. You have been a very good daddy to them."

"That doesn't make this any easier. With Nathan it's different. I see him almost every day. He's twenty minutes from home. I could practically wave to him from across the lake. But the girls, they're going to be clear across the country, Babe. New York is almost three-thousand miles away. That's definitely not a day trip."

"No, but we'll still see them. They'll be home on holidays and during the summer. And I'm sure we'll make plenty of trips to New York. You're acting like you're never going to see them again."

Randy countered, "Well, you're acting like it's no big deal."

"I'll miss them just as much as you will," she returned. "But dwelling on it and letting it consume you like this isn't going to make it any easier, Sweetie. I'm happy they have been given the opportunity to accomplish their goals and meet their dreams. They are both excited, and we should be celebrating with them."

"I'm excited for both of them, and I'm very proud of my daughters. I just wish they weren't going so damn far away."

CHAPTER FORTY-EIGHT

After returning from Bermuda, Randy felt revitalized. The beach always had that kind of effect on him, especially when he was with Jane.

He and Jim made plans to attend the local car show, but before they did, the two of them met for coffee. When Randy walked into Starbucks, he laughed at the tee-shirt Jim had on. Printed on the front was a huge photo of a baby's face. "Seriously? What the hell is that all about?"

"What?" Jim asked.

"There's a baby's face on your shirt."

Jim looked down at the imprint on his shirt. "That is my granddaughter, you son-of-a-bitch. Don't be dissin'."

"Someone's a little too proud about being a grandfather." Over top of the tee-shirt, Jim had on a black and orange Hawaiian button up shirt. He always left these unbuttoned to expose the tee-shirt underneath. In this case, it was a bit unnerving because it looked like the baby's face was peeking out from behind a palm tree. "You're not really hanging out with me all day wearing that, are you?"

"Why wouldn't I?"

Trying to get Jim to understand his crude fashion sense, Randy explained, "Because there's a baby staring at me from behind that palm tree, and it's kinda creeping me out."

"Dude, you see babies all the damn time in your specialty. You should be used to it."

Teasing him, Randy suggested, "Maybe I should plaster your face on a shirt."

"Why would you want to do that?"

In a bantering tone, he said, "So my best friend's smiling face can be with me wherever I go."

"Fuck you, Hanson!"

Jim's lack of enthusiasm made Randy chuckle. "Seriously though, was it really necessary to blow up the baby's face larger than life and slap it on your chest?"

"Yes," Jim justified. "It was very necessary. You have a problem with that?"

"No. You're the one who has to wear it. I just think it's a little grandiose. People are gonna be staring at us all day."

"Good," Jim replied. "Then they'll get to see my beautiful granddaughter, won't they?"

Randy shook his head, thinking his friend was nuts. "Here," he said, handing him a paper gift bag. "I got something for you. Perhaps an alternative to the monstrosity you are currently wearing."

Jim pulled out a white tee-shirt with the words *World's Coolest Grandpa* written on it. "This is awesome!"

"Thought you might like that."

While they finished their coffee, Jim showed Randy a bunch of pictures of his granddaughter, who was now six months old. "Little Madeline is growin' like a weed," he boasted.

Randy skimmed through the photos. "She's a cutie. She looks like Chris."

"She has her mommy's eyes though."

"Big green ones," Randy exclaimed. "Both of my girls have Jane's green eyes too. One of the many things that made me fall in love with my wife." Randy handed the pictures back to Jim. "Keep an eye on that one, Jim. She's gonna be a heartbreaker."

"We have a long way to go before we get to that point, Bro." Jim slipped the pictures back in the envelope. "How are your girls, anyway? Bet they are gettin' excited."

Randy was not looking forward to shipping his daughters off to New York in a couple months. He really didn't want them to go, but he didn't want to hold them back from pursuing their dreams either. "Don't know that I'm ready for this," he admitted. "But they are. They both have worked really hard to get where they're going. Juilliard and Columbia have been dreams of theirs since they were little. Both of them pulled it off and got into the school of their choice."

"You have really talented kids, my friend. Lauren has an amazing voice. Lacy is a badass dancer, and Nathan...that young man is a superstar on the basketball court. You should be really proud of your kids."

"I'm very proud of them. I just wonder where the hell the time went. Next thing I know, my kids are going to be graduating from college, getting married, and having babies of their own."

"Oh good. Then you can get a tee-shirt with your grandbaby's face on it," Jim said with a cheesy grin.

Randy had to laugh. "Uh, no. I don't think so. I am in no damn hurry for that to happen. Nathan better keep it in his pants and not even consider fathering a child right now."

"What would you do if Gabby was pregnant?" Jim posed hypothetically.

Randy didn't want to go there. "Jesus, Jim."

"I'm just sayin' it could happen. He is dickin' her."

"Nathan is wiser than that. But then again, it happened to you."

"Dude," Jim protested. "Really? You had to bring that up?"

"Happened to Bruce and Stephanie too. Was I the only one sensible enough to use birth control when we were younger?"

"Shut up!" Jim complained.

"You do know that if you have sex without some form of contraception, your chances of getting pregnant are pretty high."

"I'm a doctor for Christ sake, of course I know that!"

"Are you sure?" Randy teased with a chuckle. "Or maybe it's just that at the time you were so damn horny, you didn't want to take the time to wrap it up."

Jim quickly retorted, "I was young. I made a mistake. Everything about Trina was a fuckin' mistake. The only good thing that came out of that relationship was my son, and now my granddaughter. I'm gonna laugh my ass off the day you become a grandfather because your son, as you so blatantly put it, can't keep his dick in his pants. He's not that much different than you were. If I remember correctly, you slept with every damn woman you saw. If she had a hot body, a pretty face, and a wet pussy, you were all over her. You had a different chick at our apartment every damn weekend. At least Nathan is reserving his dick for one woman."

Randy really couldn't argue with that. "Ok. Valid point. And thank you for reminding me of my insensitive asshole years."

"My point is people do stupid shit in their youth," Jim argued. "Nathan is young. God forbid that happen to him and Gabby, but what would you do if it did?"

Randy didn't want to consider this possibility, but to ease Jim's curiosity, he replied, "I'd do my best to support my son. I would expect him to be a man and be responsible about it, however. If he's gonna do the deed then by god he's going to be responsible for his actions and take responsibility for the child he created. There is no way in hell I would allow my son to even consider shirking his responsibilities as a father, and if that meant I had to beat some sense into him, I would."

"Exactly," Jim plainly said. "I didn't shirk my responsibilities either. Neither did Bruce. And why?

Because we are good men who were raised better than that."

"But Gabby's on the pill, so as long as she's conscientious about taking them every day, they won't have any problems, will they?" Randy posed mockingly.

"What about your girls?" Jim asked. "You gonna put them on the pill before you ship them off?"

"Don't even go there," Randy warned. "My daughters are *not* having sex."

Jim busted out laughing. "Now I know for a fact you are not that damn naïve. You and I both know that when young woman leave home and have their first taste of independence, they're gonna have sex. Lauren and Lacy are no different."

Randy didn't like this conversation. "Dammit, Jim. What happened to my sweet little girls in ponytails?"

"It's a bitch havin' your kids grow up, isn't it?"

Randy shook his head in disbelief. "Good god they grow up fast."

"Tell me about it. My granddaughter is already six months old and I still have yet to meet her."

"When is Chris coming back to the states?"

Jim shrugged. "I have no idea. Soon I hope. I haven't even met his girlfriend yet, and I would like to see Madeline sometime before her first birthday."

"I don't blame you."

"You complain about sending your girls off to New York? Dude, try shippin' your son off to Africa. That blows."

Randy and Jane were about to put their daughters on a plane. Randy in particular was extremely apprehensive about this. He was nervous about them going off on their own, worried about their safety, and concerned about them being so far away from home. However, he felt slightly better about the situation knowing his girls were going to New York together. "Look out for each other. Keep each other safe."

"Daddy," Lacy declared. "You're doing it again."

Admitting Lacy was right, he confessed, "I'm being overprotective again, aren't I?"

"Yes."

He took in a big breath. "I'm sorry."

In an attempt to ease his anxiety, Lacy gave her father a hug.

"Be careful please," he begged, squeezing his daughter and trying to postpone this departure. "Call once in a while and let us know how you're doing."

"We will," Lacy promised.

Randy embraced Lauren with a lingering hug, as if afraid to let her go. "I love you. Let us know if you need anything."

Lauren held Randy tightly. "I love you, Daddy."

"Call when you've landed, please," Jane instructed.

"I will," Lacy answered.

The girls waved goodbye and headed toward their gate. Randy stood there in a trance, watching his girls go through the security line. They were both excited and obviously happy about taking on this new adventure in their lives. But Randy didn't move. He felt numb and suddenly couldn't breathe. When his girls were no longer in sight, he gulped hard, choking down tears.

Jane wasn't expecting him to react this way. "Randy?"

There was a hole in his heart, tearing him up inside. He closed his eyes and took a few deep breaths, trying to fight the pain. "Wow," he said softly. "This was a lot harder than I thought it was going to be."

Jane gently touched his arm. "They're going to be fine, Sweetie."

"But I'm not sure I'm gonna be."

On the airplane, Lauren could hardly contain her excitement. "Oh my god, Lace. Can you believe we are actually on our way to New York City? Broadway, here I come!"

Lacy giggled in delight. "I know. We finally get to experience life outside of Kirkland. I mean I love Seattle and all, but there's so much more out there. Opportunity is knocking on our door."

"For sure," Lauren agreed.

New York City, arguably the world's most vibrant and sprawling metropolis, occupied five boroughs—Brooklyn, the Bronx, Queens, Staten Island, and Manhattan. Manhattan was one of the most affluent neighborhoods in New York City, and was considered home to the intellectual hub, artistic workers, and wealthy business types. Both Juilliard and Columbia University were located in the Manhattan area, as were the most recognizable buildings and iconic sites that dominated the popular perception of New York City.

With Columbia University located at the northern end of Upper West Side Manhattan and Lincoln Center for the Performing Arts (where Juilliard was housed) located at the southern end, the twins would not be that far from each other. They each got settled into their dorms then spent the following day exploring the city.

Among their New York City adventures was a visit to Times Square. Times Square in Midtown Manhattan was considered part of the Theatre District, which was where most Broadway theatres were located. Other places of entertainment, such as local theaters, cinemas, recording studios, record label offices, ABC Studios, and theatrical agencies, also occupied this area. The twins enjoyed everything from souvenir shops and M&M's World LED signs and enormous billboards advertising Broadway musicals. They took a break for lunch on the red glass staircase facing Times Square, watching the crowds and flashing signs in their new environment.

After lunch, they explored Central Park, where they saw trees, flowers, shrubs, and perennials that decorated the Conservatory Garden. They climbed around on oddly shaped rock structures and discovered the many statues and fountains that covered the grounds. New York was a plethora of culture and diversity, and the Hanson twins were more than ecstatic to be here.